Magnificent MESS

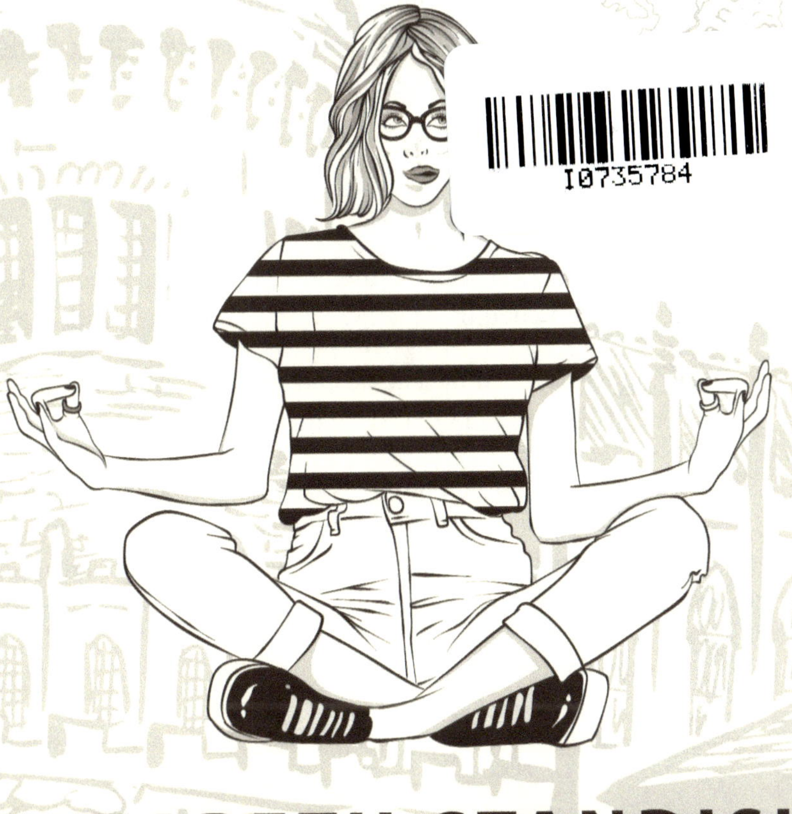

ELIZABETH STANDISH

For my parents, who read to me every night and are the reason I still cannot fall asleep without reading at least a few pages.

For all the horses who taught me how to show up, even when the going was tough: Babe, Bo, Angel, Slim, Annie, and Timer.

Chapter 1

April 7

"Shit," I muttered under my breath and tossed the letter on the counter. It slid into the stack of similarly offending papers. I bent over the counter and rested my elbows on it, grabbing my hair. Behind me, I heard the back door swing closed heavily.

"That good?"

I opened my eyes to look under my arm at the neon running shoes attached to the toned legs of my roommate and friend, Renée.

"It was the last one, too." I stood quickly, not doing my straight, straw blonde hair any favors as I flipped it back.

"Have you told her yet?" Renée picked up the pages I'd been collecting on the counter.

"No, but you know she's going to call." *Maybe I should have burned them as they came in*, I thought as I took the letters from Renée. "No, no, yes, no, maybe, no."

"How is it possible that only one wanted you?" Renée reached over me for a glass of water. "I mean, really? Only one?"

"You tell me—you're the one who got into grad school."

"In microbiology, not law school." She paused to gulp water. "Maybe we should burn them."

I had to smile. "And this is why we are friends." I glared at my cell phone when it buzzed loudly on the counter, and sighed.

How I'd beaten my mom to the coffee shop across the street from her office was beyond me, but I was relieved. Even being on time would have gotten me narrowed eyes. The shop was busy with business meetings, so I grabbed the first available table, up against a brick support column.

When she entered, it didn't matter that she was silhouetted against the bright afternoon sun. I would have recognized the way her heels punctuated the floor anywhere. Her dark hair was perfect in its smooth bob, pearls shining softly at her ears and neck. She was wearing one of her many custom grey suits and sensible but still stylish heels, making her slender frame even more imposing.

Over the din of the store, I heard her order her usual double espresso, and then she slid into the seat across from me.

"Hi, Mom." I slid the horseshoe on my necklace along the chain.

"Hello, Emma. Is that new lipstick? I'm not sure it's quite the right shade for you," she said as she held out her hand for my admission letters.

I held my breath as she flipped through them. I had already double-checked; they hadn't miraculously changed to acceptances since yesterday. Then she was handing them back.

"I am surprised. I would have thought that repeating the courses you did so poorly in would have helped, although I suppose since the poor grades are still on your transcript the admissions offices must believe you to be a higher-risk student."

Therein lay my biggest failing. Despite graduating valedictorian of my high school and getting a full-ride scholarship to college, before my freshman year was over, I'd lost my way. A course catalog full of a million new classes, and I had picked the most challenging, not realizing that I would need more than my innate intelligence to get through. Presented with a dining hall buffet, I'd more than gained the freshman fifteen. Poor grades and bad self-esteem left me half the once charismatic and brilliant girl I had been paraded around as.

Even though I had repeated my classes and recovered from academic probation, I could never regain perfection.

"Denver it is."

"We could wait for the wait-list decision to come back?" I said hopefully.

"Emmalyn, you have four rejections sitting here, from far lesser law schools than Harvard. Despite what you may hope, they will not admit you. You barely made it through college."

"That's not true! I'm on the Dean's List."

My mother shook her head. "It's better if you stay in Denver, anyway."

"Better for whom?"

"Emmalyn." Her voice took on a warning tone.

I kept my mouth shut. I knew why my mom didn't care about waiting. Going to school in Denver would make it that much easier for her to keep an eye on me, to ensure I was doing exactly as she wanted.

"I know you wanted to go somewhere else, but this must do," she decreed. "I have connections here, and the partners at my firm would be happy to assist you getting internships and as a new lawyer."

Now it was my turn to shake my head. "I don't feel good about this. I'd rather wait to see what Harvard says." *Ugh!* I did not want to go to school in the same city as her. "Maybe law school isn't even the right choice."

"That's ridiculous. You're about to be a college graduate. And you have nothing else ahead of you. You cannot float along, doing nothing. Law school is the best alternative. It will give you prestige and job opportunities, along with a good education."

"I don't know. I could get a job somewhere, get some real-world experience?"

"Doing what? Where?"

I should have known the idea would be dismissed. In my mother's eyes a break would be just another reminder of my inadequacy. "I ... I don't know. I don't even know what kind of law I would practice."

She brushed the comment away. "Of course, you'll join one of us."

I nearly screamed. The thought of joining a firm with my family members was worse than law school itself. "My whole life is planned out then, is it?"

"You need direction."

I glared at her.

"Emmalyn, listen to me," she said tersely. "You might not like this choice now, but as soon as you are past the bar exam you *will* be grateful. You'll be able to build whatever life you want for yourself."

I jabbed at the ice in my coffee. "Got my suitors lined up as well? You know arranged marriages really are a thing of the past."

"The rest of your life is not to be taken lightly. Even if you choose not to practice law, although that would be foolish, a law degree is marketable anywhere. It shows you are smart and dedicated."

She sat back and finished her espresso. "This is a good choice for you. Send in your acceptance."

I stirred my iced caramel macchiato. I should have known better than to think this would be a discussion.

"And sit up straight!" she hissed.

When the back door slammed behind me Friday afternoon, Renée was waiting, tops popped off a couple of beers. She pointed through the door I'd just come in.

I slapped on a ball cap to hold my hair down in the late spring breeze. In the backyard, the sun felt good on my skin, and the lawn squished nicely under my flip-flops.

"Sit," she pointed to one of our cheap lawn chairs, taking the other for herself. In her running shorts and sports bra, she looked just like what she was: a marathon runner. I envied her quads.

"I guess I'm going to law school. In Denver." I made a face.

"Your mom must be thrilled to have you so close."

I gave a sarcastic half laugh. "Super. I think she would have liked Harvard in name, but University of Denver does keep me close." I finished with an overly cheerful note to my voice.

My mom was right about one thing—four rejections, one wait list, only one acceptance didn't reflect well on me. Maybe worse, those results didn't live up to the family image. Both my mom and her younger brother were lawyers, following in the footsteps of my grandfather. All three of them were successful and prominent, awarded and recognized, a credit to the family name.

The zeal with which I had filled out the applications for law school had been borrowed. After dropping my pre-vet course, I'd had no real path. With nothing else in front of me, my mother's not-so-subtle suggestion of law school had seemed like a logical, if uninspiring answer.

"So what *are* you going to do?" Renée asked, nudging my ankle with her shoe. She'd led my biology lab as I started my equine science degree. I'd gone to her for help understanding the KREBs cycle of cellular metabolism, and we'd spent more time laughing than studying.

I probably should have given such a big decision more consideration, but after getting my feet back under me after my rocky start to college, I'd struggled to know what I wanted. I'd been taking Mom's advice, consciously or by habit, for years. Friends, courses, jobs—all of it had been filtered through her and scrutinized. I had always gone along with her dictates. Doing so had been easier, and mostly what she'd said had made sense. Take the AP classes, be home by ten, get a part-time job. Now I was, as she pointed out, an adult. Yet she kept insisting I do it her way. And I was still obeying her, like some well-trained dog. It made sense with a grandfather, mother, and uncle in the profession, though her work facilitating mergers and acquisitions seemed tedious to me. But she had a point—what else was I going to do?

"I don't know. This is what our family does. I'm sure I'd be expected to join the chamber of commerce or something, maybe serve on the board of some hospital."

At my side, Renée pretended to throw up.

"Stop!" I laughed, reaching out to whack her on the shoulder. "Even Dad was part of the community! I remember his exuberance when he got several of his commercial real estate clients to donate to build homeless shelters. He enjoyed going to the shelters after they were built, talking with the residents, and serving in the kitchen. Drove Mom nuts!" I smiled at the memory.

I wished he were still alive. He was the one who had encouraged me to explore everything I could while I had the chance and helped me refine the ambition and dreams I'd had as a preteen. I would have loved his balanced advice.

Renée's considered approach to problems had reminded me of my dad, and was how she'd managed to get me to understand the KREBs cycle in about ten minutes. The laughter we'd shared about other professors and TAs during that study session had led to our friendship. She had graduated from high school a year early, taken summer classes all the way along, so when we'd met, she was already a graduate TA, despite only being a year older than me. It was why we'd been roommates for the past year and a half, why she'd asked me to be a bridesmaid when we'd only known each other for eight months.

"You left pre-vet for a reason," Renée reminded me, pulling me back from my memories. "I get why you started there—vet school made sense after being raised with horses. So why did you leave?"

I'd been bound for vet school since junior high. When I applied for college, I'd hung a poster-board chart on my wall with every detail about the colleges I was applying to, what programs I was interested in, the tuition, and how I *felt* about each choice. Naturally, I'd gotten into each of those universities.

"You know why." I glared at her. In my mind played a series of clinical memories. Lancing the abscess on an elderly dog and watching his face when he finally felt some relief and bandaging the broken leg of a racehorse and then hand walking him several times a day through his rehab. Those had been wonderful moments. But I still recalled the nights I'd spent crying when a younger cat I hadn't even been responsible for, whose owner had babied him through kidney failure for months, had to be put down.

Despite my retaking all the classes I'd done poorly in, and still graduating in four years, my early-on failing GPA was the real reason my mother had taken my post-college plans so firmly in hand. I *would* remember that I was brilliant. Law school would *prove* it.

"I think you shouldn't go," she said, clanking her bottle against mine.

I slumped further down in the chair. "Mom is used to getting her way. Is fighting back worth the effort?"

"Hell yes!"

I continued as if I hadn't heard her. "I think I'll end up in the same position, and feeling apathetic. I wasted so much time. I could have been 'finding' myself during college instead of flailing around. I'm not sure I even know myself that well. It sort of feels like, 'Well, why not?'"

"That's exam fatigue talking," she said firmly.

"Yeah, I'm sure you're right," I sighed.

"As rational as it might seem, and less emotional than vet school, is sitting in an office sorting papers really what you want to do for the rest of your life?" Renée asked, grabbing the letters from the bag I hadn't set down before she'd dragged me outside, and shaking them. "You're a people person, and brilliant when you're working on a problem you find interesting. Why waste that on something you don't love?" Renée flung the letters on the ground. I had to smile at how disgusted she was for me.

"You can say that because you have Aaron, who not only lets you do the things you find interesting but encourages you to do so."

I wished, not for the first time, that I had someone as supportive as Renée's husband. His position in the military had him stationed in Washington D.C., but he'd encouraged her to get her master's in microbiology, even though it kept them apart, and he continued urging Renée to apply to the labs she was most interested in, no matter where they were.

"You have me!"

"For, like, three more weeks, when you take your masters, meet Aaron in D.C., and go to the cool viral research lab. Meanwhile, I'll graduate and, ugh!" I dropped my head back against the chair and groaned. "Move *home* for the summer."

Chapter 2

Memorial Day Weekend

"Happy graduation, Emma!" Kim raised her glass of wine to mine. We were sitting across the table from each other on the back patio at her house, while her husband John towered over the grill. "Are you ready for law school?"

"I just graduated like two weeks ago! Of course not."

"Well, are you at least excited?"

I took a sip while considering my friend. In the heat, her curly brown hair, streaked from her time in the sun, puffed dramatically around her shoulders. On anyone shorter, the haphazard curls radiating about her head would have looked ridiculous. The muscular build from working on her acreage and at her day job at Old West Preservation, a large animal shelter of sorts, didn't hurt, either.

"I'm ready for something new. Maybe I'll be excited when it gets closer. Right now, I wake up, and the sun is shining, and Mickie and Annie," I named mine and my mom's horses, "are looking over the fence at me from the backyard, and I wonder if I want to go back to school. Then I clean their stalls and I wonder what else I would do. I've been accepted, the money has been paid."

"You still have plenty of time to back out. And so what if the money's been paid? It can always be refunded if you don't start."

"I have to go. Backing out now would mean mass hysteria, arguments, yelling, disappointment." I wanted my mother to be proud of me for *something*.

"You should at least think about it."

"All right, I will," I said dismissively. Kim couldn't understand. She had met my mom, but my mom was always her most-charming self in public.

I had met Kim when she came to talk to the high school equestrian team about careers in the equine industry. She had already worked for a couple of breed associations by then. Now, she led development and fundraising at Old West Preservation, fondly referred to as The Resort, which worked with high-risk youth and hosted grade school kids to teach them about agriculture.

I had needed a big sister for the yucky parts of college, the bad dates, the overloading on credit hours, and the self-loathing that had come with my weight gain. She'd been there for a turbulent breakup, unlike my mother, who had insisted it was merely a college relationship.

"What are you doing with your summer?" John asked from his place at the grill.

"Working at Home Depot, but that's just running around money. Cleaning stalls." While my parents could have afforded to board our horses elsewhere and sent me for training, my mother believed that doing the day-to-day chores made you more invested.

Kim jumped in so fast that I wondered if they had planned the setup. "Are you over the last guy?"

I flipped a hand. "Totally. We both knew it was just fun."

"How would you feel about meeting someone new?" she asked coyly.

I raised my eyebrows at her. "Got someone in mind, do ya?"

"He's new at The Resort, he could use a friend, and I think you guys would get along great. It doesn't have to be anything serious. We could all just go out for drinks or something."

"Uh-huh."

"I would never send you out on a blind date."

"Right," I said, skeptically. "I just don't know that it's a good idea, what with school. I probably won't have time for a relationship. That's what they say, anyway. First year, they scare you to death, second year, they work you to death, third year, they bore you to death."

"Do they really say that?" she asked, horrified.

"They do. I hope it's not true, but better safe than sorry, you know. I'd really rather not risk getting sidetracked and drawing more of Mom's attention."

"Yeah, but she could hardly blame you for wanting to get laid."

"Ha!" I thought of my uptight, perfect mother giving any thought to sex—her own or mine. "All right, I will think about it. John, are you almost done fanning the flames? I'm hungry!"

Chapter 3

September 9

A couple of weeks into the start of my first semester, Kim and I sat in the coffee shop at Barnes & Noble when I felt her nudge me. I looked up at the guy she indicated at the end of the bookshelf from us.

"Not my type," I mumbled. He was tall enough but had hair that stood out every which way, probably due to the curls that hit him at the jawline. His shirt was untucked.

"Come on, he's cute! You should go talk to him."

I shook my head. "I'm going to go look at books." Stood, I tugged my floral top down to cover the gap above my jeans. Kim would just love to call this guy over.

Wandering, I found myself in the self-help section and sat down on the industrial grey carpet, perusing the books I had picked up along the way. Someone blocked my light, and I looked up. It was the same guy. Kim was right; he was good-looking, in a rugged kind of way. From my vantage point on the floor, I could see his beat-up boots and the frayed hems on his jeans.

Definitely not my type. Not the tall, skinny, baby-faced guy I normally singled out, my cookie-cutter definition of handsome. He was also not the starched-jeans-and-crisp-button-downs I'd gotten used to in college with guys coming from the family farm in Texas. Nor was he anything like the guys in law school—I'd developed an earnest appreciation for well-cut dress pants since classes had begun. And yet, despite all of that, he was attractive.

I gave him a half-hearted smile, wishing, in spite of all the differences, that he was my type.

"Hi," he said, giving me an enthusiastic smile.

"Hi," I returned. I wanted desperately to disappear into my stack of books but was paralyzed by his brilliantly ocean-blue eyes.

"I saw you earlier in the coffee shop. With my co-worker, Kim. Do you know her?" he asked haltingly.

If she was going to set me up, why couldn't she have done it the old-fashioned way, so at least I knew what I was getting into?

"Yeah." He looked at me, waiting for me to elaborate. I stared stupidly up at him, wishing he would leave; hoping, despite the frayed hems, and because of, damn them, the blue eyes, he would sit down next to me.

"I'm Patrick, by the way," he said. I blinked up at his offered hand before accepting it.

"I'm Emma."

The handshake was everything he was not. Pulled together, crisp, and in your face. It felt like static electricity vibrating inside my skin, and a flush crept up my cheeks. I promptly dropped his hand.

An awkward silence lingered for a moment, while I tried to think of something to say.

"Right," he said, sounding almost disappointed. "Well, nice to meet you, Emma. See you around."

I watched as he turned and walked down the aisle. Then I dropped my head into my hands and groaned as I saw the couple of books on top of my pile. I left them there, shoved to my feet, and set off to find Kim.

"Shit," I whispered under my breath as I turned up the main aisle. One of my mom's firm partners stood looking at a display on a center table. I kept my head turned to the side, pretending to be looking at the endcaps, as I passed him.

"Emmalyn?" he asked.

"Oh, hello!" I feigned surprise. "How are you?"

"Doing well, thank you for asking. Your mom tells us you're attending University of Denver for law school."

"I am."

He nodded. "That's a good choice for you. I'm sure you'll do your mom proud."

"So far it's much different than my animal science degree."

"Yes," he chuckled. "A more useful endeavor."

"People who take their animals for veterinary care might think differently," I said somewhat irritably.

He chuckled. "You sound like your mom with that quick response."

"Hm." I refused to agree. "I'm actually meeting someone, so if you'll excuse me."

"I'll tell your mom I saw you. Have a good day."

"You too." I hoped he wouldn't say anything to my mom. Then she'd want to know why I wasn't at the law school in the middle of the day.

I attempted a beeline for Kim, where I had left her in the coffee shop, surrounded by books on nonprofit development. She was talking to Patrick, so I ducked behind the nearest bookshelf.

When he left, I came around the other end of the shelves and sat down across from her.

"Hey!" she said brightly.

"'Hey!' That's all you've got to say for yourself? Couldn't you at least have given me a little warning?" I said urgently, my voice almost breaking. Between Patrick and my mom's partner lurking in the store, I couldn't afford to make a scene. Accomplished and impeccable, that was the image my mom displayed. Flawless. I couldn't do anything to contradict that by, say, yelling at my friend.

"You're always telling me you like meeting new people and you want to meet more. He's good with the animals at The Resort, and genuinely friendly. He's new in town and spends most of his time at work. We talked about this, you said you were open to it."

"I said I would think about it," I corrected sternly.

"Besides," she went on as if I hadn't spoken, "I thought a random meeting in the bookstore was perfectly convincing."

I had to give her that.

"Kim," I said, "I was sitting in the self-help section when he found me. With *What Can You Do With Your Law Degree?* and *10 Ways to Find Your Wonderful Self* sitting in front of me."

"Oh." She cringed. "Well, I told him that you read a lot, and that you were always researching something." She laughed a little *heh-hee-hee*, and I glared at her. Still, there had been that handshake. And the blue eyes.

I grabbed her iced coffee and sucked hard on the straw, hoping the sugar would melt away some of my curiosity-laced discomfort.

Chapter 4

September 18

By the time I was through the first few weeks of classes, it became apparent that law school would be nothing like anything I had ever prepared for, or experienced. Wistfully, I thought of the predictability of the steps of cell division. I glanced at Claire, sitting across from me at the tables in the atrium.

We'd met standing in line for the bathroom during pre-semester functions and ended up having every class together. We'd bonded speculating about why there was a condom dispenser in the women's restroom but not in the men's, over growing up with horses, and a love of baking. When we'd gone out that first weekend, I'd watched her both charm and cut people down to size with a flash of her dark brown eyes as they'd tried to guess her nationality, always assuming she was Asian until she'd teasingly but directly correct them about her Native American heritage.

Now she was bent over a case book, as I should have been. I thought about Claire's motivation. She'd already worked for a state representative whose district included an Indian reservation suffering from extreme poverty and low high school graduation rates, and was determined to make changes that would provide better economic conditions, and fund support programs.

"Time to go," she said, gathering her books and speeding down the hall. "We don't want to miss torts!" I envied her determination.

As I took my seat, I thought about how class was predictable. Each professor had a method, but they worked their way along rows, systematically calling on the next person in line.

Except today, when I was called on immediately, the professor skipping over the next person in the row, to quiz the hell out of me in the time-honored Socratic method.

"Ms. Greene, can you describe the facts of the case?"

I glided the horseshoe along the chain of my necklace. "In Whitcombe versus Hunt, the plaintiff sued for loss of his horse, when the horse fell over a fallen log on the defendant's property and broke his leg. The court ruled it was the plaintiff's responsibility to guide his horse to prevent the accident, and the defendant won."

"And what theory did the court use in issuing their ruling?"

"The plaintiff sued under strict liability, but the court ruled using contributory negligence."

"And the outcome?"

"The plaintiff not only lost his horse when it had to be put down for the broken leg, but wasn't able to recover the value of his horse either."

"Very good," the professor said, turning away to walk to the other side of the lecture hall.

"But I disagree."

"You do?" The professor paused, turning around to look at me.

I felt the guy sitting next to me jerk, and I glanced at him. "Yes. The court failed to address the issue that it was dark when the plaintiff was riding on a well-traveled footpath, and that the tree had been downed a week earlier in a storm."

"You make an excellent argument."

"Furthermore, horses are generally very careful of where they step, even when moving fast. Since the horse was familiar with the path, it would have avoided the log, not trusting to step where it wasn't sure of the footing. Therefore, by leaving the log in place and not warning his neighbors of its presence, the defendant should have been liable under strict liability."

"Well done," the professor said, attempting to hide his smile.

"Nice work in there today, Emma," Claire greeted me as we filed out of the lecture hall.

"Thanks! I got lucky getting a case I could actually say something about."

"No, I was impressed," added my seat neighbor. "I got lucky when I was skipped. How did you know that—about horses?"

"I grew up with them, and I have a bachelor's in animal science," I shrugged.

"I'm so jealous you still get to ride," Claire said. "I sold my last horse in the middle of college."

"I didn't know you both had ridden," my seatmate said.

"I rode a bit. Nothing like Emmalyn over here." Claire jerked her thumb.

"That's not true, you rode, and showed, a lot!"

"Okay, Miss Almost Olympian."

"Not exactly." I rolled my eyes.

"A couple of us from my writing group are grabbing beers tonight, do you two want to come too?" said my seatmate.

"More fun than torts!" I replied.

"Sounds good to me," Claire agreed.

Talking with my classmates was the easy part. Answering questions on demand, despite today's success, less so.

Together Claire and I headed for our next class, chatting about the cases we'd had to read the previous night. In the back of my mind, I thought about how I should be studying instead of going out. But I'd rather socialize. I could study more over the weekend, I rationalized. I needed people time, too.

Monday morning did nothing to improve my mood. I hadn't thought about my successful torts interrogation all weekend. Instead, I'd stewed about meeting Patrick. It irritated me that Kim led me blindly into such an obvious setup, and I was mad at Patrick, too, for talking to me, catching me off guard, and then leaving.

Patrick probably wasn't still thinking about why I had those books out, I reminded myself as I jammed my head through my shirt. He probably wasn't thinking about me at all. It was my own fault; if I had been in the library studying like I was supposed to, I wouldn't have made a fool of myself.

Swinging my backpack off the floor, I threw a hasty "Good morning, see ya later," to my roommate, Travis, a fellow law school student, as he came out of his room running his hand through his hair and yawning.

The problem was, Kim was right. I did want a serious boyfriend, and I was tired of my only companion at night being whatever case study I was reading for my Civil Procedure class. I wasn't sure about years two or three yet, but a month in and I could confirm that during the first year, they definitely scared you to death. Most nights I had two hundred or so pages to read, and each class met daily.

I was well on my way to dying from the sheer fright of having my grade hang on just a midterm and a final exam and wishing that boredom would hurry up and get here.

"'Morning," I called to the same guy I sat across from every morning at the law school library. He was one of the overachieving types and a 2L—a second-year law student—whose business card proclaimed him a legal intern for one of the city's largest law firms. We had no reason to speak to each other, other than morning pleasantries. Whereas I was the big bad 1L on my way to making my mark in, well, nothing other than the number of hours logged alone at night with a casebook. He shot me a disdainful look over his glasses. Perhaps my greeting was a bit too loud and chipper for the morning, but I was trying to brighten my mood. I opened my laptop and sent a morning text to Kim.

"So, what do you think of my proposition?" she wrote back. Hm. No morning pleasantries from her either.

"What proposition?"

"Read your email."

To: equestrienne@hotmail.com
From: heelsdwn@aol.com
Date: Sept 21

Subject: Why not?

I really think you should get to know Patrick. Yeah, it
might have been an awkward introduction, but now you
have that out of the way! I think you guys would have
fun together.

Great. I knew just where this was going. I slammed my laptop lid
with more force than was required, causing my study buddy to glare
at me again. I glared back and strode out of the library to my torts
class.

I finally had a break to call Kim about seven, after my nightly date
with the treadmill.

"No!" I said, after her answering machine message ended. I never
knew which phone to call. "No, I th—"

"Hi there," she chirped into my ear. She must have been waiting
for my call. "Why not? You're both outgoing, he's interested in knowing more about horses, and I think you would have fun together. He
seems very real, grounded."

As I listed the reasons—again—I didn't think this was a good
idea, starting of course with our less-than-stellar meeting, I thought
about Kim's motivations. She was always supportive, and I knew she
wanted to see me happy—just like a big sister was supposed to do.
Maybe she had a point, maybe I should give this guy a chance ... at
least to have dinner with them. *All* of them.

"Okay," I said, interrupting her.

"What?"

"I said okay. I'll meet Patrick in a normal situation. He seemed
friendly enough, and there were those blue eyes, which cannot be dis-
counted. Plus, you do know me well, so I might as well give it a shot.
At worst, it's one night away from the books."

"Great! Or I could just give you his number ..."

"Ohhh, no," I said. "I'm not letting you out of this just yet. You got me into this—you're going to keep me from looking like a fool while we check each other out. And not until first semester exams are over. A semi-blind date is *not* going to lessen my stress level."

"Sure." I could hear her placating tone, and the slight smile behind it.

The following Friday, I stood in the entryway to the Western-style restaurant and bar, Cactus Moon. Final exams were looming in front of me, I had told Kim I didn't want to meet Patrick before they were over, and yet here I was. Where was Kim, anyway?

From my post at the bottom of the steps, I saw Kim's car pull up at the edge of the sidewalk. Someone in tattered khakis tramped up the stairs and muttered, "She definitely said seven o'clock." I was so relieved to see Kim that I didn't even care who the yahoo was.

But, when Kim and I headed to the door, I realized the yahoo was Patrick.

"Emma, this is Patrick. Patrick, Emma," Kim introduced us formally.

Well, shit. He stood tall before me, his eyes bluer than I remembered. His light beard only emphasized the definition of his jawline and appeared as an extension of the mass of very curly, light reddish-brown hair he sported. He stuck out his hand, and I automatically reached for it, suddenly remembering our first handshake vividly.

"N-n-ice to meet you," I stuttered lamely.

"Again."

"Sorry?"

"We've met before, or do you not remember? You were sitting on the floor at the bookstore. You had a book about finding yourself on the top of your stack."

I managed to not wince. "Oh, right. Well, you know how it is. You automatically say the same thing whenever you meet someone, even if it's not the first time you've met. That book wasn't mine though ... it must have been left there by someone else."

"Sure." He smiled, humoring me. "Well, nice to meet you again, or see you again, whichever you prefer."

His accent sounded like Will in *Good Will Hunting*, and I wished I didn't think that was attractive. I wanted to dislike him. I wanted to not appreciate his teasing. I wanted to not find him so ... hot.

John walked up then, enveloping me in a big hug, saving me from responding. Between his height and his build, it felt like being wrapped in a down comforter. Kim was lucky. If John had a younger brother who was identical to him in every way, I wouldn't be standing here in this awkward situation. "I'm starving," he announced, "let's go eat."

"Great idea." Maybe with food in his mouth, Patrick wouldn't be so quick-witted and thus seem less attractive.

Chapter 5

October 18

Unfortunately, this turned out not to be the case. I tried not to stare, even though I assured myself he was not my type. I gave lengthy answers to all his questions, hoping he would somehow understand my inner conflict.

"How did you get from animals to law?"

I finished chewing and slowly took a swallow of beer. The truth was, I was still struggling with that one myself.

"Vet school is highly competitive. That's what I assumed I was going to do when I started college. But after my sophomore year, I didn't really know whether I wanted to do that anymore. I took a break from the intense biological classes, got a bunch of my humanities out of the way, and then ..." Then I couldn't go back. I couldn't deal with seeing any more animals in pain. "I didn't know what I wanted to do, but I knew it wasn't where my degree might take me," I finished, which sounded better than because I was told to. "What about you?"

"History, with a minor in Spanish." He picked up his own beer bottle. "Kim mentioned you've been riding all your life."

"I did grow up competing at high-level horse shows. Mickie and I, that's my horse, did hunters and jumpers like you see at the Olympics, although the fences aren't quite *that* high. I had a trainer who came to our house. It was my life, but it's impossible to make a living that way."

"Isn't law school competitive too?" Patrick asked, confused.

"Yes, but not as much as it used to be. Plus, I wasn't sure I could handle taking care of other people's animals and giving bad news over and over again." That much at least was true.

Classes were hard. And even though I had ultimately chosen not to go to vet school, those courses had been far more interesting to me. Why hadn't I decided that all those rejection letters were a sign that this was not the right direction for me? "I come from a family full of lawyers," I finished.

"Carrying on the family tradition?"

I took a drink to buy time to answer. Competition was ingrained in the family, handed down from my great-great-grandfather and his prize-winning steers on the family cattle farm, thousands of acres in rural Illinois. After he had died, my grandfather had gone to law school, leased the farm, and when my mom was seven, he gave her a show pony. My grandfather to my mother to me. I'd taken the example my mom had set and run full speed for the competition ring. I loved it, but unless I wanted to stay on track for the Olympics, it wasn't an acceptable career. Now, I was expected to take that drive to compete and shift it immediately to the courtroom, or negotiations. Unless I'd decided to rebuild the family cattle empire, agriculture wasn't prominent or powerful enough to carry on the family legacy.

"I know, it's a little anticlimactic. Maybe you'd have to know my family to understand."

Patrick nodded and picked up his beer. I didn't understand it from the inside, how could I expect him to get it from the outside looking in? Oh well, I had needed a night out. Besides, he looked a bit like a hippie. He was wearing a flannel shirt for crying out loud, and it was untucked. Not my type, I reminded myself, listing his flaws. So why did I care what he thought?

John spared me from analyzing too much. "The drink special lasts all night, so I say we go by the dance floor and have a couple more."

"Great idea!" Kim agreed.

After we migrated, the awkwardness continued. Patrick never asked me to dance, just stood leaning against the bar, nursing a beer, and talking sporadically as we watched John and Kim two-step. I mentally shook my head at him. If you were at a bar with a dance floor, shouldn't you dance? Especially if you were on a date?

But when I grabbed for my bottle and knocked it just hard enough to tip it, Patrick caught it before it could fall, enclosing the bottle and my hand in his. He might not look like he belonged on the Old West farm, but his hands were worn enough to prove he wasn't running numbers for them. He looked me in the eye, holding on for a moment, and then another, before he let go.

"Got it all right there, Slick?" he asked casually.

"Yes, just fine, thank you," I replied shortly. But despite being irritated I slid a half step closer.

"I'm not a dancer," he said, turning to look at me, "but if you wanted to go someplace else where we could just sit and talk, I'd be up for that." He was giving me a tentative smile.

"Sure."

"I still don't really know Denver all that well," he said as we walked to our cars. I'd forgotten he'd moved to Denver only at the beginning of the year.

"Do you want to follow me to my place, and we could go together?"

"Sounds great."

While Patrick followed me, I wracked my brain for a suitable location near my apartment. "Is downtown okay, I don't really have anything great in my neighborhood," I asked when he slid into the passenger seat.

"That's fine with me."

I parked near an innocuous bar with a late-night menu. As we walked up the street, shouts rang out and two guys started throwing punches. Before I realized what was happening, Patrick grabbed my arm and pulled me close to himself. I looked up at him, registering the comfortable way in which his arm slid protectively around my back. "Thanks," I smiled.

He nodded and smiled back.

Talking to Patrick was better in a quieter place. Dimmed lights made conversation less stressful than the spotlights and changing colors at Cactus Moon. Our booth had a warm yellow glow thanks to a couple of small pendant lights suspended above.

"So, AmeriCorps? At Old West Preservation?" I prompted.

"Yeah. College was a blast, but I didn't know what I wanted next. Kinda like you, it sounds. My older sister did a year in the Peace Corps and liked it. I thought, why not? I like animals and kids, and if more people understand about how important animals were to our national history and to our daily lives that can't be bad," he explained. "Plus, I needed to get away from home."

"Why?" I interrogated around a mouthful of cheesy fries.

He shrugged. "I grew up near where I went to school; high school was a private Catholic school. So was college. Pops is ... Pops. He's retired, and in tinkering mode."

"Where is home?"

"Woo-bin," he said. At my confused look, he laughed. "'Woburn' on the map. It's not far northwest of Boston proper."

I nodded, then asked, "You mentioned an older sister."

"Yep. After she finished her time in the Peace Corps, she came back to get her PhD in English. She's at Brown. I have a younger sister, too. She's in college now, doing her own thing. She's kind of a gypsy, going where the wind blows. She's really happy like that. They both seem on their right path. I don't know what mine is. I left in February, and my truck barely made it. I wrote 'Denver or bust' in the back window and it became a self-fulfilling prophecy. Guess I shouldn't have tempted the gods, since I broke down in Limon," Patrick grinned. "But I killed the time waiting for repairs finishing *The Old Man and the Sea*. It's one of my favorites."

I'd seen the little white Toyota when he'd gotten in my car. It did look like it had seen better days. I also noticed he hadn't mentioned his mom, but didn't ask. "Is it what you were expecting, The Resort?"

He turned his pint of beer around, thinking. "Sometimes. The other day, we had fourth graders on a tour. They were just the cutest things! Everyone enjoys feeding the baby goats with their fuzzy whiskers." He caught the tip of his tongue between his teeth and smiled, remembering. "But lots of days I'm fixing something. I'm not as involved with the kids or animals as I thought I'd be. It's fun tossing hay into the pens and giving everyone a pat. Billy the goat—I know, predictable—likes the spot between his horns scratched. Hard. The pig just wants you to give her food, and then go away. There are two mares in a paddock together who fight for attention."

I tried not to sigh over his obvious affection for the animals.

On the street, Patrick gave me his fleece against the chilly October night air, as we walked past a bum who smiled, said hello, and then sang to us about Cupid aiming his arrow. As we walked further, he faded, and Patrick picked up the tune. I laughed.

He shrugged. "My dad listens to the classics."

I was irritated with myself for being so tense over dinner. He was nothing like I had assumed based on how he dressed. More articulate and thoughtful. Had I thought he was going to judge me the same way my mom did? Found me wanting because I couldn't articulate what I was doing with my life? I wished the whole evening, start to finish, had been as uncomplicated as sharing fries had been.

"I have to confess, I've never listened to country music before tonight," Patrick said as we drove back to my apartment.

I winced.

"And you skip all the good songs on this album—it's Jimmy Buffett's *Songs You Know By Heart*, right?"

"You don't like 'Margaritaville?'"

"No, I do like it, but you skipped 'Come Monday,' 'One Particular Harbor,' and most importantly, 'Son of a Son of a Sailor.'"

"I have very specific requirements for a song to make it into my rotation. I'm eclectic, but discriminating."

"Maybe too discriminating. You're missing some great songs. Just listen," he requested as he flipped back through "Son of a Son of a Sailor." Great, we were sitting in my car in the parking lot at my apartment screening music.

"I don't think thi—"

"Just listen to the words. It's such a great song you keep skipping over. See, he just talked about crooks ... and now there's a reference to lawyers. Totally your kind of song."

He looked at me and I shut up, letting the rest of the song play out. "Huh. Okay, you're right. From now on, I will listen to all the songs on this CD."

He looked at me smugly and smiled. "Good. You never know what you might miss by skipping the ones that don't instantly appeal to you." Was that some kind of psychic remark directed at me? Did he know I had balked at going out with him?

We sat there a while, talking about the rest of the album. By the end of the night, "Son of a son of a son of a sailor" had worked its way into our conversation, like it was some secret code.

"This was fun tonight, I'm glad Kim arranged it."

"I am, too," I agreed.

"Would you want to go out again sometime?"

In a split second, I thought through my initial hesitation, my homework load, all the qualities he was lacking, and all the ones he had.

"I'd really like that." I smiled.

When we finally got out of the car, Patrick wrapped his arms around my shoulders, pulling me close against his chest. I felt a small frisson of possibility snapping between us.

"Goodnight, Emma, see ya latah'," he said in that attractive accent, stepping back but not letting go.

"Goodnight, Patrick. Nice to *see* you again."

He grinned at me, "Yeah, you too."

Chapter 6

October 19

"So??? How was the rest of your night?"

"Kim, it's not even seven in the morning. I didn't get to bed until three," I moaned into my cell phone and dropped my palm down on the bedspread.

"Oh-ho! Details, I want details, girl." I heard coffee hit her cup on the other end.

"It was nice, he was sweet, and I think he like, *likes* me. We found a chill bar and just talked. About why he wanted to come to The Resort, and you know, just stuff. Oh, and he reads ... Kim, he really reads." I paused, listening to her spoon clanking on the cup, stirring in cream, while I thought about how to go on without giving away too much of how I was feeling this morning. "You know, Hemingway and stuff. And you're right, he's definitely an animal person. The way he talked about talking to each of the animals every morning was so adorable."

"Hemingway and stuff.'" She slurped. "That's very descriptive of you. So that's it, he reads? What else?"

I knew she wouldn't give up until I dished. "Well, he's so not my type, ya know? But he has more depth than you'd guess by a first look. He's very friendly, but I get the sense that he doesn't share himself easily." I pushed upright in bed. "He's not as tall as anyone else I've dated."

"Six feet is not exactly short," she pointed out.

"True, but you know me—three inches taller than me has always been a requirement. Patrick just makes that. He's not my tall, skinny, no-butt prototype. There's just more to him. He's not all lanky like every other guy I've dated. He actually has muscles. Plus, all that hair," I laughed. "He's got them all on the blue eyes. So maybe different is good. And his Boston accent is fun. When we finally got out of my car, I was less unsure, but then he gave me this great big hug that was long and warm and soft, but firm, and all wrapped together ..." I trailed off remembering. "And then all that feeling of being up in the air about whether I want to get any kind of involved just dissolved."

"Yeah," she agreed emphatically, "he gives really great hugs."

"There's just something ... compelling about him. It seems like there's something he's avoiding, or at least reluctant to talk about. He told me about his sisters but was hesitant talking about his dad. He didn't talk about his mom at all. But it feels good to be with him," I concluded.

The problem wasn't, as I had insisted initially, that he wasn't my type, or even, try as I might to convince myself otherwise, that I wasn't interested. The problem was that I was very interested, despite the little voice in my head saying I didn't have time to be cavorting. It sounded remarkably like my mother's voice.

As if she read my mind, Kim added, "You two don't have to have a great love affair. But you can't keep yourself chained to your desk all the time. Patrick would bring a little levity to your life."

"When we were away from you guys, maybe the pressure, it was better," I agreed.

Nervous, sure, but comfortable. It felt like he was paying attention. I knew that we had a good connection; that somehow we had an innate understanding of each other. I wanted that. I felt lost in my current life. I didn't fit in at law school. It would be nice to have someone to talk with who got me. Maybe Patrick could be that person.

Monday morning, I sat staring out the window of the library, tapping my pen against the pages of my casebook. Despite my good class where I'd impressed the professor, I wasn't sure I belonged in law school. I'd come to realize I would need the kind of drive Claire had to get through. I was surrounded by people who had graduated from college *summa cum laude*.

"Good morning," Claire said, as she sat down across from me. "How was your da-ate?"

"Good, I think. I mean, it was good for me. We'll see. More fun than reading three thousand casebook pages, though."

"Ain't that the truth! But it's for a good cause."

"Six weeks down, two years nine months to go," I joked.

Claire laughed. "I'll see you later. I've gotta go find one of the profs before class."

It wasn't that I felt like I couldn't compete. I just wasn't sure if I cared to. I preferred that ten minutes before class. Reading cases could be interesting, although if I was honest, that probably had more to do with getting to use about eight differently colored pens to highlight. But catching up on Claire's weekend or hearing about classmates' dogs always made me smile.

I knew I was as smart as anybody there—a fact my mom hammered me over the head with, at every opportunity. The bigger question was whether I cared. I turned back to my casebook. Maybe if I did poorly on the few midterms next week, I could convince my mom to let me drop out.

In the days that followed, I feigned nonchalance to myself. Patrick hadn't called within two days of our date? I was too busy to worry about it anyway. He hadn't asked me out again? No big deal. But once he did call, it was as if we'd been just waiting to have each other to talk to, dropping little pieces of ourselves in the dark. His sisters, the horses I'd had over the years, what he missed about home, why I alternately liked and hated being an only child.

"It's late, you should go to bed," he said. I heard a *meow* in the background.

"Do you have a cat?" I asked.

"She's the neighbor's. She comes crying at my window at night, so I let her sleep with me and then let her out in the early morning." The window thunked closed.

"That's sweet," I smiled. "Good night."

I glanced at the clock as I put my phone down—we'd been on the phone for an hour. I thought guys weren't supposed to like talking on the phone?

Chapter 7

October 26

The hole-in-the-wall bar Patrick parked in front of was not the kind of place I would have picked. We law schoolers hit the pretentious bars downtown, so we could one-up each other and everyone there. Subtly, of course. This bar evoked no pretense, just a cold beer and a good jukebox. I fidgeted with my rings as he ordered a pitcher of beer for us, finally tucking my hands beneath my thighs.

I wished I could do what kids did: hand him a mud pie and instantly be friends. No worrying about whether the other person only liked sand pies—you could just walk off holding hands. Determining if I measured up, whether to his expectations or my own, was harder.

All I felt was the frisson in my body, like the top of a solder wire just heated, and over it all, his Boston accent.

"I've been trying to get rid of it," he confessed when I teased him about pahkin' the cah' in Hahvahd yahd. "There's no accent in Colorado. People look at you like you have two heads."

When his hand brushed my own while reaching for the can of peanuts, his fingers curled casually over mine. I felt the same spark from when we'd first shaken hands, but tamped it down.

"You've been to The Resort?" he asked. I nodded. "How is it different from how you grew up?" he asked.

"The Resort is very casual. Dirty, disorganized. I love how open and welcoming it is, but with thirty different 4-H kids in and out each week, and no one fully responsible for the equipment, plus being a nonprofit on a tight budget, nothing is in perfect order. At home, every piece of equipment has its own place, and my mother expected me to keep them all spotless. My chores included cleaning stalls, polishing tack, sweeping floors in our barn. Excellence was the only option."

He shook his head. "When my Pops taught me to sail, I dumped the dinghy every time for the first seven outings. Each time he'd come up laughing. My mom would pack lunch, and we'd all have a picnic while Pops and I dried off."

"Not in my house," I laughed. "My mom was my trainer when I was a kid. I think if I had fallen off repeatedly, she would have given up, and taken my pony away. It happened eventually, though. I was twelve the first time I fell off in the show ring. I got a lecture from my trainer about guiding my horse better, and one from my mother about concentrating. I think I like your dad's response better."

"Sounds like they were rough on you," Patrick said kindly, giving my fingers a small squeeze.

"They knew I could do better. So did I. My mom was demanding, but she showed horses when she was younger, too, even for a while after she became a lawyer. So, she understood exactly what I needed to do to be the best. That's a blessing and a curse. Lots of parents don't have the experience, so they're happy when their kid places. My mom did know, so it was harder to impress her. But when I was sixteen and made it to the Junior Young Rider's Championship in jumping, which is like the penultimate for youth riders, she praised me repeatedly for my hard work and dedication. Even put a photo of my win on her desk at work. It was one of the few times I really knew she was proud of me."

He sat back and whistled low.

I half smiled. "I wanted to be the best as much as she wanted me to. She's like that with law school, too. Certain that it's the right career for me, that I can be the best."

"And you're not?" His head tilted like he was really listening.

"Not so much. As strange as it might sound, I miss the time and effort—mental and physical—that it takes to be as good as I was at show jumping. Those are the big fences you see in an arena at the Olympics. Law is about making a better argument, twisting words to suit more effectively. Some days that's enough; most of the time I feel unfulfilled."

"Could you go back?" he asked, reaching for my hand again.

As I took it, I shook my head. "Not really. I still have my horse, Mickie. He and I were an amazing team, and he's still my best friend. But he's retired now, reminiscing about his glory days, getting fat in Mom's backyard. Even if I could do something else, I'm not sure what that would be. I should know what that is if I'm going to change course."

"That's got to be rough, feeling like everyone else has your life planned out for you."

I thought about what he had said as we walked back to his truck. He barely knew me, and yet he had identified my struggle exactly. Was he that perceptive or was I that transparent? After we returned to his house, we sat in his truck talking for a while. I transferred my nervous energy into checking things out, flipping the visors, and looking at all his CDs. When it got too cold to stay in the truck I stood frozen by the passenger door, heart pounding madly in my ears, nerves taking over now that the evening was ending, primed to bolt to the cover of my car.

Instead, he came and gave me one of those wonderfully consuming hugs. Face-to-face as he released me, I tried to step back, but either my body or his hands wouldn't let me. Which didn't matter when I fell into a fantastic kiss. My pulse picked up again and everything went fuzzy except the sharp outline of what was happening inside of me.

"You taste like lime," Patrick said as he broke the kiss.

"Lime?" I asked faintly.

"Probably from the Corona with lime you were drinking."

I opened my eyes and stared at him, dazed. "Oh, right, the Corona." Did I look as disoriented as I felt? When Patrick stepped close for another kiss, I simply gave myself over to the butterflies and the warm fuzzies.

With the cold seeping through my coat, I pulled back. "Well, I, um, I should leave so I can get home and read some more cases before I go to bed." God! Lame! "And, uh, I should let you go 'cause you're so cold you're shaking."

"What if I'm not shaking 'cause I'm cold? What if I'm shaking 'cause you're kissing me?"

Was that possible? "Th-then we have a different dilemma."

"Do you maybe not want to leave just yet?" he asked, his mouth so close I could feel his warm breath on my cheek.

Standing in his living room, he kissed me again, only to stop and say, "I want to make it clear, I'm sending you home tonight."

Did I look that desperate? Maybe he was taking pity on the girl who let herself get pushed around. I felt my cheeks redden. "Well, of course," I said with a tone that sounded more prim than the *well, duh,* I'd been aiming for.

He led me to his room, then left me standing there while he went in search of water or something else equally unimportant. I studied what I could see in the dark—a picture of Brandi Chastain ripping her shirt off after the US soccer team won the women's world cup in 1999 pinned to the wall, magazine clippings with quotes stuck on the back of the door: "Start where you are, use what you have, do what you can," and another, "Happiness can be found, even in the darkest of times, if one only remembers to turn on the light." Apparently, he read Harry Potter as well as classic tomes. There was a pile of shoes next to the door, a poster of Buddha on the wall, and a state-of-the-art stereo. Like his shoes, the sheets on the bed were a messy tangle.

What are you doing? a little voice nagged. I turned to see if I could sneak out just as Patrick walked through the door. Well, it had been a great kiss, so maybe more of that wouldn't be so bad.

Kissing me gently, he carefully guided me backward toward the bed. I sat abruptly when the backs of my knees bumped against the side. He came over the top of me, and I reached up for him.

What is he thinking about?

I was surprised when he voiced my thoughts out loud. "Me?" I squeaked. He nodded. "Oh, well, I was thinking about your poster of the Buddha."

"That's not Buddha, it's Ganesh, the Hindu god of intellect and wisdom, and remover of obstacles," he corrected, kissing me again.

"Oh, well, it's dark and ... and I was thinking I don't even know your last name."

"Branagan. What's yours?"

"Mine? It's," crap, what was my last name? "It's Greene. So, um," I licked my lips, "what were you thinking about?"

"How you give noisy kisses that are fun." He rolled, pulling me on top of him.

Noisy kisses that are fun, I'll give you something to think about. I focused all the nervous energy churning inside me into a kiss, deepening it, breaking it off just as it got exceptionally good.

"You're right, though," I said, pushing myself upright, "I really should get going, spending the night would not be a good idea. But I had a great time tonight, we should do it again."

"You're going to kiss me like that, and then you're just going to leave?" he asked, incredulous.

"Yep." I turned to smile smugly at him.

Patrick studied me for a moment with an amused smile. "All right," he agreed, holding out his hand to help me up. He followed me out the front door.

After I buckled my seat belt, I glanced back up at him, my breath catching. Haloed by the streetlight, with his hands in the pockets of his frayed jeans, wearing a navy sweater, Patrick looked relaxed and pleased with himself. The moment froze, the image branded in my memory. I felt the fizz of excitement for something new burn from my mouth into my stomach. The beginning of something that would deeply impact me. I had a sudden feeling, as if I were perched above the scene, watching. From that view, I could already see we were bound together.

I turned my car around to head home and called him over for one last kiss. He leaned in the door, kissed me with a hint of the frustrated anticipation I had hoped I was leaving him with.

"By the way," he whispered.

"Yes?" I asked expectantly.

"You're going the wrong way on a one-way street." He stepped back and waved, leaving me to my embarrassment.

In the morning, getting ready for class, I sang along with a favorite song on the radio about first kisses on second dates. I smiled to myself, feeling foolishly excited.

Chapter 8

October 31

Patrick called as I sat altering an old dress to create a makeshift angel costume for a law school party.

"My roommates and I are having a Halloween party, but it's the day after Halloween," he explained.

"So really it's an All Souls Day party?" I teased.

"Sure, that too. Can you drink on All Souls' Day?" he queried.

"I don't see why not."

"Great! Talk to you latah'." I shook my head as I turned back to the dress.

The next evening, my phone rang as I slid pumpkin bars into the oven. "Hello?"

"Hey, it's Patrick. I just wanted to let you know that the party is a costume party, and if you don't come in costume, my roommates and I get to create one for you."

"Things you could have told me yesterday!"

"Well, look on the bright side, Halloween's over, so if you have to buy anything, it's probably on sale," he offered.

So helpful.

Four hours later, I straightened my dress, took a deep breath, and started toward the front door. I had kept my navy-blue angel wings from the previous night but traded the flowing dress for something a little more daring. Two George W. Bushes watched me walk up the sidewalk, and I prayed I wasn't walking right past Patrick. Inside, I set down the pumpkin bars, met a roommate, and hoped finding Patrick would be easy. Otherwise, I'd be making conversation with a hundred of my closest new friends.

"Emma!" I heard, only slightly slurred, from behind me. Patrick reached to wrap his arm around me. "I'm so glad you're here! Here, everyone has to start the night off with a Jell-O shot," he said, handing me one. "See it's orange on the bottom, and green on the top, like a little pumpkin!"

Eyeing it dubiously, I gamely downed the Jell-O and reached for a beer.

"What are you supposed to be anyway?" he asked.

I held my arms out to the sides. "An angel?"

"I didn't think angels usually flashed that much leg," he stated seriously, staring where my skirt ended mid-thigh.

"What a keen observation. It is, however, Halloween, so I thought maybe I could pull it off."

"No, it's great," Patrick managed, still staring. "You look like one of those Victoria's Secret angels."

"This from the cowboy wearing a loose ring snaffle bit on his belt, instead of spurs that jingle-jangle-jingle." I mentally slapped my forehead for criticizing his costume.

"You know what that is? That's so great! No one else knows and I feel kinda silly, but I had to have something that would make that noise. But you know, and that makes it totally worth all the ridicule I got at work. Margo, come here," he said, grabbing one of his roommates and dragging her over. She was dressed as an apple tree. "Do you know what this is?" he asked, shaking his hips so the bit jangled.

"I have no idea."

"It goes in a horse's mouth to guide them, but it's loose so it jingles."

I smothered a smile as Margo raised an eyebrow while Patrick continued wiggling in the kitchen.

"Like that song—'spurs that jingle-jangle-jingle,' and Emma gets it! Isn't that just so great! My costume makes sense to someone now!"

"Suuure." She patted him on the shoulder in mock sympathy.

Later, to the background of beer, bad nineties music, and drunken dancing, I ran into Margo again, who asked how I knew everyone. I glanced behind me to confirm his presence and said I knew Patrick.

"Are you guys dating?" she asked, her eyebrows nearly hitting her hairline.

I looked at Patrick again.

"We've gone out," he offered.

I shrugged to Margo. It wasn't exactly how I would have phrased it, but we'd only had our semi-blind date two weeks earlier.

"Huh," was all she said before grabbing me and pulling me into the crowd in the living room jumping up and down to "Tubthumping."

Around three in the morning, I started looking for Patrick, wondering where he had wandered off to. I needed to go home and go to bed. When I noticed the door to his room was closed, I "accidentally" bumped into it.

"Ah-ha." I barely made out Patrick's face and arm in the dark room. I picked my way over to the bed, hoping I wouldn't trip in my heels and break my ankle. "Patrick?" He was flopped over on his side and had lost the denim shirt of his cowboy costume. "Patrick, I just came to say goodnight, I have to go home."

"Mmmph," came his muffled reply. As I leaned closer, he grabbed me around the waist and pulled me crosswise onto the bed next to him. I tried to wiggle out from under his arm, but he only pulled me tighter.

Oh well, at least I tried. Plus, if I didn't struggle, I'd get to cuddle with him. *So much for dignity or being nonchalant.*

Chapter 9

November 2

I opened one eye. Where was I? The beige wall I was facing gave me no clues. Then the arm around my back registered, and I picked my head up to see *Metallica* glowing, emblazoned across the front of the T-shirt I was sleeping on. Oh, right, Halloween party. I picked my head up a little further to see Patrick's face slack-jawed and covered in stubble. He was still wearing the bit at his belt. I put my head back down and checked out again.

Three hours later, I repeated the same exercise. This time, however, Patrick had his eyes open and was looking at me intently, as if he were trying to figure out what I was doing there. Recovering, he mumbled, "Morning," and yawned.

"You guys sure throw some party."

"I guess so. I was supposed to oversee keys, and instead, I ended up with a Victoria's Secret angel in my bed. How did that happen?"

"Well," I began, looking for a way to make my search of the house less stalker-like. "I came to say good-bye before I left, and you reached up and pulled me into bed with you. I—" I cut myself off awkwardly. We hadn't even done anything, and the morning after was weird.

"Huh. I don't remember that at all."

"I can tell." I paused, waiting for him to say something, anything that would clue me into how he was feeling. "I should probably go. Let you get on with your day." Nothing.

Not until I was strapping on my shoes did he finally say, "Here, let me get shoes, and I'll walk you to your car."

"There's no need for that," I said coolly. He looked relieved at my dismissal, and I cringed.

I shivered in my dress, standing on the front step to take a deep breath of the clearing morning air. I didn't need to feel stupid; I hadn't made a fool out of myself by sleeping with him.

The embarrassment still tugged at the bottom of my stomach as I walked into my apartment. Rather than berate myself over nothing, I grabbed my gym bag and headed out again.

I was surprised to find, given the awkward awakening and my hasty retreat, that Patrick had left a voicemail while I was on the treadmill. Rather than listen to the message, I returned his call. If he was going to break up with me I wasn't going to let him do so by voicemail.

I twisted my ring, dropped my hand, but picked up the horseshoe on my necklace while it rang.

"Hey, it's Emma. I saw you called."

"I'm sorry about this morning," he began. "I was pretty hung over, and you seemed upset when you left."

"I was. I guess I was just expecting today to begin differently."

"Uhh ... differently how? Because, I mean, if you were looking for something in particular, you should have said so."

"That's not—I mean, not that I hadn't thought about it," the words came tumbling out on a half giggle, "just that, I wasn't expect-ing that, and I ... well you were so aloof this morning, I was pretty sure you never wanted to see me again."

"Well, do you maybe want to come over and hang out?" he asked, casually.

"Sure, that'd be nice," I said, equally casual.

"Hi," I said, as I stepped cautiously over the threshold just as the sun was going down. "How are you?" Despite his friendly invitation, I didn't know what to expect. It felt like the morning after, except not.

"Hi," he returned, still unshaven from the morning, looking just as uneasy as I felt. We sat on his bed, comforter pushed to the floor on top of the tumble of shoes, talking quietly, a bit about the party, and nothing in particular. Just as he leaned over to kiss me, a huge crash resounded from the next room.

"I ... I'd better go check on that."

"Sure." The look on his face said his concern wasn't that someone was pinned under a bookcase. While I waited, I picked up a book by a Buddhist nun from the nightstand.

"I'm sorry," he said, twenty minutes later. "She's going through some stuff right now. Family stuff. I need to—to help her through some of it. I'll call you later?"

He needed to help her with family stuff? "Can I do anything to help?"

"No, I've got it."

Then, just like that morning, I was standing on his front step, in the snow that had begun on my drive over.

In my warm apartment, empty of Travis who was out on his own date, I perused my cabinets for anything that might soothe the aching throb in my heart. Was I mad at the roommate for not leaning on one of the other two females in the house—why was the only boy her go-to? Or was I mad at Patrick for ditching me to go be with her? Why would he do that? My cupboards were bare of anything helpful.

My cell phone shrieked, shattering the silence of the apartment. "Hello?" I asked, suspicious.

"Hi." Patrick's voice flowed out of the little speaker. "I'm so sorry about that. Her family is kind of falling apart, and she's struggling. How are you?"

"Well, I'm eating olives because there was no alcohol and no chocolate in the house."

"That bad?"

"Worse than you might think, because I looked for chocolate— and I don't even like it."

"I'm sorry," Patrick said again.

"She needed a friend, and I can appreciate that. There was a time not too long ago when I could have used the same thing from someone."

"Is that why you were upset?"

I took a deep breath, preparing myself. "No. It's because I really like you, and I love hanging out with you, and this evening makes me question where it's been feeling like things are going between us. What I had started to assume. And that scares me a lot."

"Wow," he breathed, "You're pretty brutally honest for a girl."

I closed my eyes. "I'm just tired of playing games."

"You haven't played any with me."

"That's because I don't want to with you."

"It's still kind of early. I could come over?" His voice was halfway hopeful.

"That would be really nice."

"I'll see you soon." I could hear the smile in his voice.

I squealed quietly to myself, then sighed. I knew myself. Sometime while drinking Corona on our first real date, I had decided Patrick was "It." I was in big trouble.

I jumped when Patrick knocked, but rushed for the door. "Hi!"

"Hi," he said, coming to hug me.

I let myself sink into the floatiness I always felt when he hugged me, but didn't object when he pulled back enough to kiss me.

"I'm sorry. She's a mess, but I shouldn't have asked you to leave."

"You're here now. Will you come in?" I asked, taking his hand to lead him to my bedroom.

As I closed my room door Patrick rushed forward, kissing me thoroughly. "I had bettah' plans tonight than comforting my roommate," he said between kisses.

"You had a plan, huh?" I pushed my hands under the edge of his always untucked shirt.

"I did. Do." He pushed my sweatshirt over my head.

"Will I like this plan?" I asked, undoing the buttons on his flannel shirt.

"I hope so," he answered, kissing my neck.

"I already know you can kiss ..."

In response his hands tightened on my back, pulling me toward himself as he walked backward toward my bed. "Is this okay?"

"Mm-hmm," I hummed, never letting him stop kissing me.

I woke before my alarm, aware of Patrick, smiling to myself in the dark. I felt so light, but I knew that wouldn't last long.

"Good morning," he said quietly from behind me.

"Good morning," I returned, rolling to face him.

"I'm sorry again about last night. But I'm glad you let me come over."

"Me too."

"Are you free tonight? This was fun. Maybe we could do dinner and ..."

I grinned. "Actually, I am."

When I closed the front door behind Patrick a bit later, I rested my head against it. I knew I had lied to myself. I wanted something serious. Instead, I said I wanted something fun and casual, but really, I was not a girl who jumped from relationship to relationship. Not that I didn't want passion. But my heart, oh my heart, needed something more predictable and anchoring. Could this be it?

Chapter 10

November 5

During my early morning library time, I stared out the window, ignoring my casebook, replaying my nights with Patrick. My cell phone danced on the table. With a glance at the caller ID, heaviness surged to my stomach.

"Hi, Mom," I answered tiredly, getting up to leave the library. After my midterms had come back, I was even more worried about having only one more exam to get a decent grade.

"Emma. I haven't heard from you in a few days. I wanted to be sure you were all right."

I paused. What was I going to tell her? That I'd been kicked out of the house of the guy I was seeing, that she didn't know about, so that he could comfort another woman? That she wouldn't be pleased with my midterm results? That the same guy had then made it up to me, and we'd barely slept?

She didn't wait for me to choose an area. "How were your midterms last week?"

"Fine."

"What were your grades, Emma?"

"I mostly got C's, a couple of B's. Okay, I guess," I said as I left the library to pace the along the windowed hall.

"That's not even close to 'okay'! You should have gotten all A's. Why didn't you study more?"

"I did study, Mom!" I stopped in the hall, running the horseshoe along its chain. "I don't think I'm cut out for this. I think I want to withdraw." I rushed through the words, conscious I'd just implied I was a failure who wanted to drop out. "All my classmates have an enthusiasm and drive I don't."

Before I could finish my thought, she was running over me. "You think you're not good enough because you're not applying yourself. Graduate school is very different from college. You will actually have to do your homework."

Ouch.

"No, it's not that. I just ..." I dropped my hand from my necklace. "I'm discouraged. It's too hard. Not in a good, challenging kind of way," I rushed on, "but in a maddening, beating me down kind of way. All I do is study. I'm not having any fun; I don't understand how it all fits together. More, I don't really want to," I finished on a sigh.

"Law school isn't supposed to be fun. Your grandmother always said she only saw the back of Grandfather's head for three years. It's early still. Everyone feels like this at some point during grad school. Just keep going, you'll learn to like the law."

"Mom, this is my life." I turned around and started back down the hall.

"And you're my daughter. What would people think if you dropped out? If you can't even finish a semester?"

"That I have a mind of my own and know what I want for myself." It came out as a question.

"And what exactly is that?"

"I don't know. Yet. But I'll figure it out."

"Absurd. We've talked about this. You can't just go floating through life with no plan. Law school gives you opportunities you wouldn't otherwise have."

I stared out the window, letting the green grass and bright flowers outside unfocus in my gaze. Apparently it was too much to ask that she understand my frustration, or that I was questioning this path.

I escaped the library that afternoon, stealing a few hours to ride Mickie when Mom wouldn't be around. A few precious hours to myself. While I brushed him and put away tack, I chatted with Kim on the phone.

"Patrick and I were talking for an hour every night for like two weeks. Then poof, nothing in the last week. I can't let myself get hurt," I told her.

"Why didn't you call him?"

"Because. I'm afraid if I call him first, he'll think I'm pushing him." I paused, the brush resting on Mickie's back. "You know, when this started, it was just going to be nice and relaxed."

"I know. You've sounded different recently, talking about Patrick. Lighter. Like he makes you happy."

"He does! And I need that. Easy. Fun. Relaxed. Maybe I'm over-thinking. Mom and I had a crappy conversation about school. I told her I want to leave, and she basically said it was a phase."

"Way to bury the lede! You want to drop out?"

"I do."

"Are you going to?"

"I don't know. My midterms weren't great—virtually all C's. And I hate it. She will not entertain another conversation about it, though. I still don't know what I would do if I did drop out." As I patted Mickie on his forehead, he shoved his nose into my chest, knocking me back a step. "Maybe I'll wait and see how this semester finishes. If I study harder, maybe I can do better on the finals."

"You could just drop out and not tell her. Or at least not ask for her permission." When I didn't respond, she continued. "I can't pretend to understand your relationship with your mom. But if you want to drop out, you can come live with us, so at least you don't have to move home. If you want my opinion, I think you should."

"Thanks." She was right, but then I'd be totally on my own. My mother would ostracize me. If she stopped paying for law school, she'd also stop paying my rent. I had no ready job, and as my mom kept pointing out, no real direction. I scratched Mickie's forehead harder, and he bobbed his head in appreciation.

"So you're freaking out. Life feels serious and laborious, being with Patrick isn't as effortless as you'd like, and you have nowhere to let off steam."

"Exactly. I wanted something fun, but steady. Uncomplicated."

"You deserve that, Ems."

"Yeah, but that's not what I'm in the middle of. Ugh, I'm in the middle of falling for him. And I don't want to be here. Nor do I want to get so deeply entrenched that getting out becomes a land war." I gave a small half laugh.

"Famous last words."

When Patrick called the next evening to see if I wanted to get something to eat, my insides leaped. *No, no,* I calmly explained to all my parts that were dancing around. *We are going to take this nice and slow and be rational about this. Just because we think we are falling for him, doesn't mean we actually are.* My insides danced around some more. *Right, so long as we've got that clear.* Of course I said yes, and went to figure out what to wear.

He turned up on my doorstep looking more desirable than I remembered. I stood on my toes to kiss him, leaning in, wanting him more than I could have imagined.

"Suddenly I'm not particularly hungry," he said, lifting me off my feet and wrapping my legs around his waist.

"You know, I'm not either." I kissed him harder, wanting to be closer to him.

"Bedroom?"

"Yes," I panted, fingers fumbling with the buttons on his shirt as he walked in that direction. He set me down to pull my shirt over my head and strip off my jeans. I stood in front of him, stripped down to my underwear.

"Well, now that you have me mostly naked, what are you going to do with me?"

"Hmm ... did you say 'mostly'?" he grinned, catching the tip of his tongue between his teeth, his eyes teasing, as he picked me up, then dropped me soundly on the bed.

I reached to pull him down to me, hungry for him. He leaned down to lick my ear.

I giggled. "That tickles!"

"Well, I'll just have to move on," he said, and then inched his way down my neck.

I woke abruptly at 2:13 a.m., tucked in closely to Patrick, shoulder to hip to ankle, as he slept soundly with his arm thrown over me. I smiled in the dark, relishing the feeling.

Then, my unleashed brain took a sharp turn toward the fact that we hadn't been talking every night recently. I wondered if he was seeing someone else, and that's why he didn't always call. We hadn't talked about being exclusive or if that was even something either of us were ready for. And then there were nights, like tonight, when we couldn't get close enough to each other. It felt hot and cold. Or was I imagining things? "Catastrophizing," my mother would have labeled it.

After staring at the wall for a half-hour, I wiggled out from under Patrick's arm to get some water and in the dark tripped over Patrick's boots, collapsing in laughter.

He opened one eye and examined me sprawled on the floor, laughing my head off, and said in a voice heavy with sleep, "I suppose I should be glad you're not used to walking around shoes."

Chapter 11

November 19

Patrick was sitting at the kitchen table when his roommate Margo let me in, her mouth in an O of surprise. "Nice boots," she commented.

"You sure got all prettied up to go out," Patrick observed, staring at my boots and skirt.

"Law school drinks." I smiled to myself, thinking back to the happy hour I'd just come from. Someone in the cramped booth had said happy hour was always better when I was there. I focused on the pile of clothes and mud-covered work boots by Patrick's bare feet. "That's a mess."

"Tractor engine seized. I spent the day lying on the ground taking it apart."

"You look like you need a night off as much as I did."

"I thought that's what I was for," he said with a wicked grin, but something didn't quite feel right. In the couple of weeks since he'd rushed to his roommate's aid, and we'd then spent the weekend together, I'd felt us seesawing. Feeling out our respective feelings, I went over to get a hug. "You're freezing cold."

"Very astute. It's cold outside." He wrapped me even tighter in his arms and I relaxed. Maybe I was just making things up. He let go and tugged on my hand, "Let's warm you up."

I followed him into his bedroom, where the local jazz station was playing on the stereo. He turned around and put his arms around me again, and we started swaying with the music playing softly in the background. One song ended and the next came on, Billie Holiday crooning tenderly about familiar places.

As the song faded into something else soft and slow and appropriate for a cold winter night, Patrick pulled back and started to push up my sweater. "Patrick, you know," I said, voice low and teasing, "that's got a zipper on it."

He stopped tugging on the hem of the cardigan. "Scandalous!" A wicked gleam lit his eyes as he reached for the zipper pull. "But you know," he paused his unzipping, "if I take this off, it's going to be even colder, and you'll probably have to stay. Just so you don't get frostbite and all."

"That seems reasonable," I agreed solemnly.

"Good," he said, jerking it the rest of the way down.

The Tuesday before Thanksgiving, morning brought me back to reality with a jolt. Claire was asleep next to me and there was a half-empty bottle of rum on my nightstand.

We, and our law school cohort, had partied our asses off, celebrating surviving the first semester. For a few hours, I hadn't thought about the fact that finals were still ahead, or that I needed to ace basically everything to get my grades up. I'd ignored the unease that still hung over me from Mom's constant critique and numerous calls.

Slowly I got out of bed. My head didn't feel like it was going to fall off. *Hmmm ... maybe I hadn't had as much as the evidence suggested.* I padded out to the living area, where I found Travis passed out in the recliner. He woke up as I knocked around the kitchen.

"Mmm ... coffee," he said in a blurred voice. "Thanks, Ems." He sat upright in the recliner and reached for the mug I handed him.

Claire joined me in the kitchen a couple of hours later, just as I pulled a quiche from the oven. "Morning," she said, stifling a yawn. "Mmm, that smells good. Did you bake this morning?! Are you going to feed me?"

"I already forced her to make that promise," Travis stated proudly from where he was packing his backpack to leave for the week.

"Thank you!" Claire said.

I laughed. "Given how awful you look, yes, I will feed you. Both. But while classes may be over, we still have finals." I pointed at Claire. "So promise that we will study with dedication today. I'm going to fail if I don't finally learn some of this stuff!"

She yawned again. "Okay, but only if *you* promise to tell me how you managed to get out of last night without a hangover." I laughed and handed her a bottle of aspirin and a glass of water.

Travis grabbed a gigantic piece of quiche. "Have a good Thanksgiving, Ems, see you next week," he called as he banged out the door.

A few hours later, I took a hot shower and returned to my notes. I sincerely hoped that all this studying would pay off. I was starting to sink into the nerves of finals when there was a knock at the door.

I opened it to find Patrick on my doorstep with a bouquet. "Oh! It's you. What are you doing here?"

He took a step back from the doorway. "Well, I could just go home if I'm interrupting something."

"No, silly," I grabbed the front of his shirt. "But I wasn't expecting you for a couple of hours."

"I wanted to surprise you. I thought we could eat in, just be together." He held up a bag from my favorite Chinese restaurant.

I stepped back to let him into the apartment. My insides were dancing around again, and the blood fizzed through my veins in excitement. "Let's have a picnic! Travis left to go home for Thanksgiving this morning, so he won't be around tonight."

Patrick grinned at me over his shoulder and wiggled his eyebrows. "So he won't mind if I lick plum sauce off you?"

"I'm sure he won't."

"Good," he said, coming over to lift the edge of my shirt and smear some on my stomach.

"Patrick," I laughed as he followed up with his tongue. "Fine, all's fair," I pulled his shirt off and grabbed another package.

It took no time for us to strip each other, uncovering new spots to dab on and lick off sauce.

"This is the last of it," Patrick said.

"There won't be any left for dinner."

"I'm okay with that," he said, drawing his thumb just under my collarbone.

An hour later we sat on the floor, me in an old T-shirt and Patrick in his boxers, finishing the last of dinner. I watched Patrick as he read his fortune.

"How's my girl?" he asked, leaning over to kiss me on the nose.

"Good." I smiled. "Is that what I am?"

"What?"

"Your girl?"

In the long silence, I steeled myself. "As much as I don't like disappointing you ... I call the mares my girl, too," he said with a grin.

Ouch. A cold sensation of the disappointment he didn't want me to have flooded my body.

"Hmmm," I said, infusing the sound with as much skepticism as possible.

At least I'd get some distance from this new source of inadequacy while spending Thanksgiving with my grandparents in Chicago.

At six the next morning my alarm clock turned the radio on, unfurling Jimmy Buffett asking why we ever go home.

Chapter 12

November 22

"I heard you had a date," Mom commented as we buckled into our flight to O'Hare.

"Excuse me?"

"One of the junior partners mentioned he'd seen you walking downtown. Holding hands." She said it like I could catch the plague.

"That's what people do."

"He said he was surprised, since the guy you were with clearly wasn't an attorney."

It was like she had spies following me around. "I'm not sure it's good for two people who both like to be right to be in a relationship. Besides, I find many of my classmates to be arrogant."

"What does he do?" she queried, her disdain for what someone who hadn't been wearing a suit probably did burying my smugness at my comeback.

"His *name* is Patrick. And he's in AmeriCorps."

"Oh, Emmalyn." She all but rolled her eyes.

I stared pointedly at Mom as I shook out the book I'd been about to open.

"Shouldn't you be using this as study time?"

"I've heard it's a good idea to give your brain time to absorb information," I replied sweetly.

When we got to my grandparents', I retreated.

I stared out the window in the unused study, curled up in an oversized leather club chair. I had been there for days, avoiding my mom's questions and scrutiny by reading notes and going over rules, only taking breaks to go for a mind-clearing run, as the chilly air hung heavily around the house in an exclusive northern suburb. My mom stepped through the door, holding out a glass of wine for me.

"You've been unusually quiet this week," she observed.

"Yeah, well, you know, finals and all that. Gotta be ready!" I feigned brightness.

"How are you feeling about them?"

It surprised me how genuine her question sounded. "I don't know," I shrugged, closing the casebook. "Some areas I know, I know, others not so much. I'm hoping what I do know will help overcome what I don't. Or that all this cramming will prove fruitful."

"Cramming never works, you know that."

I smothered a snort at the irony of the advice, balanced against her admonition on the plane. "No, I know. I'm sure I know it better than I think I do. I just don't feel ready. It's so different from college. Animal science was practical, you know; this is so theoretical. I know it all fits together, but I can't always see how."

"You'll do well. I'm glad to see that you're past the point you were a few weeks ago. Joe, one of the partners asked about you last week. I was proud to be able to tell him how hard you are working. I told you it was just a phase. I know you're not a quitter." She patted my knee and walked away.

I rolled my eyes at her back. I might not have been a quitter, but the closer I got to finals, the more I questioned why I was there. I wanted to march out to the living room and declare to them all that I was dropping out.

They would have been horrified at my rebellion. My mother for obvious reasons. But I could imagine my grandmother gasping in shock; how dare I question the authority of my mother. Next to her, I envisioned my grandfather shaking his head of perfectly combed white hair at my foolishness.

But here was the problem: I was a good girl. I'd never once been so much as sent to the principal's office. Straight A's. Honors courses. My few boyfriends had all had a seal of approval. And now law school. A ticker tape of checked boxes.

The older I got, the less I could be myself unless that made Mom look good. The unspoken agreement to always measure up to the highest standards no longer felt like a challenge worth meeting. Maybe it had never been.

Chapter 13

December 13

By the time I returned home from Thanksgiving, I had run out
of the capacity to feel disappointed in myself, and my brain was
crammed full of facts and theories. After I unpacked, I called Patrick
and left a message. He didn't return my call until much later, and then
only stayed on the phone long enough to tell me he didn't want to
talk. All the resolve I'd had upon returning from my grandparents'
house drained away, and I went to bed feeling deflated.

I didn't have time to feel sorry for myself, though. With my first
go around with law school finals upon me, I didn't even have time to
sleep.

"Sorry I didn't call you back sooner," he said in a voicemail, three
days later. I almost hadn't noticed. When I returned his call, he apolo-
gized again. "It's been a little hectic around here, with one roommate
leaving, and a new one coming in. How about we grab dinner?"

"I'd love to, but I have my Civil Procedure final in two days, and I
can't afford any time off right now."

"Oh." He sounded disappointed. "Well, how about that night,
after your final?"

The evening after my CivPro final, a casual dinner of burgers and beer let me unwind, and even relax away some of the finals-induced stress. "This was nice, thanks," I said around a mouthful of French fries.

"You really sounded like you needed it. Rough exam?"

"God, they all are. It's like how can they ask a question in the most twisted way possible, or it's the most nuanced thing you spent like five minutes on during the semester?"

"Do you think you did okay?"

"Maybe? I don't know. It's like when I was studying—some of it I know I knew. The rest of it I just took the best guess I could."

"Well, that sounds ... fun."

"Yeah," I laughed, "never go to law school, it's murder on your sanity."

"How's the rest of it, other than finals?"

"Enh. Mom is haranguing me about my grades, I want to drop out, I still miss riding, and I hate my life." I pulled a face. "I just wish it were easier, that there was some clear alternative. I'm okay if all I do is keep my head down, but if I don't ... Plus, I need to find an internship or something for summer. Preferably at a prestigious law firm so my mother can point out how *well* I'm doing."

Patrick nudged my pint glass closer. "My sister says the same thing. Not the dropping out part, but how hard her doctorate is. She said she wanted to quit several times, but then something would come together, and she'd be able to keep going."

That made sense to me. I bumped Patrick's shoulder with mine. "Thanks for listening to me bitch."

He bumped my shoulder back. "You're welcome."

As we stepped out into the brisk night air, I slid my hand in his pocket and he took it in his, giving it a squeeze. I turned to smile at him. He stared at me.

"What?" I asked, rubbing my nose. "Do I have ketchup on my face?"

"No, I just like looking at you. You're awful cute."

Heat and affection swelled inside my chest. "Oh." I stared back. "Thanks." He leaned over and kissed me on the nose.

Maybe it was just the stress of finals that had me imagining rock-iness in our relationship. Here he was rescuing me from them. My knight in tattered khakis.

A week later, finals were over. No rest for the weary though, as I packed a suitcase for Christmas with my grandparents and New Year's with Renée.

"Hello?" I answered as I tossed another sweater into my suitcase.

"Hey, it's me," Patrick answered.

"Oh, *hi*," I enthused back, "I was just thinking about you." Last week's exams had flattened me, both mentally and physically. But Patrick had kept me entertained with brief phone calls on each of the long days. I was looking forward to going out with him and law school friends to celebrate the completion of our first semester. "What are you up to?"

"I just got back from The Resort."

"Really? I thought you had today off."

"I was supposed to, but one of the horses got caught up in the fence and I got called to see if I could get the fence out. It turns out she had been there all night and lost a lot of blood. We called the vet, but her leg was so bad he couldn't do anything. She would never have been the same. We had to put her down."

"Oh, Patrick, I'm so sorry." I sank on to the edge of my bed, heart squeezing in sorrow, thinking how he knew every horse's name and favorite spot to be scratched. He cared about them like he did the neighbor's cat. This was exactly the reason I'd opted out of being a vet. "I know how much those horses mean to you. Did no one see her last night on rounds?"

"Apparently not. It was Steven on duty last night, and we've had some problems with him recently. I don't think he was doing rounds like he was supposed to, and that's why no one saw her until this morning." I heard the shush of fabric and imagined him pulling off his sweatshirt. "Anyway, I just called to say that I don't think we should get together tonight. I'm beat, and I've been outside in the freezing cold and snow all day. I'm covered in blood and I just want to retreat for the rest of the night."

I understood, of course. I probably wouldn't want to see anyone either, especially a bunch of drunken, celebratory law students. "I leave tomorrow morning. And then you're not back from Boston until mid-January. I won't see you for almost a month."

"I know. I'm really sorry about that. But I just can't be social tonight."

"Well, what if it was just you and I? We don't have to go out."

"No," he said, surprisingly vehement. "You've earned this celebration and the right to go out with your friends. I'm not taking that away from you. You go out without me tonight, and when you get back, you and I will celebrate then."

"I really want to see you. Please come over, at least for a little bit." The silence between us stretched out. I knew I was begging, and I hated that, trying to not cry.

"Okay, I'll come over, and we'll go out for one drink. Then you have to go back out with your friends for the rest of the night."

"Okay. I'll see you soon?" I asked tentatively.

Patrick sighed. "Yeah, I'll be there in about an hour."

An hour and a half later, I was pacing my living room wondering where Patrick was. Travis had already left for the bar, saying he would grab a large table we could all sit at. Had another horse gotten hurt? Had he decided not to come after all? Maybe I had pushed too far, and he was just not coming. Could he be breaking up with me?

I was reaching for my phone when there was a knock at the door. "Oh!" I cried upon opening it. Patrick looked more tired than I'd ever seen him before. I pulled him inside, wrapping my arms around him, holding him tight. He looked as though someone had ripped his heart out, and I wanted to hug the life back into him.

"Hi," he sighed. "Sorry I'm late. I'm just moving slowly."

"I'm glad you're here. But you look awful. Are you sure you want to go out? We don't have to go anywhere. We can just order in and veg on the couch." I suddenly didn't want to go anywhere, I just wanted to stay home with him and cuddle in bed. I'd have five more semesters to celebrate. I could put one off for him.

"Yes. You earned this. We have to go out for a drink. Besides, all your friends are expecting you. We can't let them down." He smiled wanly.

"Yeah, no, I am making the decision. We are not going out. Yes," I said before he could protest, "it is the end of my first semester of law school. But there will be more, and I will be just as relieved to be done with all of them. I want to spend tonight with you. And frankly, you look like you could use a friend." I watched him not responding. "Let's just order in."

"Pizza? I know that's not very sexy."

"Doesn't matter. Pizza sounds great to me! Easy, and you can take the leftovers home." I punched in numbers and made a quick request. Patrick watched me bustling to the kitchen for beers. "Can you just sit down for a minute?"

"Sure."

Together we sat on my bed, him quiet, me running my hand through his hair. I realized we'd never had a gentle moment like that before.

"It just hurts, to think of her suffering all night," Patrick said softly.

"I know."

"It was like that when my mom died. She was in bed for months, hooked up to machines, slowly wasting away. She never said it, but you could tell she was suffering."

"When did she die?" I held my breath. He'd never talked about his mom before.

"When I was a junior in high school. She told me and my sisters that she would be there for our graduations and to dance at our weddings. She died nine months later. She was fun. Easy to talk to. She was always there for us. Pops got reclusive. He's better now, but aged fast in that first year. My older sister was already away in college, and I was left to hold up my younger sister."

I could barely breathe. I knew how he felt, although my dad hadn't suffered. "My dad died when I was in high school, too. Hit and run. We rarely talk about him, but after he died, my mom became edgier, harder, more demanding. I'm so sorry, Patrick." I leaned forward to kiss him on the forehead. There were no tears, he was just staring straight ahead.

"That's why I don't dance. The Buddhists teach that all life is impermanent, and to hold on to it is suffering. I want to embrace that philosophy, but I think she'd be upset to not be able to participate, and I always think about how she doesn't get to do anything ever again."

"Don't they also say that nothing ever ends, it is only transformed, and that the best way to honor our loved ones is to allow them that transformation?"

"I know, but ..."

Yes, but letting go when we felt like we had been deprived was hard. I wished I had better wisdom for him. I knew that feeling of being gypped. We might be on opposite ends of the emoting spectrum, but I knew the anguish at the well of grief, and how it could come to swallow you at any moment.

We spent the evening in bed cuddling and talking quietly. I missed my dad, but Patrick clearly still held all the pain from his mom's death as if it were fresh.

In the early morning light, I threw the last of my things in my suitcase and headed for the door. Travis had left me a note on the kitchen table when he'd come in very late, or very early. I scribbled a response that Patrick was still sound asleep in my room.

Travis was a great guy, and he wouldn't care. He was a good friend, solid and easy to talk to. And studious. My mother would have approved of him.

I took a last tour of my room to make sure I wasn't forgetting anything. "No, don't get up," I whispered as Patrick mumbled something at me. "Just keep sleeping. We'll talk soon. Have a merry Christmas," I said, kissing him on the cheek.

Chapter 14

December 23

Claire was late picking me up to drive to the airport, causing me to sprint across the airport while pulling my suitcase and two carry-on bags.

"Hi," I panted, "sorry I'm late. Getting all the suitcases in the car took some maneuvering."

"Can I see your ID, please?" the lady at the check-in counter asked.

"Um, yeah, it's here somewhere," I said, frantically patting my pants pockets for my wallet. *Oh shit.* "Um, hold on just a minute." I patted some more, avoiding eye contact with my mother. Finally I had to look up. "I'm sorry. I don't have my license. I was packing and I ... I seem to have misplaced it."

"Emma!" I could hear the harsh edge of disapproval in my mother's voice.

"I know, Mom. Last night didn't really go as planned." She didn't need to know more than that. It didn't matter that she hadn't met Patrick; she didn't need to, to know she didn't like him.

I could feel her taking in my late arrival, my disheveled state of dress, and complete disorganization. Of course, even at six in the morning, she looked perfect. Tailored flannel dress pants, a pressed button-down. Her only concession to casualness was the loafers she had on in lieu of her normal heels.

I ignored the scrutiny to focus on checking in. "I have my student ID. Will that work?" I asked desperately.

"Sure will," the check-in lady smiled brightly as she finished printing boarding passes. "Here you go, have a nice trip."

My mom grabbed my arm and steered me away from the counter. "You were so late we now have to rush to make our flight."

"We'll be fine, Mom. We'll even be able to get coffee," I said with a fake smile.

After navigating security, I left her at the gate with our bags and went for the promised coffee.

"A quad latte, six sugars, and extra milk, and a double espresso black," I requested, sagging against the counter. Maybe her favorite drink could calm her down.

Buckled safely into my seat, I put my headphones in and pulled an eye mask down in an attempt to thwart any comments my mother might have.

"I can't believe you," she hissed. "You almost didn't make the flight."

So much for coffee as appeasement. "I might have been a few minutes late meeting you, but I did not miss the flight." I pushed my eye mask up over one eye to glare at her. "And if I had, I would have figured it out."

"You were still late! That is unacceptable! How is that going to look to potential employers if you can't show up on time for appointments?"

"Oh, come on!" I said, noticing that although first class was full, everyone was concentrating on putting luggage away and not us. "I was a few minutes late due to circumstances beyond my control. I did not miss the flight. We weren't even running behind. Comparing this to an interview is ridiculous!"

"If you can't get to the airport on time, how do you expect me to believe you can be responsible about anything else?" she snarled. As usual, my small slight was a catastrophe in her eyes. "You were probably out late, drinking, with that Patrick, weren't you?"

"As a matter of fact, I was with Patrick, but we weren't drinking. Not that it's any of your business," I shot back.

"Of course it's my business. He works as a farmhand. That is not good enough for you, which you know but refuse to acknowledge!"

I had known as soon as she'd said someone had seen us together this would come up again. "He's doing a year of service," I ground out. "And he's a nice person, who's good to me. That is *all* that matters. Stop judging him ... and me!"

"That is *not* all that matters. If you are going to be a successful attorney you need to be with, and married, to someone who is equally successful and intelligent."

"You have no idea how successful Patrick may or may not be once he's finished. Didn't you, approvingly, tell me that one of the partner's kids went into the Peace Corps after college?"

"Working for a non-governmental agency, not some nonprofit that can barely pay him."

"Like I'm some Jane Austen heroine who has to be saved from potential poverty," I said sarcastically.

"You know how much your father's friendly approach to business drove me crazy. It was totally inappropriate, and I was judged for it, too. I cannot fathom why you can't comprehend the importance of a good match."

"Dad was a good businessman and people liked him!" I kept my voice quiet, too, but was no less angry. "You don't have to be a shark to be successful. And maybe I don't want to be a lawyer anyway! I'm going to sleep," I said, putting my earbuds in. "Oh, and yes, I think finals went well, thanks for asking."

Now I had a headache. This was not how I had envisioned my semester break starting.

After last night, I knew Patrick and I were fine. Still, something about a month apart after the closeness we'd shared weighed on me. I carried Patrick's grief heavy in my heart, and it felt as if the sadness might overwhelm us. I shifted to my side as much as I could and tuned out everything but the song.

Chapter 15

New Year's Week

Although I had been duty-bound to spend the Christmas holiday with family, I escaped to Renée's for New Year's week.

The wind and snow swirled around me in front of the Manchester airport, where Renée picked me up. She had gone to New England to be with Aaron at his new assignment.

"You made it just in time before it gets really cold and snowy!" she said, hugging me through our heavy winter coats.

"I'm so glad you guys were around."

"Like where would we go?" she rolled her eyes. Her life since graduation had changed too, and now she was a manager in one of the microbiology labs at the University of New Hampshire. "Besides, it always feels like Christmas when it's supposed to."

"And the house," I said as we pulled up the drive. "Wow, Renée, this is beautiful!" The 1830s farmhouse, on the New Hampshire seacoast, was surrounded by woods, now covered in snow.

While having a traditional New Year's celebration had been great, it was the days after that I was most grateful for. The tide melted away the snow that fell on the beach, and I ran there every morning, my breath coming in gusts of steam. I ticked off each exhale as a sign of progress, even if it was the only way I was seeing any.

"What's wrong?" Renée asked one morning. I glanced up from where I was prying off my snow-covered shoes. "You're scowling."

"I was thinking about Patrick while I was running. Again."

"Want to talk about it?" she asked, handing me hot coffee piled with marshmallows. I smiled seeing them.

"When I left Denver for Christmas everything between us was okay." I began, following her to the living room. "We had that good conversation the night before I left. There isn't any real reason to feel the way I do."

"But?"

"But we haven't talked at all. I know he's not great with his cell phone—he still grumbles that The Resort can reach him whenever they want."

"Sometimes I feel the same about the lab," she said dryly.

"And me about Mom!" I wiggled my toes in front of the fire-place, enjoying my relaxing muscles after the cold run. "It's just every time I think about him, there's this heaviness in my stomach. Like we're not actually okay."

"I know you don't want me to say this, but the best thing you can do is to try to stop worrying."

I made a face, and she chuckled.

"Enjoy hanging out. He'll either trust you and reach out, or he won't. I know that's hard for you, but there isn't anything you can do about it."

"I just—I don't know how. I don't know how to not control things. It's how I've stayed ahead of Mom, you know?"

"Patrick isn't your mom; he doesn't need to be controlled. And if you try, speaking from experience, he'll retreat. Agonizing about him and your relationship won't change anything."

Back at home, doing laundry and organizing for classes, I lived inside the warm bubble of her pragmatic support and advice. And Renée had been right; I heard from Patrick not long after I got back to Denver.

Over dinner shortly after we'd both returned, he told cheerful stories of the couple of weeks he'd been home, we'd traded notes about how we'd spent the same winter storm, and then we'd gone back to his place for a more satisfying reunion.

As January rolled in, so did the National Western Stock Show. For over one hundred years, Denver had played host to cowboys and livestock for two weeks. What had begun as a way for stockmen to learn feeding and breeding techniques, and buy, sell, or show livestock, became, over time, a booming economic influx for the city, eventually adding horse shows that were a stop on all the national circuits.

I had competed there until just the year before. Things looked different as a spectator. As I strolled around the concourse above the main arena, something I'd never had time to do, nostalgia and longing washed over me.

Done right, competition was all consuming. Hours training, practicing individual elements, how tight to make this turn, extra encouragement to get over the jump that's just three inches higher. It was a mental exercise as much as a physical one. The bond I had with Mickie was as strong as any I had with a human friend. I'd spent hours beyond training grooming him, cleaning the barn, retrieving feed, and organizing for the next show. Then suddenly we'd be in the competition arena, facing jumps of four to five feet, the sounds from the stands receding as we focused on the route ahead, and the individual challenge of each obstacle.

Without financial support or a high-paying job, the possibility of going back to that kind of high-level competition was nearly impossible. I had been using the rationale that going to law school would give me the kind of career that would allow me to get back to showing. But who was I kidding? Once I graduated, there would be even less time for horses than I had now. With eighty-hour workweeks in some high-rise office building, I'd be lucky to even see my horse, let alone have the time to dedicate to being show ready. That is, if I could even get a job.

I didn't want to be studying, or in class; I wanted to be here, competing. Being at Stock Show wasn't going to help me get my grades up, but in this moment, I didn't care.

About halfway around the concourse, I came to The Resort's interactive booth, with the Old West Preservation banner arcing over it. Patrick was there, along with another volunteer, talking with a visitor. I browsed at the next booth, wondering if I should just return the way I had come.

"Emmalyn!" Patrick called as he finished answering a question.

I hesitated. "Hey there, how's it going?" I'd only seen Patrick once since we had both returned from our holiday trips. Would he think it was weird I was here? I had missed him the whole time, but I was afraid he hadn't missed me at all.

"I'm glad to see you!" he said, wrapping me in one of his wonderful hugs. All the tension left my body. "It's a little boring. I'm assured this will change in the next few days. We'll see about that."

"It will, and weekends will be packed." We walked slowly around the concourse, passing vendors of tack, custom caps and jackets, and one extensive area for custom English riding boots. I knew I ought to be leaving, heading back to class, but I couldn't yet force myself to do so. "Claire called earlier. She and her roommates are going for dinner downtown tonight. Want to come?"

I crossed my fingers that he would. None of my law school friends had met him yet, and they were starting to think he was a figment of my imagination.

Patrick hesitated. "I suppose that will work."

I slowly released the breath I'd been holding.

As we walked into the modern restaurant later that evening, where a waterfall behind the bar was illuminated by blue, I worried about melding these two halves of my life. Patrick's relaxed casualness jarred with Claire's skirt and heels, against the modern backdrop, leaving me cold with a sense of dread I couldn't quite shake.

Coming back from the bathroom, I saw Claire at the end of the bar talking pointedly with Patrick, frowning as she listened, and Patrick with a nearly blank face.

"You should probably check on the dewormer you are using at The Resort," I heard Claire say. "There was litigation on the one you're using for causing awful cases of colic that led to death."

"Are you still in school mode?" I teased Claire, coming to slide my arm around Patrick.

"Just trying to help Patrick do his job better."

"I'm sure you're not the only one who knows about that lawsuit." Patrick could take care of himself, but I wondered what had made Claire so forceful in the first place.

Until the next morning, when Claire called me as I drove into school. "Emma, he was so rude, making lawyer jokes."

"We were all joking with each other. What did you expect him to do, have a philosophical conversation? Talk proximate causation? He was perfectly nice. What were you talking to him about all evening at the bar?"

"Well, I tried to talk to him about horses, but he wasn't responsive to that."

"Claire, he's not a horse guy—he's not like you and me, he wasn't raised with horses. Just because he works with them doesn't mean that's his thing. I don't want to talk about class when I get home, why would he want to talk about work when he's not there?"

"I don't care. He was meeting your friends for the first time and should have been trying to win them over. He just doesn't seem to fit your life."

"You're the only person in law school who could possibly understand how he *does* fit. I thought you would." I turned the radio up to block my anger as I finished my drive.

I really should have felt cheerful about my life. Patrick and I hadn't had any of the stiltedness I was afraid would happen after our holiday separation, and who cared what Claire thought anyway? Who cared if there was a nagging voice that wondered if she was right, that I was two different people and rapidly becoming more the lawyer than the dedicated horse girl? The sun was shining, and I wasn't going to my hated Property class. I belted out the song right along with Sheryl Crow, singing about being happy and life not being so bad.

When I got to the library, Travis was there working, so I sat down across from him. Claire came in shortly afterward. "Can we go somewhere and talk?"

"No, I need to work. I'm behind on case studies for Contracts. We can talk later."

"Fine." She turned smartly on her heel and strode away.

I sighed as I watched her go.

Travis looked up from his reading. "Are you okay?"

"No. Claire thinks Patrick is a jerk, and that he's rude and not right for me. She sounds like my mother." My stomach tightened at the thought.

"Well, that's crazy," Travis said. "He's a great guy. Different from the type that go to law school, but a good guy. Maybe Claire is just having a bad day."

I smiled thinly. "Thanks Travis, you're a good friend."

"Good friend nothing. I like Patrick. If you end up breaking up, can I date him?"

I laughed out loud. "I don't think he's your type," I said, winking at him.

"Damn. That long hair really does it for me."

"Ha-ha." I grinned in spite of myself.

Chapter 16

January 15

I wasn't sure if I wanted to reminisce about the joy of competing or if it was a backward desire to torture myself with what I was missing, but when Mom suggested we go watch some of the jumping at Stock Show, I agreed. Together we walked through the show barn. Well-known names from my time competing jumped out from the heavy embroidered banners that adorned aisle end caps, or were suspended at the head of an aisle the horses were stalled in.

"Emma!"

I turned to find Kelsey, a former competition friend, rushing down the main aisle toward me.

"I wondered if I might see you here. Mrs. Greene," she acknowledged. She took in my jeans and vest. "Are you not competing this year?"

"I started law school last fall."

"Oh! That's a shame, I was really looking forward to beating you again this year." Kelsey's brown eyes sparkled with mischief.

Suddenly I was back in a moment six years earlier, the two of us the last ones standing in the lineup for awards at a qualifying competition for the Junior Young Rider Championship. That had been a big summer, of winning consistently and turning sixteen. I felt the exhilaration and joy of that moment, followed closely by grief that I wasn't also getting ready to compete tonight. I had one more year before I aged out, but instead of getting ready for tonight's competition, I had studied case books diligently to take the night off to observe. In my mind I saw myself sitting at a desk over a stack of papers, trophy plaques from decades ago gathering dust on the walls. My whole world reduced to mementos. "Mickie's enjoying some downtime. But good luck tonight!" I said as brightly as I could manage. "I'm sure you'll be as great as ever."

"Thanks, Emma. Good luck in law school."

Mom and I turned back toward the stands. "You know she was never as good as you, she only beat you because you downed that rail," my mom noted rather unfairly.

I turned away from the flash from my past and headed toward the stands, catching glimpses of what my life had been like. A young girl got a leg up and someone polished barn dirt off boots. A bright chestnut reminded me of my first show pony when I was five. I had seen Kelsey here last year, at what had been my last competition. Applause from the main arena registered, washing over the memories of completing that final course perfectly, of winning everything one last time before I was forced into early retirement. I smiled to myself for a moment, then saw the jeans on my legs where breeches should have been, and the memory faded.

I shook myself as I followed my mom into the stands. The arena was freshly dragged, the fences pristine under the brilliant lights. Brightly colored, the jumps sported arches, fans, multicolored poles, two standards set close together to create the wider spread of an oxer, and obstacles set a mere stride apart. I'd grabbed a course map from a table earlier, and unconsciously started planning how I would have executed the course.

When the next round of competition began, the lights over the spectators dimmed. As one, the crowd leaned forward, gasped, or applauded. Mom and I leaned together, commenting on a turn here, a too-late cue there, analyzing how big to make that turn on the end, and at how much of an angle to take that fence in the middle before having to make a tight turn back for the next.

Show jumping was the ultimate balance between speed and grace. Ride your course too cautiously in an effort to keep it clean, to not tick a rail and have it come crashing out of the cups holding it up, to not have your horse refuse a fence, and you might cross the timer seconds too slow and accumulate penalties. On the other hand, ride too fast, and your execution might be reckless, knocking rails willy-nilly, or as I had seen in more than one case, collapsing an entire fence.

More applause. "It's a shame she was so careful with her execution," Mom said, "those time penalties will cost that girl a placing."

I wished I were out there. Then I would know what I was doing, what my goal was.

"Mmm," I agreed, "still, she had a beautiful ride. Oh, there's Kelsey!"

I watched Kelsey make a slow, easy circle, collecting her horse, getting in sync. Then she passed through the flags marking the timer line, and I saw it as we had been, matched point for point going into the final round of qualifying competition for the Young Rider Championship when I was sixteen ...

And then I wasn't watching anymore, I was riding with her, feeling the horse under me as he lifted his front feet and pushed powerfully from behind, that momentary suspension midair where it felt like you were flying, and then an athletic landing before speeding on to the next jump. The sensation of power moving around a course blurred with the memory from our qualifying round—Mickie slipping just the tiniest bit as he lifted off, hearing his toe catch the back rail of the oxer, the two stands of the fence set four feet apart, and knowing without hearing the rail hit the ground that those four faults had cost me first place. It had been a near-perfect round. I had finished with half a second to spare; I hadn't been reckless, and the photos later revealed how flawless our form had been. But my mother had only seen the jumping faults, the 0.1 percent imperfection.

Kelsey had won that round, edging me out in total points, and I had placed second overall in the competition. To my mother it didn't matter that I had still qualified for the Championship; all that mattered was the red ribbon fluttering from Mickie's bridle.

When applause exploded, and the crowd surged to their feet around me, I was yanked back to the present. I joined in, but felt lost in space and time, both excited for my friend now, and hollowed from the loss all those years ago.

"Kelsey has improved since we last saw her," my mom observed as we clapped for the awards.

We were still talking about it at breakfast the next morning, after I spent the night with Mom. I looked around the kitchen and into the dining room, knowing that outside, the property was quiet.

The camaraderie from the night before, critiquing each ride, the nostalgia of plotting how each of us would have approached the course, had bonded us again. As we sat drinking coffee, talking about the good rides and the bad from the night before, reliving memories of my shows, Mom said calmly, "I have been thinking about Mickie and Annie." I looked out the bay window of the breakfast area, but they were still in the barn with their own breakfasts. The area we lived in had been rural Denver until the 1960s, when it was subdivided into several-acre parcels. I'd still been in grade school when my parents had bought the seven acres and built the house and barn with an indoor arena for our show horses. "I don't have the time to take care of things, and the barn needs maintenance if we're going to keep horses here. We both know you don't have time to ride anymore. I think we should sell the horses. Mickie and Annie still have good years in them for the right owner."

"I'm not getting rid of Mickie!"

"I know this is a hard choice, but it's not realistic for them to stay here."

"But what will we do without them?" I asked, appalled. I had never not had a horse in the backyard.

"I will continue to work, you will study, and gradually it will become a memory."

I could only stare at her, clutching my coffee mug. "But ..."

"You don't honestly think they can stay here indefinitely, do you?"

I had, actually.

What she was saying wasn't wrong, though. She was firm in this, but also kind. She hadn't had much time in her life without a horse, either. While the idea felt like a personal attack, that was selfish; it was personal for her, too. In that, at least we were the same.

"No, what you're saying makes sense," I admitted. "I just didn't think I'd have to think about it until graduation, I guess. I know what a responsibility they are."

"The only way we could consider keeping them here in retirement until you graduate is if you moved back home and could help with chores and upkeep," she allowed.

Ugh. Moving back home but having my horse. What an awful choice.

"We don't have to decide immediately, but I do think it should be soon."

I nodded, tears sliding silently down my cheeks. At least there was understanding in this decision. It wasn't a matter of *if*, I knew, but when.

Chapter 17

January 18

What had been, even just last week, a place for me to revel in the sounds and smells that brought back the happiest times of growing up, was now a punch in the gut. A disheartening reminder of all I was going to lose. I fought with myself nearly every morning. Going to classes would be better for me and would keep me from getting so dispirited. But every time I drove the interstate to the Stock Show complex, I was relieved to be in the stands instead of in a lecture hall.

My mother was right, though; neither of us had time for the horses, even to ride casually with any consistency, and I felt guilty for letting their talents go to waste. Both Mickie and Annie were too old for serious competition, but they still had life in them. I'd had Mickie for nine years, longer than any other horse I'd owned. He was my best friend and partner—what would I do without the option to go see him whenever I felt like it?

A nagging voice in the back of my head, that sounded exactly like my mother's, said I should be at the library, I should not be skipping classes, that it didn't matter if I was studying in the stands, as that wasn't quality studying. I told it to shut up and go away, swiping at quiet tears.

I called Kim from where I sat in the stands, watching class after class of horse show, detailing the pros and cons of moving the horses somewhere else. They'd be well cared for and appreciated. It would be a big change. They could teach some other kids to ride. I'd be alone in the world.

"I see you, sitting in the stands with your backpack," she said instead of hello. I'd known she was splitting her time between the office and Stock Show but didn't know her schedule.

"Guilty."

"This will be the last year I come," I said when she sat down next to me a few minutes later.

Kim handed me a plate of fries. "You'll come to watch in the future."

"It'll be gut-wrenching, thinking of the life I gave away."

"I bet it would be more nostalgic than anything," she said, wrapping her arm around my shoulders. "What if you donated the horses somewhere you knew people, where you could still go visit and maybe even ride?"

"Like where?"

"Like The Resort! Girl, I swear."

"What about Patrick?" I asked.

"What about him?"

"I think he thinks I'm coming to Stock Show because of him. What would he think if I sent our horses there and started coming to The Resort?"

"He'd probably think you were finding a good home for them and supporting where your big sister works. And once he met them, he'd love them as much as I do. Mickie especially!"

"I doubt he'd feel that way. The other night he told me I couldn't spend the night until Stock Show is over. He doesn't want to see me. I wouldn't be surprised if he's going to break up with me because he feels like I've been stalking him."

I could almost hear Kim's eyes roll. "Stock Show is almost over, so you'll get to test that theory soon enough. Where is all this insecurity coming from, anyway? Is it just the thought of losing the horses?"

"No. Yes. Maybe. Hell, I don't know." I took a deep breath, smelling the cold air, arena dirt, and the grease left from the fries. "It's just, every once in a while, he pulls away. Not all the way, just back. And I don't know why. Is it my interpretation, or is he actually hesitating? And he's not telling me what's going on in his head, so I'm freaking out even more. Is he scared of getting too close, or am I doing something wrong? I wanted a serious but easy relationship. He's not easy, but I'm in too deep now. Maybe I'm just making it all up, some weird defense mechanism, in case he does break up with me, then I won't be so hurt."

I stepped into Patrick's house three nights later. "Come in here and close the door," he said. "I have an important question to ask you. And if the answer isn't what I want to hear, feel free to lie."

"Uhhh ... okay?" I crept around the corner and cautiously closed the door.

"Are these yours?" he asked, holding up a pair of grey cotton thong underwear.

I doubled over laughing. "No," I said, gasping for breath, "sorry, they're not. Please tell me you did laundry with one of your roommates and you found them wrapped up in your sheets."

"Are you sure they're not yours? They're pretty tiny."

"As flattering as that is, no, they are most definitely not mine." I was still giggling.

"Come here," he whispered, "I want to check for myself to make sure you didn't leave them in here earlier."

I stepped over to the side of the bed, and he reached for my jeans. "I want you," I whispered to him.

"Where?" His hands slid inside the edge of the waist, checking, as he'd promised, that the underwear wasn't mine.

Where? Everywhere. I could feel my blood pressure rising, my body generating more heat. The laughter from the underwear mix-up had released whatever tension I had been carrying around with me.

"I want you ... I just, I want you."

Patrick's response was to pull me forward, on top of him, and then it was my turn to unbutton his jeans as he flicked open the clasp on my bra.

Later, curled up against his chest, I squeezed my eyes shut, remembering and feeling everything—the physical sensations, *and* the emotions all over again. When I opened them again, I was still curled up with Patrick's arm around me.

"I need to ask you something," I whispered in the dark.

"Okay," Patrick said, uncertain.

I took a deep breath. He had been impressed by my honesty before, and I clung to that. "Do you think I'm stalking you?"

"Define stalking?"

I took a deep breath. "By being at Stock Show every day. You know, stopping to say hi, spending most of the day there."

"Well, are you? Hunting me down?" he queried.

"Do you think I am?" Was I trying to talk to him, or evading?

"I didn't. I might now." But there was a teasing note in his voice. "I don't know why you're there all the time, since I assume you have class you should be in."

"I should, I do. But it's Stock Show, and it smells like home. It's the start of every competitive season. I miss it, and I hate law school." I was horrified to feel tears roll out the corner of my eye toward his chest.

"You never said specifically you'd competed there, but I assumed you had."

"Do you think, or does it seem like I'm stalking you?"

"No. You swing by and say hi, but you never stay long. I like that part of the day best; when you come say hello," Patrick said softly.

"You do?"

"I do."

"I thought I was, I don't know, bothering you. Or that you might think I was keeping tabs on you."

"You've been going there a lot longer than I have. You fit in there, people don't look at you when you walk into the barns. They just see another crazy-psycho-horse-chick." I could almost feel him winking.

"You said I couldn't spend the night until it was over, so I assumed ..."

"That I don't get enough sleep when you're over here," he finished.

Oh.

"The only reason you're here now is because I don't have to work tomorrow. If it makes you happy then keep doing it; and keep coming to say hi."

I stretched up to kiss him on the cheek.

"You know how much I hate the last day of Stock Show, how sad it makes me," I relayed to Renée over the phone Sunday night. "But today I dragged Claire with me, and showed her The Resort's interactive exhibits. Sort of one last hurrah. You know, in case I never go again." Claire and I had glossed over our disagreement about Patrick, and I'd decided it wasn't worth my time to chase it down. Despite our similar backgrounds, she was very much on the lawyer track, while I wished I were still competing. Maybe she couldn't understand that having a boyfriend who worked in that world made me feel less torn.

"Wise choice, to soak up all the memories you can."

"When Claire and I stopped by the booth, Patrick said he assumed Claire and I were up to trouble."

"Well, you are, with all your messaging commentary back and forth about your fellow students during class, and laughing in the library."

"Indeed. But we're not saying anything about that out loud," I laughed. And then I said, "I just keep thinking 'what is he doing with me?' and wondering when he's going to realize how much of a loser I am and dump me."

"Emma!" Renée scolded.

"Well, look at me. My life is a mess of wussy choices and no follow-through. It took me weeks to have a simple conversation that should have been more of an 'oh by the way'."

"Hello! None of you know what the hell you're doing. That's why they all choose AmeriCorps, and you got pushed into law school."

"You're not floundering," I pointed out.

"That's because I had the good fortune to get a job that matches my interests right out of grad school. My responsibilities don't include 'figure out what to do with my life.' Being vulnerable is hard. You should be proud of yourself for talking to Patrick instead of hiding from him."

"I'm in love with him, you know," I said quietly.

"I know you are. He obviously gets you, so just relax and have fun with him."

"We used to talk every day, before Christmas. He'd call and wake me up a couple hours after I went to sleep, and we'd talk for an hour or so, about our days, the horses at The Resort, how much reading I'd had. Mom, his dad, and sisters. Everything and nothing." I was lying in the dark, staring at the ceiling, almost talking to myself. "When was the last time we did that? The last time we went out, or stayed in for that matter, just the two of us?"

"When he wasn't working fifteen-hour days, and you weren't involved in the holidays with family and there was time," Renée reminded me, logical. "You will again."

Chapter 18

January 28

While driving home from classes, "Margaritaville" played on the radio. My spidey senses tingled, and I automatically turned the radio down. Before the volume was off, Patrick's ringtone began.

"Are you watching *The Bachelor* tonight?" he asked immediately.

"Hello to you too. And, no."

"Good. My *female* roommates are watching it and I don't want to be here for it," he explained, giving me a good picture of just how he felt about it. "Do you want to go do something else?"

"Yes! I'm driving home, so I'll come to you instead."

When I pulled up in front, Patrick hopped in my car. "Where to?" I asked.

"I don't care. Maybe downtown, and we can wander."

As I drove us the few miles, we filled each other in on how the end of Stock Show had been for each of us.

"I don't think a lot of my professors even noticed I was hardly there for two weeks," I explained. "Most of my classes have over a hundred people in them." I hit a dead end and turned right. "But my mother, God! You would have thought it was the end of the world!"

"Maybe she has a poin— what are you doing?!" Patrick exclaimed.

"I'm trying to get a little closer to the Sixteenth Street Mall before I park."

"But you're going the wrong way down a one-way street. Again."

I slammed on the brakes. It was a little-traveled street, but still, I was going the wrong way. I stared out my windshield for a moment. "It must be you. I only do this around you. You're so distracting I get all confused and break traffic laws."

"Uh-huh," he said, the words infused with skepticism. "Find a place to park. I'm not sure I want to be in a car with you any longer!"

I found an empty parking space, and we walked up the pedestrian-only zone. It was warm for January. The cold snap from Stock Show had come and gone, and the day had been a sunny sixty degrees. I celebrated the fine evening weather by jumping back and forth from bench to bench in the middle of the Mall.

"You seem a lot more relaxed than a couple weeks ago," he observed.

I shrugged. I didn't want to tell him how nervous I had been after not seeing him very often and not talking to him every evening like we had before Christmas. He didn't need to know all my neuroses, and I was glad when he didn't push further. "Life with Mom has been relatively peaceful these days. By which I mean I haven't talked to her much." That was also true, although not the larger part of why I had loosened up.

I looked over at him, took in the long hair and the bandana, the loose jeans and the leisurely walk, and felt the butterflies flapping excitedly. I jumped down off the bench to walk next to him, only to realize he had stopped walking.

"What?" I frowned, looking over my shoulder to where he stood.

He took another step forward to come up next to me, slid his arms around my waist, and bent to kiss me. "I really missed you during Stock Show," he said when he stepped back.

"How much did you miss me?"

"Let me show you," and he leaned down to kiss me again. I let myself relax into the moment, enjoying without thinking.

By unspoken agreement, I didn't take Patrick back to his place, and we headed for mine. Listening to the radio in my car, in the parking lot at my apartment, we turned on our sides to face each other and talk. "You know how you said you missed me during Stock Show?" Patrick nodded. "Me too. I missed my boyfriend. I didn't want to say anything because I didn't want you to think I was needy …" I trailed off at the look on his face.

"I'd rather, we're not—labels are just words," he finished.

"We're not together? After five months?"

"That doesn't change the fact that I missed talking to you every night, too." He paused. "Can we go upstairs?"

The connection we'd shared all evening dissolved, and I felt his energy pull away from me. Protesting would only make him more defensive. "You don't like my cramped little car?"

"Well, she's great and all, but it'll be hard to get your sweater off. Plus, I don't want to abuse her virgin eyes!"

Patrick and I rarely emailed; there was no need. But a couple of weeks later a brief message showed up in my inbox, distracting me from White Acre and Black Acre in my property lecture.

Emmalyn, it read. *I was afraid I'd forget if I waited to call. I can't do a movie Saturday like we'd planned. Party at a co-worker's that I forgot about. Latah*

And he couldn't take me because …?

People knew we were dating! Kim was my big sister, and she was going. Several of his co-workers knew me. It wasn't like it would be a big deal. If he really wanted to see me, why couldn't he take me, or not go?

I felt itchy, out of place in my skin, angry at being left out of Patrick's life. So, when Claire suggested we go downtown for drinks, I put on my knee-high boots and we hit the newest martini bar.

"Hello, California," I heard from behind me. I turned around to look up to a nondescript, reasonably attractive, former-frat-boy type. Well, I had said I wanted a distraction from my worries.

"That's interesting, I've never been mistaken for a state before," I nearly snarled. Apparently, the martini wasn't relaxing me as much as I thought.

"It must be your haircut ... very California." He reached out to touch the tips of the sunny swing left after I'd cut off sixteen or so inches at the beginning of the year. "How do you pull that off here in laid-back Colorado?"

"I'm sure it's because I'm not a ski bum," I said more calmly.

"I'm Jeff," he said, extending his hand, smiling to show off his perfect teeth. Inwardly, I rolled my eyes.

"Jeff. I'm Liza," I offered my hand and the pseudonym I used when I was not interested. Except four rounds later, I was interested. In something. So much so that when he suggested we find some place quieter, I slipped out the door with him.

Claire was standing on the patio talking to someone else and grabbed my wrist as we walked past. "Where do you think you're going? You're my *ride!*"

The feel of my arm being pulled behind me snapped me into the present, and I breathed in the frigid February night air, clearing the buzz from my brain. I looked at Claire, then at the former-frat-boy. *What the hell? I don't even like this guy.*

"She's right," I looked at him. "I can't just leave my friend here. Sorry," I shrugged, not really meaning it.

"Bitch." He stomped off up the street.

"Thanks," I breathed into Claire's ear as I hugged her.

"Come on, time for food," she decreed, saying a hasty good-bye to whomever she'd been talking with, and guiding me a couple blocks Sam's No. 3.

She was quiet until we had placed our orders. "What the hell was that about?"

My hands rose and fell, my mouth opened to say something, but all I could do was shake my head. I wasn't ashamed, per se. I was young, and I wanted someone to pay attention to me.

"The Emma I know would never make out with some random guy in some random bar. She would have let him buy her some drinks, flirted harmlessly, and then left with her friend. She would not leave her friend without a word."

"What the hell is wrong with me?" I dropped my head back against the seat behind me, then picked it up again to look at her. "That was like the twenty-something version of a temper tantrum!"

"Yes, it was."

I kept repeating the question over and over in my head as I showered and climbed into bed. No answer came. I loved Patrick; I was happy with him. *But was I?* Yes, I enjoyed being with him. But he seemed to swing wildly between hot and cold. Was I that desperate for attention that I couldn't be satisfied with what he gave me, or was the relationship as unpredictable as it felt?

When I woke up the next morning, I decided what I needed was some good big sister time.

"I'm coming over," I announced via text.

"See you soon," was her reply.

I was glad to be at Kim's kitchen table, confessing my errors from the previous evening, with a mug of steaming coffee.

"I don't know what is going on. I'm so lost. Everything is so up and down between us."

"You realize you're blowing it out of proportion, right?" Kim followed the coffee cup with a sugar bowl and creamer.

"That's why I'm here!" I said, throwing my hands up. "It feels real, and very big."

"You're both young." She reached to bring my hands down. "You're bound to have some misunderstandings."

"Explain please. Because right now the relationship feels unpredictable. Sometimes we won't talk for days, and there was the whole month over the holidays, followed by Stock Show. It feels like something's missing." I fisted my hands in the hair at the sides of my head, looking at the table. "But I have no idea what."

"Maybe you're just ready for more from the relationship." Her hand appeared in my peripheral vision, as if she were reaching to comfort me. "You assumed he thought you were stalking him at Stock Show, but he said he actually was missing you. He's not badgering you to spend more time with him because he knows you have to study. But maybe not spending more time together is keeping you guys from going deeper."

I raised my head and watched Kim calmly pour both of us more coffee. She'd braided her hair, and with her curls mostly tamed, she looked even more serene than usual.

I stirred cream and sugar into mine while I continued. "I want to tell him that I feel left out, because he didn't take me with him to the party you all went to. I want to ask him if I'm imagining that I'm not important to him."

"I did think it was odd that you didn't come with him to the party."

"I just don't get why he acts one way or another. It's like I'm missing something."

"Another indication it might be time to get to know each other on a new level."

"I think if I try to do that he'll freak out. We were together after Stock Show, and I called him my boyfriend. His response was to say labels are just words."

"And words are important to a lawyer."

I hadn't thought of it like that, but that was true. "How can he not be my boyfriend after five months?"

"If it bothers you that much then you definitely need to have a conversation with him. You have every right to know what he thinks the status is at this point."

"I just hate not knowing what he's thinking," I said, wrapping my hands around the warm mug for comfort. "What if I'm just clingy? Or he's not everything I'm looking for, and I'm the problem. We seem to drift apart a lot, but then we end up talking and it's always better after that."

"His behavior is a little avoidant. Maybe there's a legitimate reason for that, maybe he's just a jerk. Either way, a real conversation would probably help a lot."

Chapter 19

February 17

I'd been avoiding Mom and a decision about the horses, pushing it from my mind while I legitimately spent time studying. Despite the weeks since I'd last been over, everything was the same—flowers in the cut crystal vase on the front entry table, not a speck of dust in sight, china on the dining table. Planned and perfect. Predictably, dinner was a roasted skinless chicken breast, probably weighed to four ounces each, and a large salad with vinaigrette. Nothing sweet.

I wandered through the living room, touching the fireplace mantle, the bookshelves, and running my hand along the back of the sofa. Everything had a place in my memory. The antique brass lamps had been in my room at my grandparents' house when I was young; the round flat knob had fit my small thumb perfectly. I had helped pick out the drapes when Mom and Dad had first built the house. This was my home; it always would be. I was glad I didn't live here, but it was full of memories, and I missed it. Was some part of my former self still in residence here who would know better how I felt about everything?

My mother joined me in the living room. "I have been thinking about the horses more, recently."

I nodded. I wasn't surprised she was bringing it up.

"Have you given it any more thought?" she asked.

"I have. I do understand what you're saying. But I'm afraid I'll lose touch with that part of myself. What if this is the last time I have a horse? I don't know who I am without being someone who rides," I admitted.

"It has been a defining part of who you are, and for good reason, with your dedication and successes."

While my fellow students were being shuttled to and from tennis practice, or home watching TV after school, I'd been perfecting my jump approaches, grooming, and cleaning the barn or my tack. Lessons had always been a challenge I wanted to rise to. She hadn't had to force me into the show ring; I'd raced for it. I'd been given the chance to ride, to compete, and though it was something Mom and I had shared, I'd put my full self into doing so, a thing I loved for itself, for the bond I'd shared with each horse and the partnership that was unique between myself and each trusty steed.

Flashes of the perfect sunsets I'd seen while leaning on the broom, looking out the front door of the barn at the end of the day, sped through my memory. The way that Mickie looked at me, his striking, dappled dark grey coat and pewter mane and tail sparking in sunlight, a different expression for each part of our day. Ears forward and interested in what fun new thing we would do together. He had always been game for whatever I asked of him. I'd snuck him treats like he was a dog as I had done my chores. Although Annie hadn't cost as much as Mickie, she moved with the same fluidity and grace, her dark brown hair and black highlights making her seem even larger than she was.

I needed the acknowledgment and was glad that for a moment my mother was just *Mom*. Tears fell. "Maybe it is time to move on," I admitted between sniffs. Would I lose myself and what was left of my independence when they did go? "But can they go somewhere like The Resort, so at least I can still see Mickie?"

"I think that is a wonderful idea," she said, brushing my hair out of my face. I'd always liked that, seated or standing, we were eye to eye. "We don't have to do anything immediately, we can wait until the summer," she offered. "And let's think about taking a trip this summer to mark the end of this time in our lives. Maybe Paris!"

I nodded, blew my nose, and took a fortifying drink of the wine. "Can I stay here tonight?" I wanted to pretend, just for a minute, that I was a girl again, and everything would be okay after a good night's sleep in my old bed.

"Of course."

Over the next few weeks, I barricaded myself at the library. If I wasn't there, I was likely at the desk I'd studied at during high school. Somehow being around Mom was a comfort right now. I could hop on Mickie for a quick ride, brush him while he ate dinner, go back in to study, have someone else think about food for me, and crash hard at night.

The few nights I wasn't at Mom's, I was with Patrick. She and I didn't talk about him, perhaps both of us nursing the current affection between us.

Patrick and I were finding a rhythm, slowly digging deeper into the pockets of each other. He told me about his sisters, and I told him about learning to drive with my dad, him standing behind me on the small tractor we'd had, until I could go full speed weaving between the trees. He gave me tips on how to improve my pie crust, tricks he'd learned from his mother. I felt bonded in a new way, like I was being introduced to his whole family, even if I could never meet his mom.

I invited him for drinks with Travis and Claire. In a more casual setting, Claire was relaxed and less interrogatory. It turned out the two of them could talk about pro football, which calmed everybody down.

I had taken Kim's advice to heart. If the relationship was going to go anywhere, Patrick and I needed to be involved in each other's lives. We were both trying.

For St. Patrick's Day, Kim and I convinced John to go out for dinner, so the four of us hit a neighborhood pub for Guinness and fish and chips.

"You decided to stay, huh?" John asked Patrick.

"I did. When my AmeriCorps service year ended, President Jim asked me himself, and I couldn't very well turn that offer down," Patrick explained.

"And I, for one, am very glad," I chimed in, leaning over to kiss Patrick on the cheek.

"I'd miss all the fuzzy pony butts. I couldn't very well just leave them," he joked.

"And we are very grateful that you decided to stay. Or at least I am. I was not looking forward to having to break in a new office mate!" Kim added.

We finished dinner before the crowds could get too rowdy, and said our good-byes on the sidewalk. I stretched up on my tiptoes to hug John.

"Be careful, Ems," he said, close to my ear.

I pulled back with a furrowed brow.

"Patrick wasn't nearly so receptive of your 'glad you stayed' enthusiasm and kiss as I think he should have been." I shook my head, still not understanding. John continued, "I know you're in deep with him—Kim has told me, and I can see it. Just watching him tonight, Patrick doesn't seem as committed. You're my wife's little sister. Keep your eyes open."

Chapter 20

March 21

I danced around the kitchen, baking cookies. Travis watched, amused, but he was grateful for the distraction too, and the sweets.

At the end of three days over three feet of wet spring snow had fallen, dropping tree branches and plugging residential streets. I had tried calling Patrick several times to see how stir-crazy their house was going, but got no response until the afternoon after the snow stopped. Patrick returned my calls shortly after the last batch of shamrock-shaped sugar cookies came out of the oven.

"Hi!" I answered. "I was wondering if you were still alive."

"Yeah. I'm dead tired, but I'm still alive. I got stranded at The Resort with all the snow."

"That must have been nice and cozy."

"Not really, it was a pretty hellish few days ..." I responded, but he cut me off. "Listen, I'm freezing cold, but I could really use some company. Do you think you could come up here and hang out for a little while?"

Spatula paused midair, I listened to the tightness in his voice. "Sure. Is everything all right?"

"Not really. I'll explain when you get here."

"Oh, okay. Depending on th—"

"Thanks. I'll see you soon," he said and hung up.

"Well, that was weird," I said as I closed my phone.

"What's that?" Travis munched one of the still-warm cookies.

"Patrick just asked if I would come over, and then sort of hung up on me. I wonder what happened out at The Resort these past couple of days."

Forty-five minutes later I opened the front door to Patrick's house. He stared hollowly at the blank TV.

"There's beer on the back porch if you want one." Three cans sat on the table in front of him already.

When I returned and handed him one, he glanced at me with a blank face.

"Do you want to talk about it?" Whatever the hell *it* was.

"No."

I picked up my beer and held the icy can in my hands. I settled in to wait him out. Patrick liked a beer after work as much as the next guy, but he wasn't a heavy drinker.

Finally, out of the blue, he turned and looked at me. For a long time. I wondered if he had gotten tired of staring at the dark TV. But he was studying my face intently. Suddenly he leaned over and kissed me.

"Oh!" I exclaimed when he broke the kiss.

He pulled me close to him and cuddled around me, then just as suddenly let go. I got up for another beer as much for myself as for him. He studied every move I made as I came back into the living room. As I set the beers down, he reached for my hand and tugged hard enough to have me sprawling into his lap.

I looked up at his face. It was set, the corners of his eyes and his mouth tight. I sat up, straddling him, and looked at him more care-fully, placing my hands on either side of his face to tip it up toward me. He regarded me as intently as I studied him, trying to discern what was hurting him the most. Slowly, giving him plenty of time to retreat, I laid my lips gently on his. I waited. There was no response. I opened my eyes slightly. He was still staring at me. I pulled back a little but met resistance from his hands. I bent down again and kissed him softly.

It was like unleashing a storm. Patrick ran his hands down my hair a couple of times, kissing me fiercely as he held my hips in place. Then just as suddenly, he jerked back, pushing me away from him.

"No," he commanded.

"No, what?" I asked. I wasn't even sure what had just happened.

"No, I can't do this. This is wrong."

Aside from being curious as to what was going on in his head, I was turned on. "Wrong why?"

He shook his head. "It's my fault. I didn't want to be alone here tonight with my thoughts, but I shouldn't have asked you to come over. I didn't know who else to call, but I shouldn't take advantage of who you are this way."

"While that's a very admirable explanation, I still don't know why I'm here, or what happened, or why you're so upset. Tell me what's going on. I'm your friend, and you wanted me here for a reason," I insisted.

"This will only lead to bad places," Patrick stated.

"Mm-hmm."

"Are you sure?"

"Do I look unsure?" I asked, sitting back a little.

"Well, no," he admitted.

I sat and waited. I knew what I wanted, but I was fairly sure that Patrick was so upset about whatever had happened that he didn't know what *he* wanted. "If you just want my company, I will stay for as long as you want, or leave now. This is, after all, your house," I added.

He tugged on my hand. Finally, a clear signal. I leaned forward again and waited for him to close the distance between us. When he kissed me, I felt magnetized, like I had a purpose.

Patrick stood up, setting me on the floor to back me into his room, where the local jazz station was playing softly. He stood there, holding me tightly. "Thank you for coming over."

"I am always here for you."

"Yeah," he sighed.

Billie Holiday started on the radio, and we swayed in the dark, as she crooned to us the same song about familiar places. We had been here before, and I could feel his internal war between pushing away and pulling me closer.

His mood didn't match the soft music though, and before long he yanked me to the bed, with none of his usual playfulness. He kicked his boots off, pushed his own jeans away, and then grabbed mine, yanking them off my hips. He pulled me upright and grabbed my shirt as well. I gasped as he thrust into me, his hands curled around my shoulders. Desperate, I pulled him closer as he buried his face in my neck and his fingers dug into my shoulders.

"We were all taking shifts making rounds to check on the animals." He inhaled and exhaled quickly, and I felt him turn the key on whatever box he kept things locked in in his head. "It was cold and snowy, and the wind had kicked up enough that at times it was hard to see. It was Wednesday evening, before dark, but the sun was setting." So basically a blizzard, I recalled. "You know the big pond out in the big pasture?"

"Yeah."

Patrick paused for a few minutes. "One of the horses had broken through at the edge and was stuck partway in and partway out. It was Steven's shift. I don't know why he didn't use the walkie-talkie and call us for help. Or come back up to the office. But he tried to get the horse by himself. It looked like he went out onto the pond and tried to push the horse to give him some help getting up out of the water. The horse got out okay, but Steven was in the water waist-deep. He was wearing heavy Carhartts against the cold. But his hat and gloves were in his pockets. The coroner said his jacket and overalls probably soaked up the water very quickly, so even though he dragged himself to the edge of the pond, he was too cold to move. He didn't stand a chance in the storm."

This was more than I had expected. A little destruction, some injury, maybe a lot of blood. Those I would have been ready for. Not, however, one of The Resort volunteers being killed. "Oh, Patrick. I'm so sorry." I hugged Patrick to me and let him burrow in.

"We weren't even really friends. But I was the manager, you know. He was my responsibility." I could tell he was on the verge of tears. But no matter how bad it was Patrick would not cry. I hugged him tighter, and he curled as close to me as he could while he shook with unshed tears and sadness.

We stayed like that, not talking anymore. It wasn't a question of if he would blame himself, but how much. He had been in charge, as he had noted. I knew he felt responsible, even if there was nothing he could have done. And buried under all of that, his abhorrence of suffering. I still knew little about his mom, except how hard it was for Patrick to see her in pain.

Finally, I felt Patrick relax into sleep. I watched the light in the room change as the sun came up. Selfish though it might have been, I was glad for something, anything, to have happened to help him to realize that we were more than just dating for five months. I wanted him to realize he needed me, that we were allies, and that these trials proved we were good for each other.

The rest of the story I got from Kim the next day. Patrick and the other volunteer who had gotten snowed in on Monday night finally decided to go check and see what was taking Steven so long. That's when they found him. It was so cold that the pond had started to refreeze over where he had fallen through. They had to leave him there until Friday, when the police and ambulance could finally get through the roads to The Resort. Patrick's phone call to me had come just as he had left after dealing with all the legalities. My question, if he was still alive, had not been well timed.

Chapter 21

March 31

In the weeks that followed, I watched Patrick carefully, wondering what I could do to make him feel better. We went to the funeral for Steven together and I held his hand while the priest recited, "ashes to ashes, and dust to dust." Looking around at the gathered crowd I saw only Kim with tears in her eyes, everyone else still in shock. Patrick stood in stony-faced silence. I could feel the rigidity and tension of every muscle in his body.

When Kim took my hand at the reception afterward all I could do was shake my head, fighting my own tears.

She glanced across the room where Patrick stood talking with The Resort's President Jim. He had his hand on Patrick's shoulder, who, in turn, was staring straight ahead, probably not hearing any of what Jim was saying.

"How is he?"

"About as well as he looks right now. I know that logically he knows there was nothing to be done. But he's bearing all the guilt, anyway. I'm afraid he might just float away, that he'll never be the same."

Kim put her arm around my shoulders and squeezed. "Why don't you come over next weekend—just you—and we'll have some sister time."

"Yeah. I could really use that."

For the first time since I had enrolled, law school became a haven. The library was its usual quiet self, but classes were interesting. Now that we students had been together for eight months, we were more comfortable with each other, the professors, and their teaching styles. Heated discussions happened frequently, and I needed them so that I could speak without censoring myself.

"Emma," my criminal law professor called after class one day.

"Yes?"

"What are your plans for the summer?"

Most students looked for an internship. Some took classes or worked other jobs. "I'm trying to find an internship. But it's competitive, you know."

"It is. You seem to have a special touch with criminal law. Is it an area you're interested in?"

"I hadn't given it much thought. My mother is an attorney too. Mergers," I explained. "Her father and brother are corporate lawyers."

"Ah, family legacy," she nodded, comprehending exactly. "How would you feel about joining my firm for the summer?"

"Really?" I asked, my face showing my confusion. "Aren't there others ...?"

"Sure, other people have higher grades. But your arguments in class have been passionate. That's required for criminal defense. And I suspect that you're more of a people person than they are. These are people we represent; we need lawyers who can see the clients' humanity, even when they are charged with felonies."

"Wow. I'd be honored!"

"Why don't you stop by the firm next Friday, and we can get you set up," she instructed, as she walked out the classroom door.

I stood staring after her for a minute. She was my favorite professor. Now I had an internship lined up, I could stop stressing about that. I might even enjoy it, instead of being chained to a cubicle desk, fact-checking another attorney's work.

I couldn't wait to tell my mother. I even bought tiny little pieces of cake to take to dinner at her house to celebrate with. I should have known better.

"Great news, Mom!" I cried as I burst through the front door of her house. "I got an internship for the summer! Here, I brought something to celebrate with." I set the treats on the counter.

"Emma, you know we only do sweets for special occasions."

"Yeah, but I thought this qualified." Her expression said *I'll decide.* "It came out of the blue. My criminal law professor asked me after class if I was interested in working with her firm. She thought I had a good feel for criminal defense."

"Criminal defense? Really, Emma."

"She's well respected at the law school, and she's a great teacher. I'm excited about it!"

"And will this internship pay well?"

I hadn't thought to ask about that at all. "We didn't get into details," I hedged.

My mother shook her head at my ineptitude. "You don't know if you'll be able to support yourself this summer, and you found a job unrelated to working in a corporate setting. Emma, you know better. You know you need to be building your resume and your visibility with high-quality, prominent cases."

"Her law firm does that!" I mentioned a couple of the newsworthy trials my professor had been counsel for.

"Not notorious, Emma, prominent. I suppose you've already accepted without taking the time to talk with me about it. You should keep applying for other internships. Although it would be poor form to back out now, I'm sure your professor would understand if one of the top litigation firms offered you a position with a salary."

"Mom, she asked me because she thinks I'm good at this, and I'd be good with the clients. That's an honor."

"Lovely. My daughter works well with criminals but doesn't have what it takes to go after the most prestigious summer associateships."

Nice guilt trip, Mom. "Would you pass the asparagus, please?"

Patrick, however, thought the idea was great. I was glad to see him responding to something. Since Steven's funeral, he seemed to be going through the motions, dragging himself through chores and conversations. "Think of all the good you'll be able to do! That's why we have a criminal system, right, so people can get trials and have facts presented? Innocent until proven guilty, right?"

"Yes, exactly! My mother doesn't see it that way. Of course. Guilty until proven innocent for her."

"That can't really be true."

"But it is. It's like this. Here my professor specifically asked me, but she doesn't see that as a compliment. It's almost a black mark against me. I just want her, for once, to say that I did something well. It's so frustrating to work hard and not get any recognition!"

I knew in my mother's eyes I was guilty of bad grades until I got good ones, so Claire, Travis, and I spent the early days of May taking up an entire table in the library or spreading our books out across the apartment coffee table, quizzing each other with flashcards we'd made through the semester.

By the time we got to finals in mid-May, I felt prepared.

I high-fived Claire as we walked into our last exam for the year.

Two hours later, the last timer for the last final of our first year went off. We logged off our computers, packed them up, and left the building. Claire, Travis and I, and a few others headed for the bar.

"That was terrible!" Claire exclaimed.

"Even worse than the first semester," Travis agreed.

"I'm so glad it's over. Finally some downtime." I flopped into a chair on the patio.

"Doesn't your internship start on Monday?" Claire asked.

I dropped my head backward. "Whaaaaa! I hate law school!"

"But for now, we drink!" someone added.

Chapter 22

Memorial Day

Although I had technically started my internship immediately after finals, I hadn't done the kind of furious writing I assumed I would. I'd filled out court paperwork and shadowed each of the attorneys for one day, attended hearings, and managed the binders full of exhibits.

Next week, my professor told me, I would start working on researching specific legal issues, write memos, and if that went well, write sections of motions that would be filed with the court.

Some of that paperwork, she told me, I would sign my name to, as a student attorney supervised by a practicing attorney, just as I had given my name at court. I didn't mention it to my mom, but if I'd gone to work with one of *her* contacts, my name would never have appeared in a record.

I hadn't looked for a different internship, as she had commanded. And each time she had asked about it, I had put her off, saying that my applications were still pending, that I hadn't heard anything. I didn't bother telling her I was getting paid. The amount was less than she would have liked, and definitely less than I would have made working in a big firm like hers. I was in, and even she couldn't argue.

I rather liked my associateship. Meeting new people and sitting in on client interviews was interesting. Often they were held at the jail. I didn't think I had any shot of helping any of these people, but I developed a genuine appreciation for the criminal justice system and why the range of sentencing options was necessary.

Patrick was usually curious about what I was doing, so I told stories about the clients' stories, or talked about the rationale used to plead a case versus take it to trial.

"Are they all guilty, like the public assumes?" he asked one night, as we sat on his couch drinking beer.

"No, of course not. But most of them are guilty of making a wrong choice."

"Doesn't that mean that they are still guilty?"

"Perhaps technically. But we have one client, he's just nineteen, who was orphaned at eleven. He grew up by himself, on the streets, eating out of the trash, stealing to get some money, and then shot a cop one night thinking it was someone coming to beat him up in the abandoned garage he was living in."

"How is he not guilty?" Patrick frowned deep lines forming around his mouth.

"Self-defense for one. Also, he was seventeen at the time and had never had someone to support him. He really didn't know he had other options besides run, steal, defend." I gestured forward with my bottle in a half shrug.

"That's sad!"

"It is. I tried to explain it to Mom the other day, but she got hung up on the technical side of things. I wouldn't want her on a jury! She missed the humanity of the situation, and insisted he could have made a different choice at any point."

"Do you like it?" he asked.

"I do. I probably don't want to do it as my career, but it's engrossing. I am learning so much about people. Each of these clients have a story," I mused, staring off into the distance for a moment. "I wish I could wave a wand and fix whatever it is that's holding them back."

A week later while driving home from the courthouse, I picked up a call from Kim.

"He's very excited," she said of President Jim. "Logically, he knows we don't do lessons for any of the kind of showing you did, but I think he went a little crazy imagining having such high-end horses in the program." She giggled. "You should have seen him striding around, all puffed up like he'd brokered this big deal."

I had asked Kim to find out if I'd be leaving my horse behind forever. "What did he say about me coming to ride?"

"He said it would be fine if you still wanted to ride out here. And if you wanted to come train any of the other horses while you were at it, that would be 'just fine too'." Her overemphasis told me just how thrilled Jim was with the idea.

I breathed an audible sigh of relief.

"I know you don't want to think about it, but we have to do the paperwork before we can come pick up Mickie and Annie. I think your mom thought the end of the month."

I felt the tears pricking behind my eyes and let out a slow breath. *Only two more weeks.* Would I still be able to call myself a horse girl? A crazy-psycho-horse-chick, as Patrick called me and Kim.

When Kim and the horse trailer were out of sight, I went back to the barn to close up. Saddles and bridles were still hanging in neat bags on the walls. The aisle was clean from being swept that morning. We'd strip the stalls tomorrow, and the leftover hay and grain would get picked up by someone from The Resort next week.

"It's quieter in here now," Mom observed from the front door, startling me from my pensiveness.

"Too quiet." I watched smudges of my former self around us, as a little girl learning how to ride, as an adolescent learning about the nuances of competition, and my teenage self using everything she'd learned to take on bigger and bigger challenges. Each of them were carrying out the chores of measuring out feed—something I'd loved doing when I was about five or six years old—mucking stalls, or cleaning tack. It was like watching a film of ghosts of the past. "I feel empty, like the definition of myself is gone," I finally said.

The quiet continued before she eventually said, "I think it will feel that way for a while. When I gave up horses during law school, I wasn't sure I'd ever be able to have them again. I may never, now. But you will, once you finish and put a couple of years in. You will." She reached down and squeezed my hand, startling me. "Let's go have a glass of wine. You're staying tonight?"

I nodded. Words would have given the tears an escape.

Lying in my bed that night, I searched the trophies and ribbons on the walls in the moonlight. I thought of my dad driving our trailer hours to shows each summer. Sunglasses on against the glare off the road, cassette tapes replaced by CDs of Oldies music. Would Mom and I be the same? Our love of horses and competition had been the one thing I knew I could count on as common ground. With that gone, where did that leave us?

A few days after the horses left, I walked into the darkness of the office building at The Resort out of the bright sunshine glare.

"Oh! Hi." Patrick said, startled, coming out of his office. I hadn't told him I was stopping by.

"Hey," I answered, looking around the open space at the walls lined with riding helmets and posters of different breeds of horses.

Patrick came over to hug me. "Why are you—?"

"To see Kim. And my ponies," I replied, avoiding looking at him. I wasn't sure if I was avoiding his reaction specifically, or my emotions.

"She's at the arena. I'll take you down there." As we walked across the property, Patrick seemed on the verge of saying something. "Do you want to have dinner tonight?"

"Really?" I blinked furiously at the threatening tears. "Yes, I would love that. Thank you."

He arrived before I expected that evening. "Before we go anywhere, I want to say something."

"Okay ..."

"I ... I'm trying. I suck at this. I keep thinking about Steven and how great you were for me. Then I think about my mom, and I turn it off." I tilted my head, questioning, and he continued. "I don't know how to react. I know what it's like to lose a pet, but not to give one away. I felt like it shouldn't be a big deal because you'd probably still be able to see them. But seeing them come off the trailer—Mickie is clearly used to you settling him in—it finally occurred to me that this might be harder."

"Thank you," I breathed. "It felt like you thought I was overreacting. Maybe I did. Am. But this has been my whole life. I wanted you to understand that, and maybe you can't."

"Not like you need me to, no," he said, taking my hand. "Even though I still have a job here, I'm never sure how long that will last. You know how thin of a string The Resort operates on. That makes me nervous, makes it hard to plan."

"I get that."

"Just keep being patient with me. I'm trying," he repeated. "I'm sorry I haven't been more supportive."

"Just you saying that makes me feel better. Thank you," I squeezed his hand.

"I understand bettah' now than I did when you first brought it up. Sometimes we have to let go even when it hurts to do so. This is a very real loss for you and ... and loss is hard," he finished without looking at me.

There was an army marching time, in very heavy shoes, across my forehead, and the police had turned on their spotlights full bore at my face. I opened my eyes cautiously. No, there was no midnight search of the apartment going on, it was merely the sun poking its happy head above the horizon. It was just shy of seven a.m. My contacts were glued to the insides of my eyelids. I reached gratefully for the glass of water on the nightstand next to me, only to miss and knock it over. "Damn it," I swore softly.

After dinner, Patrick and I sat drinking. I passed out after he helped me stumble upstairs and into bed sometime around three in the morning.

Patrick bent over to pick up the glass and handed me a fresh one as I gingerly pushed myself upright. I closed my eyes again and prayed my head wouldn't explode.

I opened them at a new sound, magnified to tympanic levels, and turned to see Travis shuffling down the hall.

"Feel better?" Patrick asked, sitting down next to me.

"Ha!" I barked, then grabbed my head. "No, but at least I can't even think about the horses right now."

"Travis offered to make us all hash browns and eggs."

"I could kiss him!"

"What about me?" Patrick feigned offense.

"You too. Sorry about last night. Thank you for taking care of me. I feel rotten, but I think maybe I needed that."

"You did. Probably deserved it too."

When my cell phone rang the next afternoon, I was glad that my mother hadn't been calling a day earlier. "Surprise!" she greeted me. "I bought tickets to Paris!"

"What?"

"You were so upset after the horses left, and we had talked about it months ago. Last night I made the decision that we would go. It will do us both good. We have tickets, first class of course, and a reservation at the Ritz."

I almost laughed out loud. "When are we going?"

"The last week before your second-year classes start."

Were we already talking about second year? "Sounds great, Mom!" I forced the excitement into my voice. In truth, it did sound like fun, and we'd always been great travel companions. I was just still raw from the last couple of weeks.

"I can't wait to take you to the spa!" she enthused, sounding for a moment like a spoiled trophy wife.

Chapter 23

June 17

Logically I knew the horses weren't completely gone, and I'd always have the opportunity to go see them. In truth, it was comforting they were somewhere they would be appreciated and of service. It helped assuage some of the guilt. I did my best to ignore the sadness, plowing my way into the internship, working at least as hard there as I ever had for classes.

My dad had always called me his little firecracker, bright and explosive, teasing that I was fearless. I didn't feel much like that anymore. I let the internship consume me, and distract me from one more loss of my old life. In each new courtroom, I was introduced as the intern for the firm, sometimes allowed to make a brief statement or conduct a short bit of questioning. I began to know all the judges and have them know me. A few had asked, "Are you Virginia Greene's daughter?" which frustrated me. Maybe if I had gone to Harvard, I could have had a whole city to myself. But slowly the judges and clerks started to recognize me as myself and say hello in hallways. One judge even complimented my style and skill for an opening statement.

In many ways, presenting a client's experiences and arguments was just like showing: display your best case. It was thrilling to command the attention of an entire courtroom, just as in the show ring. But I struggled with the paperwork every day and wondered how much of the fun was because I was getting praised.

On the phone, I told Renée that my mother was taking us on vacation. This trip felt like the kind of frivolous escape she would have never condoned if I had suggested it.

"This hadn't occurred to me until just now, but I think she's unhappy with her own life," Renée stated. "And being in control, being a perfectionist, is a distraction from that."

I contemplated the swirls in the ceiling paint, comforted by the quiet solitude of my room. Travis was out with the law firm he was working for, playing golf. "Maybe?"

"So the logical outcome is this: she's clearly distressed by her life, and as her daughter you've grown up with that. So that's what you think life is supposed to look or feel like. Not quite content."

I sighed. "Sometimes I just want to say, 'fuck it all' and go on my merry way. But then what, what would I do?"

"Maybe it doesn't matter what you would do instead. Just chuck it and figure your life out as you go, like the rest of us," Renée suggested.

Chapter 24

July 7

"Hey," I said, pulling the door open to Patrick.

"Hi." I felt a wall he'd erected slam into me as he walked through the door.

"How are you tonight?"

"Fine."

I frowned at his one-word answers and abandoned my move to kiss him. Instead, I followed him to my bedroom, where he sat on the floor with his back against the wall.

I'd known yesterday, as I'd run on the treadmill, tears threatening, that this was coming. And now the moment was here. Patrick's apology and attempt at understanding my grief about retiring Mickie and Annie had seemed sincere in the moment. But nothing had changed, the warmth he'd brought dissolving in the wake of Steven's death.

A heaviness filled the space between us, waiting for someone to cut through it.

"I ... this is .... I don't know where to start," he began. "You know how we all have energy in and around us?" He didn't wait for me to respond, but plowed on. "In interactions there's a give and take of energy, especially in relationships. I've been reading recently about this energy exchange. And how if you aren't developed enough as a person you feed off the energy of whomever you're in a relationship with, to try to make yourself complete."

I nodded, wondering where he was going.

"I keep giving to you, you keep taking from me. It makes me feel good for a while to buoy you up. But you have so much drama."

I frowned. I knew I could be sensitive about things, like the horses leaving or Mom's influence in my life, but dramatic? How could he feel like he was always giving to me, when I was the one who was always trying to prop him up, make sure he was okay?

"You're always saying how hard your life is. Everything is 'poor Emma.'"

"Poor Emma? Like it's a one-way street?"

"If you're struggling, you want me to fix it for you. You complain about how hard things are. How much reading for classes, how much time you have to study, what your Mom said—do you know what I'd give to have my Mom giving me guidance?"

"So I'm not supposed to share what's going on in my life? I'm not allowed to be upset or frustrated?"

"You want people to feel sorry for you. Then they'll fix it, and you won't have to take care of yourself. I just can't keep propping you up anymore."

The breath of shock caught in the back of my mouth. "And this from a guy who refuses to have any feelings, about any freaking thing!" I yelled.

He let out a deep breath from where he sat, propped against the wall. "There's a hole in my chest," he said more quietly. "I keep trying to fill it."

I looked at him closely for the first time, maybe since our first date. He'd always stayed slightly apart from me, I realized.

"I know," I agreed more calmly. "That's what happens when you lose a parent you're close to. We were young, still figuring out how to be who we are." I had been right, assuming his detachment was a product of his stunted emotional state. I'd assumed that he would grow out of that and open up. But maybe he wouldn't. Or couldn't.

I stayed seated on my bed. Maybe this was as good as it was going to get.

"Now I can. I have the courage to face what I've been hiding from. You did that, Emmalyn, with your smile and your alternate take on things, you shined light in places that had been dark for a long time. Now I can see them and move forward. You did that," Patrick repeated.

"Really?" My brow furrowed. "With my drama and my need to be taken care of, I made you do a complete self-assessment? And that's causing you to break up with me?" In a corner of my brain, a Kenny Chesney song comparing drinking and loving started playing.

"It's not because you aren't fun to hang out with," Patrick said, almost excited, and completely ignoring his non-logic. "'Cause you are. You smile a lot, and you laugh easily. I still want to be friends."

"Friends?" I nodded automatically, trying to comprehend. I swallowed the tears in my throat.

We fell silent for a while. That damn song kept playing in my head. "You should probably go," I said.

I let him out of the apartment and fell against the door sobbing, unsure if I was more angry or heartbroken. When Travis came home, he poured us each tequila, straight. I passed out on the couch, the room spinning whenever I closed my eyes, everything appearing in triplicate when they were open.

Infinitely better than reality.

Breakups happen, people move on, I told myself. I had plenty to do to keep me busy. My internship kept me engaged enough that I didn't have the time to think about Patrick.

About two weeks later, when all my research and writing on one case became a section of the brief submitted to the Colorado Court of Appeals, I realized I was numb. I should have been ecstatic, jumping up and down, celebrating. My work being fully accepted, getting to cosign the brief for filing, was a big deal.

But nothing penetrated. I wanted to share the excitement with Patrick. I could barely eat. Everything I tried to swallow got stuck above the unshed tears. I stopped sleeping, instead lying awake, missing him.

What had I been doing before Kim introduced us? I wanted to say that I was miserable. But I hadn't been. I kept telling myself that story, though, lying to myself in some kind of self-flagellation.

I left my phone on "just in case" he might call late at night like he used to. I knew he wouldn't. I didn't have that tingly feeling I got when I knew he was going to call. There'd been no Jimmy Buffett on the radio.

On the drive to and from work, I wondered if he missed me half as much as I missed him.

"And how are you doing now?" Kim asked.

As if laying my arms and head on the kitchen table didn't give it away. I had talked to her the morning after Patrick broke up with me, but nothing would substitute for time at her house. "Huunnnnhhhh-hhh ..." I moaned into the wood. I sat up abruptly. "Screw Patrick."

Kim chuckled.

"Or at least that's how I feel today. Yesterday, it was all I could do to drag myself out of bed. I don't know *why*. And despite Mom's comments that Patrick 'wasn't your type,' and 'not good enough,' that this 'was inevitable and it's better this way,' I actually can't wait to go to Paris with her in a couple weeks."

"This is my fault," Kim admitted.

"Sure is!" I said without any bitterness in my voice.

"I misjudged him completely. He seemed so dependable and kind. How did I get it so wrong?" she mused.

"We both misread him. I don't think you got it wrong. It's not your fault—he *is* dependable when there's nothing deep required of him. And I'm guessing you didn't talk about energy fields."

"Heh. Nope!"

"Can I ask you something—and I want you to be honest." She nodded. "Patrick said I was a drama queen, that I'm 'poor Emma,' and want people to pity me. Do you think that's true?" I heard my voice rise with insecurity.

"Like how?" Kim frowned, confused.

"He said because I talk about how much work law school is, or rant about Mom, or whatever."

"No." Kim's palm hit the table, and I smothered a giggle at how much like Renée she'd reacted. "You vent—everyone does it. When we have a bad day, or John does it about frustrating clients. What are you supposed to do, not talk about what's going on in your life?"

"That's what I asked!"

"Yeah, no." She shook her head. "That's his issue if he thinks you're a drama queen. I'm surprised, because when we used to office together he'd bitch about stuff, like the tractor, which is always breaking."

"It felt like reverse psychoanalysis. He never says anything! He won't tell me what's going on with him, he doesn't share what he's feeling, and he thinks it's all *my* fault that it was hard to be together?" I took a breath and plowed on. "Like he was so easy to be with. Maybe if he didn't think everything was his fault, or if he would just move on from his mom's death! I mean I get that's awful, and he was still in high school, but come on—we're in our twenties, you can't use it as an excuse forever!"

"Good girl!" Kim all but cheered.

"Despite that," I sighed, "sometimes I still want him back. I miss being able to hang out with him with no pretense."

"Absolutely. That's one of the best things about a good relationship."

"Half the time I'm trying to figure out a way to get him back. Could I have been less and held on to more? And then I think, there were so many times I wanted to push through the shell he puts up when he doesn't want to be bothered. But every time, I backed down because I didn't want him to get mad or uncomfortable and break up with me. Being less would have made me ... nothing. And look how far being *not* pushy got me!"

"Are you happier not having to deal with Patrick's inconsistency?" Kim asked.

I considered the question. I had written Patrick's comments off, but they had hurt me. My mom also occasionally accused me of not wanting to take responsibility for my life. Secretly, I was afraid he was right. That *they* were right. Did not wanting to be in law school mean I was looking to be rescued?

"I don't know what I am. Sometimes it's like, I want my old life back. But I'm not even sure what that is. Was. Was it when Patrick and I were first dating? Before we met? Before I started law school?"

"Do you want to figure it out?" Kim asked gently.

"Maybe. I *am* unhappy. There was so much push and pull with Patrick, not enough consistency. I thought we were good together. He was easy to be with, and he was fun. But he was also hard to fully relax with. What if I wanted the feeling of completeness more than I wanted to be happy? What if I've been lying to myself this whole time?"

Chapter 25

August 22

On our first day in Paris, my mother and I rode the tram to the top of the Eiffel Tower. We also went back on our last night to watch it sparkle golden against a sky fading from deep purple to grey-black. As I glanced at her, looking up at the twinkling lights, I caught a glimpse of who she had been when my dad was still alive, her face open and filled with wonder. For just a minute, a woman lost in something beautiful. I hadn't been old enough to appreciate it at the time, but in this moment, I remembered her looking at him like this.

For an entire week, we had done nothing but eat crepes with no thought to the calorie count, drink champagne, pop in and out of museums, and shop for new shoes. Being in France had softened her around the edges, and she had laughed more. She'd talked about the past, the trips she and my dad had taken, and herself. I hardly remembered this side of my mother, but she had once been like this more often, and I realized how very much I missed her. It was the first time I had felt peaceful in at least a year.

From the window in our suite, we looked over the Vendôme Column, and the city shining with secrets. "To a very successful year." My mother raised her glass of champagne. I raised mine back. "You have handled the transition beautifully. Law school is hard. I wanted to drop out too, after my first year."

"You did?" I gasped, turning to her from the window. I couldn't imagine such a thing.

"Yes, but I surely could not prove your grandmother right that I was too headstrong to be a professional." Mom grinned like we were sharing a secret.

I stifled a laugh. Then I looked at her carefully. I had always believed she just thought she was *right*. What if it was a defense against her mother? Their relationship was not warm, but I'd always thought that was because my grandparents' generation didn't show emotion. Now I wondered if it was something more.

"I know that giving up the horses was hard, but it's the right thing for now. You'll see that in time."

"I feel like they were all we had left in common. What if there's nothing we ever share again?" To say it out loud was terrifying.

"We will find new things. When you graduate, we'll both be lawyers. Someday you'll have children and maybe you'll teach them to ride."

"It feels like I have nothing left tying me to who I am." Mentioning Patrick was out of the question. I wasn't over it, and I wasn't sure I ever would be, but Mom wouldn't understand that. I didn't even know if he was part of what I was missing right now.

"You're in transition. Give it time. I wasn't thrilled with your internship choice, but you seem to be doing well there. By graduation, you'll wonder where the time went, and you'll be a whole new person!"

Somehow she always knew what was going on with me at work or school—the benefit of being connected to every player in the legal community. I wasn't sure I wanted to be her kind of new person. But on the other hand, being different from where I was now might feel good.

I didn't want a pep talk. I wanted her to hug me and tell me it would all work out, that it would get easier, or I would get more interested. But talking was what she was capable of, and the acknowledgment that it hadn't been all cake and roses for her either was a comfort.

I managed to avoid Patrick for more than a month after returning. Paris hadn't solved my problems, but it had given me some perspective and some space to get my emotions off the rollercoaster they'd been riding.

I was careful to try to visit Mickie and Annie only when I thought Patrick would not be at The Resort. But President Jim had fallen in love with Annie and had practically begged me to come to a wine tasting fundraiser, where I was sure to run into Patrick.

I put on my sexiest respectable outfit and sprayed on the new perfume I'd purchased on the Champs-Elysées like armor. I might feel steadier, but that didn't mean I didn't still want Patrick to want me.

I thought I'd beaten him to the restaurant, but as I turned the corner to the entrance, he was on the sidewalk a few squares away. I froze, hand on the handle.

Even with his blank face and the sun glinting off his sunglasses, hiding his eyes, I could tell he was assessing me. "Nice dress," he said, his hand coming to rest over mine.

With the feeling of him pressed around my shoulder, I couldn't move. Patrick inhaled, his body tense. And then the door opened from the inside, startling us both out of our bubble.

Inside Patrick walked away quickly. I looked down to smooth my dress, took a steadying inhale, and then looked out into the room, a smile plastered to my face.

"Emma!" I turned at the sound of my name. "Over here!"

Ruth Eichorn, one of The Resort's biggest potential donors, waved at me from near the shrimp cocktail. I hurried over and exchanged air kisses. She smelled of Chanel and looked like old money. Everyone at The Resort knew she was dedicated to the cause, but was waiting to see if it would be worth her while to make a larger contribution—if her money could, and would be put to good use.

"Mrs. Eichorn, it's so good to see you. I'm so glad you could make it tonight."

"It's Ruth, honey," she insisted in her smoky, French-accented voice. "Nonsense, I wouldn't have missed it. Plus, I wanted to see what your trip to Paris had done for you," she stated.

"I— How—?"

"Honey, you know there are no secrets at Old West Preservation. If you'd wanted to keep your travels quiet you shouldn't have told anyone. Except that Patrick boy. I'm sure he could keep a secret if necessary." She raised one perfectly arched brow at me.

I swallowed. "Well, yes. I just didn't realize you'd been out there recently. You know, to um, to talk to anyone."

"Jim can't stop talking about the addition your horses have made to the program, and I like the idea that the contributions I have made are supporting them. Besides, I like to keep tabs on where my money is being spent, and hard workers like Patrick are part of that."

Perhaps I could distract her. "Paris was wonderful, but I don't have to tell you that."

Ruth laughed a throaty laugh. "Yes, darling. Paris is wonderful. But what I want to know is why you aren't paying more attention to that young man over there who can't keep his eyes off of you."

I turned to look over my shoulder. Patrick was standing about halfway across the room. Despite the suits around him, and his co-workers in chinos, he was still wearing his beat-up khakis. His one concession to the event was a button-down shirt, still untucked. He was decidedly *not* looking at me. "Mrs ... Ruth, I don't know what you're talking about."

"Sure you do. You're just too scared to do anything about it. But I can keep a secret too, when necessary," she said in a half whisper. "Go say something to him. You're a worldly woman now. You can pull off whatever you like."

On some levels she was right. As a rule, people didn't scare me. No one, that is, except Patrick.

"By the way," she said, interrupting my daydream about saying something witty and flirty to Patrick that would make him laugh and realize how much better off we were together, "that perfume, which I know you didn't buy in the States, is the perfect scent for you."

My head snapped around.

She gave me a knowing smile.

At the end of the evening, Kim came up to me. "Jim wants to speak with you," she said.

"Me?" I squeaked. I couldn't think of a thing that I had done that would provoke a response. I chewed over all the things I could possibly have done wrong as I walked the length of the room. Patrick stood at the wine bar next to where President Jim was waiting for me. Great. Now whatever I got chastised for, he would hear it, and probably never let me forget about it.

"Emma," Jim boomed, "well done tonight, well done." He took my hand, pumped it up and down.

"I'm sorry. I must have missed something. What did I do?"

"What didn't you do is more the question." His voice was loud in the small space. Even if Patrick had been on the other end of the hall, he would have heard every word. "I talked to more than a dozen patrons and potential patrons who said you were the best part of their evening."

"Oh." I blinked. This was not what I had expected to hear. I could see Patrick and a few others had stopped talking and were listening intently.

"That's all you've got to say for yourself after all the money you raised for us this evening?"

"Um, well, I guess I didn't think of it like that. I was just talking to people, you know?" God, I sounded dumb. Definitely not a soon-to-be-lawyer. Or a world traveler.

"Since I haven't been able to convince Ruth Eichorn to donate more than a couple thousand at a time to us in the last three years, with substantially more than just a little party small talk, I guess I don't."

"Mrs. Eichorn donated?" I asked, incredulous.

"Well, yes," Jim stated, as if it was the most logical thing. "I was sure you knew, that she had mentioned it to you."

"Actually, she didn't."

"You can count yourself the sole person responsible for Ruth Eichorn's generous donation of a quarter of a million dollars."

I choked on my drink.

"Congratulations, Emma, I don't know how you did it, but you are something else."

Chapter 26

September 23

"Emma! Wait!" Patrick yelled at me.

"Yeah?" My hair hung wet and limp as I walked across the parking lot at The Resort, clinging to my face in the rain. Not only had I, apparently single-handedly, gotten Ruth to donate, but President Jim had been rather insistent that I come work some of the lesson horses. I should have said no, but instead, I'd said yes gleefully. I had worked eight horses, and I was ready for a hot shower, some hot soup, and my warm bed.

With more homework than I'd thought was possible, I finally understood why second year was described as "work you to death." And the professors expected you to have better answers, too. I carved out a weekend or a few hours most weeks for The Resort, but it also meant I lost downtime with friends, like Claire.

Patrick came up short in front of me. "Oh," he said, looking at my scowling face. "Well, I just wanted to say congrats."

"For what?" I turned back around and started walking toward my car again.

"You know, for that donation you got for The Resort."

"Yeah. Thanks."

"Aren't you excited about it?" he asked.

"Thrilled."

"Why don't you sound happier about it?"

"Because, Patrick," I yelled, opening my car door and whirling around to face him, "I am tired. I'm also soaked, muddy, and hungry! I have an exam on Wednesday and a paper due next Monday. I have spent twelve hours a day, for the past seven weeks, in the library. I have no life, I never see the outside of my apartment or the library. And I need to get laid! Okay?"

"Oh yeah. Yeah, sure." He took a step back, his face changing from excitement to confusion. "Well, have a good night."

I got in the car, wrenched the door out of his grasp, and slammed it shut. I gunned it out of the parking lot. At the stoplight, I laid my head on the steering wheel and cried. I hated my life.

"Emma," Mom said in her most reasonable tone, "I know that you like spending time at The Resort, and that it's been helpful for you to be able to continue to see Mickie there, but it's time to move on."

"I don't spend much time out there at all." I had my phone tucked in my back pocket, ear buds in , while I folded laundry. Never a moment of time lost to idle hands.

"You are spending too much time out there. You shouldn't be seeing Patrick anymore, that's not good for you mentally. All of your time should be in the library or studying at home."

It wasn't that I told her everything; it was just that she was particularly good at putting pieces together. Probably President Jim had mentioned my "volunteering" to a mutual acquaintance. Six degrees of separation didn't occur around my mother—it was more like two. I knew a couple of professors in college had reported back to her, but getting my grades up had gotten her off my back. And, in college, I'd been far enough away geographically to avoid most of the day-to-day meddling.

"You know you need to have excellent grades to get the kind of job that you want for next summer—and after you graduate," she added. My grades had been fine, but not stellar, and only stellar was acceptable.

"Mom, this is something I need to do for my sanity. You know as well as I do that being with the horses is good mentally *and* physically. I'm almost done with laundry, and I need to get back to studying, as you pointed out."

After the laundry was folded and put away, I sat down with a cup of coffee and considered. If last year had stressed me, my second year of graduate work was making me irritable, miserable, cranky, tired, and hopeless. What if I didn't want the kind of job Mom wanted me to have? What if I didn't want to practice law at all? What if I didn't even want to finish? *Yeah right*, I said scornfully to myself, *you don't have the courage to drop out and you know it*. Maybe I needed a change of scenery to sort through things.

I picked up the phone and called Renée, then booked plane reservations for the next week, and emailed professors to tell them that I would be gone for two weeks. I chose not to say anything to my mother. I knew she'd only yell that I was being irresponsible. But keeping her in the dark would also mean she couldn't influence my drastic change of scenery. I could sort through all my thoughts and my options unfettered.

A week later, I stood in the middle of a hay field directing traffic and assigning volunteers to various flatbed trucks. The Resort had gotten a last-minute call from a rancher offering his last cutting of hay of the season. When the volunteers were all headed to their various sections, I flagged down the truck Patrick was driving and hopped on the running board to drive to the next field. It was the second day of gathering bales across several hundred acres. Patrick handed me a water bottle through the open window.

"Thanks," I panted. It was close to 80 degrees, thanks to a long Indian summer and the altitude.

"You look like you could use it. You look like you could use a margarita even more."

"God, yes!" He grinned back at me. I turned to watch where he was driving us. "I could use a ride to the airport tomorrow, about nine, can you take me?"

"Sure. Where are you going?"

"New Hampshire seacoast. I'm back November eleventh, could you pick me up too?"

I knew it was a bad idea for him to be my ride. The trip was supposed to get me away from him as much as give me space from school, but I was also a consummate glutton for punishment. And Patrick was my favorite form of overindulgence. Although I'd told Mom I was going to The Resort for myself, and even though I went mostly when I thought Patrick wouldn't be there, I wasn't trying as hard as I should have been to avoid him. When I did run into him, he was remarkably accommodating, behaving as if nothing had changed between us. Same easy smile, same great hugs. Same sexual tension, at least for me.

At the next field, several more trucks pulled in behind us. We got down and headed to the back of the trailer to throw hay bales up to the guy stacking them. I was wearing out. I looked up as two more trucks with full trailers honked as they drove past. Patrick waved as they headed back to The Resort.

Two volunteers approached as Patrick was opening the door to get back in the truck. "How much more of this do we have to do?" I heard one ask.

"Until this field is entirely picked up. This is the last field we've got."

I turned, purposely not looking toward the conversation, stretching my back, waiting for Patrick to pull forward toward the next bales.

"But I'm exhausted!" whined the guy. The girl, a pretty little slip of a thing, who I was surprised had volunteered for such physical labor added, "And it's hot out here."

"Do you see that girl back there at the end of the trailer?" Patrick asked them.

They looked at me. "Yeah."

"She has been here all day. She was here all day yesterday. She has thrown more hay than both of you combined, just today. So unless you'd like to explain to her why you get to sit down, when you have only been doing this for six hours—six lazy hours I might add," he said with an edge, "then I suggest you get back to work."

They considered this for a moment before ambling off, grumbling between themselves. I was sure they had reasoned, correctly, that if they did not get back to work, Patrick would not credit all their community service hours.

Ten minutes later, I sat in the cab as we drove to the next section of the field, secretly smiling to myself. But flattery was how I'd gotten roped into helping with the hay in the first place. He'd called, nearly begging for my help. I'd declined. But he really needed me; he was going to be busy driving and coordinating volunteers.

But I was strong! And virtuous! I declined again, stating he didn't want me there. I'd be more of a hindrance than a help, as I wasn't strong enough to throw hay all day long.

"Don't give me that crap, Emmalyn. I have seen you naked. You are perfectly capable of throwing hay all day long and then some."

I was weak! I had caved!

The truck stopped, and I opened my eyes, reaching for the door. Patrick's hand was on my arm. I turned to look at it, then back up at him. "What?"

"You stay here for the rest of the day. You've done plenty already."

"Those kids will stack the hay all wrong. It'll be a mess."

"Emmalyn," he said, his voice low. "Stay in the truck and drink some water."

"Fine," I sighed as he got out. I knew my face was flushed, but I was fine, and I knew that he knew this. Still. Sitting in the air-conditioned truck cab felt good. I put my head back against the rest. "Fine," I repeated to the empty cab.

Chapter 27

October 25

I looked out the plane window the next morning, watching bags being loaded. I was so tired, and not only from throwing hay for two days. I felt like I was coming apart inside. Patrick had been so chummy lately, since I had snapped at him after the fundraiser, really. Friendly and kind, giving me his all-consuming hugs, teasing, and occasionally grabbing my hand. All the things I missed. I said I wanted our relationship to be over, and at the same time couldn't keep my distance.

I rested my head against the cool window, reminiscing about the previous night. When Patrick had taken me home, he hadn't just dropped me, he'd come in and we'd shared a beer. It was one of those moments where we sat in silence, and I'd happened to look over to find him looking at me. The kiss that followed hadn't been rushed, it was more like we had been apart for a long time and were looking forward to being back together again. Even the urgency with which we had undressed each other had been tender, and I recalled the way he had run his hand up and down my side, the feel of his rough palm exhilarating, a familiar touch that both soothed and stoked. When we finally joined, he'd said "Emmalyn" so carefully I knew just how much he had missed me, too.

What was *wrong* with me? I shook my head. I wanted to start over, give myself a new beginning. It felt like I was ready for a significant change, maybe even leaving Denver. If I could push restart somewhere else, maybe I could be a new person, or at least find myself again. If I weren't in their realm every day, maybe I'd be able to get out from Mom's influence, her my-way-is-the-only-way, and to shake the last vestiges of Patrick's hold on me.

"There are only two things I know," I said on my third morning at Renée's as we scrunched over stones and frosted fallen leaves in the driveway, heading for town a mile away. "One is that I'm miserable, the other is that I'm not getting over Patrick."

The old farmhouse was comfortable, with its wide-plank oak floors and stone fireplaces. It felt as solid as it had when I'd visited at the new year, fitting in to the town and the nearby beach, the ocean, and waves. But I'd needed to get outside.

"Why?" Renée asked, opening the door to the coffee shop for me. I loved this area. The proximity to Boston and its history, the neighbors Renée waved to in town, the sense of belonging, somewhere, that I felt.

"I keep asking myself the same thing." I turned to order. "Columbe winter toast, extra cream and sugar. 'Why can't you just move on, Emmalyn?' I want to," I added, after Renée had ordered and paid. "Or at least some part of me wants to. Or maybe it's better to say I don't know *why* that part of me is." I brightened as I was handed my coffee but frowned again when I turned toward Renée.

Renée looked at me skeptically. "You're making yourself miserable trying to find an answer when maybe there isn't one."

I detoured around her. "He thinks I'm a mess, when clearly he's the one floundering. I mean I am, too, but that's all about law school and Mom and being my own person. I miss him—that he gets me and lets me be myself."

"He doesn't though! You said he's a mess. He made you the bad guy in the breakup!" Renée's coffee sloshed as she poked her cup toward me. "Maybe you've built up a fantasy about who he is. A coping mechanism for all the other BS."

"He accepts me for who I am," I argued as we walked outside and down the street. Even through the running pants Renée was wearing, I could see the outline of her muscles. "If I dropped out, he'd still be my friend, he wouldn't judge me."

"I wouldn't judge you if that's what you decided to do!"

"As my best friend, you're required to support me," I joked. "And then there is the fact of law school, which I'm not engaged with. I want to do something I love, but I don't even know what that is."

"Let's be real. All of this is about your mom. Even though you love Patrick, he's as much an eff-off to your mom as he is someone you have great connection with. As soon as you open a case book, your whole demeanor changes." Renée paused on the sidewalk and mimicked me, her shoulders at her ears, hunched forward, a heavy scowl gracing her face. After a moment she dropped the posture. "It looks like you're fighting a battle."

"I just, it feels like everything I've ever done has been in pursuit of a blessing from my mother. It feels disloyal to even say that." Worse, saying it made me feel untethered from reality. "I want the kind of life that you and Aaron have, that bond."

"You can have it. But you'll have to let go of a lot of things to get there. Most of all, that need for approval. And the need to do things, like stay with guys who aren't a good match for you, just to spite your mom. And before you say anything, I think Patrick is a good right-now boyfriend. With a lot of unidentified baggage, and you deserve better."

I sighed. "I hate that you might be right."

She gave me an overblown grin.

Ten days later, I stood at the end of the drive looking back at the house. I had imagined a place like this time and again, wishing but never knowing where it was. I'd spent every day running and turning my choices over in my head. I breathed in the crisp air ripe with the tang of falling leaves, coming back from a last run. I didn't want to leave, and I wanted to come back as soon as I could.

Chapter 28

November 11

Patrick stood by my baggage claim carousel and waved. He looked tired, but the stubble on his cheek still made me want to crawl into bed with him and rub my cheek along his. I raised my hand to give a half-hearted wave back. As I approached, he pulled my bright pink bag off the carousel and started walking toward me.

"Truck's just outside," he told me, putting his arm around my shoulders and squeezing. "How's the nervous breakdown?"

"Oh, you know. Fine. I—" I started to say that I had missed him. "I'm not really glad to be back just yet. Still processing, I guess." He gave me a sympathetic hug and nod.

We drove about ten miles in silence.

"So, what did you learn about yourself on this trip?"

"What?" I asked distractedly, pulling myself from a meditation on the dry grass flying by the truck window. "Oh," I looked over at Patrick, wrist slung comfortably over the steering wheel. "I think it's probably too in depth to talk about right now."

"Yeah," he sighed. "We lost another horse at The Resort." Past the edge of his sunglasses, I could see a tear at the corner of his eye.

I wanted to reach out and touch him, but was afraid of his reaction, and my own. Would I be able to hold the pieces of myself together if I started offering them out again?

Silence stretched out between us. I should never have had him pick me up.

"What are you doing tonight?" I asked, running over Patrick's telephone greeting less than a week later. The need for distance didn't keep me from continuing to put myself in stupid situations, but there was no one else I wanted to share this with.

"Eating dinner?"

"I got tickets to the KISS/Aerosmith concert!" KISS ranked right up there in Patrick's favorite bands, and before he'd broken up with me, we had been mooning about how wouldn't it be great if we weren't broke and could buy tickets.

"You bought tickets? I thought it was sold out."

"It is. One of my classmates *gave* them to me. Wanna go?"

"Hell yeah, I wanna go! What time? Wait, she gave them to you?"

"Yeah, I know, crazy—and they're good seats." I looked at the tickets. "Um, opening band at six thirty, then KISS after that."

"Why don't I meet you at your place about seven," he suggested.

Standing inside the outdoor concert bowl, I remembered concerts in high school and college, with girlfriends screaming over Matchbox Twenty. There were screams again tonight, as KISS sang songs like "Rock and Roll All Nite" and "Beth," that I hadn't known were theirs.

When Aerosmith—hello, Steven Tyler!—took the stage, I cheered along with the crowd. As I sang along with my favorite song, Patrick maneuvered me in front of himself, surprising me when he put his arms around my waist and swayed to the tune.

Even as it happened, the feel of his arms around me, pulling me back against his chest, and my head resting on his shoulder, listening to the words instructing us to sing, sing about everything—today, tomorrow, yesterday, next year, happiness, and sadness—made me wistful, like the last glimpse of something remarkable. I wanted to follow the instructions—I wanted to dream on and on. I wanted my dreams about Patrick and me to come true.

But then the concert was over, and the lights came on, illuminating just how far apart my dreams and my reality were.

We sat people watching as the audience filed out. "Wow! Look at those!" Patrick exclaimed.

"What? Oh, the thigh highs—yeah what about them?" A girl wearing KISS-inspired silver shoes, black thigh highs, and a very short skirt walked by a few rows down.

"You should wear some of those. But only if you wanted to, you know, get in real trouble with a guy. I mean, with guys in general ..."

"I know. That's why I wear them," I said wryly.

"You've worn those? How come I've never seen them?" he asked, feigning insult.

"Because you've never paid attention!"

"I'm sure I would have noticed those."

"I've worn them a few times when we've gone out; my skirts just aren't that short. And it was usually nights when you elected to go home rather than spend the night." I shrugged to brush off the fresh disappointment.

"Really? I wish I had known, that's something I would have liked to see ..." He trailed off, imagining, then realized what he was saying.

I raised an eyebrow at him.

"Just, you have nice legs," he said, looking away from me.

Back in the cab of his truck, Patrick dug around looking for a CD. "Here it is!" he shouted triumphantly.

"Here's what?" I asked.

"You'll hear." He inserted the CD. All of a sudden, Jimmy Buffett was saying you couldn't describe a KISS concert unless you had seen one.

I laughed. "A Jimmy Buffett song for every occasion. And sage advice," I agreed, as I pulled up my sweatshirt.

"Are you taking your clothes off in my truck?"

I paused with my sweatshirt halfway over my head. "Uh, nooo," I said through the heavy material.

"That's a relief, because otherwise we'd probably crash into a light post."

"Right," I agreed, carefully folding the sweatshirt. How was I supposed to take that, especially after our conversation about thigh highs? The silence between us was heavy, even tense, Jimmy Buffett repeating himself in the background. We were both waiting for the other to make a move.

When we'd been sitting in the parking lot at my apartment for a half hour, Patrick put his hand under my chin and lifted it so I had to look at him. "Emmalyn, I think you are lying to me." The words I'd been saying fled from my brain, and I felt the blood drain from my face.

"Wh-what are you talking about?"

"I think you are avoiding telling me the truth about something."

"That's ridiculous! I never lie to you." Although, I admitted to myself, I didn't always tell him the entire truth.

"Really?" He paused and seemed to consider this for a minute. "Emmalyn, do you want to fool around?"

Shit. I looked him directly in the eye. "Yes," I said, my voice full of false confidence.

Patrick dropped his hand like he'd been scalded. He'd expected me to lie about wanting him. "Come on, I'll walk you to your door."

I shoved the passenger door open and stalked up the sidewalk. At the door to the apartment, Patrick gave my stiff body his typical big hug and turned back toward his truck.

"You are such a tease," I said, not quite under my breath.

Patrick stopped, turning around slowly, and asked, "What was that?"

"Oh, you heard me," I spat at him.

"I did. I'm not sure I understood."

"You're all touchy-feely all night. You dance with me and then you ask if I want to fool around and then you just want to *leave?* What exactly is it that you want from me anyway—just *tell me!*"

"I don't think sleeping together would be a good idea just now. Especially for you."

"Oh, so now you get to make decisions about what's best for me? How chivalrous! Why don't you just admit you want me too and stop judging me for it. At least I was honest when you asked!" I stomped up the steps and slammed the door behind me, the sidelights rattling.

Chapter 29

December 3

For weeks, we deliberately avoided each other. We'd see each other across the field and divert eye contact. Christmas was coming, though, and I knew it would bring big changes. I had heard rumors that Patrick was going home for a long holiday, and it was unknown if he would be coming back. I wasn't sure how I felt about this prospect. I knew I should be grateful he was removing himself from my proximity. But I didn't want him to go. And if one of us was going to leave, it should be me, so that my exodus could make the statement that I was the one who was done.

I was driving home in the dark from a review session when Patrick's home number flashed on my screen. "Hello?" I answered tentatively.

"Hey, Emma! How are you doing?"

It was not Patrick, as I had hoped and feared, but Margo.

"You know that Patrick's leaving this weekend to head home for a while." It was not a question, but rather a statement, as if this was something I had known for weeks.

"Sure."

"We're throwing a little going away party for him tonight. You should come!" She sounded sure that this was going to be a fun send-off. "Everyone is meeting before he gets home from work so we can surprise him."

I thought about how cold and tired he would be, and how much he would just want to come home, take a hot shower, and have a beer. But his roommates were trying to do something nice.

"Well, I don't know if that's such a great idea. I mean I'm all the way on the other side of town ..." I was grasping at straws. I *really* wanted to go and help send him off. Plus, I was going to be *really* sad and didn't think that I *really* wanted to share that sadness with fifty people I didn't know well.

"Oh, you should come. He'd be bummed if you didn't!"

She said it so sincerely I wanted to believe her, even if after yelling at him and calling him a liar, I wasn't sure it was true. On the other hand, I couldn't help but hold out hope that she knew something. And if this truly was my last opportunity to see him for who could say how long, I didn't want to miss it. "What time?"

"You should be here by six thirty. And if you could bring a little something to share, that'd be great."

"Okay," I said, rushing into my apartment. It was colder now than when I had left the law school, and snowing. I closed my phone and banged my shoes on the floor mat, then promptly slipped on the linoleum with my next step, landing on my elbow. The spot vibrated, but I massaged the place, assuring myself that I had just bruised it, and rushed off.

"Here you go," I said, handing over the bowl of guacamole when I walked in their front door a couple of hours later. "Listen, do you guys have any ibuprofen?" My elbow throbbed. Not unlike my head. Together they made a nice drum line in my body. I swallowed the pills gratefully. There were about twenty people milling about, some signing a huge sheet of brown packing paper, others just enjoying a beer and catching up.

I already wanted to go home and avoid all these people, most of whom I didn't know, the tension between Patrick and I, the sadness ... all of it. I didn't want to cry in front of anyone here.

Abruptly the front door swung open, and Patrick stopped short, letting frigid air in, as he took in all the people and the going away signage. A couple of people yelled, "Surprise!" He glanced around the room and locked eyes with me, his expression halfway between fear and a sneer. I shrugged.

He recovered quickly. "Hey, guys, what's all this mess in my clean living room?" A couple of people laughed—the living room was never what anyone would call picked up. "Looks like this party is for me. If you'll all just excuse me for a moment."

He walked through the kitchen toward the basement, snagging me by the wrist as he went. I had a split second in which to decide to either go quietly or make a scene. In deference to the roommates who were trying to do something nice, I chose the former.

In the downstairs living room, Patrick released me. I stopped at the bottom of the stairs. "Oh no, you're coming with me," he said, pulling me into his room and slamming the door behind him. "WHAT is going on here? Did you do this?"

"Did I do what?" I asked contemptuously.

"This party."

I had known this was a bad idea. But at least it hadn't been my bad idea. "No. As a matter of fact, I'm merely a guest this evening. Your roommates called and invited me. They were of the opinion that you would want to see me. Now, as I am a guest, I think I'll return to the festivities upstairs." I reached for the doorknob, only to have him pull me back from the door, and up against him.

"What?!" I snarled.

"My roommates invited you?" I could tell he didn't entirely believe me.

"Yes. In fact, Margo seemed to think that you would be most upset if I didn't come. I thought the gesture of a going away party was a nice one, so I agreed to come. Even though I *knew* this is exactly how you would react."

"You knew how I was going to react, did you?" he asked, mocking me, daring me.

"Ye—" His mouth closed over mine and for a split second everything went blank. Then I shoved him hard, and he stumbled backward a couple of steps. The silence was deafening.

"Well, well," he said softly, "not the reaction either of us was expecting as it turns out."

I turned and yanked open the door. Maybe I could sneak out the back door. I was hurt, and afraid I might lose it at any moment, and I didn't want anyone to see that. But mostly, I just wanted to be alone with my grief.

I was in the dark living room when I heard him softly call me: "Emmalyn. Wait. Please?" I'd heard the sadness before, but never the sound of fear or apology. I stopped and he came up behind me to give me a hug. "I'm sorry. I'm a little on edge right now. Th-things are not going well at The Resort, I don't know if leaving Denver is the right thing, but I'm not sure that staying is, either. To be honest, I've kind of suspected my roommates were planning something. And then, I wasn't expecting to see you here tonight, so everything just kind of exploded. Apparently, I decided to take it out on you." He gestured to where we'd been kissing moments earlier.

In the darkness, I closed my eyes, and everything around us became part of that pinpoint. The music and the chatter from upstairs, how his arms felt around me, the sadness that engulfed me, the pain in my elbow, and the dark pressing on us. I walked out of the circle of his arms and back into his bedroom, where I laid down on the edge of his bed and curled up. "They'll be expecting you back upstairs soon."

"I've got to take a shower. Will you take one with me?"

"Patrick, they are all going to notice if I come back upstairs with wet hair." Inwardly, I rolled my eyes.

He paused for a moment. "Wait right here!" he said suddenly, and then took off up the stairs. Moments later he was back. "Okay, now sit on the floor in front of the couch."

I was sure I wasn't going to like whatever happened next, but did as I was told. He set a plastic cup of beer on the table in front of me and sat on the couch behind me. Just as I started to turn to ask him what was going on, he grabbed the cup sideways, knocking beer all over the place. I yelped.

"Brilliant!" he exclaimed.

Margo came to the top of the stairs, "Is everything all right?"

"Yes," I called back, "Your idiot roommate just spilled his entire beer on me, is all."

"Sorry," Patrick called up. "I am an idiot. Do you have an extra shirt Emma can borrow? Hers is going to need to go through the wash so she doesn't smell like a keg." He leaned over and sniffed loudly at my hair. "And so is she!"

I turned around, staring in disbelief. Patrick winked at me before he leaned over and kissed me again. Despite the chill from being soaked in beer, I warmed up.

Patrick jumped up as footsteps came down the stairs. He met Margo at the bottom step. I sat by the couch looking and feeling like a drowned rat. "Thanks, Margo, you're great."

"Obviously Patrick doesn't understand being a girl," She walked over to where I was sitting, and winked, "So here's lotion and some mascara." I smiled.

When she was gone Patrick asked again, "So now will you take a shower with me?"

This time I did roll my eyes at him. "Well, since you went to all that *trouble*, I suppose that would only be the polite thing to do."

The light in the bathroom was glaring after the semi-darkness of the living room, so I closed my eyes against it, letting Patrick peel clothes off me. He stepped out into the hall and threw my shirt and sweater in the washing machine. I had my back to the door when he came back in.

"Emmalyn! What is that?"

"What is what?"

"That huge bruise on your elbow?"

I twisted my arm around to see what he was talking about. And sure enough, where I had landed on the floor I had a goose egg and a large, very dark bruise forming. "Oh, that."

"What do you mean, 'Oh that'?"

"I fell earlier this evening and landed on my elbow. Hurts like a sonofabitch, too."

"Do you need to go to the ER or something? Did you break anything?"

"No, I'm pretty sure I didn't break anything, nothing feels weird. But you should have seen me making the guacamole earlier!"

"That's not funny," he said, pulling me into the shower. The hot water stung my elbow and then dissolved the throbbing almost immediately. Only to be replaced by throbbing in other areas of my body that both resolved and intensified when Patrick kissed me.

When he turned off the water, I trailed after him.

"Here," he said, handing me an ace wrap from the linen closet.

"I'm fine."

"Wrap your elbow."

I yanked the roll from his hand, and struggled to get a loop started on myself.

"Emmalyn," Patrick said, taking over, "you should know better; you've spent your whole life dealing with horses."

"Whatever." I rolled my eyes, but added, "Thank you."

Together we went back upstairs. Under the fluorescent lights of the kitchen, the reality of Patrick's imminent departure was forced back on me. He had returned to being standoffish, chilling the places where moments ago he had been warm against me, leaving a cold spot where his presence had made an impression on my life, even though he hadn't yet left the state.

Around ten o'clock, I couldn't stand it any longer—being ignored was making everything worse. Walking slowly around the room, I said good-bye to the few people I knew. I touched Patrick on the arm as I put my coat on. "I have to go. I have more review sessions tomorrow," I lied.

"Oh, right. Well, um," he turned and looked at whatever girl he had been talking to.

"It's all right. Have a safe trip, Patrick," I said quietly.

I was on the front step, in the snow. Again. But this time he reappeared in the doorway, "Wait, let me at least walk you to your car."

"All right." We crunched over the snow together. "Were you going to tell me that you had decided to go back? Before you actually left?"

"I wanted to. I didn't know how, though. Since my AmeriCorps year ended, things have been chaotic at The Resort. I don't always get paid on time, the pens aren't always safe. Even with Ruth Eichorn's donation—which I still think was amazing you got—it's thin. She put restrictions on how we could use it, not that I blame her. I was supposed to know better what I was doing with my life by now. Instead, I feel more lost than ever. I don't know when—if—I'll be back."

I glanced up at him but looking into his brilliantly blue eyes was too hard, so I dropped my gaze to the snow-covered street.

"And then there's all this ... he waved his arms around, "between you and me. I'm going to miss you too, you know," he admitted quietly.

I nodded—it was all I could manage while we looked at each other for another minute. He looked away first.

"Here," I said, and handed him a loose ring Snaffle bit keychain. "What is this?"

"It's a loose ring Snaffle."

"I know. But why?"

"Just a little bit to remember me by," I gave an exaggerated silly grin. He reached out and enveloped me in one of his hugs.

"Take care of my truck while I'm gone, will ya?" he said to my scarf.

"What do you mean?"

"You know, take her out, drive her around, let the horses run." Over the summer he'd traded in the little white truck that had barely made it to Denver for a black half-ton pickup. He was proud of graduating to what I teased was "a real truck." "She likes you. And I trust you with her."

"Oh." This, I knew, was as close as I was ever going to get to an out-and-out declaration of feeling. "Well, she's awful cute, so I suppose I can manage," I kidded.

"Shhh! Don't let her hear you say that!" We grinned at each other. He hugged me again.

I started the car. "Be safe. Say hi to Pops." He slammed the door and nodded at me with stoicism.

I drove around to the other side of the block, put the car in park, laid my head on the steering wheel, and sobbed.

When I got home, I crawled into bed, but lay awake in the chill quiet, the starlight seeping through the blinds. I wanted to sleep, to disappear, but knew it wouldn't come. The darkness throbbed around me, a deep, black abyss opening in front of me. As I lay there, I thought about what Patrick had said, that there was so much between us. We both felt it, a tie that bound us, for better or worse. The more I tried to hold on to Patrick, the less I felt like doing so was a choice.

This was why I needed leave. It was also why I had to stay.

Chapter 30

January 1

The grey light behind my closed eyelids was unfamiliar. Cautiously I opened them, wondering if I had done something dumb for New Year's Eve. No, I realized, recognizing my old bedroom, I was at my mom's, buried under the covers as if I were hiding. With the door closed I could pretend I was still asleep for a little while, but judging by the amount of light filtering through the blinds it wouldn't be too much longer before my mother was knocking on the door, asking if I was awake.

I flung the covers back, pulled on sweatpants, and found my slippers. I'd had other invitations for the big new year celebration, but I hadn't really had the emotional energy to go out into the crowds. Instead, I'd decided to head home, hunker down with a fire, some wine, and filet mignon. In truth, I had looked forward to it, and the night had been relaxing, with no talk of school or Patrick or jobs or grades.

"Good morning!" Mom called from the other side of the island, handing me a steaming cup of coffee.

"And Happy New Year!" I agreed, dumping sugar and cream into the mug.

"That is so unhealthy. Maybe you should wean yourself off the sugar for one of your resolutions."

And there it was, three minutes into the morning, judgment, and ways to improve. I was immediately glad I had shed my college weight, so I didn't have to hear about that too.

"Not everyone likes to torture themselves with bitterness in the morning."

"What classes are you taking this semester?" she wanted to know.

"I have the rest of Constitutional Law, and then the mandated ethics class that has to be done before third year. Evidence. Oh, I'm taking International Law!" I said, settling into the couch.

She nodded, "Proctor is well respected, that's a good choice," she agreed. "If you do well, he'll be a good reference for you for a summer associateship."

"I might not get a job this summer. I think I'd like to study abroad."

"You can't do that! You need all the real-world experience you can get so you'll be that much more qualified than your peers. I won't allow it!"

"I think it's a clever idea." I didn't know why I had given away my hand so early. I had known she wouldn't like the idea. Maybe some part of me had thought that if I had more time to convince her, she would come around. "If I decide to do something with international law, having all that time abroad would be really beneficial!" I was excited.

"You're not going into international law. What would you do there? No, you need to focus on trial skills so that you're ready to litigate after graduation," she said as if she were picking the color of socks.

"What?" I asked, startled.

"That's the best way to use your skills and your law degree. I don't know why this is surprising to you."

Even though I had done well in public speaking in high school and college, that didn't mean I needed, or wanted to be, a trial attorney. "Sorry, I didn't realize you had decided what I was going to do for the rest of my life."

"Emma, I can't believe that you haven't thought of this yourself. You are an excellent speaker. Being in court is logical for you."

"And what if that's not what I want? I'm good with people, why couldn't I be successful negotiating deals for international corporations—or working for the UN!"

"That's ridiculous. You can't work for the UN in Denver."

I hid behind my coffee mug. Apparently not only was my whole career planned, but also where I would live. I should have known.

As I left Mom's the next day, a van fishtailed as it turned the corner in front of me. Swerving to avoid it, I slid across the black ice, my little car slamming sideways into a tree. Happy New Year to me.

Through it all, one small thought glimmered in the back of my mind. *I could just use Patrick's truck. He did ask me to make sure she got out and about.* And though I knew using the truck instead of getting a rental car would keep me tied to him, a small part of me wanted the connection.

I called him. He didn't answer. I left a voicemail. I waited.

To: equestrienne@hotmail.com
From: pbranagan@oldwestpreservation.org
Date: Jan 5

Subject: live by the caller id ...

Hey Emmalyn,

Ain't it weird though? I'm in Mass, minding my own business, and I start thinking about you. Lots of wise people would say that that would be enough reason to call, especially because it wasn't like I heard a song that reminded me of you or saw someone wearing a snaffle on their belt. But there you were, peering over my shoulder for four sunrises and sets, and finally I call and whaddayaknow, there was a reason to call when I first started thinking of you. Obviously I should have. Hey, no one is perfect.

I'm glad you're all right. And I guess I'm sorry I didn't call. Car accidents are scary, even when someone walks away fine and can talk about it like it's a totally normal thing ... it ain't. I hope you're ok with it. I'm sorry The Little Car is in intensive care, I hope that she gets better soon.

So otherwise, how are things? Your car is probably at the top of the list, but what about Christmas? And New Year's? And presents, did you get presents? Holidays here were grand. We tried to get all the pre-Christmas season crammed into one afternoon. I'm still trying to recover. We started the day at 5 and kept going until 2am. Wooooh! But the whole fam was together, and it was cool having everyone and it's cool to be in New England, and my dad has been at times overwhelmed by Branagans but more often happy to have us here, and the weather has been typically atypical and life is just a big hoot you know?

Sometimes I miss Denver, especially The Resort. And sometimes I think I don't miss it as much. Sometimes I feel I need to get out of here, sometimes I can't remember why I left, but no feeling is around long enough to qualify, you know? I don't really know what I'm doing, and if I talk to my sis that's not only ok, it's ideal, but if I talk to my dad it's madness, especially if it doesn't have a 401(k)! Does any of this make sense?

I'm glad that you are ok and that your spirits weren't too marred by the accident. Have fun driving around the big truck like a crazy-psycho-horse-chick!

Patrick

I had known I could count on Patrick, for this at least. When I closed the truck's door behind me the first time, I paused to breathe the unique scent in—car wax, alfalfa hay, arena dirt, and the remnants of the cherry air freshener that had been hanging from the rearview mirror for months.

Driving his truck meant we stayed somewhat in communication, and he told me that he'd be back mid-February. He still didn't know what he was doing long term, but if he was moving, he needed to get his things. And if he wasn't, well, at least he didn't have to move it all back across the country again.

Knowing he was coming back didn't give me as much peace as I had thought it would. I still spent my free time on the hamster wheel of missing him, wishing he were already back in Denver, being glad he was gone so I could have space, wanting him to call so I could hear the comforting flow of his voice, hoping he didn't so I could get clear of him, all while anticipating the next hug from him.

I spent my days in the library reading casebooks, doing exercises, writing, and reading more, so much more. The shortest day I spent at school was fourteen hours. I was exhausted, but I wanted it this way. If I was too tired to feel, then I couldn't feel sad.

To: pbranagan@oldwestpreservation.org
From: equestrienne@hotmail.com
Date: Jan 20

Subject: and die by the caller id ...

I've been putting off replying to this email for some reason. Probably 'cause I wanted to talk to you. But I heard
Jimmy on the radio last night and I decided that that
was a good enough reason to finally break the absten-
tion.

The Little Car is still in the shop. She probably won't be
done until just before you get back. Thanks for letting
me drive the big truck around. We had a pretty bad
snowstorm here on Sunday night. I was scared to drive
to school the next day. I think that if I had been driving
The Little Car it would have been fine, but I kept thinking that I was just going to slide off the road and wreck
your truck too. I thought I was fine with slamming into a
tree. Guess I was wrong.

See you when you get back—speaking of which do you
have a ride from the airport? If not, be glad to give you
one in repayment.

latah'

EL ☺

I heard Jimmy Buffett and Kenny Chesney on the radio, and then spent the rest of the day waiting with bated breath for Patrick to call. Every time, he did. It was driving me mad, prompting ridiculous fantasies I could feel everywhere but my heart.

When he finally did appear, we met at The Resort. As we hopped into the truck I sat in the passenger seat, feeling everything about him soaking back into me.

"What's wrong?"

"Nothing."

"Emmalyn, what's wrong?"

"Nothing."

"Okay, I don't have the energy to pull it out of you, so maybe you could just share it, instead of making me work."

"Patrick, there's nothing wrong. I'm just sitting here with you. I'm really happy you're back, and so glad to see you. I really, really missed you."

There was a long pause. "Oh." I waited as he paused again. "Oh."

"It's really good to have you back."

As soon as it was out of my mouth, I froze. I hadn't intended to say anything like that, but it was freeing in its own way. I was tired of tamping down how I felt so he was okay. And yet, I didn't want to lose the friendship because I had made him uncomfortable. He might be incapable of opening up enough to love me back the way that I wanted, but he understood me and let me be me.

"Oh. I—that's unexpected."

"Is it?"

"I just don't feel the same."

"We're not friends—good friends?"

"We are, I just—I don't know how I feel," he said, shaking his head. I couldn't tell if it was at himself, or at my revelation.

Chapter 31

February 14

I propped myself against the wall in my bedroom, staring across the room. I said Patrick's name out loud to myself, testing how it sounded, how it felt. I heard Travis come in, pause in front of the closed door to my room, and then move past.

My phone rang, startling me out of my ruminations. "He-hello?" I asked, swallowing my tears.

"Hey, Emmalyn! Happy Valentine's Day!" I held the phone away from my head and looked at the caller ID in disbelief. This could *not* be happening. "Oh, it's you."

"Of course it's me. I wanted to wish you a Happy Valentine's Day."

"Gee, thanks."

"What's wrong?"

"You want to make sure to wish me Happy Valentine's Day? The holiday reserved for lovers? Sure, everything is fine."

"It doesn't have to be just for lovers. It can be for friends, too."

"You didn't really seem to like my confession of how good of a friend I thought you were. I saw you one time while you were here. And I'm pretty sure you were only pretending you wanted to see me."

"I did want to see you! I'm just feeling very conflicted. Home wasn't as helpful for sorting things out as I would have liked."

"Maybe you could sort those things out first." I paused, hoping I wasn't ending things right then. "I don't really want to talk to you right now."

"Right." He sounded like his spirits were slightly flattened. Well, good.

I waited until the next day to call Kim, not wanting to interrupt her Valentine's Day.

"Why won't he go away?" I said as soon as she picked up.

"What did he do this time?" she asked, clearly humoring me. No need to clarify who I was talking about.

"That idiot called me yesterday. On Valentine's Day!! What is wrong with him?"

"Ah."

"Surely, he would have known what a kick to the gut that would have been? Tell a girl you don't want to date her, but you want to stay friends, then you say you're not sure you even feel friendship. He had to have known that would hurt my feelings. Right?"

"Not necessarily. This is, after all, Patrick, one of the most emotionally stunted, stuck, unable-to-see-things-from-another-person's-perspective people. Compassionate and clueless at the same time."

Such a good description. "It's just so frustrating because every time I start to get over him and move on, he pulls this kind of shit. He says he wants me to move on, and then he always does this, every time. What's his problem?"

"I'd say he doesn't want you to move on. But he doesn't want to feel guilty for stringing you along, even though he knows that he is. So he coats it in him wanting the best for you, when really he's only looking out for himself."

"AAARRGGGHGHGH!!!"

"Yep, that's exactly it!" she laughed. "But you have to get off the ride. You have to let him go, let that pull to each other you two have dissolve, or you're going to just keep being miserable."

"That's depressing. Both the miserable part, and the getting over him part." I sighed. "And I don't want to," I exaggerated my whine. "Ugh. I hate when you're right. This is all your fault!"

A month later, I sat in class pretending to take notes but really daydreaming, wishing I could spend the day with Patrick, but also remembering last year's St. Paddy's Day, when snow fell like it does out east, and Patrick got stuck at The Resort and pulled a dead body out of frigid water.

I shoved my hesitancy aside and called him. "Hey," I said quietly when he answered.

"Hi."

"How ya holding up?"

"Fine," he lied. I could hear a catch in the back of his throat.

"Do you want to talk about it?"

"No."

"Maybe you should anyway," I pushed, knowing he would hate it, but wondering if it wouldn't be good for him to be forced to face things. When he didn't say anything, I commented, "Sad. Maybe a little guilty? Hurting in all the other places you don't want to think about."

"I said I don't want to talk about it!"

"I know."

"Go away." I heard the crack of a can in the background.

That hurt as much as anything. I didn't want him to be alone. "All right. I'm here," I reminded him. The line went dead.

Rather than start crying, I called Kim.

"Hey lady," she said, cheerfully.

"Hi," I let out a long breath.

The tone of Kim's voice changed. "It's a crappy day for all of us."

"I just got off the phone with Patrick. He wouldn't talk to me. Granted I was pushing him to acknowledge his feelings ..."

"But he never talks about them, and you're worried about him, and he's your friend, and you're still in love with him, and you're worried about yourself too."

The silence stretched out between us, my emotions vibrating along the telephone wire. "Yeah," I exhaled. "Yeah."

Kim's voice continued as I reflected on the previous year. I'd always been susceptible to anniversaries.

"You're not listening, are you?" She already knew the answer.

"No, I'm not. I'm sorry."

"It's okay, I understand you're all over the place right now. Go home early today, stop at the store, and buy some Häagen-Dazs ice cream and a bottle of wine. Have a glass for me and then cue up *Legally Blonde* for the three thousandth time."

"Okay," I whimpered. "Okay." I took a deep breath. "Okay. I'm leaving now," I sniffed, recomposing myself.

"Good girl. Call me tomorrow."

An hour later I slid into scalding hot water.

I wondered, in that abstract way we think about things that are a puzzle that we don't actually want to solve, if he couldn't let go of me because I was a habit he was too tired to break. Was the same true for me? Were we still attached because we were each so fragile we didn't have the fortitude to sever the connection?

Chapter 32

April 13

In the old days, contracts consisted of two identical copies, one written on the top and the other on the bottom half of a page. The page was cut on an irregular line, leaving a jagged edge. To confirm the validity of a contract, the two halves could later be fitted together. Patrick and I were like that: one tooth missing; such a close match, but not authenticated.

I glanced up from my studying. The big window in the library I routinely sat next to was spattered with rain, making me exhale softly. I wished I had the kind of time that Patrick had: a couple of months to think about things. But on second thought, if I did have that kind of time, I'd turn introspective. I'd think and think and think and think. About the fact that I didn't know what I wanted, which was where I'd been at the end of college, and how I'd ended up where I was now. About how much I wanted out of life, and from Patrick, and how I didn't know how to get any of it. About all the things I was trying not to think about.

I didn't want the time to think about these things, or to have to admit to myself that I was at least as mad at myself as anyone else. I was halfway through law school and even I could admit that dropping out now would be irresponsible. But I didn't want to be the obedient daughter anymore. I wanted to tell Mom how much I didn't care at all what her opinions of me were. Even though, of course, I did.

No, it was a good thing I didn't have the time to think.

I didn't want to get the summer associateship that was expected of me. Logically it would mean income, and would look good on my resume. I wanted to run away from responsibility; to have an adventure, get out of the comfort zone I had so effectively boxed myself into. I wanted something I had never had before: space and time to clear my head; an opportunity to find myself as myself.

I switched over to the webpage I'd been looking at earlier, describing the law school study abroad programs available across the country. While I'd been asking classmates who'd been abroad last summer what they had liked best, a professor had mentioned that a student could transfer to a different law school in their third year, and be a visiting student in a new place. Anywhere. I could do both! Study abroad and visiting student.

I turned to face out the window again, considering. I could go somewhere far away, yet near friends. I immediately thought of how I had felt along the seacoast, the calming rhythmic crash and *shhh* of waves coming in and pulling away. I could choose one of Boston's nine law schools—city, suburbs, ivy league, or not.

My days were filled with the consistency of classes, library, gym, watching out the window, and dreaming I was back on the coast. I flipped from tab to tab on my computer, and a new email in my refreshed inbox caught my eye. I decided to reply immediately.

To: pbranagan@oldwestpreservation.org
From: equestrienne@hotmail.com
Date: Apr 22

Subject: Re: Hellooo .....

I wrote a paper last summer that my professor shared
with a colleague. The colleague liked it so much, I've just
found out, that now he wants me to work for him. So,
I've been offered an internship with a small firm in town
for next year, which will likely lead to a job with them
after I graduate. If not, a full year's internship, paid of
course, will open other doors. You'd ask me if I really

want to do it. I think the work would be interesting, and that would be nice. It wouldn't be an area of law that Mom loves for me (bankruptcy), but neither would she hate it. It would be good, solid experience. I don't think it would be as fun as last summer's criminal law stint, but I don't know that I have time to be choosy. Anyway, I'm still thinking about it. Finals are only a couple of weeks away now, but I can put off any decisions until that's done.

Tuesday is the last day of classes for the semester. Yikes! Finals start May 3rd. And then May 6th I'm done.

Anyway, hope all is well with you.

Talk to you sooner than later.

EL ☺

To: equestrienne@hotmail.com
From: pbranagan@oldwestpreservation.org
Date: Apr 25

Subject: re: Helloooo ....

Wow. That is quite the turn around! Finals, Nobel-prize-winning writing, last-minute job offers, it was like a Hollywood movie! You started as an overworked law student and now you'll be raking in the big bucks!

The honey do list dad created has a fatal flaw—it's incomplete. That might sound like less work for yours truly, but it doesn't quite work that way. Yesterday we were to begin painting, but when he turned on the hose faucet to fill a bucket, it took like a half an hour to fill. Closer investigation revealed a crack in the inside of the silcock (no, that's not a dirty word, but I still don't like saying it ...) so I had to go to the hardware store (hah-dweh-uh stow-uh) to get a new ... errr ... faucet. I figured while I was there I should get the parts I needed to fix the tub, which has been leaking. So I had to find the leak, and figure out what I needed, then go to the store (half an hour round trip if you don't dawdle). Then turning the water off to the house here is an adventure, and ... and ... and ... etc. It took nearly all damned day to fix the two silly things. Then the cordless drill wasn't working, and so I had to take it all apart and figure it out ... I never lifted a paintbrush. It's raining today, which curbs any attempts to paint, so dad's a little distraught about checking things off the list, but he's finding ways to stay busy. Home is good.

Glad to hear about Denver, and I'm glad so much is working in your favor!

Latah!

Patrick

I felt a renewed sense of missing him. And I wished he would miss me, too.

But I also wasn't sure I missed Patrick as he was now. He was still all the things I loved about him. But his inability to decide on a course challenged me. Was he avoidant because he didn't feel connected to me anymore, or because he didn't even feel connected to himself? I missed the guy I used to know, not the one who had gotten lost.

I stared at my computer screen, Patrick's return words blurring.

I would have loved to be able to share with my mother the way that I had once shared with my dad. Fully. All of it—practical, rational feelings, and also my full spectrum of emotions. But she wasn't interested in my experiences or reflections. She only wanted facts. GPA, credit hours, new people met and their titles. I wanted someone to *care* about my day.

Each day I found myself watching out the same window, my mind wandering, returning to the same subject of Patrick and our friendship—past, present, possible future.

In between study sessions, my mind wandered back and forth between last minute plans for the summer and the fact that Patrick had stopped in Denver for a few days on his way to a new job in Utah but hadn't bothered to call. It was anyone's guess as to if or when he might be back.

And then I had a depressing thought. What if loneliness was all I had left of him?

A week after my email to Patrick, I made a decision. I did not have a conversation with my mother until it was over and done with, until I'd had my acceptance to the study abroad program in Ireland in hand.

When I told her, she screamed and yelled. "I did not raise you to be a lazy, irresponsible, semi-adult. I expect you to work hard for what you earn, and to do it the right way. Flitting about an island for eight weeks does not fit in your plans for your life."

"*Your* plans," I reminded her. "My plans have yet to be fully formed. I am doing this for me. Because for once I would like to do something that was my choice, and my choice alone. Not something I got your permission for."

"You're so ungrateful for the things I have done for you and the sacrifices I have made! And you repay me by confirming just how lousy of a student you really are!"

I stalked my way through finals, glaring at anyone who got too close to my study seat in the library, wishing we had real lockers so I could slam them closed.

By the time finals were over she was still shouting, but not as often or as loudly. Despite the reduction in frequency and volume, I was ready to put about 5,000 miles between us.

Chapter 33

May 16

When I arrived in Shannon, Ireland, and made my way to the meeting point, I encountered a group of some thirty-odd people milling around with various amounts of luggage.

"You must be Emmalyn," a rotund man in his sixties said loudly.

"Emma." I shook his hand.

"Professor Hood."

"I noticed," I said dryly. His full, but neat, grey beard looked exactly like his photo, and he sported a University of Virginia Law polo shirt.

I stood to the side, watching a group of guys tell stories about their flights. One girl in a skirt and short heels had cornered a few other guys. Some feet away stood a young, but clearly, married couple. Two others, also wearing UVA gear, held hands but were part of the larger group conversation.

Together with our suitcases, we were herded towards the bus.

Professor Hood grabbed the bus mic as we pulled forward. "I know you're all tired, but before you fall asleep, we're going to go around the bus and introduce ourselves. Yes, just like we're in kindergarten. Name and what school you're from."

Groans came from the back of the bus. I counted thirty-three people plus the two profs. Only five of us were not from UVA.

After I unpacked in the cottage I'd been assigned to, I walked outside and looked over the houses on the other side of the road to the blue water of Dingle Bay. I sighed with contentment, stretched, then turned around and started up the rise to the cottage whose lawn was full of the guys who'd been clustered together at the airport.

"Is this a boys-only club?" I asked, as I approached.

Several of them answered together, "Yeah," but then laughed.

"You have to make her feel welcome. I don't want the visitors feeling left out!" Professor Hood said. "Or you'll all fail. Go get her a beer!"

"Here," someone said, pulling up an empty chair.

"Thanks." I glanced over as he handed me a beer, startled to see a genuine smile and kind brown eyes. I hesitated briefly before I stuck out my hand. "Emma."

"Alex." He smiled more. His long runner's legs stuck out from his shorts as he leaned back in his chair.

No other girls joined us. I let myself be excited that maybe I would get to hang out with "the boys" by myself for the entire trip.

A few days later we all piled back onto another bus and took a tour around the Peninsula. I'd picked this study abroad in particular because it was with a good school, and the classes were internationally focused, but also because it traveled. Ten days here, a week there, a quick weekend, and another few weeks there, with sightseeing included.

Ancient sites turned to ruins littered the peninsula's landscape, but the Gallarus Oratory, used as a church over eight hundred years ago, was completely intact. As I stood in the grey semi-darkness, I set my hand on the wall. I was unprepared for the energy that was still humming in the stone walls, and jerked my hand away. Taking a moment to steady myself, I set my hand against the wall again and absorbed the constant hum left by the thousands of souls that must have passed through the small building.

Outside, Alex and I posed for a picture. He was quieter than the rest of the group and had a thoughtful response in nearly every class.

All I knew about him was that he was from Richmond, Virginia. Then, one night's Guinness on the lawn turned into drinking games until around midnight in Alex's cottage. We sat by each other, bumping elbows and sharing cheese off a plate, while the game progressed around the table, all of us getting progressively sloppier in the quarters we were tossing at the Solo cup.

He stood up from the chair next to me, and tugged on my hand. I looked at him, questioning, but he gave a small jerk of his head toward the stairs.

"Wow, you've made yourself right at home here," I said as I let the doorjamb hold me up. His suitcase was neatly tucked in the corner, shoes lined up near the door. The door to the armoire stood open, and his shirts were neatly hung.

"It's more than a few days, might as well unpack," he shrugged, shoving off his T-shirt and pushing down his jeans to reveal boxers with dogs in party hats.

I didn't know what he wanted from me. I had assumed he wanted to sleep with me, but he wasn't acting like it.

"Com'ere," he gestured.

I walked carefully over to the bed and sat next to him. He leaned over and kissed me on the cheek. I wasn't sure what to do next. I didn't want to seem so desperate that I would just jump in bed with him. But he was right there. Immediate.

Alex stood to peel back the covers, gesturing I should get in first.

I gave in to curiosity and peeled off my jeans. But the problem with drinking games is that inevitably, everyone falls asleep. Or at least Alex did.

I lay in the dark thinking about what this might mean. Did he want to sleep with me but was too tired? Was he looking for a summer fling—was I, for that matter? As the sky turned to the leaded grey that heralded the coming dawn, I slipped downstairs. A few guys were passed out in chairs and on the couch. Someone was slumped over at the kitchen table, head pillowed on his arms.

The morning air was cool, and breathing it brought clarity. It wasn't like our joint departure from the kitchen had been secretive. I had wanted company, but what had Alex wanted? I didn't want to have some rash decision hanging over me, tainting the remainder of the summer. I didn't want to ruin the group dynamic that was shaping up nicely. More importantly, I didn't want to ruin the trip for myself by getting into something that ultimately turned sour before our program was up. What I wanted was to not be lonely.

I stretched up into the last of the dawn before heading back to my cottage. I decided not to decide, to merely wait. That in and of itself was a change for me.

"About last night ..." Alex began the next evening, having sought me out as I left my cottage.

"Yeah. What was that?"

"You're nice, I wanted to spend some time alone with you. It wasn't about sex. Clearly," he laughed at himself. "You're an unknown commodity, being one of a couple of outsiders."

"Aww, I like you too, Alex," I teased.

"Friends?"

"Friends," I agreed.

I'd clicked through web pages with photos showing the areas near where we were staying: rolling green hills, stone fences, misty clouds. Quintessential Ireland stuff. And horses. There had been photos of people in horse-drawn carts and riding at the Gap of Dunloe. It was supposed to be one of the most majestic sights in Ireland. So, on a day off from classes, I took the bus to Killarney. I figured some much-needed time on horseback wouldn't hurt my spiritual equilibrium.

I spent a good chunk of that bus ride beating myself up for inserting male drama into my peaceful time in Ireland. Even though I knew there wasn't any actual drama. Still, I ran possible consequences through my head. If I would be branded the "loose" girl, if going with Alex, even though nothing had happened, would impact the other friendships I had started to form. Then I was mad at myself for letting the thoughts overtake the day. I was supposed to be getting my act back together so I could return to Colorado with some semblance of balance in my life.

I faced the whitewashed building that said "Kate Kearney's Cottage," overwhelmed by the people coming and going. Off to the side of the dirt yard stood horses hitched to small carts, and a few tied up. Behind the cottage rose a granite hill covered in trees and gorse—not a mountain like I was used to, but big enough.

"Hello, can I help you?" I turned around to find a guy about my age with burnished chestnut hair and an easy smile. Between the work boots, knit sweater, and reddened cheeks, I could tell he spent a lot of time in this yard. "Well, I was wanting to ride up the Gap?" I explained.

"Do you know how to ride?" he asked.

"Yeah, I do."

He led me over to where the horses were tied. "Do you want me to go with you?" he asked in his Irish accent before I could mount.

"If you want to, that would be nice." What was I saying? This was supposed to be alone, get-back-to-center, away-from-boys time. He jumped on the horse next to me and we set off at a leisurely pace. "I'm Tim," he said as we began up the hill.

"Emma," I offered. I let the horse I was on plod along, enjoying the hills that rose on either side of the narrow road. A wide stream rushed over rocks, the road winding along its route. I turned my face to the sun. Not even in its wettest springs had Denver had a single day this green. It was peaceful feeling the swing of the horse's stride under me, riding but not thinking about the performance of riding.

When we finally crested what the Irish referred to as a mountain, the view took my breath away. The guidebooks hadn't lied. In front of me, the hills continued, dropping and then rising again, covered in all the shades of green. I felt both lost and found. Like this was where I was supposed to be, that I had discovered something I had been looking for, but couldn't yet inhabit.

Tim didn't push me to hurry up and go back. He stood with the horses while I stared, trying not to cry about something I couldn't even name.

We swung up on the horses and walked back down the hill. Tim pointed out other overlooks, a stone house that had been in his family for five generations, and told me that the valley we rode through was called the Black Valley because it hadn't had electricity until the 1980s.

"Do you want to continue back at a walk?" Tim asked when we were partway down.

"No, we can pick it up a little," I offered. We set off at a trot, but soon we were galloping down the road. I felt like my younger self, the one who had loved jumping huge fences just for the feeling of freedom sailing above the ground for a few precious seconds brought. Fingers of the wind whipped my hair back, streaming through the strands. As we crossed the stone bridge, the cool air rose up to greet us. By unspoken agreement Tim and I raced each other, urging our horses a fraction faster. For those twenty minutes, while we galloped out of the glacial hills, nothing else mattered.

We came screaming into the dirt yard, pulling up short of the horses and carts, startling tourists.

"Well, my guess was wrong, you can ride!"

I smiled. "I was just enjoying my time. I haven't ridden in a few months, and it's so beautiful here, I wanted to remember every little detail."

Tim nodded. "Do you want to get a beer?"

I nodded back as I slid off and loosened my horse's girth.

"You don't have to do that, that's my job," Tim said to me.

I shrugged, "Habit."

He chuckled. "I'll meet you over at the pub."

I sat at one of the tables, enjoying the sun and the feeling of muscles well used. "For you," Tim said, setting a Guinness in front of me. People he knew drifted in and out of our conversation. A weather-beaten man in his late sixties sat down, chatting briefly with Tim in Irish. Whatever it was they were saying, it was clearly about me.

Hours later, as the sun was finishing setting, Tim called a cab to take me to the bus station. "Here," he said, handing me a piece of green paper with his phone number on it. "If you're back in Killarney, let me know, we'll go riding again."

I smiled, outside and in. "Thank you for a lovely afternoon."

"Thank you," he returned, kissing me on the cheek.

As I rode the bus back to Dingle, I thought about the longing I'd felt standing at the top of the Gap. What *was* the longing? It wasn't for Patrick, but it was for something that I'd thought maybe he could fill. It had felt so right. Like I was in exactly the right spot.

I needed to go back to Denver and be able to face Patrick level-headed. It was clear I couldn't keep him out of my mind, or even out of my heart entirely. But maybe if I could identify what had prompted that feeling of groundedness I could recreate it back home.

Chapter 34

June 5

A week later students and professors alike loaded our suitcases and ourselves back onto a bus to drive to a small island off the northern coast of Ireland, where we would spend a long weekend. I fell asleep somewhere along the way and dreamed a vivid, intense, and wishful dream about Patrick coming to visit me in Ireland.

After our initial greeting, Patrick and I had stood there, no clue what to do. The dream had been so vivid, as if it wasn't just a dream, but reality. I hadn't even told him I was leaving for the summer. That awkwardness I'd felt in the dream wasn't just my imagination; it was how we truly acted.

I woke up as we pulled into the parking lot at the Cliffs of Moher, shaking off the dream, reconciling the real world, where I had been flexing long unused muscles of flirtation, with the disappointment I felt waking up. It was challenging living from moment to moment.

A couple of nights after we arrived in Derry, the whole group headed out. After two days of nonstop lectures on international law, we deserved it. The bar had good music to dance to, but I needed to get away from the people that I had spent the last three weeks with.

"Are you not having a good time?" someone asked.

"What?"

"You don't look like you're having a good night." The guy stepped into my personal space.

"No, just hot." I turned away from him to the bartender. "I'll have a Guinness, please."

"You should let me buy that for you."

"No, thanks." He took a step closer. I grabbed my beer, throwing my coins on the bar top, and turned away quickly.

He didn't seem to take the hint and followed me through the crowds. I glanced behind me to see if I'd lost him and when I turned around Alex was walking toward me.

"You okay?" he asked, brow furrowed.

"Just some guy who doesn't know that 'no I don't want you to buy my beer' means 'please go away.'"

"Tall, muscular, rugby-player looking guy?"

"Yes. Is he still there?"

"Yep. But don't worry, I've got you," Alex said, sliding his arm around my waist.

As I looked up into his face, his eyes met mine. All I heard was my heartbeat in my ears. Until a hand came down onto my shoulder.

Alex pulled his gaze away from mine to look at the person belonging to the hand. "I believe the lady said no thank you." Another moment, and the hand released.

"Thank you," I said, my free hand reaching around Alex's back to hug him.

An email awaited me the next morning.

To: equestrienne@hotmail.com
From: pbranagan@oldwestpreservation.org
Date: Jun 10

Subject: RE: Ireland Week 3

Mickie looks much cuter in his summer coat than the winter shag. Why do I say that? Well, I was thinking it when I was looking at him the other day and thought I'd tell his mom. Why was I looking at him the other day? Because I was rebuilding his pen. Why was I rebuilding his pen? Well, it needed it.

And because I'm in Denver. Because I got fired from the canyon trail-guiding job. After two weeks.

What now? I don't know. As your weekly emails to us all back here in the lowly States prove, the world is wide open (except parts of Utah).

I'll keep you posted.

Latah,

Patrick

I wandered through Dublin, our third and final residence, until I reached Ha'penny Bridge. The graceful arch of the pedestrian bridge looked out over the River Liffey, colorful houses on one end, and the beginnings of the Temple Bar neighborhood on the other. Forearms resting on the side of the bridge, I contemplated the email and why he'd sent it. The tears that had been pricking leaked out and slid quietly down my cheeks.

Given how often I didn't talk to Patrick and how little effort he made, I wondered why I even still bothered. I didn't want to have to work this hard at something. What if I didn't want to fight my way through law school and then along a partnership track somewhere? What if all I wanted was a job I could go to, someone to come home to, and some pets?

I pulled out the green slip of paper with Tim's number on it. With my Irish cell phone, it would be a simple matter to phone him, take a bus the few hours back to Killarney. And what about that moment with Alex in the bar, protecting me from the overzealous rugby player? I rubbed my thumb across the paper. That day with Tim had been one of my best days in a long time.

What if that was what I wanted—a nice quiet life? Horses, fresh air. A cute guy. Thinking about that kind of contentment made the tears fall faster.

The water rushing under me was soothing. I wanted to live somewhere I could find a peaceful place like this, somewhere I could sit and search my soul. For the answers, but also for the *questions* I needed to ask.

"Hey," Alex said from behind my shoulder.

At the sound of his voice, I jerked back, simultaneously shoving the paper in my pocket and rubbing the tears off my cheeks. "God, Alex, you scared the crap out of me."

"Where were you? You looked pretty far away."

"I don't even know," I said, shaking my head at myself. I frowned at him. "How did you find me here?"

"You've seemed a little quiet recently, so I've been paying more attention to you," he explained, leaning on the railing next to me. "Then today, when I decided to take a walk after classes were over, here you were, looking lonely. It's got to be hard, no matter how cool everyone is, to be the only non-UVA'r."

Even though I wasn't the *only* person from outside the home school, I took the cover story. "Yeah. I'm not exactly homesick, but you're right, it's a little lonely at times. Then there's the couples, too." I gave him a wry smile.

"If it would make you feel better, I'll pretend to be your boyfriend," he teased, bumping my shoulder with his as we leaned on the railing.

"I'm pretty sure they've all figured out that we're not dating, or even sleeping together," I laughed.

"Hm, I suppose not," he agreed.

I found myself gazing up into his face. He was a little over six feet, with well-cut brown hair. He was lean, but muscular, and there were those legs I'd noticed on our first day. I managed to not sigh.

Anyone would have found him attractive. He looked exactly like who my mother would have picked out for me. But he wasn't arrogant or loud with his opinions and intelligence. He was rational and calm, and he enjoyed the puzzle of law more than most. He had the kindest eyes, the color of slow-roasted light coffee.

Something I couldn't quite define made him appealing and relaxing to be around. Like even the world's biggest problems could be solved, if they were approached calmly.

"Why don't I just hold your hand while we walk back to campus, and I convince you to break out of your solitary mode for a night and come on a pub crawl with us? And by us, I mean everyone, including the professors."

"Now that sounds entertaining!"

Chapter 35

July 4

On the day of my birthday, I woke up feeling more alone than I had any other day of the summer. I was glad to be exploring and away from home, but my birthday had always meant summer rituals with my mom. If I was home, we would be at my grandparents', just like every year, watching the fireworks display at their country club, drinking iced tea, and having a custom cake for my birthday. I hadn't realized how important those things were to me. I felt like I was missing out somehow. Missing cousins, and the momentary relaxation of the holiday, missing out on summer. I lay in bed, watching the rain spatter against the window, feeling nostalgic and sorry for myself. Here, I would have no one to help make tonight special, even if we managed to celebrate the holiday.

I called my mom, who answered despite the time difference. "Happy birthday, Emma."

"Thanks, Mom." I smiled on my end.

"Are you meeting any interesting people?" It was her standard query, especially after I had told her that we had toured some courts and met a few lawyers here.

"No, just partying every night," I said dryly.

"That's not amusing, Emma. You need to be using this to your advantage to make connections. If you are serious about practicing international law, though I still think that's a waste, you need to make all the connections you can." Even early in the morning, just woken up, and on vacation, she was full of lecture-y advice.

"I really just called to say hi, Mom. Not to be told what to do. It's a holiday at home, you know. And my birthday."

"Yes, I know."

"Right. Well, I don't have much to add that wasn't in my last weekly email back. I'm—" I didn't know what to say. I was homesick? Missing her? Lonely? All of those were true, but not exactly.

"Are you alright?" she finally asked.

"Yes. No. Yes. Just a little lonely today."

"Maybe if you had stayed home you wouldn't be feeling this way. You'd be at work and have responsibilities. You'd be networking at social hours and meeting more of your peers."

Maybe if I'd stayed home, I'd be more miserable. But I knew I'd have been just as lonely. I wanted affection. I wanted Patrick back, I wanted Alex; I wanted to go home, I wanted to stay. I wanted to be sure about what the hell I wanted!

"Tell me what you're doing today," I changed the subject.

As she described the same things we did at my grandparents' every summer, I lost myself in the memories. Hot, muggy days. Thunderstorms enjoyed on the screened-in porch. Swimming at the country club, or walking to the well-preserved downtown for iced coffee. I could see it all perfectly in my mind's eye.

"I'm worried about you," I heard my mom say.

"Why?"

"You don't seem very focused. I wonder if you're going to make it. I love you, and I want you to do well." That was a strong declaration of feeling.

"I'm going to be fine. Do a sparkler for me tonight. I love you."

After she hung up and the call disconnected, I kept the phone to my ear, listening to the silence for some time. Then I pushed myself out of bed and resolved to stop feeling sorry for myself.

I was proven wrong about being lonely for my birthday when the wife of one of the professors produced a bright yellow sheet cake at the pub we most often frequented.

"What's this cake?" asked a local at the table nearby.

"It's this young lady's birthday," Professor Hood gestured to me.

"It's a fine day for a birthday," the local raised his beer to me.

When the candles were lit, our table neighbor nudged his companions, who made a rowdy addition to the round of "Happy Birthday." Across the table, Alex raised his whisky to me, and I raised mine back with a grin, feeling less lonely than I had in months.

The next morning I received an email from Harvard's law school, saying that my application to attend as a visiting student had been accepted.

A few days after that, I received an email from Patrick that began "Hey, Darlin'," and wished me a belated birthday. As much as I relished it, I knew the affection wouldn't last. I was almost ready to go back home—torn between loving this experience, and feeling ready to start something new.

I paced the green outside my dorm building at our Dublin campus, waiting for Mom to pick up the phone. "I got an acceptance to Harvard!" I exclaimed as soon as she said hello, burying the lede a bit. Maybe starting with the big name would soften her reaction.

"For what?"

"I found out at the end of last semester that a lot of schools accept visiting students for the third year. You know how upset I was when they waited-listed me. Well, now I get to go, anyway!"

"I don't get it. You want to transfer schools? How's that going to affect your credits and your graduation date?"

"It's not a transfer. They call it being a visiting student. I'm still enrolled in Denver, I keep paying the same tuition, to Denver, and then they credit my transcript with the credits from Harvard! Like that summer in college I took a couple of math classes online," I explained. I would have preferred to wait until I was home to tell her, but there wasn't time for that. Honestly, I would have preferred to not tell her at all, but I thought moving across the country probably deserved some notification.

"I don't think that's a great idea. What are potential employers going to think if you change schools just before you are done? That doesn't show follow-through."

I rolled my eyes on my end. "It is not a transfer, Mom. It's like summer school. I will still graduate from Denver. I will still get a single diploma with all my credits on one transcript. And I'll be in Boston! Think of all the networking I can do outside of Denver!"

"No," she stated flatly, "I won't let you do it."

"Mom, my tuition money is already in place, there's nothing else to do. It's very easy. Renée has already offered I can stay with them, at least until I find a place of my own."

"I won't allow it!" she yelled, as if saying the words louder would make them true.

"What do you mean you won't allow it?" I demanded. I was almost yelling back. A few people who were outside enjoying the afternoon looked my way. I took a deep breath.

"You may not go! This is entirely your fault. If you had just gotten over Patrick, we wouldn't be having this conversation, you wouldn't be wanting to chase him all over the country!" she yelled again.

"Patrick is in Denver, for your information, not in Boston. Not that that matters for my decision." Patrick did matter. More than I wanted him to. But I knew that going to Boston, finally getting to go to Harvard, was the right choice. "It's really not your decision to make about whether I go or not!"

I had really hoped this would be different. That the fact I was going to Harvard would make it easier. I wanted her to say, "Oh, that's great! I know how much you wanted to go there; this sounds like a good compromise." But who was I kidding? It wasn't her plan, I'd be too far outside her sphere of influence; therefore, it didn't get her approval.

It wasn't so hard to say good-bye to the people I had met in the program. But leaving Alex created a hole. I didn't realize how important he had become until suddenly he was no longer going to be there.

Everyone else was flying out of Dublin to go home, but I had wanted a last couple of days to myself, so had elected to take a bus the four hours back to Galway. As I'd packed, I'd found myself considering Tim's phone number again. But what good would a one-night stand do?

"Have a safe trip," Alex instructed as he loaded my suitcase into the cab I took to the bus station.

"I will, you too," I agreed, looking anywhere but at him.

"Stay in touch," he ordered, pulling me into his arms. Instantly I was back in the moment in the bar, his arm around my waist, protecting me.

"I will," I promised with a quick sniff, blinking furiously to banish the tears before Alex could see them. I would miss his unfailing politeness, pulling out chairs even as the other guys plopped down in theirs. His quick and intelligent responses in class. I would miss him checking in on me. Miss his friendship. As the cab pulled away, I rested my head against the glass, watching raindrops streak past me. The bus ride gave me the opportunity to say good-bye to the rolling fields and the forty shades of green, to think about the summer and what I was heading home to, and what lay ahead generally. For the first time since I had met Patrick, I could see that there were other possibilities out there.

Patrick called almost as soon as I was home, like I had some homing beacon on me that let him know I was close. I was wary. I wasn't sure I wanted to see him, cautious of bursting the bubble I had built around myself.

Chapter 36

August 7

I flip-flopped for a week about getting a beer with Patrick—ignore him completely or see what he wanted? I wanted so badly to hold on to the image and feeling of Alex, but he hadn't even kissed me. Whereas Patrick almost assuredly wanted to.

Together we drove the two hours to Wyoming, to Cheyenne Frontier Days, the rodeo equivalent of Stock Show. In his two-plus years of living in Denver he'd adapted nicely to cowboys, country music, boots, and horses.

The Kenny Chesney concert began with a video of Jimmy Buffett throwing beachy things at the camera: flip-flops, a beach ball, margaritas, a pineapple.

As we stood in line for more beer, Kenny played the first few notes of the song that always made me think of Patrick. I turned around to him, singing along about first kisses and second dates.

He grinned at me.

"Cheers," I said, lifting my plastic cup.

"Cheers," he echoed.

Patrick turned me to face him squarely and put his arms around my waist. I wrapped my arms around his neck, savoring just this moment, the chance to dance with him even if I knew he would write it off as concert dancing.

When the concert was over, we grabbed one more beer, and I dragged him over to the Ferris wheel. Soon we were suspended over Frontier Days, looking at all the lights.

I wish I could say it had been incredibly romantic, that something amazing had happened up there. But it didn't. We were just two people suspended above the glow of revelry below us. The magical spell the concert had cast loosened its grip with each step we took away from the rodeo grounds. At the car, I opened the doors, turned it on to start the A/C, and George Strait came out of the speakers, singing about easy coming and easy going. I turned around and held my arms up, to ask for another dance.

"Emmalyn, you know I don't dance," he insisted.

I forced myself to ignore my irritation, since we had been dancing just minutes ago. "Okay, so then just hold me." He obliged and put his arms around me while the song finished.

"Hey ..." Patrick said, as he turned to put his seatbelt on.

"Yes?" I asked, turning to him. One look at his brilliant blue eyes, and lust went straight through me.

He leaned in. I did too. And then he kissed me, pulling me as close as the seatbelts would allow. "You're trouble, you know."

"You are, too," I said breathlessly, kissing him again. Then he pulled back from me, and we were just two people in a car.

I waited to turn out of the parking lot, the local country station pumping out songs for the crowds leaving Frontier Days. They all seemed to relate to Patrick and me somehow, I thought, as the next song came on—Sara Evans singing about the suds in the bucket while waiting for her prince in his white truck.

"I used to know a guy that drove a white pickup," I said somewhat sadly.

"Yeah? What happened to him?" Out of the corner of my eye I watched Patrick looking at me. The light changed, and I accelerated.

"I think he went away, I'm not sure," I said as I headed on to the highway. We were not far along I-25 headed back to Denver when Patrick put his hand on my knee. I eyed his hand surreptitiously. The further south we drove, the further north his hand strayed. I was wound tight like a bobbin thread, hands gripping the wheel as we bantered back and forth, and I tried to not pull off into an open field and have my way with him.

"Do you want to do this?" I asked as we drove through the north side of Denver, waving my hand around.

"Only if you do."

"Right." We were flying down the highway while I barely kept hold of what was left of my reason.

An hour later, I lay flat on my back in Patrick's bed, shaking.

"I can't do this," I whispered. It wasn't because I didn't want to. Definitely not that.

"I'm glad," I heard from the darkness. I rolled over and looked at Patrick. "I mean, I'm glad that you feel comfortable enough to say that to me this isn't what you want."

"Oh, I want."

He watched me until he said, "You're different from the last time I saw you."

"I know," I said almost to myself. "Do you want me to go?" I asked eventually.

"No. I want you to stay."

I rolled over to my other side, facing away from him.

The next morning, we woke up wrapped around each other. Only in sleep were we true to our feelings.

Chapter 37

August 16

I looked up as my mother walked into my childhood bedroom. Boxes littered the floor, half packed with clothes, books, and linens. There was already a stack on the landing at the top of the stairs. I had dumped everything there when I left for Ireland. Now I had to sort out the nightmare.

"I see you're still going through with moving to Boston."

"Of course, I am. It's what I want, and it's a great opportunity."

"It's a foolish choice. No one will take you seriously! I can't believe you are throwing away all the groundwork you have laid here for your career!"

"You mean the internship I had last summer you didn't approve of?" I snapped.

"I mean all the connections you have here."

"You mean all the connections *you* have here."

"I can't believe you would just throw all of this away! For some ridiculous fantasy about graduating from Harvard."

"I would have thought that you would have liked to see me make some new connections through an Ivy League school." I stopped what I was doing, resting my hands on the edge of the box, and took a deep breath while looking at the ceiling. "I'm making a choice for myself about my life. If it backfires, that's mine to deal with. But maybe it works out better than you think."

"No one there will know you, or care about some transfer student."

"I don't want to live under your watch, Mom." Her gasp filled the space where I took a breath. "I want to figure out who I am on my own. I will never have another opportunity like this."

She tried one last time to bend me to her will. "I thought I raised you to be more respectful than that." She nearly glared at me.

"You also demonstrated how to be strong willed and do things my own way. If you want to blame me, you should start with yourself," I shot back. I was tired of having this same conversation. I should have gone straight from Ireland to Boston.

She looked at me for one long moment before turning on her heel.

My phone chimed on the floor next to me. I watched her retreating back for another minute before looking to see two more texts from Patrick, the latest in a barrage over the last two days.

"I haven't seen you since the County Fair. I wanted to say thanks again for your help," Patrick said as I settled on to his couch. The Resort had needed an extra driver shuttling horses back and forth for the 4-H show, and who better to call for help than trusty old Emma? I'd been happy to help at the time, but now I wondered why I had. If they'd really been tight, Kim would have asked me.

"It was fun, a trip down memory lane." We clinked our bottles together. "That used to be my whole life. Sometimes—" Tears sprang into my eyes, my mother's criticisms ringing in my ears. "S-s-sometimes I don't know what I'm doing in law school. I don't know how to be a lawyer. I get horses, and competition and mucking stalls, and physical labor ..." I sniffed.

"Whoa, whoa, slow down here!" Patrick's voice was slightly panicked as he pulled me closer and put an arm around me. I gratefully curled into him.

"Even now, after hearing your stories, and watching you ride at The Resort, I still don't have a clear picture of what it was like. I know it was all of who you were for a long time."

"Sometimes being there just sucks. But most of the time it's a way for me to keep a little piece of that life with me. And I still get to see Mickie," I smiled wetly.

With Patrick stroking my arm, I calmed down and pushed back. "Thanks, sorry, I'm just stressed, and obviously missing showing!"

"It must be hard to still be around the thing you love the most and not fully participating."

"It's a different kind of participation. Maybe what Mom felt like when I was the one showing, and she was watching."

Patrick snorted. "I've seen you look at some of those horses like you'd like to push the kid riding it off and execute the pattern yourself. Perfectly."

"Maybe," I laughed. I was startled when Patrick swallowed my amusement in a kiss. Then my shirt came off.

What am I doing? Why did I go so willingly to Patrick's bed? Did I want to be there? I pondered as, at three in the morning, we rolled toward each other again. *Even if it does feel good.*

When the alarm went off at six thirty, both of us groaned.

"I don't want to get out of bed. I don't want to go anywhere. Can you make it go away? Can we just stay here all day?"

I thought about the look on President Jim's face when he realized neither of us had shown up. The confusion about where we were, hardworking Patrick, and dependable Emma. Where were they? How come neither of them showed up? "I think they would notice if neither of us showed up today."

"I suppose. O-kay," he said, rolling out of bed. I watched him walk naked into the bathroom and sighed appreciatively.

By lunchtime, both our eyes were crossing. We were overseeing a group of animal science students in a day of volunteered maintenance at The Resort, painting fences, and it was easily ninety-five degrees outside. "Anna, would you help me carry the other cooler back down here from the building?" I asked one of the volunteers.

"Sure!" she said brightly, bounding over the tomato plants with a backward glance.

On our walk back, she attacked. "How well do you know that Patrick guy?"

How to answer this question politely ... "Pretty well."

"He's really nice and seems like he'd be *a lot* of fun!" she proclaimed.

I shot her a pointed look. "You have *no* idea." She dropped it immediately. Patrick proved my pointed look shortly after lunch by grabbing me from behind and painting up the back of my leg.

"So that girl, Anna? I think she was flirting with me today," Patrick commented as we washed paintbrushes at the end of the day.

"She might very well have been." *Nonchalance, nonchalance*, I chanted silently.

"She was cute."

Someone just shoot me now. "Mm-hmm."

"Why? Did she say something?"

"Actually, she did."

"Why didn't you say something? Friends are supposed to help each other out."

I jerked open the door on his truck to get in. "Are you kidding me?"

"No?"

"Patrick, do you remember who you woke up with this morning? Do you remember who *you were inside of last night?*"

"Well, yeah, but that's just fun. It's not like we're serious or anything."

"Wow. Just—wow. You really are a grade-A asshole!"

When I slammed the door to the Little Car a few minutes later, I took a deep breath. Only a few more days. Then I'd be free of the torture of seeing and not seeing him. It was such a relief to know that even if he called me, there would be nothing he could do about it, I would be two thousand miles away.

Chapter 38

September 23

I had been in Boston for less than a month, but I was more than half in love with the city. Every day I took my run through the towering trees of the Boston Common, past the Frog Pond, and out along the stately houses of Beacon Street. Sometimes I'd go into the thumb of the city sticking out into the harbor, and run past the Old North Church, stopping for coffee in Faneuil Hall on the way home. Or down the path along the Charles River. The changing of the leaves was unlike anything I'd ever seen in Denver, reds and golds that didn't exist among all our pine trees. Classes felt different in old, hallowed buildings. I stopped wearing whatever was handy and began putting on cute tops and heels. I found a new spot in this library and paid closer attention to cases and lectures than I ever had before. I wondered, not infrequently, how much more I would have liked law school if I had been here, a place I had wanted to be, from the beginning. My classmates were different, too. Most of them were from the East Coast, and had long histories with the area or the school. A few classmates' families had houses on Cape Cod or Nantucket.

My apartment was tiny, and expensive, but the floor-to-ceiling windows faced the Green, and I could just barely see it over the tops of the buildings between. I didn't mind the daily commute to Cambridge.

"Emma! You made it!"

"Of course I made it, I planned this whole thing." I took a playful swing at one of my classmates as I neared our tailgate site outside the Jimmy Buffett concert.

"Okay, fair, you do have the best organizational skills of any of us here. Speaking of which, we're almost out of beer," Rob said.

"Out!? How long have you guys been here?"

"Long enough," he shrugged. "I was about to make a beer run across the street. Can you be an extra set of hands?"

"I suppose," I sighed dramatically.

It took a mere twenty minutes as the liquor store was quite literally across the street. "I don't know, I suppose I'll go into corporate law like the old man, but I really love criminal," Rob was saying as we hauled cases of Sam Adams.

"Emma!" I heard behind me. I ignored the call, as Rob asked me if I had figured out what I was going to specialize in, knowing that except the people I was tailgating with, there wasn't anyone else in Boston who knew me.

But the call came again, then was bellowed right behind me just before a hand came down on my shoulder.

I whirled around, swinging the case of bottles I was holding as a weapon. I flicked my gaze up, and found myself looking at Patrick.

"Emmalyn!" he cried.

I felt my eyes widen involuntarily and was glad I had the case of beer to prevent him from hugging me. "You—what are you doing here?" Rob had turned around to see why I had stopped.

"I'm in town visiting Pops, and my friends had an extra ticket. A better question is what are *you* doing here? Shouldn't you be in class, or something?" he joked warily.

"Emma?"

"Yeah," I said, glancing around. "Rob, this is Patrick, an old friend from Denver." I saw Patrick flinch at the dismissal but ignored it. "This is Rob, one of my new law school friends."

"Hey, man. Emma doesn't talk much about Denver, so it's nice to see some proof she didn't make up an interesting back story." He laughed at his own joke. "I'll take both cases, Emma."

After Rob walked off, I turned back to Patrick. "I'm finishing law school at Harvard."

"You ... you just left?"

I shrugged. "I needed a change. Anyway, how's Pops? How long are you in town for?"

"Long enough for us to get a drink and for you to tell me what's really going on. Why didn't you tell me you were leaving?"

"I just ... couldn't. Listen, I need to get back. I don't want to miss out on my beer, ya know," I joked. I watched his face tighten just a fraction. "There's a big group of us," I gestured down the aisle. "Um, call me?" I suggested tentatively.

Patrick gave a curt nod.

I felt heavy walking into the stadium. This should have been something Patrick and I did together. Ages ago we might have, if we had ever managed to keep the lightness our relationship had had in the beginning. The whole point of moving out here had been to have a fresh start, to get away from a lot of things, Patrick not the least among them. Which was precisely why I hadn't told him. But part of me wanted to believe that running into Patrick this way, randomly, was a sign of some kind, the Universe opening up with a glorious *ahhhhh* that enlightened us both.

It was almost a week before I could force myself to confront what I'd done and tell Kim. "Patrick and I slept together," I said before she could finish saying hello. "Again."

"*What?* I just saw him this morning, so how did that happen? And I mean that literally!"

"It was ... uncomfortable. I ran into him at the Jimmy Buffett concert here, out with a bunch of friends. Patrick saw me and grabbed me," I explained, remembering the way the butterflies had roared up when I realized who it was. "He wanted an explanation, so I gave him one. Even though I'm not sure he deserved it."

"And?"

"I told him to call me; I didn't expect he actually would. So I agreed to meet him at this little neighborhood pub he suggested. Good pizza, and beer. Dark wood, low lighting. He filled me in on The Resort, most of which I already knew from you. I told him about deciding to do Harvard for my last year."

"Did he say anything about you not telling him?"

"He did, but I think he was hesitant to probe deeper. I don't know if I'm sorry for not telling him; I needed to escape. Now it feels like instead of taking a chance to start anew, I just cut and ran. Like a coward who refused to face her fears, instead of making a choice to step away from something so destructive."

"No, don't do that to yourself. You've been talking about this since you were there a year ago, it's not like you woke up one morning and decided to run away."

I nodded on my end. "When we were finished with dinner, I don't really know what happened. The next thing I knew we were back at my place, and after that I just remember clothes flying everywhere," I explained, resigned.

"No hesitation?"

"Nope. I would have remembered that part," I gave a half laugh. "It was amazing too, which is of course, all the better. Or all the worse. And now, I just keep running back and forth along the teeter-totter from 'that was a stupid-ass idea' to 'wow, I'm really glad I did that!' Not confused, but not ready to let it rest. Somehow though, in my heart, it feels like things are sorting themselves out."

"How does sleeping with him make things clearer?"

"It feels like a sign."

I heard a little humming growl from Kim's end of the line.

"I know, it's stupid. I think I just want it, him, us, so badly that I want it to mean something. If it didn't, why would he have been there, at that concert, at the same time, in the same tailgating row, just fifteen or so spaces down from us?"

"Maybe so you get a choice? To make sure you mean it that you want to move on? You've always understood that the Universe places choices in front of us," she suggested.

"Maybe ... I suck at making choices for myself. Law school, this thing with Patrick. I feel so frustrated and defeated that I can't seem to get it right. Boston was about creating space for myself, and Patrick blasted—I *let* Patrick blast," I corrected myself, "right through that. Maybe it's just random. Or maybe it's a test I just failed miserably."

Chapter 39

Thanksgiving Weekend

Kim was right. I had been longing to get back to New England for the last year. A few leaves still clung to trees as I drove to Renée and Aaron's, rubies and citrines fluttering in the breeze. I felt the same way I had when I'd been to see them last fall: hopeful. Everything about where I now lived felt full of possibilities.

There was a box of wine in the trunk, and I would be stopping to pick up supplies for the pies Renée had requested. Sunglasses firmly in place, I sang along with the radio, every view as I drove along making me smile.

"Hello!" I called, crunching over leaves and acorns on the driveway, inhaling the musty and slightly sweet tang my footfalls churned up.

"Hey, slacker, you made it!" Aaron greeted me with a warm hug.

"Just barely. I've been so buried in books I didn't realize how early it gets dark these days. I thought I was just so dedicated I was studying really late."

"Renée is in the kitchen; I'll grab the rest of your stuff."

"Thanks, Aaron," I said. "Renée!"

"Dinner is ready, and then you're going straight to bed!" she said, coming around the corner with flyaway hair and sweatpants that showcased her well-toned glutes.

"Yes, Mom," I teased.

"Seriously, you look beat."

"I am. I've been studying a lot. And networking, and going to law school social functions, and still running of course."

"Good thing you're here and it's a holiday, or I might have to burn your books to get your attention."

I laughed, "Not this weekend. I'm looking forward to a long weekend of eating, drinking, playing games, and relaxing."

The next morning Renée greeted me with a steaming cup of coffee, light and sweet, just the way I liked it. After the second cup, I set to work making enough pies for the group of twenty or so friends and family coming for Thanksgiving. While they baked we sat with more coffee, until the timer on the oven and the doorbell went off at the same time.

"Would you get the door?" Renée asked as she got up to get the oven.

"Got i—" I swung the door open and stared.

"I realize it's not the usual weather for this time of year, but it's still not exactly balmy out here. Do you want to let me in?" the person at the door asked.

Renée came rushing over, pulling oven mitts off her hands. "Alex! It's so great you're here. We weren't sure if you were going to make it. This is my friend Emma, we went to college together," she said.

I stared, tripping over my own feet as Renée subtly pulled me out of the doorway, my brain trying to compute if this could really be the same guy. But it was, the same Alex. Same lean, athletic build, same distance to look up into his face, same warm voice, same well-cut dark brown hair, same kind eyes. Our summer together came rushing back—pints of beer, late nights talking, almost sleeping together. When I'd left Ireland I'd put the summer, and Alex, in a box. My focus was my third year, Harvard, good grades. Trying to keep Patrick locked in his box.

"We've actually met, although I'm not sure whether she remembers me or not," he teased.

I pulled myself together and closed my mouth. "Well, *of course* I remember you! I was just, you know, really surprised when I opened the door." Questions raced through my brain. How did Renée know Alex? Alex-from-Ireland-Alex? A pleasant twist to the weekend, but a twist, nonetheless. I had been prepared for drinking and pigging out, girl time with Renée, hanging out in sweats. I certainly couldn't do that now.

"I set up an air mattress for you ...," Renée was saying when I tuned back into the conversation. She was also leading us toward the fireplace in the living room.

"Thanks, I appreciate it. I'll have to head back Saturday morning, but I managed to give the firm the slip for the weekend."

"What firm?" I asked. As far as I knew, Alex and I were both on track to graduate at the same time.

"The law firm I'm working for in Boston."

"Boston? Wait, aren't you a 3L?"

"No. I took a lighter load after my first year so I could help take care of my grandma. I was a few credits short of graduating, so I took UVA's Ireland study abroad to pick up the last hours I needed. I actually finished when the program did. For now, I'm just grunt work at the firm, but when I pass the bar exam in February, it'll be a different story," he grinned.

"We know him because Alex was working on a government contract that Aaron was involved in negotiating from the other end. Procurement stuff." Renée made a gagging face. "He really liked Alex, and who wouldn't, so when Aaron's in Boston, Alex puts him up."

The weekend passed comfortably, with raucous laughter at every turn. Unlike any Thanksgiving my family would have had, there were no china plates or antique silverware. In the damp and chilly air, collected around the table or the fireplace, everyone was relaxed. The dishes lingered in the sink while the group played board games, friendly insults traded along with the pies. It felt like the kind of family I had always longed for.

Friday, Alex and I spent the day wandering through the woods that bordered the seacoast, and then came back into town to sit and have coffee. All the nerves I'd felt opening the door to him had faded. He was as comfortable and confident as I remembered, good-natured—and gentlemanly, I noted as he opened the coffee shop door and pulled out my chair.

"I chose UVA simply so I could stay close to GiGi. She'd never seemed old when we were kids."

"We?"

"I have an older brother and sister, both of them live in California, though, married with kids. My sister and her wife just adopted their third."

"Third!?"

"Mom and dad are thrilled to have more grandkids. They travel out to California often, but they retired to Savannah about five years ago. That's the other reason I went to UVA. I couldn't leave GiGi by herself."

It was so incredibly sweet to think of Alex driving his grandmother to see her doctor or holding her hand if she had to have surgery.

"She died last year, just before I left for Ireland."

"Oh, Alex," I said, reaching to set my hand on his, "I'm so sorry. She sounds like she was an amazing woman, and I'm really glad she had you."

"She really was," he nodded, swallowing hard. "I learned a lot about life from her."

When I waved as Alex pulled out of the driveway the next morning, I was surprised how much I missed him already. He'd asked for my number as he'd loaded his suitcase, saying, "Let's try to stay in touch this time." The kindness he had shown me in Ireland was just an extension of his whole personality. I felt none of the angst I'd ever felt around Patrick. We could have talked all weekend, I mused, as I drove back to the city. I wondered if he had a girlfriend. Probably; guys like him always did. Whoever she was, she was very lucky.

Chapter 40

December 2

"Your finals end on the thirteenth. I don't understand why you have to wait a week to come home. It's Christmas, after all."

"Well, honestly, with finals, I haven't had any time to do Christmas shopping. I need to pack, and before that laundry—unless you're okay with me wearing sweats at Christmas dinner," I joked.

"You're just making excuses! You know I need you here before the rest of the family gets here," Mom reminded me for about the fortieth time.

"Yes, I know you do. But you don't need me twelve days before Christmas. Grandmother and Grandfather won't be there until the twenty-second anyway. Bobby can help just as well as I can," I said, reminding her that her brother was an adult as well. "I need to do some things here before I'll be ready to come home."

"Like what?" she snapped.

"Like the Christmas shopping I mentioned." What I really wanted was some time alone. I had been surprisingly unconcerned about finals, knowing I was prepared this semester. I wanted to go out with my classmates for a drink, get pedicures with Renée, and take five minutes to myself.

"You can do that in Denver just as well as you can do it in Boston."

"No, Mom. I will not be coming back immediately after finals. I'll come home on the eighteenth. And take the early flight and be home before noon. I can't stay as long as you want, but I will be there for Christmas and New Year's, like I promised. And remember, I have that fundraiser for The Resort on the nineteenth."

"You are just trying to make this harder for me! Everything you do is all about you, you can't help me at all!" And we were back to shrieking.

"Mom," I said tiredly, "stop yelling. It makes me want to not come back at all."

Then she started crying. She rarely cried, only doing so when nothing else worked. Usually, her tears did work, guilt for not being the daughter she wanted outweighing my own desires. But at the end of a long semester, the ploy was exhausting, and I was tired of bending to her will. I had already compromised, agreeing to stay past the new year, but not for my entire break.

The plane ride gave me a few hours to settle from the semester. The lead-up to finals hadn't been the frenzied kind of preparation I had experienced my first year. I had been, and was still, well aware that if this time as a visiting student was to be remembered by my mother, or myself for that matter, as anything other than a whim, I needed to approach the exams differently.

I'd made a core group of friends, formed a study group, and found myself competing just as fiercely as everyone else. There was competition about everything. Not just to be good, but to be the best, and secure the most coveted internships, jobs, or highest pay. But this time, I found the competition invigorating, just as it had been in my decades of showing. As it turned out, in the right environment, law school was no longer overwhelming, it was galvanizing. And I had secured one of those internships, giving me much-needed experience, as well as a decent amount of extra cash.

Aside from Christmas, there were other festivities to attend. The Resort had chosen a holiday evening to thank its biggest donors and encourage more donations. I dressed carefully. Patrick would be there, Kim had forewarned me. Other than his emails, which I hadn't returned, I hadn't spoken to him since our rendezvous.

I pulled on a navy skirt. Then a pair of thigh highs. I felt like I was dressing for battle. Finally, a red camisole with cream lace trim, and stilettos.

Despite being prepared for Patrick, I was relieved to see that Kim and John were already in the ballroom of the theater, where we'd see the Rockettes, chatting with past donors. As was President Jim, who greeted me warmly, as if I were still his star fundraiser. Seconds before Patrick greeted me, I felt my whole back prickle.

"Emmalyn!" he said, hugging me, as if we had just seen each other. "You look very nice tonight."

"Thank you." I glanced down, taking him in. He was the most dressed up I'd ever seen him, but his khakis were still frayed. I had a pang for how we'd once been. I turned back to Kim.

Patrick immediately hugged her and shook John's hand.

John gave me a quizzical look, but I shook my head. "Here, Emma, want some of this really fancy salad?" He offered me a small skewer with a ball of mozzarella, half a cherry tomato, and a basil leaf on it.

"I'd love some!" I was going to be the coolest, most popular girl tonight, and Patrick would be sorry he was missing out.

"Just don't use it for anything other than picking your teeth." John pulled the skewer out of my reach.

Patrick tried to catch my eye a few times, but I actively avoided him, chatting with anyone else. When he came to stand beside me, wrapping an arm around my shoulders, telling a donor how I was about to graduate from law school, I kept a smile plastered on my face.

Instead of ignoring me, like I'd thought he would, he was always next to me, jovial and friendly. It was maddening that he was behaving as if we were just buddies from The Resort. One quick look had me wanting him all over again. How much was simply physical attraction, remembered lust from our time together, and leftover threads of emotions tying us to one another? What I felt now sat differently in my body. A dull ache around my heart and a pounding pulse.

At intermission, John bought me a drink.

"When did you start drinking whisky?" Patrick wanted to know.

"When I was in Ireland, the motherland of whisky."

John must have seen impending trouble in my eyes because he quickly changed the subject. "So how are the animals out at The Resort, Patrick? Emma, did you know Patrick is back working his magic at The Resort?" He knew that I knew.

"Oh, great. We had a couple of horses delivered this week for their thirty-day trial period, and they seem to be settling in nicely. Of course, that's more mouths to feed, but they seem to be good horses to add to the programs."

"That's really good to hear." John had surely heard all of this from Kim already, but he didn't show it. Tones sounded, indicating the end of the intermission.

"Here," I said to Patrick. "You've been eyeing it all during intermission, go ahead and finish it," I handed him my drink.

He tossed it back, then hissed through his teeth. "Jesus that's strong!"

"That's how I like it." I turned on my heel and stalked back into the theater.

After the show, someone suggested we unwind from talking The Resort up all night. As we crossed the street, Patrick called up to me. "Emmalyn, is this that place where we saw the homeless guy?"

I briefly closed my eyes to calm myself before answering. "Yes."

"Cool," he said, resuming his conversation. The corner where we had been serenaded on our first date. I didn't want to remember, but it was somehow worse that *he* did.

The group pitched in to shove tables together, and when the musical chairs ended, I was sitting next to Patrick. I ignored him, running around the memories like obstacles.

"See that guy over there?" Patrick nudged me as we stood to put on jackets. I followed his gaze. "That guy, with the veddy niiice blue shirt that's all tucked in properly?"

"Yeah?"

"Would you still talk to me if I started tucking in my shirt?" Patrick teased.

I wanted to laugh—that was the most ridiculous proposition I'd ever heard. Patrick would start tucking his shirt in when the pigs at The Resort could fly. Slowly I turned to look at him. And there he was, the same guy I had fallen for two years earlier, with the open face, looking to be accepted. "You'd have to be talking to me at all, for me to keep talking to you."

"After I saw you in September, I didn't know what to say to you," he said quietly. "I thought you might call, or something, and then you didn't."

"Third year is very stressful."

"Can I hug you?"

I lifted one shoulder in acquiescence, and felt his arms come around my waist. I sighed, my head on his shoulder, resistance fleeing.

"My ride left earlier," he said as he stepped back. "Can you give me a lift home?"

All that avoidance and protection only to end up alone with him. Resigned, I followed him into the house, into his room, multicolored Christmas lights strung around the ceiling. I stood with my back to Patrick, listening to him pull off his shirt and khakis.

Moments later he was behind me, hugging me close to him. "You smell good. Like that night of the fundraiser."

Score one for Mrs. Eichorn.

"Emmalyn," he said quietly, his breath soft against my ear.

Fuck. I wanted to scream and cry that it wasn't fair what he kept doing to me. I wanted to finish this and be done with it almost as badly as I wanted to jump him.

"Emmalyn," he said to my silence, "you didn't talk to me at all tonight. You wouldn't even look at me."

I wished he'd stop saying my name. "Yeah. Well. It's like not you've always been so considerate of me, either." My voice was quiet too, like ice, trying to hold it all together.

"That hurt. Lay down here with me for a little while." His fingers twined with mine against my skirt.

Shit.

"I'm so worn out by all of this. I can't read you anymore."

"I'm not sure I've ever been able to read you," I said, concentrating on keeping the twinkle lights from blurring, hoping I wouldn't cave, any more than I already had.

"You know who the last person I kissed was?" he asked. I shook my head. "You." And then he kissed me softly, as if trying to apologize. *Double shit.*

"Good morning, sleepy head." Patrick kissed me on the forehead the next morning. I was curled up against his side, head resting in the curve of his shoulder.

"'Morning," I mumbled against his skin, refusing to tilt my head and look at him.

"Let's get breakfast, I'm starving."

"Right," I pushed myself out of bed and refastened my various hooks and buttons, padding upstairs behind Patrick, into the kitchen.

Standing at the sink, drinking a cup of coffee, stood what had to be a roommate. The kind of housemate every guy fantasizes about having around. She was round in all the places Sir Mixalot said were important. I instantly disliked her.

"Emma, this is Bayless."

"Good morning," I said, watching her closely out of narrowed eyes.

"I'm headed out for a run. Nice to meet you," Bayless waved. As she walked past, her head came to my nose, and I recalled Patrick's comment, ages ago, that I was the tallest girl he'd ever kissed.

Over waffles at a nearby diner, Patrick laid his hand over mine. "I hate that you're in Boston."

"Do you?" I was genuinely curious.

He nodded. "I miss you. But you're not here. Not like you used to be." I knew he wasn't talking about the two thousand miles between the cities where we lived.

"I'm different. Boston has been good for me. And I know better now what I don't want." I paused, studying his face. "Why am I here, Patrick? Why did you want me to go home with you last night?"

"That's why I don't call as much anymore," he said, not answering my question. "You have a new life, and I don't know if I am part of yours anymore."

"That's so unfair! You can't just toggle me on and off like a light switch! What gives you the right to decide if I can or should talk to you? If you don't want to be friends anymore, fine. But we both know that's not true."

"I just thought that not calling you would be easier for you, you know, less distracting." He couldn't even look at me to make the lie convincing.

"No, you didn't. You thought it was easier for you, but now you don't want to deal with those consequences. You're uncomfortable with the depth of our relationship, but instead of being straight about it, instead of saying you were done with the relationship and moving on, which you clearly aren't, you decided, for me, that there should be no communication. That's ridiculous. If I want someone to tell me what to do, I'll ask my mother."

I was outside before I realized Patrick was right behind me, arms around me. I let him, just for one minute, soaking up everything I could, before I pushed out of his hold.

This was exactly why I had left. I had been so sure that going to Boston wasn't about Patrick, but, in fact, it was. I had left Denver to get away from him, from this. I laid my head on my steering wheel, crying, angry with him for always, always jerking me around. Even more upset with myself for letting him.

My life in Boston was peaceful without him. And here I had let myself undo all that hard work. I handed him every opportunity to make it right, all the while knowing that he'd only crush me again.

"Hey, Emma!" Travis waved jovially from his seat at the bar.

"Hey. It's so good to see you." We hugged each other sideways as I slid onto the barstool next to him. "How are you? How's the last year?"

"The food isn't nearly as good since you left, but I'm surviving. Here." He skated a pint in front of me. "Otherwise, things are pretty much the same. I'm doing an internship this year, Seventeenth Street law firm and everything."

"Travis, that's great! Is it awful, are they mean to you?"

"No, they're pretty nice, actually. I do a lot of depositions. I think I have a decent shot at a job after graduation, too. How's 'Hahvahd?'"

"Really good, actually. I love it there. Different, so different! But in a good way. I too have an internship, but it's with a boutique firm, and I don't think it will lead to a job. So, unlike you, I have no idea what I'm going to do after graduation."

"We've still got four months, right?"

"I hope so!"

"So," he lowered his voice conspiratorially, "any Patrick sightings?"

Semi-reluctantly, I filled Travis in on running into Patrick in Boston, and then our reunion and showdown the day before.

"Seems like things always get heated up, for better or for worse, when you and Patrick are around each other." He paused, as if deciding whether to continue. "I only say this 'cause I care, but you know, the best thing would probably be to just get him out of your life. He causes you nothing but pain and anxiety."

"Well, I did move two thousand miles away."

"What's the current count of the number of times Patrick has told you he can 'never' talk to you again?" Travis queried. "My calculations are at 187 times, but I'm sure I've missed a few." I missed having him as a roommate. "Why does he keep saying that when it obviously doesn't mean anything?" Travis wondered out loud.

"Hey, you're the guy, you tell me!" I stated. "Remember, you're supposed to be my inside track into whatever the hell might be his motivations."

"Yeah, well, this one's got me stumped, I'm afraid. Unless it's the sex."

I dropped my head back and groaned. "Please don't send me out of here thinking that he's just using me for sex!"

"Sorry, Ems." He grinned at me.

Chapter 41

January 10

I sat in the wide sill of one of my big windows, my Chinese takeout getting cold on the kitchen table. Snow was falling softly on the city, big, heavy flakes that made me happy.

My departure from Denver had been anything but the end-of-holiday warm fuzzies. My grandparents also didn't understand how I had transferred to Harvard for my last year, even though I had explained repeatedly that I hadn't transferred.

"I had hoped being home over Christmas would show you just how silly this transfer to Harvard is. I took you to the firm's holiday party, and everyone there was so generous to you. I'm sure if you just asked, any of the partners would take you on for an internship for your last year. And then you'd have a job once you graduate," had been my mother's parting shot.

Never mind that the partners had barely spoken to me except while I was being dragged around by my mother, repeatedly introduced as "my daughter, Emmalyn," never my name first. "I don't think any of them could pick me out of a lineup," I'd said.

"Well, that's your fault, for not being more aggressive pursuing them. You can't just expect people to hand you a job." Wasn't that what she had just suggested they would do?

"I'm at Harvard until graduation, Mom. It's been a much better experience for me, and I do have an internship already," I reminded her.

"Well, you can't expect that to last. And I miss you so much! I never see you now, and the house is so big without you here!" she'd choked out.

It had been a relief to get back to my little space in Boston. It was modest compared to everything in Denver, but it was all mine, and so was the city. It saddened me that my mother couldn't see that Boston was the right place for me, that she didn't recognize how much fuller of a person I was from my time here. Her surety that she knew what was best for me, and that she neither wanted nor needed my input on my life, was disheartening. I had left her standing on the front porch, the image of her crumpled face embedded in my memory. Her desire for me to stay, to get an internship and a job through one of her contacts, was all about her. None of it was about who I was becoming, the choices that were best for me.

Mom was right; my internship wouldn't lead to a job after graduation. But not for the reasons she assumed. I'd applied for the job with a small boutique firm knowing they weren't looking to hire anyone, but needing experience and income. The five to ten hours I worked each week didn't interfere with my studies, and water law let me see how agencies functioned and sometimes attend hearings. Not glamorous, but consistent and different from the corporate world Mom inhabited. I stared past the blue circle on my computer screen spinning into eternity, waiting for a city webpage to load, wishing I was still on spring break. Naturally Patrick had called on my last night, while I sat on the beach listening to the waves. I'd forced myself to let it go to voicemail. Involuntarily my hand went to my phone as the blue circle hazed in my vision. Its sudden vibration startled me out of the memory. When I lifted my hand, my phone showed a Boston number I didn't recognize.

I cleared my throat, in case it was someone from the firm. "This is Emma."

"Oh good, you answered. Hey, Emma, it's Alex."

"Alex, wow, hey. What's up?"

"I know we said we'd stay in touch, and then I didn't call, but so much time has passed I wasn't sure ... Anyway." He paused, and I heard him inhale. "I wondered if you wanted to grab a drink. You know, St. Paddy's Day and all."

"That's as good an excuse as any." I clicked closed the webpage that still wouldn't load.

Six hours later, Alex and I scooted into a relatively quiet back booth at The Burren, our third pub, named for the rocky west coast of Ireland. The stacked rock wall behind me looked like the stone fences I remembered from our long drives around the countryside. In the front, near the window, an Irish band of white-haired men fiddled, and someone's bodhran thumped.

It was after midnight, but the partiers would continue until the wee hours of the morning. I sat sideways on the bench, my feet stretched out in front of me, sipping some specially aged Bushmills. Alex faced me, intent on the conversation.

"I'm so glad you called," I told him.

"I wish I had sooner. I kept thinking how much fun it would be to grab dinner sometime, but I thought that might be a little too forward. I, uh, wasn't sure if you were seeing anyone."

"Well, it's not like we just met that one weekend over Thanksgiving," I teased.

"True. Still, it's been a while," Alex hedged.

"All the more reason I'm glad you called," I said, reaching my hand toward his on the table. I flagged down our server and ordered another round.

"Remember that night we sat around drinking with the profs until nearly sunrise?" I asked as the server set our lowball glasses down.

"God, Professor Hood was so over the edge, wandering out onto the courtyard with his whisky, singing 'Molly Malone' at the top of his lungs. Cockles and mussels, alive, alive oh!" Alex belted out, arms wheeling in the booth, imitating Professor's Hood four a.m. off-key bellowing.

"Oh God, he was hysterical," I nearly wheezed. I wiped tears at Alex's impression. "So drunk! Sweet Molly Malone!" I waved my glass similarly.

"Not that any of us were sober enough to realize we were just as bad. Who had the drum?"

I blanked. "I have no idea," I laughed. "Someone had a drum?"

"I think it was an overturned mixing bowl." Alex started laughing again.

When we'd both caught our breath Alex raised his glass again, steadily, to mine. "Here's to that. And reconnecting."

"Agreed. I'm having a fun, non-dramatic time."

"Not dramatic?" He gave a curious frown.

Oops. "You know how law school can be, how excessive things can be, how into themselves lawyers can get," I brushed off my misstep.

"Oh, you mean like that one girl from Ireland who kept calling you out on how you were so different from those of us who came from UVA, when she was the one who wore skirts every day?"

"'That one girl.' Like you didn't notice she spent the whole summer flirting with you, trying to walk next to you," I joked.

"What? She did? No way! I wish I had known," he said.

"Guys can be so oblivious sometimes! Why do you wish you had known?"

"So I could have been more attentive to ignoring her, of course."

My eyes widened, and I burst out laughing, garnering a self-conscious smile from Alex.

Before the bars closed and the drunken crowds were disgorged on to the streets en masse, Alex walked me home.

"Can we do this again?" I asked, feeling slightly unsure as the evening ended.

"Definitely," Alex said, giving me a tentative hug. I tightened my arms around his torso just fractionally, not wanting to let go. "I won't wait so long to call."

I was smiling widely as I stepped out of the hold. Our fingers hovered near each other, and I felt anticipation build, a tingling in the palm of my hand.

Chapter 42

April 23

With only three weeks left in the semester, in all of law school, I was worn out. I cared even less now about the outcome than I had when I started. Even once this was over, the end was still months off, with the bar exam.

"Em, are you ready?" Rob asked. Since the Jimmy Buffett concert, Rob and I had spent countless hours with a small group quizzing each other, and trading papers to critique. We fell in step walking toward our corporation's class final.

"I'm going to go set up a shell corporation after this and hide myself away from my student loan lenders."

"Great idea! Can we be partners?"

"Only if we both survive finals," I joked, walking through the door Rob held open.

"See you in the library."

"I saved my spot. Dirty travel mug and a smelly sweatshirt. It's my lucky spot!"

Rob laughed.

I slid my hand into my jeans pocket, fingering the penny that had been on the table Alex and I had shared at the back of The Burren, as if by bringing up a positive memory I'd have better luck on the exam.

"Keep writing until time is up," had been his advice. So I did just that, thoughtfully filling in bubbles to match my multiple-choice answers. Pausing to collect my thoughts as I wrote about the benefits of an S-Corp versus a C-Corp. When the professor called, "Time," I sat back, satisfied with what I had written.

I trudged home, heated some leftovers, and sat down at my table to prepare for the next exam.

But my mind kept drifting to Alex. We had gone out a couple more times, as fun and easy as it had been in Ireland. He'd also been a sympathetic ear about the last-minute stressors of grades, resumes, interviews, disillusionment, and the specter of the bar exam ahead. How we interacted had been subtly shifting over the six weeks since our impromptu St. Patrick's Day evening, and even in the midst of the finals push, I kept expecting something to happen, some comment to be made, an admission that he was feeling just a little more than friendly toward me.

But nothing had.

I woke up from a restless nap the next afternoon. I'd been half awake anyway, asking myself flashcard questions in my head, thinking about what would come next. My lease ended at the end of May.

I flipped over onto my stomach, head pillowed on my hands, watching out the window. "You had a plan when you came here," I whispered to myself. "And you did it."

I could put a check mark in front of each accomplishment. Settle myself, get good grades, have a new experience. But staying in Boston had never been part of my original plan. I had a moving van rented. My registration for the bar study course and the bar exam in Colorado were both complete. Denver was ready for me to pick up where I had left off and begin practicing law.

I sat up and pulled the arbitration casebook across the bed.

Then, miraculously, it was all finished. Not a single remaining argument was left to be made. I was relieved the exam boxes were checked, but I felt a bit bereft. I'd worked hard at Harvard, participating in a way I didn't know I had wanted to. Now all that was left was to go home, leave behind the friends I'd made, and the crimson Harvard regalia they'd all be wearing. I'd graduate with all the friends, and maybe the old parts of myself, I'd left behind. What would I do when I got there?

Alex, though, was another matter, I thought, as I pondered what earrings to wear. He said he was taking me out for dinner to celebrate the end, and he'd said to dress up. I was probably overdressed, but I didn't care. I was ready to get fancy after all the time I'd spent surrounded by paper and books, hunched over my computer the past few weeks.

I decided on the sapphire studs my dad had given me for my sixteenth birthday just as the release for the front door buzzed. I looked around my small space—it was a mess. But that couldn't be helped. I stepped carefully over a pile of casebooks ready to be sold back and opened the door for Alex, wearing a dark charcoal suit.

I felt less overdressed. "Um. Wow." He wore a light blue dress shirt and a maroon tie; his hair even more neatly styled than usual. It was all I could do to keep from drooling.

"I could say the same thing!" he said, looking at the fitted, strapless, navy dress. His gaze caught my eye, then skipped over my shoulder. "What's all this?"

"Packing," I made a face.

"So soon?" He looked alarmed.

"Graduation is next week, so ... Yeah."

Alex recovered quickly. "Then we'll make the most of tonight while we have it," he said, reaching for my hand. He'd tugged on my hand when we stood on Ha'penny Bridge, but the way he held my hand now wasn't a joke.

My building didn't have a doorman, but the next one down did, and Alex had convinced him to watch his car while he came to retrieve me. The doorman, greying and in his sixties, smiled indulgently at what he obviously thought was a very serious couple going somewhere fancy and important.

He wasn't far off, as Alex had chosen a small French restaurant in upscale Chelsea. Red banquette-style chairs pulled up to white linen-topped tables, and heavy white plates stood ready. I noticed the pattern on the silver was the same as my grandparents' antique set, passed down to the family from the 1800s.

We sat by a mullioned window with an ivory candle in an antique holder casting romantic light over our glasses of wine.

"I hadn't realized you intended to leave," Alex said as we shared Grand Marnier crème brûlée.

I looked out the window to the cobblestones shining in the street, unable to look at him. "I hadn't realized I might want to stay. I had a mission coming here, and I accomplished it."

"You could stay, you know."

"I could. But my lease is up in a couple of weeks, I'm registered for the Colorado bar classes, and to take it out there."

"So? You and Renée are close enough, you could live with them for the summer, while you study, right? It's just money, you could register to take the bar out here."

His response caught me off guard. "Could it be done? Sure." And in that moment, all I wanted was to stay. "But convincing my mother, who is the one with said money, might not be worth the fight."

"It'll be a shame for you to leave. You seem to really like it out here. I'll be sad." Alex put on a comical frown, and I laughed.

"Sure, sure," I humored him.

"No, really. I will be." He set his hand over mine. "I didn't realize that you were leaving so soon. Actually, I didn't realize that you were leaving at all." His gaze caught mine, and I was hooked, remembering the feel of his arm as he'd protected me in Derry. "I thought I was going to have loads more time with you." The look on his face said he was questioning my excuses.

I saw concern in his eyes as I felt warmth in my chest. He did have feelings for me. And now I was about to leave. Shit!

It felt like everything was out of my control. I did want to stay in Boston; I loved it here. Plus, I was tired of defending myself from my mom's criticisms. I wanted to be able to just sweep in and prove her wrong. And then, there was Alex. Damn it.

"Will you come back?" he asked quietly. We both knew he wasn't just asking about vacations.

"I hope so."

On my last night in Boston, Renée stayed with me in a hotel room, eating pizza out of a box and drinking cheap champagne. She and Aaron had come down the day before to help with the last flurry of activity and to supervise the guys I'd hired to load the U-Haul.

"I have to say," she said, picking up another slice, "I'm surprised you're going back."

"You sound just like Alex." I accused her.

"What do you mean? Did he say something?"

"He did, he took me out for a really nice dinner the other night to celebrate my last finals ever!"

"Oh reeeally?"

"Oh really, what? Spill it." I jabbed the plastic knife at her.

"Well, it's just," she said with a shrug, "that Aaron met Alex not long after he'd come back from Ireland. He'd come up on weekends sometimes, stay with us, and would tell us all about his time there. He mentioned a girl a couple of times. We didn't realize until Thanksgiving that it was you!"

I stared at her in total disbelief.

"I guess he finally decided to do something about his regrets of not courting you in Ireland," Renée added, refolding her pizza slice, as if she hadn't just dropped a bomb in our conversation.

"Why didn't you tell me?! I mean, at least after he called me out of the blue."

"It wasn't for me to say. Alex has his own time frame, we've discovered. Besides, you had just gotten back from spring break, and you looked like you were finally grounded again. I didn't want to throw anything else at you just as you were getting to the big finale," she explained.

I couldn't fault her reasoning.

"So what are you going to do now?"

I had been wondering the same thing for two days. "Nothing. Go back to Denver, take the bar exam, see what still fits and what doesn't. I'm not going to stay in Boston just for him."

"Staying wouldn't be about Alex, you know that as well as I do. You should be making yourself happy. You're almost twenty-five. And about to be handed a doctorate. Why are you going back for your mom? She's done nothing but make you miserable since college!"

"I know all of those things! I do. But there have been too many decisions I made based on Patrick. I'm reminding myself that doing so now, based on Alex, who I'm not even in a relationship with, would be really stupid."

"And what about all those decisions you've made based on what your mom thinks?"

"That's not the same thing!"

"In the grand scheme of things, yes it is! And you've made all your own decisions over and over this past year. You can do this. Aaron and I are here for you, you can stay with us, or we can help you find a new place in the city, whatever you want. We are here for you. And Alex too."

All I could do was shake my head, staring at the bedspread, tears dropping on the paper plate. "I couldn't even see him again. He didn't ask, but I knew he wanted to, and I—" I sobbed in a breath— "I couldn't suggest it." I gulped and cleared my throat. "Self-preservation." I looked up at Renée with a tear-stained face.

Chapter 43

May 24

The drive back to Denver felt like an eternity although it was only a few days. I just wanted my diploma so I could know I was done.

When I arrived, Patrick insisted on taking me out for a welcome home and celebratory meal. *What harm could it come to?* I reasoned with myself for the three hundredth time as I drove to meet him.

"That's a really pretty ring. Very you," he complimented.

I'd bought it on one of my last days in Boston, on a whim. "Thanks. I spent hours one day doing some retail therapy—I mean, celebration. See, one diamond for each year of hell I went through!"

"How appropriate."

"Yeah, I'm a big fan." I held it up in front of me, like girls do, admiring it from all angles.

"You should put that on your left hand."

I started. What? "What?" *WHAT?* When I jerked my gaze toward him, Patrick was casually watching me.

"You should put that on your left hand. Really confuse everybody. Here, like this," he said, taking my right hand, pulling the ring off, picking up my left hand, and sliding the ring on.

Oh. My. God.

Two days later, I was still wearing the ring on my left hand because I couldn't bear the thought of taking it off and putting it back where it belonged. I had once wanted a ring from him, fantasized about it, but never had I imagined anything like this.

I held up my hand and twisted it left and right, catching the glare from the hockey arena's lights, weighing all of it. It felt like being in a small boat in a storm at sea. What should have been a nice period on the end of a long road suddenly felt like a series of dots leading into the unknown.

"Pomp and Circumstance" startled me out of my reflection, and my friends and I began our processional.

Each graduate's name was read, followed by their accolades. I listened to the things my classmates had accomplished during our tenure.

"Claire Campton," came the announcement, "American Jurisprudence Award for Evidence, Trial Practice, Indigenous Rights, and Native American Law. Inducted into the Order of St. Ives."

Wow! I had known that Claire had done well in some of her specialty classes, but not that she had gotten the highest grades. And Order of St. Ives was the top ten percent of the graduating class. I screamed myself hoarse for her.

"Emmalyn Greene." I put one foot in front of the next on the steps to the stage. "Clayton J. Harding Award for Academic Achievement."

I jerked my head around from where I was shaking the hand of the dean. I knew I had done extremely well my third year, in Boston, *at Harvard*, but I had not had a great start to law school.

As if reading my mind, the next person to shake my hand said, "That's the point." I focused on her—the criminal law professor who had given me my first internship. "You deserve it, Emma. I know because I nominated you."

I stared at her, momentarily frozen by the gravity of being acknowledged. She squeezed the hand she was still holding.

I didn't recall anything else after being handed my diploma.

At the party on the front lawn, my mom grabbed me, crying, telling me how proud she was. I was still in a daze. Patrick was the last to hug me, and he didn't let go, which was good. I wasn't sure I could hold myself up.

Claire came running over and we hugged each other hard, both crying. She was headed to Cleveland, where she already had a job waiting.

"Can you believe it, that we made it?" I asked.

"From theorizing about condom dispensers to graduates! Who would have thought! And Emma, really, academic achievement? What the hell happened in Boston?"

"I—I don't know!" I shook my head in disbelief.

In the evening, I called Alex. "I watched the whole thing online. You were amazing, Emma!"

"Hardly," I snorted. "All I did was walk across the stage."

"But academic achievement! See, I knew Boston was good for you." I could almost see his teasing grin.

"You don't mind that it says I was terrible to begin with?" Not that it mattered; it wasn't like we were dating.

"If you'd been acing everything, would you have come to Boston? No, I don't mind. And I'm really proud of you," he finished quietly.

Chapter 44

May 26

I was curled into myself on the balcony, knees drawn up into a ball, with a glass of whisky on the table next to me. It was a gorgeous evening. Warm and a lovely sunset shifting colors over the mountains. And yet ...

And yet there was a continuous flow of tears I couldn't seem to dry or stop. On the one hand, I was delighted by all the friends who had come to my graduation party. It was nice to see so many people I hadn't had a chance to spend much time with over the last year. But now that it was over, I sincerely wished that sunset was the pinks and purples over Boston Harbor, not the reds and oranges over mountain peaks.

I heard the garage door open and close, then my mom's heels hit the hardwood floors. She didn't appear in the doorway immediately, and I wiped at my face more diligently, trying to remove all evidence I'd been crying. Stubbornly, the faster and harder I swiped, the more tears came to the surface. A few minutes later, Mom was back in tailored shorts and a polo shirt, her normal casual attire.

"Hi," I said, plastering a smile on my face. "Nice evening, huh?"

"It is. How was the class today?"

I'd started my bar review classes the Friday before graduation. No rest for the weary. "Fine. There's so much information I don't know how they think they can cover it all in six days. There are about five hundred of us crammed into a ballroom at the hotel."

"Hm."

"The bathroom lines at breaks are ridiculous."

"You could find a different restroom," she suggested.

"There are still a lot of people."

"Why are you crying? That is what you were out here doing, isn't it?" she accused.

"Oh, you know, just stuff," I said vaguely. Patrick and the ring. Missing Alex and Boston. Wondering if I had made a mistake coming back. "I guess because I'm glad law school is over, and it's like an end of an era, so it's also a little sad."

"I suppose that's fair," she said as she sat in the deck chair next to me. "A bit of feeling empty after all the work you've put in the past three years. I'm sure it doesn't help that you had to pack and return to Denver virtually on top of your finals out east. All hurry, hurry and then all of a sudden, it's graduation."

"Yes!" I said, nodding emphatically, soaking in the rapport. "It feels like it's all over and now I have nothing!"

"But you have your study sessions," she reminded me, not even looking at me.

"Sure, although that's not *quite* the same." I turned away from her to face the sunset too.

"It should be. You should be approaching them with the same determination that you did your classes if you want to pass the exam. Law school may be over, but you're not an attorney yet."

As if I wasn't keenly aware of that.

"Even so, you still have several months in front of you. So, even if you are feeling adrift, there's no real reason to be sad. Now that your schooling, and all that ridiculous traveling you did, is over, you can concentrate on becoming a lawyer. Imagine the life you'll have now! You can get a new car, buy a nice house, find someone to date who suits who you really are. You'll be a real catch now, for all those eligible bachelors you'll be working with."

I shouldn't have been surprised. As if *poof!* graduation happened and now I would be bestowed with these magical gifts.

"That's not how it works, Mom, you know that. First, I have to get a job," I ticked off on my index finger, trying to make a point. "Well, first I have to pass the exam, then I have to get a job. Then said job will probably require me to work insane hours, so I won't really have time for all these guys you think will be falling at my feet. Besides," I shrugged, "I'm not even sure I want to practice law."

"Not practice law?" Now she was looking at me. Both confusion and disgust on her face. "That's ridiculous. What else would you do with a law degree? All that time and money wasted. And you're very good at it, that award you got at graduation should tell you that."

"No, Mom. My award said I'd had the most progress in my academics. That means I sucked the most and improved the most, not that I'm good at it. I don't even really like the practice of law. I've been telling you that I hate it since I told you that I wanted to drop out partway through my first semester. But I didn't want to let you down." The tears were starting again.

"Just what exactly do you think you would do instead of being a lawyer?"

"I don't know! But I don't want to practice law, I don't want to be a lawyer, and I never h-ave!" My breath caught as I laid out my truth.

"I can't believe this. You are being utterly ridiculous. Of course you want to be a lawyer, why else would you have gone to law school?" Her look of disbelief said she truly didn't understand.

"Mom," I shifted my chair to face her more fully, "I have told you since my first weeks of law school I didn't want to be there, that I didn't want to be a lawyer. You knew that, and you told me to do it anyway! This should not be a surprising revelation. Unless you were ignoring everything I said."

"I don't ignore you." She flipped her hand, flicking away the accusation as if it were a gnat.

"I stayed in law school to make you happy. And you don't care that I'm miserable and have been for three years." I downed the rest of my whisky. "I need to go." I walked decisively off the deck, leaving my mother mentally gaping at where her obedient daughter had gone.

"Hey," I said into the phone when I'd gotten down the street toward the canal that ran through our neighborhood. "Is this a good time?"

"Sure. What's wrong?"

"Nothing I—" I swallowed the tears and anger that were fighting to rise up.

"Emma," Alex said with a small warning note in his voice. "I can hear it in the way you sound."

"Mom and I had a ... disagreement about how I should be feeling after law school. And—"

"And you never wanted to go," Alex finished for me.

"Yes." Had I told him that? Had he just known? "Doesn't matter; I did go, and I finished, and it is something to be proud of. So now it's on to bar prep. I just wanted to hear a friendly voice."

"Friendly voice, activated," he said in an exaggerated, peppy robot voice. "What would you like to talk about today!"

"Oh, just keep talking like that," I laughed.

When we hung up twenty minutes later, I felt lighter.

On the Sunday of Memorial Day weekend, I drove out to Kim's. Even though we had seven acres, her ten with only a few neighbors made it feel like home had felt when I was a kid, before the city had built up around us. Alex had sent me a few silly texts—pictures of robots mostly, with cheesy captions like, "Have a sunshiny day!" But I was still feeling off-kilter. Mom had frozen me out since I'd told her I had never wanted to go to law school, and I could see she was going to carry her anger around for a while.

I walked around the side of Kim's house to her small barn, where she was feeding chickens and horses, her hair poufed around her shoulders in the heat.

"That good?" she asked, as I reached through the paddock fence to pet a dusty neck. "Come on, let's get a drink," she added, gently taking my arm when I didn't answer.

In the sunroom they had added in the last year, John poured us each a beer. "Cheers!" he said before retreating.

"And déjà vu," Kim said as we clinked glasses.

For a moment I was puzzled, then laughed. "I guess so, huh?"

"Down to the same weekend as college graduation." She paused as she took a sip. "I'm so proud of you! You really pushed through the last year and came out on top."

"I don't know about on top. Maybe," I hedged at the consternation on her face.

"But I don't have anybody to set you up with this time," she laughed.

"And thank God for that!" I teased back.

"And?" she prompted when my face lost its smile.

"And I don't know what. Mom and I had a, a disagreement, I guess. I told her, again, that I didn't want to be a lawyer. It was like I'd never said anything, like she didn't hear anything I said for the last three years. And naturally, I'm a disappointment for not wanting to practice law. You were right all along; I should have just dropped out."

"Well ..." she said with a shrug of her shoulders. Then she pointed at her chest. "Big sister."

"So true," I laughed. "And then there's Patrick. In truth, I didn't expect him to come to graduation."

"I wasn't surprised to see him—you two are important to each other."

I gave her a dry look. "And then ..." I filled her in on him moving my ring from one hand to the other.

"He did *what?*! That's strange, even for him."

"Especially for him." I shook my head. "I can't seem to anticipate where he's going to come from next. It makes me want to leave again. I know I could cut him out of my life for good, even staying here." I paused, twisting the offending ring, which I'd put back on my right hand as soon as I'd talked to Alex. "When I had the ring on my left hand, I imagined what it would be like if it were there every day, if we really were together, if he really did want me more than when it was convenient for him. And you know," I looked Kim in the eye,

"I couldn't come up with a scenario in which that would be feasible. Mostly I just kept feeling sick to my stomach. I wanted to want it. But I don't anymore. That makes me a little sad. Like letting go of something you were anticipating."

Kim caught my gaze again. "You were so driven the past couple of years by your empathy for the sadness that he feels. But it made you miserable."

I gave a wry smile. "Patrick was right after all. I was trying to give and give to him—I was trying to fill up that hole inside of him."

Kim nodded emphatically. "But it didn't work because he felt guilty accepting it. I think he knew, even knows, he's never going to be who you thought he could be."

I sighed out a breath, feeling the truth of what Kim had just said.

"And now for the big question: what are you going to do about Boston? You can't stay here; you have to go back."

I felt the pinpricks of tears behind my eyes. Kim got up to get Kleenex off the counter.

"You have three choices," she said as she tossed the box in front of me. "You can suck it up and take the bar exam here. Or you can be brave and register for the exam in Massachusetts. Or be really brave and tell her to take a flying leap." After a pause she added, "I hate to agree with your mother here, but it does seem silly to have gotten all the way through law school and not at least take the bar exam."

"I know. I can't not take it, that would be stupid." I tossed several used Kleenex on the floor. "I have to find a job as a lawyer. I literally can't afford not to. Kim, I have almost a quarter of a million in student loans. I don't have a choice anymore. I can't make enough money to live doing anything else." A fearful hitch of breath punctuated my words.

"So be a big girl and take it in Massachusetts."

"I don't know if I want to take it there."

"Oh, bullshit!" I recoiled at Kim's vehemence. "You miss Boston, you miss living there, you miss Alex, and you miss being happy."

"I do!" I said fervently. "But I had my moment of rebellion."

Kim pulled her hair back in frustration, the violent curls pushing into a pouf as big as her head, until she let them go with an explosive breath out. "Why would you get licensed here if you don't want to be here!"

"Because I'm a coward. I went to Boston, I did the thing she didn't want me to do."

"And you were successful out there!"

"Kim, I didn't imagine it would be like this," I said quietly. "I didn't know I could feel so conflicted about two guys at once, or that I would not want to be here. Or that it was possible to both want to please Mom, and not care what she thinks. I'm tired of fighting her on everything! And taking the Mass bar would be another big fight. I know this makes absolutely no sense, but I keep thinking that one of these days I'm going to do something so right that she'll have no choice but to approve of me," I finished on a sigh.

Chapter 45

June 20

After studying for a month, the bar exam was only another month away. Each day I became more terrified.

"I don't think I'm going to be ready," I said to Alex on what had become a weekly Sunday night call. "I'm worried I won't have studied everything by the time the exam gets here."

"You will."

"I'm terrified. If I'm not ready, then none of it will have made a difference," I fretted.

"Ems, you're going to do great. Just keep practicing multiple-choice questions and reviewing the logic on them." I heard something bump and then liquid in a glass. Maybe wine.

"My mom has said I'm going to fail." Thinking of her derisive, accusatory voice brought the fizz of tears to my throat again.

"Maybe she thinks she's motivating you."

I snorted. "If so, she should know better. Tell me something good."

"You're doing a great job studying, and you're going to pass."

"Alex!" And then, quietly, "Thank you."

When we hung up, I lay on the couch in the room I had turned into an office to study in, my head propped on the arm, thinking two things at once. First, how different Alex was from Patrick, whom I hadn't heard from since graduation. Patient with my weekly bouts of fear, and unfailingly positive. And second, Mom didn't have any reason to say I was going to fail. Just an expectation that once again I wouldn't be good enough. I could ignore it while studying, but despite Alex's assurances, in the back of my mind, I wondered if she might be right.

I sent Kim a text. "Trail ride this week?"

The outings we went on every week or so were keeping me grounded, reminding me that there was one thing I was really good at.

"Happy birthday, Emma," President Jim said, as he handed sparklers out to the group of Resort staff and volunteers gathered in a city park for fireworks.

"Thanks," I said, turning away from Kim and John to take a sparkler.

"It's your birthday?" Bayless the Bitch asked breathlessly, breaking into my moment. Petty though it might have been, I relished the private moniker I'd given her.

"Tomorrow."

"Wow, you were born on the Fourth of July? That's so cool!" She sounded like a teenager.

"Yep! Sure is!" I said, overly cheerful. The last time I had seen her had been in Patrick's backyard, where I'd fallen asleep after graduation. I hadn't liked the way she'd looked at him then, and it was obvious now that she wasn't at the barbeque just because she'd been out to The Resort a couple of times. Kim had told me, though, that Bayless was more of a hindrance than a help.

I felt the hitch in my stomach that was jealousy. Even though no one had told me, I had known that they were dating. I'd sensed the beginnings of a relationship even as far back as the morning I'd met her in January—a casualness beyond that of roommates.

"We're all rooting for you, Emma," President Jim continued. "I have no doubt you'll be as good of a lawyer as you've been a friend to The Resort. Patrick," he called, bringing him closer, "just because Emma is a lawyer doesn't mean you should stop calling on her! The two of you make a remarkable team."

"Yes, sir," Patrick agreed, eyes locked on mine. The part of me that was deeply embedded in him tossed her hair and said, *He may be sleeping with you, Bayless the Bitch, but he and I are bound together.*

"You can always ask me, I'm available to help!" Bayless stuck her hand out to President Jim.

"And who are you?" he questioned, looking her up and down.

"Bayless. I'm Patrick's ... uh, roommate. I can do anything Emma can't find the time for."

"Hmm ..."

"Thanks, Jim, you guys will be the first to know how the exam goes!" I turned back around to Kim and John and rolled my eyes, then looked over my shoulder to watch Bayless trail past Patrick in President Jim's wake.

"She has no clue," John agreed. "Is she always like that?"

Kim nodded emphatically. "It's like she's trying to become Emma. Patrick was muttering about wishing Emma was available for a load of hay and Bayless literally said, 'I can do it just as well.'"

"Interesting. Well, we know you can't be replaced," John said, putting his arm around my shoulders to give me a squeeze.

"Emmalyn!" We turned at the sound of Patrick's voice, and Kim and John faded away from us.

"The bar exam, it's going to be hard, right?"

"Terrifyingly so!"

"Take this with you, he'll keep you company." Patrick placed a small but heavy ball in my hand. When I uncurled my fingers, I saw a tiny statue of Ganesh. "You know, patron of students, remover of obstacles." He caught his tongue between his teeth and smiled.

I felt the breath whoosh out of me, instantly back in his bedroom after our first real date, the poster of Ganesh on the wall, feeling the possibility and hope I'd felt then. I looked up at him from where the elephant sat in my palm. "Thanks, Patrick, that's really thoughtful." I reached to hug him, the familiar feeling engulfing me. "He'll bring me good luck."

I spent the last two weeks cramming as much I could into my brain, flipping through flashcards, and doing practice exam after practice exam. Then just as suddenly as the end of finals had come, so did the bar.

When I walked into Denver's convention center, rows of applicants splayed out before me. Hundreds of my peers, and those from other schools, were seated down the long hall, a seat between each person.

That first day, we bent our heads over Scantron sheets, filling bubbles as we'd done our entire academic careers. Two hundred questions, with a time allotment that gave an average of 1.8 minutes per question.

When I walked in on the second day, I was prepared for the sight of all the people I'd be competing against for jobs. I applied my task to the eight essay questions, flipping through the exam booklet to see which areas I knew and which I could only hope I remembered enough.

That night, the adrenaline still hummed in my veins like electricity, and I lay awake despite the exhaustion. I questioned if I'd given the right answer to this question or that, suddenly feeling the sinking of knowing the part I'd left off the essay I'd struggled with.

I gave up at 1:43 in the morning and reached for my phone. Fingers poised over the keys, I debated who to text. Patrick or Alex, Patrick or Alex. I pushed Patrick out of my head. Alex's last text from the morning of the first day lit up my screen in the dark.

You're gonna do great!

"I hope it went okay. I wish ..." I had started to type, I wished he was here, but thought better of it. He was in Boston. I was in Denver. It didn't matter what I wished.

Two days later, my mom and I flew out to Chicago for our postponed annual summer vacation. The first day had been blissfully relaxed, sitting by the pool, drinking iced tea, and reading. Exactly what I needed to unwind.

Then a different story emerged. On the other side of the kitchen, my mother and her mother were engaged in a screaming match. Mom and Grandfather had been having a heated but civil conversation about my mom's role at her law firm. Then Grandmother had joined in.

"That's enough!" I yelled, slamming the lowball of whisky I'd been drinking on the counter. It barely registered when the glass shattered. They looked up at me in surprise, oblivious to the fact that I had been in the room witnessing their meltdown.

"Just shut up!" I hollered again, grabbing my phone off the counter and running from the room, the house. I slammed the heavy front door with as much strength as I could manage, setting the heavy door knocker banging.

I ran to the park across the road and sank on to the edge of the fountain I'd thrown pennies into on every visit since I was a little girl. Sobbing, I punched buttons on my phone. *Please pick up, please pick up.*

"Emma, I was just thinking about you," Alex said. He sounded like he was right next to me, genuinely glad to hear from me, the tenor of his voice familiar. I squeezed my eyes shut. If I concentrated, I could feel him sitting next to me. Why hadn't I stayed in Boston?

When I opened my eyes again, I watched blood seeping from my hand. "I cut my hand. I broke the glass and c-cut my hand." My breath hitched as I remembered the events.

"Whoa. Are you okay? Where are you?"

"My grandparents' h-house."

"Take a deep breath." I complied. "Okay, now let it out slowly ... Good. Now again."

A few more and I calmed down enough to talk. I told him about the argument. "I don't even know what the disagreement was, only that they were yelling, and it was loud, and I was, I don't know, scared maybe? I'm so tired of conflict. Everything with Mom is a fight. And I can't believe I yelled at them! I'm too well bred to rage. That's not how we behave."

"I think you learned it by watching," he remarked dryly. "Do you need stitches on your hand?"

I looked at my hand and realized I was hardly bleeding at all. "No, I don't." Just having Alex on the other end was enough for me to continue taking deep breaths, calming down, tears stopping. "Thanks," I said quietly.

"You're welcome. Do you want me to call you later?" he offered.

"Yes!" I grabbed on to his offer like a lifeline.

My mom came walking down the driveway and picked me up from the fountain. My grandmother was following her.

"Are you ready to come in yet?" Mom asked.

"Not really. I'd rather sit on the porch."

"Sure." She handed me Kleenex, and for a moment we were united.

"Hey!" my grandmother said as we walked past her, her voice sharp, "It's time to stop crying."

I glared at her, insolence and fury pulsing through me. "I'll be done when I'm ready to be done." Her mouth opened, as if to say something, but she had no reply, and I didn't stop to let her gather one.

The whole event had been a new experience. Our family was stoic and proper, not emotional or prone to fighting. Yet today, only my grandfather had maintained the façade. What else didn't I know about my family?

I didn't have to ask for an explanation. "I told Grandfather that I'm leaving my firm," Mom explained after we sat on the wicker couch on the porch.

"You are?" I asked, incredulous.

"Yes, I have had a better offer from someone who used to be a partner with us but joined a different firm several years ago."

"But you're a founding partner. Why would you leave a firm you helped start?"

"Because the managing partner is not managing in a way that I approve of, and most of the other partners have sided with him. Grandfather had the same question you did. A bit stronger reaction, though," she smiled wryly.

"Why is Grandmother fuming?"

"She believes that I should let the men of the firm handle it. When I helped found the firm fifteen years ago, she thought I was stepping out of my place. Women are meant to do as they're told, even when they have their own career. Since I'm leaving, her biases are coming up again. As I'm sure you've learned, the law can bring strong passions with it. Grandmother thinks I should leave well enough alone, keep my head down. And keeping your head down," Mom added, "includes not reacting, even when you're upset."

I sat back and considered this, curling up with my mother's arm around my shoulders. That would explain why Grandmother was upset I was crying but had not batted an eye at the raised voices that had caused my tears. Had she always been that way? It sounded like it. Had my mother never been allowed to express herself?

After the screaming match, the vacation was tense. I kept to myself, curling up in corners to read, or escaping to the country club. When I returned to Denver, I sent emails about jobs, both permanent and contract, and escaped to The Resort. Kim called and asked me to assist on a group lesson she was teaching. She'd promised she would keep Patrick away from me. But here I was, looking out the window of the equipment room, and there was Patrick.

He wasn't but twenty feet away, working on the tractor. I didn't want to go talk to him. But I was struck by how much I wanted to touch him, to see if he was real, or if I just imagined the whole thing.

I felt the tears burn behind my eyes. It was, once, real. It was, once, everything.

My vision blurred, causing me to blink, refocusing on the dirt on the outside of the windowpane. I felt like I had just experienced a slideshow of faded memories, good times twenty years ago, but now with little meaning. I blinked again and Patrick was gone.

Chapter 46

October 17

I scrolled the list of names on the bar exam webpage, searching again for mine in the list of people who had passed. Maybe I had missed it the first five times.

The initial blow had me reaching to call Patrick. Old habits died hard. When my phone rang, I reluctantly tore my eyes away from the computer and glanced at the caller ID.

Alex. *Shit.*

"Hey, you!" I said brightly.

"Hey, yourself," he answered, subdued. "How are you holding up?"

I paused, wondering if I should pretend I hadn't checked the results yet, that I didn't know why he was calling. "Oh, you know. Just peachy!"

"Want to talk about it?"

"What is there to say?" I said, defeated.

"How about yes?" he suggested.

"To what? Taking it again? I think I'd rather slit my wrists, thanks."

"How about something a little less dramatic. Maybe some dinner?"

"Cute. You know I'd love that." I smiled, then squeezed my eyes shut tight so that the tears wouldn't escape. I would not cry, I would *not*.

"So it's a date then?"

I laughed, "Sure."

"Good, now go answer the door."

"Why?" I asked, even as I heard the doorbell ring. "What!" I raced down the stairs. "What are you doing here!?" I cried into the phone, but Alex was facing me across the threshold. Navy suit, paisley tie. But it was Alex, sunglasses pushed up on his head. I noticed the way his shirt fell over his chest and was momentarily distracted by how *good* he looked. Strong and lean and sure. Had I forgotten in my months away, distracted by the occasional Patrick sighting? "No, really, what are you doing here!" I took in the way he was looking at me, with, was that longing? The heat in his gaze seemed like it.

"Taking you to dinner, as promised." One side of his mouth quirked up in a sexy half smile.

"But what are you doing here?" I repeated.

Alex shrugged. "I thought, win or lose, you might want some company. So, we'll have some dinner, and a drink."

"I can't believe you're here," I sounded like a broken record, but I flung myself at him anyway. "I'm so glad you're here."

"Come on, I know you have better clothes than that. Put on something fancy and we'll get away."

I jerked away, horrified that I was standing there in ripped yoga pants, a T-shirt that had long since seen better days, flyaway hair, and no makeup. "Oh my God."

He laughed. "You look great—like you!"

I cringed. "Just wait here. I mean, come in, and—um, the living room is through there." I pointed down the entrance hall before running up the stairs.

I grabbed heels, a wrap dress, and makeup. *God, I need makeup*, I thought as I glanced in my mirror. I ran a brush through my straw-like hair, made all the worse by the dry air, twisting it around into a fancy chignon. A spray of my favorite French perfume and I tore back down the stairs.

Forty-five minutes after he'd appeared on my doorstep, Alex helped me out of the rental car at valet, and we stepped on to a polished slate floor. One wall of the restaurant held a dimly lit display of wines, and in the middle, the bar top was gleaming white marble. Smoked glass covered the tabletops. On the outside we looked like a chic couple out for a midweek dinner, ready to order slick martinis and nibble on canapés. Inside I felt like a schoolgirl let out to see the boys from the neighboring school. Alex ushered me ahead of him, and I could barely feel the touch of his hand on my lower back. I was about as far removed from Patrick as I could imagine, had I been aiming.

A slice of wistfulness flashed through me. Where was he? Would he have taken me for a beer if I had called him saying I hadn't passed? I fisted my hand by my side, then released the tension. This was no time for that—tonight was special. Alex had flown all the way out here to see that I was not alone for my bar results, whatever they might have been. A friendship like that was hard to find, and what-ever Patrick and I might once have been, we had certainly never been this good to each other.

It was like being back in Boston, grabbing drinks together at the end of a long week. Except I was wearing stilettos and a slinky dress, and Alex had a suit on. I knew it was his regular attire at work, but I'd only seen him like this when we'd gone out just before I'd left. Like then, I was aware that this was for me. And yet it was somehow still the same as grabbing a pint, having some nachos, while keeping an eye on whatever game was on in whatever bar we were in.

I felt both special and normal.

When the server brought a whisky at the end of dinner, he reached across the table for my wrist. "You know this changes noth-ing about you, right?"

I tried to pull away.

"Emma." His hand pressed more firmly on mine. "I mean it. You are still the same person you were yesterday. Do not think that just because you didn't pass that it means anything about you."

"Right, thanks," I mumbled, unable to look him in the eye.

Alex didn't push, just squeezed my hand, then let go and sat back.

After we finished our drinks, he drove me back to my mother's. "My best advice," he said as he hugged me, "is to take a few days. Live your life like the results aren't out yet."

"Pretend everything is okay since I have lawyer-like work, even though it's not a permanent position?"

"Go for runs," Alex continued as if he hadn't heard me, "call Renée 'cause she's your friend, not because of the unimportant exam."

I nodded, unwilling to let him go.

He let go and stepped back, softly touching a kiss on my lips.

I crept up to my bedroom and lay down, hands clutched at my heart, giddy and tingly. I couldn't believe that Alex had come all this way, just for me, just for one night, just for ... a friend? Did friends give kisses, even small ones? If this was the standard for friendships, I had to admit Patrick and I had never even been friends.

The morning was a different story altogether. I'd barely had a hit of caffeine when Mom brought up the exam results.

"I see you failed the bar exam," she said as she stalked into the kitchen, already dressed for the day, newspaper under her arm.

I kept my eyes on my mug.

"Would you like to explain yourself?"

"I don't have an answer. I did all the right things, I just ..."

"Clearly you *didn't* do all the right things! You are so completely irresponsible." She slammed the newspaper onto the countertop. "All you've done since the exam was over is lay around on the couch, doing whatever you damn well please, not even bothering to try to find a real job, while I work to support you! All you do is make poor decisions. I told you that you shouldn't have gone to Boston!"

I wasn't lying around; I had the contract work I'd found in the weeks after the bar exam, was paying her rent, and my year in Boston had been my best year of law school. Forgotten was the graduation award that said so.

"You know," I said as calmly as possible, "I already feel like a failure, and the yelling isn't really making me want to do anything to prove you wrong."

"Well, you are!"

In all my life, I had never been so hurt. This was exactly what I had always been afraid of. That despite being a straight-A student, having scholarships, not only graduating from law school but being honored for how hard I had worked, it had all been for nothing. I took a deep breath, looking her straight in the eye. "What can I do so you won't believe I'm a failure?"

Mom just stood staring at me, as if the question didn't have an answer.

I set my mug down carefully. "It doesn't really matter; it's how you act toward me that shows your real feelings," I said calmly. In some back corner of my mind, I acknowledged this was how our relationship had been for as long as I could remember: her saying hurtful things but disallowing a reaction. Much like, I imagined, Grandmother had been with her.

"I do not. Stop putting words into my mouth," she said angrily, punctuating each word with a jab or her finger toward me. "I don't think you're a failure, but you need to take responsibility for your actions. You can't be irresponsible for the rest of your life."

"You just said you did! Two minutes ago. I said I already felt like a failure, and you said I was! Do you really not remember that?" I glared at her, waiting for her to deny it.

"I said you failed the bar exam," she said rationally. This time she picked the paper up and took a step around the table. Like she was going for coffee and that was the end of the discussion.

"UUUrrghh!" I screeched, grabbing my phone. "That's it. This conversation is over!" I stomped out of the kitchen like a sixteen-year-old who'd just had the car revoked.

"Emma, wait, come back here. We are not finished!"

"Fuck you, and fuck your attitude too," I screamed at her, crashing up the stairs to slam the door to my room and curl up on my bed sobbing.

A bit later she opened the door. "Get out of the house." Like she was suggesting, "Let's go for a walk."

"No." We did this two or three more times.

"Fine, then if you don't leave, I'm going to call the cops," she threatened. I laughed hysterically. For one minute, as she studied me from the doorway, I thought she might drag me off the bed.

She slammed the door, and I sobbed harder. Finally, I picked myself up and packed my laptop and enough clothes for a week. I got in my car and drove away.

In the car I punched Alex's number, hoping he wouldn't already be on the airplane.

"I hate her!" I said as soon as he picked up. "She just—I tried so hard, and it's never enough for her, I'm never perfect." I sniffed hugely and in my car, rubbed the back of my hand under my nose.

"Your mom?" Alex guessed.

"Yes," I cried around the bubble in my throat.

"Moms can be like that." In the background, I heard a garble of voices. I imagined him standing at the gate, a single small carry-on in his hand.

"I'll bet your mom wasn't."

"No. But I didn't have a family legacy of lawyers. And I have siblings to pull focus away from any one of us." When I didn't answer, he continued. "Your bar results change nothing about you. Maybe her reaction isn't about you; maybe it's about her."

I heard a beep of a ticket scanned in the background, and I breathed through the space while he spoke to the gate agent.

"Thanks for talking to me, Alex. And thanks for coming out, helping me celebrate my failure."

"Your 'not pass'," he corrected. "I'll call you when I'm home."

I'd been at Kim's for two days before Mom finally called me. I was reluctant to answer, but Kim's advice that she should at least know I was alive guilted me into accepting it.

"Yes," I answered, toneless.

"Are you okay?" she wanted to know.

"Define 'okay.'"

"Are you safe?"

"Yes."

"Are you coming home?" she asked, much more timidly.

"No." When she didn't say anything, I asked, "Is that all?"

"Yes." Disappointment was clear in her voice. If she had expected contrition, I wasn't giving it.

Kim sat down beside me when I set my phone down. Silent tears cascaded down my cheeks and she put her arm around my shoulders. "You know you can stay here as long as you want, right?" I could only nod in response.

At the end of the week, I repacked my bag, took my laptop off the table I'd been using to work from while I stayed with Kim, and took the direct route home.

It was a perfect Indian summer day, the sky a pure unrelieved blue, made all the more fragile by the heat. Days like this, full of emotions needing an outlet, I wanted to spend stripping stalls and polishing tack. But there were no more horses to tend, so I settled for a sweaty run, while I considered what it was that I really wanted.

When Mom stopped in the doorway to my makeshift office, I calmly got up, closed the door on her, and went back to the memo I was writing.

Apathy overwhelmed the afternoons in the following days. I'd go for a run, then lie staring as the ceiling fan spun round and round. I tried diligently to focus on the future and block out all thoughts of failure, laziness, fear, anger, and frustration. Where was my drive? I used to be ambitious, to want to accomplish things, to have a life I loved. Several days later, I jumped up from my bed, grabbed a piece of paper, and started scribbling notes about what I could do to get unstuck. Top of the list was to connect with the law firm I was doing contract work for. But they beat me to the punch, an email the next morning asking me to spend the week in the office, as a trial for a permanent position.

I launched myself into the week. When I came into the kitchen the first morning, Mom looked up from the *Wall Street Journal*, startled. "Where are you going dressed like that?"

At the counter, with my back to her, I smirked. "To work. See you later," I said, taking my travel mug with me to the front door.

I came prepared to the trial with research and notes, and sat diligently in a cubicle, writing whatever the partners asked for. I ran errands to the courthouse, filed papers, and caught mistakes. At the end of the week, I felt like I'd accomplished nothing.

As I packed up my bag, the managing partner, Todd, stopped by my cubicle, resting his arm on the edge of the wall. "Thanks for being here this week, Emma. Would you like to stay on like this for the rest of the month?"

"Sure, yeah that would be great!" I heard myself say.

As I watched Todd's retreating back, I wondered what I was doing. Worse than feeling like I'd done nothing all week, I was less interested in the firm than I had been before being in the fancy downtown suite.

"Why is this so hard?" I asked Kim over the phone as I drove home in Friday's rush hour traffic. "I don't have any clarity about whether this is the right place for me. I'm sure I've overthinking it, but I assumed I'd just know."

"The real question is, what are you going to do, what do you want?" Kim reminded me. I imagined her pouring herself a glass of wine and shaking her head in sympathy. Renée would have done a facepalm at my denseness.

"Keep doing the work, tell Mom it was a good trial, find something else."

"Sure. That's a plan. Except for it doesn't deal with the fact that you're miserable here, you didn't pass the bar exam, you miss Boston, and you miss Alex."

"When you put it like that!"

"You know I'm only looking out for you, wanting you to be happy," she reminded me.

"I know, big sis, I know."

"So ...?"

Oh, so it wasn't a rhetorical question about what I was going to do. *Dammit.*

"I don't know ... I—"

"You're mis-er-able," she chided. "The past few months, even before the bar results were released, I watched you sliding backward. I'm just saying, you should think about when you were happiest. That's not here, or now."

You think I should move back, don't you, take the bar in Massachusetts? What would I tell my mother? She'd have a fit."

"Who cares!? It's not like you've never done anything that made her mad before, so why do you still care so much? Think about yourself, Emma! You didn't go to Boston for a year because you like seafood. Alex didn't fly out to take you to dinner because you two are friends."

When she put it like that ...

On the last Monday in October, a large manila envelope appeared in the mailbox, addressed to me, from the board of bar examiners. I eyed it warily from the other side of the kitchen. Inside was the decision on my appeal.

"No time like the present," I said to myself, and carefully slit the envelope open. The rationale was clearly detailed. It didn't matter. The result was the same. I still failed.

I left the packet sitting on the counter for my mother to review for herself.

"I see there's no new outcome," she said when she came into the living room that evening.

"Nope."

"I had such high hopes the appeal would be successful. All that work, all that time, all for nothing."

I didn't reply—what could I say? She wasn't wrong; it had been a lot of work, and the outcome still resulted in me not being a full-fledged attorney.

"You'll just have to take it again, it's the only solution." She dropped the pages on the table in front of me. "This mustn't be the end," she said with determination.

"I need some time, Mom," I said, thinking she was taking it harder than me. At least there wasn't any yelling.

I couldn't even think about doing it again. The emotional stress of studying, of waiting to take the exam, taking it, waiting for the results, all over again. It seemed unfathomable. If I could just get through to the other side of Thanksgiving, then I would think about what came next. Of course Mom wanted me to take it again, of course she did. But I wanted to decide for myself. I wanted to know the right choice for *me*.

Chapter 47

November 22

"Emma, we all enjoyed having you here for the last month," Todd said, as we sat in his office the Monday before Thanksgiving. "We'd like for you to come join us on a full-time basis."

This was it. My first real job offer. Everything I had been waiting for. He ran through the numbers: salary, bonuses, benefits, time off, 401(k) plan. It was everything I had worked for over the last three and a half years. A well-respected firm, a great salary. I was post-graduation, and I needed a job. And they were offering it to me, despite the fact I wasn't yet licensed. It was everything I was supposed to want.

Instead, I found myself saying, "I've really loved working with you guys, both remotely and in the office. I'm flattered by the offer, but it's not the right fit for me. I'm sorry."

"I understand." He paused, looking thoughtful. "I recognize in you how I felt early in my career, ready for an opportunity, but also looking for a place that makes sense. We would like to keep working with you, though, until we can find someone permanent."

"I appreciate the opportunity to do that." I breathed a sigh of relief. I had spent the last few weeks trying to convince myself I should take an offer if they made one. But I knew. If I had to be a lawyer, I needed to be doing something I loved. I needed that much of a consolation prize.

I ignored the voice berating me for my choice as Mom and I flew to Chicago, and retreated to the study to avoid slipping and mentioning the offer in conversation. Away from my relatives, I called Alex. "Happy Turkey Day!"

"Ems! I was just thinking about last year. It was exactly a year ago, to the hour, that we had Thanksgiving together."

"You were paying that close attention, were you?" I shifted in the club chair, sitting sideways with my back against one arm.

"Not at the clock, no. Mostly I was just looking at you."

"Mm-hm. Nice try, Romeo," I kidded.

"Well, maybe not exactly," he repeated, "but I was surprised. I tried to make up for it over the next couple of days."

"I think you did." A memory of laughing together, walking down a sidewalk strewn with leaves, flooded my senses.

But he wasn't giving up that easily. "Not that you noticed." I could hear a smile in his voice.

I started to protest, but he was right, I hadn't been paying much attention to how he was interacting with me. I couldn't even say *in hindsight* ...

"Doesn't matter now. It was a great weekend, and I feel fortunate it happened the way it did. It was nice to see you again."

"Oh-ho, just 'nice' to see me?" Alex chided.

"Well, you know." I grinned into my phone.

"Speaking of seeing me, when do I get to see you again?"

"I don't know. Soon? I'd really like to see you. That you came for the bar results was ... it really meant a lot," I finished quietly.

"Maybe you could visit Renée and Aaron. And I could just happen to visit them again at the same time."

I shifted in the chair again, sitting upright and cross-legged. "I got my bar appeal results back. I failed, again."

"I'm really sorry, Emma. That sucks."

"It does. I'm so frustrated, I'm trying so hard, and nothing will stick." A shadow in the door caught my eye, and I glanced up while

I kept talking. "I studied and studied, even with Mom telling me she thought I wouldn't pass. And then I didn't, and it feels like fulfilling all of her worst predictions about me." My grandfather stepped into the doorway, holding a few folders in his hand, filling the frame. "Hold on, Alex."

"I saw you study, Emmalyn, you did all the right things," Grandfather said. "Sometimes we get tripped up by just a tiny detail."

"Thank you," I whispered. "I just feel like such a failure."

"You know," he said thoughtfully, "your mom didn't pass on her first try, either." At my widened eyes he added, "I guess she didn't think to tell you that part. She always has been a perfectionist."

"But aren't you?"

"Hell no. I learned a long time ago perfection is unattainable, so you do your very best. You put all your effort into it, but that doesn't mean it's perfect. That's what you did, Emmalyn, and you know that." He continued down the hall.

I didn't know what to say. My entire world had been turned upside down with three sentences. To not be perfect was an option? The best effort was enough?

"Sounds like you have at least one other supporter besides me," Alex chuckled.

"I was offered a job with the firm I've been doing contract work with, just a couple of days ago."

"Oh." Disappointment rang in his voice.

"I turned it down."

"You did?" Both hope and suspicion.

"Yeah. It didn't feel quite right. Maybe it wasn't even my best effort," I joked. "I want more. And I'm going to have to be persistent to get it, since I have to take the bar exam again—somewhere!"

"Hmmm ..."

There was silence between us. I didn't know what else to say, so I waited for him to say or ask something. I was still reeling from my grandfather's pep talk.

"Do you still think you'll retake it in Colorado?"

What if my best was something else entirely from what anyone else thought it should look like? There was no clear solution. My mother was right to a certain degree. I did have a better network in Denver, thanks to her. But I didn't want to be there, I wanted to be in Boston. And I also didn't want to be there just because of Alex.

A big sigh escaped my mouth. "I don't know, Alex. I don't know what the right choice is. It's not like a study abroad, you know?"

"I do. I just want you to make whatever choice will make you happiest."

I closed my eyes. How many times had Patrick not said that to me? On how many occasions had I wished he would have so that I could have said, "You, you make me happy"? And now, here, was someone I could say that to. But I couldn't. Gun shy.

"Can we talk about something else?"

"Sure, of course. I'm sorry, I didn't mean to upset you."

"You didn't. There's just a lot to think about," I said on an exhale.

When we were back in Denver a few days later, I lay in bed at Mom's house. One prize ribbon stood out, twisted along the wall. It had haunted me for years. The ugly brown of an eighth place.

I could still feel the ride in my body. The shift in my balance as Mickie and I had downed several rails in a row, then taken a fence at too sharp an angle. The jostle as he landed, gripping with my legs to stay on. Holding my breath as Mickie headed for the second fence in the combination, a single stride ahead of us, and hoping Mickie would do what he knew how to while I just held on. The slid to the right after we landed, nearly falling off entirely, but pulling myself upright through sheer force of will as Mickie continued galloping away from his landing.

I felt the memory of downing the top rail off the next two jumps as Mickie and I got back in sync. We'd finished the last three fences nearly perfectly. How I'd placed at all still baffled me. When I closed my eyes against the ribbon, I could still feel the adrenaline flooding my body as we crossed the timer line.

Mom had been angry, but also surprisingly complimentary of my determination to stay in the saddle.

Staring at that ribbon now, I had a new thought. Each of the awards, big or small, represented a challenge I had overcome. Although the placing had been low, that round had been one of the most rewarding rides I'd ever had. Despite the challenge, I had managed not only to stay on, but I hadn't let it affect the remainder of the courses Mickie and I had faced over the weekend. I'd done well enough to overcome my rough ride, and stay in the top three overall.

What if this bar failure was that first fence, all over again? Maybe this was my opportunity to regain my seat and move forward successfully. I'd learned from that go around to never think it was over, to never assume that my worst was the worst. It wasn't so much about not giving up. It was more like, if I just did the things I knew how to do, the ending would be better than I expected.

What I knew how to do was plan, execute, and compete. Right now, the competition was about whose vision for my life would win out. Mine, or my mother's.

I banged through Kim's front door a few days later, letting the screen door slam behind me and pushing the solid door hard to force it past the air trapped between them. "Big sister time. I need your input."

"Even if you're not going to take it?" she called from the kitchen. She didn't bat an eye at my arrival.

"Even if."

I came to a stop behind where she stood at the counter. "You know I always think about what you suggest. But we're probably on the same page for this one. I just need to talk it through. My grandfather told me that my mom didn't pass the bar on her first time either."

"Whoa!" She jerked upright from where she'd been loading the dishwasher.

"That's what I said, too," I agreed, coming around to stand on the opposite side of the island. "And Alex heard, because I was on the phone with him. At the end of our conversation he commented, he said he wants me to do whatever makes me happy."

"Good!"

"It got me thinking about Patrick—"

"Ohhhh. No!"

"Stop! Will you just let me finish?" I laughed.

She pressed her lips together as if to seal them and waved me forward.

"It got me thinking about how never once did he ever say anything like that to me. He never wanted me to be happy. I mean, he didn't want me to be unhappy, and I always felt freer with him than with Mom. *But* he never asked, 'What do you think is right for you?' or 'How do you feel about X?' And I spent a lot of energy doing things I thought would make him happy, or perhaps push him so he'd find contentment. For the first time, someone wants to back me, support me, in whatever decision I make that makes me happy."

My hands, in motion this whole time, fluttered to the countertop.

"But?" Kim asked, watching me carefully.

"It's not so much a 'but' as it is a hesitation. I want to go back to Boston. You were right, I was much happier there. But," I smiled at her, "but, how much of that happiness was because of Alex? How much of this decision is based on thinking I can leave everything here behind and be a different person again—or was that the real me out there? Am I making the decision for me, and me alone, or am I making it based on a guy—again."

"I think that it doesn't matter if going to Boston is about Alex, so long as it isn't *all* about Alex. You were happier there; I could see it in you. I'm relieved you turned down the job. So go. Take the bar exam. Stay with Renée. Spend more time with Alex. Study, and study some more. Pass the bar exam because you want to be there, not because you're forcing yourself to get through it. If it doesn't work out the way you think it will, that's okay too, because it will work out."

"Are you sure?" I asked, biting my lip.

"Yes. I am sure. And if your mom kicks you out again, you can stay here until you leave."

"Are you sure about that too?"

"Hell yes! What else are big sisters for, if not defying Mom?"

Which meant all that was left to do was tell Mom. Renée had been thrilled to have me come back, and I was sure she was already prepping my room.

So now, here I was, sitting at the kitchen table. My fingers itched to spin the wine glass between my fingers, but I refused to show weakness. I could only put my choice out there and hope for a good ending. Mom sat across from me, as if we had just finished any normal evening meal.

"I don't really know how to say this so I'm just going to come right out and say it," I began. "I'm moving back to Boston, and I'm going to take the Massachusetts bar exam in February, instead of retaking the Colorado."

"You're what?" Rather than incredulity, it was more like she hadn't heard me. I said it again. My mother laughed at me. "And just what do you think you're going to do there?"

"Study for the bar exam, take it, pass, get a job."

She laughed again, but when I didn't join in the joke, her face became blank, then hardened. "If you don't take the Colorado bar exam, I won't cosign the bar study loan. I won't pay for you to sit around doing nothing again while you pretend to study." I could almost hear her adding, *So now what do you think you're going to do, missy?*

She shoved back from the table and stormed out of the kitchen, a cloud of fury and resentment trailing in her wake.

"Getting mad won't change my decision," I called after her.

Late that night I lay in bed staring at the ceiling. I needed to find a way to have that conversation with Mom again. I needed to figure out what to say, how to say it, and how to have her accept, if not necessarily agree.

Chapter 48

December 18

Mugs of coffee sat on the coffee table in the living room in front of Mom and I, a tin of Christmas cookies open.

"I've been thinking," I began.

"About Boston," she finished.

I was surprised she had anticipated what I was going to say. I picked up a snowflake and nibbled on an arm. "Yes," I finally answered. "I know you aren't in favor of me going out there to take the bar exam, but I need to do this. For myself."

"You're right, I'm not only not in favor, but strongly opposed. You don't know anyone, professionally, out there. How will you get a job? Where will you live while you're studying?"

"Those are all questions every other person who has done something new has had to face. Do you think so little of me, believe I'm so dependent on you?"

"I won't sign another bar study loan."

So many judgments. It was like standing in the brilliant light of the sun, blinded and unable to see if there was anyone else out there.

"It doesn't matter. I don't need you to. I'll live with Renée and her husband, take only what I really need with me. And if something comes up, I'll figure it out."

"That's not a plan, that's a prayer."

My mother, the control freak. Hoarding her toys when others wanted to play, too. Wanting to know the end before it began. Everything, and everyone, in its place.

"I have considered my options, and this is what I am doing." I paused. "You know, sometimes I wonder if the reason I did so well in my third year was because I didn't have you hovering over me, holding me back from trying new things for fear I might embarrass you by not being perfect."

Her mouth formed a small O, as if she didn't know what should come out. Good.

"I just need to know that I can leave my things here."

For a moment she hesitated, and I could hear her wavering between saying yes, which would mean accepting, at least on some level, what I was going to do, what I wanted to do, and saying no just to make things difficult.

"I suppose that's fine. It's not like there isn't any room for it." She smiled tightly. "I can't believe you're just going to go out there and take advantage of Renée. That's not how friends treat each other."

There was the rub, the next way I was wrong. "I'm not taking advantage of her. She and I have worked it out."

"It's not like you have any money to pay her rent. Especially without a loan."

"I'm not completely without resources."

In fact, I had a great setup. I had savings from the contract work I'd been doing, and surprisingly, the firm had decided to keep me on even once they'd hired someone. Todd, the managing partner, said they valued my work.

"I just want you to think about how much you have taken advantage of me, and my generosity the past few years, and now you're about to do the same thing to a friend."

I rolled my eyes at her. "I pay you rent, Mom!"

My mother closed her eyes and shook her head on a sigh. "You should have graduated with Claire, at the top of your class. Despite my support, you didn't graduate with honors, and you haven't passed the bar exam."

"You knew I was unhappy. The whole time, you knew I was miserable and slogging my way through. You know, even if you won't admit it, that I've done nothing without your approval. You've never taken any ownership for your role in that, refuse to acknowledge that you keep pushing on someone until they give in."

"Your accomplishments, academically, while you were in Boston prove you were able to do it. You just weren't working hard enough when you were here!" she accused me.

"Maybe that's because I was happier there and didn't have to contend with having you yelling at me all the time!" I heard the shriek in my own voice but didn't care. The conversation had started so well. How did it always end up like this, with the two of us screaming at each other?

"You can't blame me for your laziness!"

"Okay, I'm done. I wanted to give you the courtesy of sitting down and talking with you about what I had decided, but clearly, you still refuse to see me as an adult capable of making her own decisions." I stood and walked out of the living room.

I didn't need her approval, and I fought the feeling of maternal disappointment. I had stood up for myself. I hadn't backed down, hadn't let the fear of that disappointment overtake my agency.

I thought Renée had been right, Mom was unhappy. Aside from Paris, I couldn't remember the last time I had seen her genuinely smiling. I felt bad for her for that, but I couldn't make her happy, just like she couldn't force me to be content here, either.

How many times had I thought *I think I'll go to Boston?* Between my first visit to Renée and my third year, I must have thought about it every week. Even when going back had seemed impossible after graduation, it was still in the back of my mind. I hated that I had let the fear of ostracism stop me from doing something that brought me joy.

How many times since I had come back had I thought *I could start a new life?*

Alex offered to help me drive back east, but I turned him down. I wasn't leaving Denver to be with him—I was leaving to be with myself. I needed a clean break, and I needed to do it on my own.

I left two days after Christmas.

The Christmas tree was still up at Mom's, the lights strung along the front of the house glowing in the dark of the early morning as I pulled out of the driveway.

We had fought again the night before—her saying that I didn't have to go, that I was still making the wrong choice, that I shouldn't be going because how would I ever get my career together now, with no one there to introduce me around. *I think that I'm just tired*, I'd rationalized as the tears had crept down my cheeks during the argument.

And a new one: that I was just going because of Alex, even as in the next breath she insisted I was going because that's where Patrick was from, and I hoped to win him back.

Leaving had been harder than I'd imagined. How do you fight that kind of blaming, even as you are sad to leave the person behind? We had both been in tears—no matter how we might fight, my mother was still my mom, and I would miss her. Just as I knew she would miss me. But the choice was right. I needed a new town to leave all of this behind.

My decision could be summed up as simply as saying I was tired of the sunsets that everyone in Denver bragged about. I needed a sunrise, a new beginning.

I thought about pushing hard to get to Renée's in two days, but after hitting some nasty weather driving across Ohio to Claire's, I was just as glad I hadn't.

The door to Claire's house practically blew open in front of me, the snow flung against it like little BB's. Her job had proved a good fit, and Claire had recently renegotiated payments on the mineral rights of a nearby Indian reservation. The additional funds would allow a new health clinic to be built and support college scholarships for tribal members.

The lovely two-story Victorian-inspired house with the Mercedes coupe in the garage told me she wasn't just playing at her job. Once again, I felt a stab of envy for her dedication and direction.

I would have liked to spend more time with her, and on the other hand, I was just as glad to leave behind the reminders of my failings. I set off on the third leg of my trip, arriving barely ahead of the next wave of snow.

I arrived hours after dark. The lights that decorated Renée and Aaron's front yard glowed through the snow that drifted up in a wave along the roof. Wreaths still hung in the tops of the double-hung windows, the traditional New England window candles welcoming me back. Aaron had cleared a narrow path through the snow drifts across the yard.

I was back in the room I stayed in when I had come up to visit over weekends. It was even more charming than usual. Renée wasn't frilly in her tastes, but the two-hundred-year-old house had seemed to require some frills. The side tables were both antique, topped with linen and lace-edged mats, hurricane lantern-inspired lamps on top of those. The comforter was, I knew, down, and a cream-colored duvet covered it, lace along the edges. Even the curtains were lace, arched over the wide windowsills. Pine-scented candles were glowing, waiting for me. I sat down on the comforter and began to cry.

Part of it was travel fatigue, I knew. But a bigger part was relief at finally being here, finally being where I felt welcomed and at home.

I was glad to agree with the song. *Yes, I think I will go to Boston.*

Renée shoved me into a hot shower after she found me still sitting on the bed, crying, an hour after my arrival. When I got out, she was waiting with hot toddies and we sat by the fireplace, reminiscing about our college days, and talking about the future until finally, around three in the morning, I'd felt like I could sleep.

I cried over my eggs and bacon in the morning, and as Renée started another pot of coffee Aaron abandoned us in the kitchen to the frosty winter air. Logically, I knew it was grief over all that I was leaving behind, and despite my insistence that I didn't care, Mom's disapproval. After refueling, I went back to bed for a few more hours. Another long hot shower—my remaining bags had magically appeared in my room while I had been crying over my breakfast—had washed away most of the rest of the fatigue. I wasn't ready to ring in the New Year just yet, but I was ready to start celebrating *my* new year.

Chapter 49

December 31

We didn't go into Boston for New Year's Eve, as I had assumed we would. It didn't matter much to me—there would be many more times to do that. Instead, Renée and Aaron hosted game night for a few neighbor friends. And, of course, Alex.

Alex arrived before anyone else, stomping snow from his boots and carrying a box of party goodies, which he promptly dumped on the couch with a clatter of glass, to come hug me. He smelled like cold air, and when he stepped back to look at me fully, I gave him a lop-sided grin.

"Oh God, it's good to see you," I said, my voice muffled when he crushed me to himself again. I had called him each night along my drive, but it wasn't the same.

"I felt like you were never going to get up here. I'm glad you got here safely and didn't slide into a snowbank!"

I choked out a laugh over the tears that had started to slide down my cheeks.

"I have to look at you again," Alex said, pulling back, holding my face in his hands. "Oh, but you're crying, what's wrong?"

His concern felt good. "Nothing's wrong. I'm just so glad to see you. I really, really missed my friend," I said, hugging him tight again. I felt him stiffen and then relax.

"If you two aren't careful we're going to have to use a crowbar," Renée teased against the door jamb to the kitchen, but I could see over Alex's shoulder that she had a big smile on her face, too.

"Sorry. Sorry," I repeated, swiping at the tears I couldn't stop.

"It's such a happy reunion I hate to break it up, but there's still more to be done before the *actual* guests arrive."

Alex stepped back quickly. "Right, I'll go help Aaron bring in firewood. Rum and whisky for the ladies are in the box here." He vanished outside.

"That was a warm welcome," Renée commented, picking up the box Alex had dropped.

"God it's good to see him! I had no idea how much I had missed him."

"Why did you call him your friend?"

"Because he is?" I looked at Renée sideways.

"We both know he's more than that." At the counter, she set the box down and turned toward me. "And you're more than that to him, too."

"Maybe, but it's not like we've talked about that."

"I hate to call my friend who holds a doctorate stupid, but ..." she said with her hands on her hips.

"But what?"

"But!" she rolled her eyes at me, "he didn't fly to Denver after the bar because you guys are friends. I mean, you've slept together and stuff."

"What are you talking about?" I asked, really looking at her now. "Alex and I haven't slept together."

"You haven't?"

"No." It came out as a half laugh. "We haven't even really kissed."

"What!"

I shrugged.

"You moved most of the way across the country for a guy you haven't even kissed??" she demanded.

"I moved out here for me, because I'm happy here. I did not move out here for Alex." I smiled. "Mostly."

"Ah-ha! So you *do* like him!" Renée said with a finger jab at me.

"Of course I do. You knew that, we talked about it. We just," I shrugged, a bit helpless, "he never did anything about it, and I didn't know. And despite everything that happened while I was here, last year Patrick was still hanging out in the back of my mind. Sometimes he's still there," I confessed.

"It's hard to let go of what we thought we wanted," Renée agreed.

"It's getting easier."

"Here's to that, and a new year," she said, handing me a mug of hot cider and sliding Alex's rum down the counter. "Ah, I hope you don't mind, since I thought you guys were already," she coughed, "you know, I had planned on you guys sharing a bedroom."

"I think we can manage for a couple nights." I pressed my lips together, holding back my giddiness.

Hours and many, many drinks later, when the ten people crowding into Renée's living room had had their fill of cards, streamers, and horns, I dragged myself upstairs, followed closely by Alex.

He had showered in the adjoining bathroom after splitting and hauling in wood with Aaron, but we hadn't yet been in the room together. All of a sudden, there we were. Scents of vanilla and cinnamon mixed with the pine, the pumpkin pie we'd had as dessert, and the faint hint of wood smoke as it was carried away from the house.

"Right, well, I'll grab a comforter from the hall closet and sleep on the floor," Alex stated.

I was nervous too, but covered it with bravado. "Don't be silly. We can sleep in the same bed, you know."

"Are you sure?"

"Yes, I'm sure. Why not?"

"Well, you know," I watched him swallow, self-conscious. I'd never seen Alex this nervous. "Because of that one other time we spent the night together. In Ireland."

"Get in bed," I rolled my eyes at him.

But once we were under the covers, tired as I was, heavy as I could see his eyelids were, neither of us could sleep, so we lay there watching each other. The lace edging on the duvet and hanging at the windows suddenly struck me as a sharp counterpoint to our modern arrangement.

"So. Is that why you didn't invite me back to your hotel when you came to visit me in October?" I ventured.

"Is what why?"

"Whatever it is about Ireland that you think you remember."

"I don't know. Maybe." Silence hung around us once more. Finally: "Why did you call me your friend?"

Our voices were quiet in the darkened room.

"Because you are," I answered simply. "Why did you come to see me after the bar?"

"Why did you move back here?" he countered.

"Because I'm happy here, in Boston, on the coast. You know what I mean."

"Was I part of that? At all?"

Touché. "Of course you were. Are."

"Then why did you call me your friend?"

"What would you prefer I call you?" I asked, reaching out to brush back the hank of hair that had fallen over his eye. I had never touched him like that. I felt a bit like tonight was our first bundling, in an old New England setting, a tradition in which the suitor was permitted to spend the night, provided he was wrapped in extra bedding with his hands by his sides.

"I don't know," Alex admitted, but grabbed my wrist as I was pulling my hand away. "Do that again?"

I tucked the piece of hair behind his ear again, but this time he moved to kiss me, gently. When I didn't pull away, he kissed me again, asking less cautiously. Everything I'd been holding on to for months—disappointment, fear, desire, anger with myself, my mother, with Patrick, whatever the hell as-yet-unlabeled feelings I had for Alex—came charging to the surface. I didn't just answer his tentative kiss, I *responded*.

His hand went automatically to my waist, pulling me closely against him. I didn't know if it had been there all along, or if my response had been the magic switch, but pressed close to him I could feel his next question.

So much for bundling.

In the morning we weren't quite so relaxed. It felt like each of us was waiting for the other person to make the next move. The sex was more than great—Aaron had shot me a wink over breakfast biscuits—but beyond that, there was no further conversation.

The morning after that, after a less hesitant but still cautious night together, I walked Alex out to his car, kissed him soundly, hugged him harder than ever, and wished both that he could stay, and that he would just leave.

"Godspeed with the studies. We'll talk."

I nodded against his shoulder. Then I waved as he drove away, already wondering if he was wondering if sleeping together had been a huge mistake. What were we going to talk about? And when?

"Don't worry," Renée said when I came back in with a clouded face. "Aaron said he was quite cheerful when he came down before you. He's been his normal self, so whatever it is can't be bad."

"I just thought he'd be more touchy-feely."

"It took you two how long to even kiss, and you expect he'll all of a sudden be completely different?"

"Hmph."

"Let's have one last day of curling up by the fireside before you have to be locked in your room."

Chapter 50

February 25

Second time's a charm they say, right? For a month and a half all I'd done was study, watch lectures, practice multiple-choice, and write essays, over and over again. I hadn't seen Alex at all during those six weeks, and yet here I was, staying at his place for the next couple of nights so I wouldn't have the hour-long drive from Renée's house to the testing center.

Renée and Aaron had driven me down and would come back for me in a few days. I wanted to study more—maybe that had been my downfall last time, stopping my studying the day before the exam. Maybe if I kept reviewing the proper way of things, I would come out on top this time.

I was overruled and nearly dragged to a quiet, homey restaurant a few blocks from Alex's condo.

"I shall have a martini tonight," I proclaimed.

"You're so fried you'll only need one," Aaron razzed.

"And so, I shall make it a good one!" I glanced at the drink menu. "Ooh! The Lucky Cat! And I shall sign my memo essays, 'Lucky Cat!'"

"A fine choice," Alex agreed, taking the menu and ordering chicken marsala for me.

After dinner, my chauffeurs left directly to go home, while Alex and I walked the few blocks to his place. I knew we wouldn't talk tonight. That was fine with me. I just wanted to go to sleep.

When we came through the front door, I was surprised to see a pillow and blankets on the couch. Seeing my look, Alex explained, "Those are not for you. Those are for me. I'm sleeping on the couch tonight and tomorrow. You need your beauty sleep."

"Do I look as strung out on A's, B's, C's, and D's as I feel? I'll have you know I could probably recite the entire uniform probate code right now if you asked."

"Yes, rest. For your beautiful brain." He turned my chin up and kissed me lightly.

I softened, relaxed, and nearly fell asleep standing up.

The scene at the Massachusetts bar was nearly identical to the one I'd walked into in July. I scribbled, wrote, erased, and wrote again, sure that every answer was wrong. I felt worse than I had seven months prior. But every time I came to a spot where I didn't know where to go next, I regurgitated every tiny thing I could remember about the subject that I thought might be even slightly relevant.

By the end of the day, I was tired but energized. I was almost looking forward to the next day. I picked up the phone and called Alex immediately. As soon as we hung up, my phone rang again, still on vibrate from the exam, and I didn't bother to look at it as I answered while hopping on the T.

"Hello!"

"Emmalyn, hi."

I jerked the phone away from my head and looked at the caller ID, bracing myself as the train lurched forward. Sure enough, my ears weren't lying. It *was* Patrick. He'd called me the night of the Super Bowl, excited about the Patriots' win, reminiscing about Vinatieri's famous field goals, and speculating about whether Tom Brady would retire.

"Hi?"

He all but begged for my help with a semi-load of hay. "What do you mean you're not in town?" he demanded. His reaction wasn't anger like my mother's had been, but rather disbelief. "But what about Mickie? And your mom? And, and ..."

"I'm happier out here," I said simply.

As the train lurched along, stopping and starting at platforms, I listened to Patrick talk about The Resort. "I really just wanted to say, I hope it went well today," he said eventually. When I didn't say anything, he rushed on, "Kim mentioned the date passing. I just wanted to say I hope it went well and good luck tomorrow."

Oh? "Thanks. I don't think it went badly, but I feel like I gave it my best." I stepped on to the sidewalk and headed up the street.

"That's great, Emmalyn."

"What's up with you? Beyond The Resort, I mean." I had slowed my walk back to Alex's. It seemed unlikely that Patrick had called only to wish me luck.

"Oh, you know. Not much, just stuff."

"Stuff?"

"Well, yeah, you know. Some stuff has come up with Bayless that I need to take care of."

"Oh?" I asked, feigning indifferent curiosity.

"You know how it goes. I need to sit down with her and deal with this." If he was looking for sympathy, I didn't have any. But I could understand how he felt. "Yep, I do know. Just be honest. Good luck with it. I'm almost back from the testing center and I need to get something to eat."

"Right, of course. Well, like I said, good luck with the rest of it."

"You know, if they removed all the girls with straight blonde hair, it'd be nothing but guys in here," Alex remarked as we filed into the concert venue. As a reward, Alex had gotten us tickets to see David Gray for the day after I finished the bar.

"Can I stay?" I asked, somewhat tentatively. My wheat-colored hair was hanging straight down my back, stubborn as ever in its refusal to do anything else.

He leaned back to study my hair, then looked closely at my face. "Sure." He looked back at the stage.

We still hadn't talked about anything other than the exam and I was starting to wonder if we ever would. "Are you mad at me?" I blurted.

He looked at me again, much more intently this time, tilted his head, and didn't answer right away. "It's not so much blonde as it is all these bits of gold." A greater non-answer I'd never heard, but it was better than what I had feared. This time he didn't look away.

I stared back at him. "Can you please stop undressing me with your eyes? Unless, of course, you're going to make good on it." He blinked, then started laughing, pulling me sideways into his chest to hug me.

Finally, David Gray took the stage, and in the dark, Alex started a shoving war with his leg. I grabbed his leg to make him stop. I let go, and he started again. I grabbed his leg, a little higher, and stuck my tongue out at him. He pretended to be shocked. As quickly as it began, it was over again.

When the encore song began, I stood up. "I love this song," I said. Alex pulled me in front of him to put his arms around me.

The melody of "This Year's Love" rose and fell, reminding me of everything I'd been through. All my highs and lows, my last few years, captured in the words, illuminated on the stage. All the time I'd spent alone, waiting, and hoping that this time I would get it right, that this year would be the year I fixed my relationship with Patrick, or got over him, or whatever was supposed to happen. I'd been high on his hugs, forgetting the damage he could inflict with a single careless shrug, and how often I had felt like I just couldn't go on.

But here was something new, if unknown, that had potential. I didn't know any better now than I had at New Year's what was going on between me and Alex. I cleared my throat against the threatening tightness.

I wanted to know for sure. If I let myself, I could fall back into that sensation of spinning in circles, time and again, the same circle, feeling giddy but getting sick. I thought, maybe, no I hoped—much more dangerous—that Alex might more than care for me. Did I dare hope that he loved me? I wanted to know for sure, even as I was wary of putting myself in a position to find out the answer. But maybe, just maybe, he could kiss me on a midnight street, and my heart could get swept off of its feet. Maybe, I let myself hope, life could be so sweet.

Ensconced on Alex's plush, steel-grey couch after the show, a glass of wine in each of our hands, I felt comfortable. And yet not quite. It wasn't that I felt like something was wrong between us—not that jittery nervousness when you can sense that you and a friend aren't quite on the same page. It was more of a feeling of expectation.

"So."

"So," Alex parroted. "Did you like the concert?"

"I loved it," I beamed at him. "David Gray reminds me of one of those string tension animals. You know the kind, where you press the button in the bottom of their stand, and the string loses its tension and the animals collapse, you release it, and they snap back upright. He's like that when he's playing the guitar."

Alex threw back his head to laugh. "He sure is, that's a great analogy. I love how your brain works."

"You haven't talked to me much since the exam. Or since New Year's, for that matter. Do you ..." I trailed off, unable to think what I wanted to ask him. Did he have regrets about sleeping together? Did he want to talk about it? Was he just being nice to let me stay here for a few days for the exam and old times' sake?

"I don't know. I don't know what I want," he interrupted my internal questioning. "I mean, I do! Because oh my God, the sex. Not that it's only about that," he rushed on.

I laughed at him, setting my hand on his wrist. "Alex. I know. I know it's not just about the sex."

"Okay." He let out a breath. I'm not sure he was even aware he'd been holding. In his eyes I saw the same uncertainty I felt, and maybe the same hope. "I have such a good time being with you. Your friendship is important to me, but then New Years', and ... I'm not saying any of this very well. Hm. You're also kind of like a sister because you don't take my crap all seriously like a girlfriend, or at least not like any girlfriend I've ever had."

A quick, nervous sip of wine, and he kept going. "I come home from work and all I want to do is talk to you, and you're not here. And yeah, we talked on the phone a lot, but you were there, in Colorado, working and interviewing and taking the bar exam, and planning a life there, and—"

"I wasn't doing much planning; I was mostly winging it."

"When you were here for your third year it never occurred to me that you wouldn't stay when you were done. I'm troubled by the possibility that you might decide, even if—when—you pass the bar here, that you'll decide to leave again."

"Alex," I squeezed his wrist, "I had no idea. But, if you thought I was in Denver to stay, why come at all?" That was something I would have done, reached out, tried to maintain a connection, even if I thought it would fail. Alex was more practical than me.

"I don't have a satisfying answer for that. Like I could convince you to come back with me, even though I knew you weren't ready to think about that. Like I could get the job I interviewed for while I was out there, and maybe move out there. Like ..."

"You interviewed for a job? In *Denver*?" With each question, my eyes widened further.

"Well, yeah, because what if you didn't want to leave?" His hand turned over under my wrist and held on.

"Why didn't you tell me? All that time I thought we were just good friends. I wished we were more, but I had no idea you had real feelings for me."

"I have. For a long time. Maybe since Ireland. But while you were here your third year—I knew you had been seeing someone in Denver, and then it seemed presumptuous to tell you about the interview."

"What would you have done if they had offered you the job?"

"I don't know. All I knew for sure was that I missed hanging out with you. I didn't even know if we were compatible like that."

I raised my eyebrows.

"Clearly we're compatible like *that*, but I, we, didn't even know that until seven weeks ago."

"Been counting, have you?" I gave a cheeky grin.

"Yes!" he exclaimed, making me laugh with nerves and lust.

"Okay, my turn. I don't have any good answers either. I know I missed you all the time, too. I would think 'man I miss my drinking buddy,' and then that never sounded right. Saying that I missed my friend didn't quite sound right either. I'm not planning on leaving the area any time soon. I'm so much happier here than I ever was in Denver. I don't know how that's going to look. I've been so focused on the bar exam that there hasn't been time, any headspace, for anything else. All I know for sure is that I missed you, I missed how I feel with you. I feel so settled being back here. As for the rest ..." I shrugged.

"In that case, would you like to go out for dinner tomorrow night? On an actual date?"

"Are we going to sleep together before our date?"

"That's up to you."

"I think that you should come share the bed with me. It's the least I can do for kicking you out of it for four nights."

In the end, Alex and I did not have sex that first night we slept together. Nor did we over the next several months. He took me on dates, he came to visit me in New Hampshire, we went for walks, and we made out. Oh boy, did we make out! It felt like being courted, expertly, and so much so that as winter gave way to spring, I didn't even feel the sting of turned-down job applications.

Chapter 51

April 8

The morning of my interview, as I drove the winding roads, canopied by trees just starting to bud, I could not get Patrick out of my mind. I hadn't thought about him in more than passing since his call during the bar. I chalked my mood up to the location, my past wishes, and a tug of what I had once felt, and concentrated on the task at hand.

The interview went incredibly well, and I felt confident they would offer me a job.

Afterward, I went back to Renée's, changed, and headed to the beach. As I stepped on to the cool sand, sunlight sparked little shocks of silver off the grains. If I got this job what might it mean? Would I stay living with Renée and Aaron? Would I move in with Alex? I decided not to think about that, and listened to the sound of the waves rushing up on the beach, pulling my coat a little tighter against the still chilly air. Still, Patrick remained on my mind, an uneasiness that I couldn't lose even in the rhythmic splash of the waves. I gave in and called Kim.

"You're not crazy," she said. "I was going to wait to tell you this until later, because you don't need this in your head right now ..."

"What!?" I asked desperately.

"Patrick was fired yesterday." The flatness in her voice told me all I needed to know. No *wonder* he'd been in my head so much. "He called me himself to tell me—after about eight other people had. He didn't say much, just that he was still in shock. He mentioned he was staying through when his dad comes to visit mid-September, but other than that, he doesn't know."

"I don't think he'll stay."

"He mentioned that they just signed a year-long lease on a house. He and Bayless have gotten pretty serious ..."

"Oh."

"I'm sorry you called. I didn't want to tell you until your interviews were done. You really don't need this right now," she repeated.

"It's fine. It's just this thing we have. He's not injured or dying, I can deal. And anyway, I'm glad to talk to you. I have good news!"

"You got the job!"

"Ha-ha. If only it happened that quickly. No, but I did find out that I passed the bar exam!" I sang. "Results were released yesterday."

"You did? Well of course you did, but you did! When's the swearing-in ceremony? I want to come out."

"Don't be silly, it's only a couple of hours."

"No, I'm serious. Do you suppose Renée would mind if you had a roommate for a week?"

"Kim, that's silly. I would love it, of course, but it's silly."

"Then I could finally meet this mysterious Alex ..."

To: equestrienne@hotmail.com
From: pbranagan@oldwestpreservation.org
Date: Apr 29

Subject: please read this

Emmalyn!

Hi. I'm not sure how much of the goings on at The Resort you keep updated on, but recent events have had some dramatic changes you should know about. As you well know, The Resort is struggling financially. The most recent victim in the mismanagement of The Resort was me. They "let me go."

I was stunned, shocked, caught totally off guard. When Jim asked me to have a meeting with him and our head instructor, I got ready by finding dewormer on sale online and making a list of necessary repairs for the truck and tractor. I felt like an ass sitting there with that stuff in my lap while listening to Jim try to explain it as totally a financial decision. They call it "laid off," but it feels like fired. It was a week ago this past Tuesday, and I'm slowly climbing out of my shell and letting the world know. My next move is unclear.

I'm telling you this because you have been a longtime friend to both me, and The Resort and you ought to know. Truly, I should have told you sooner. Please forgive my tardy note. I'm not sure if I'm more embarrassed, or hurt, or sad, or what's going on.

Sorry about the Friday morning bombshell. I've been thinking about telling you for almost two weeks now and thinking of you every time I turn a corner at The Resort. I hope you are well and I'm sorry again to be the bearer of grim news.

your friend,

Patrick

I found it hard to believe that he was thinking of me at every corner. But he wouldn't have said it if it weren't true. I headed back to the beach, where the sand was still packed and cold from the night's air.

Under the cupped iron bowl that was the sky over the ocean, I ran, knowing I must face facts. Part of me was still running from fear I might be this same person, stuck in this same place, forever. And from the depth of the connection Patrick and I shared, neither of us were willing to accept it.

But mostly I kept running to keep safe the secret that I would do almost anything to be loved. To be seen for myself, not for who I could be to the next person. And I was tired of running.

It didn't take long to hear back on the interview. I'd been deemed "unqualified" for the job in less than two weeks, the sting of that word greater than the loss of the job itself. At the email in my inbox, I walked to the beach, where I sat, jobless, facing the wind coming in off the sea. The rejection felt like it proved every harsh comment my mother had ever made about my worthiness.

When I saw Alex a week later, I could tell he was concerned about me, but I didn't want to talk about it. For fear of being needy. Just one more person I had disappointed. I was sure he hadn't signed on to date someone who couldn't pass the bar in one try, and certainly not one who couldn't get a job.

Alex was kind and understanding, exactly what I needed. How could he be so patient and generous, so accepting that I was doing my best when I couldn't even find that kind of grace for myself? That it was taking so long to get just one job offer only proved that I wasn't good enough after all. Everything felt like a million grains of sand spilled across the roadway, crushed under the feet of the next person to cross the street.

Chapter 52

May 23

Kim had been insistent, as had I, up to the very end, when I finally gave in. Arguing with her and trying to convince her not to come out for my swearing-in took too much energy. And frankly, I missed her.

Alex was out of town on business—depositions in L.A.—but he promised he would be back for the event. I was fine with that. I wanted Kim all to myself before she started giving Alex tips about me.

Although Kim and Renée had never met, hearing them together, they might as well have known each other for years. On the first morning, they each took an arm and led me to the car. It was like being managed by two athletes—Kim on one side, standing tall over me, hair scooped back into a bushy ponytail, and Renée on the other, powering us forward with her strong lower half, her bright orange sunglasses wrapping around her face.

After we'd been in the car for about an hour, we pulled into a paved driveway with a smallish sign advertising the winery tucked behind a tall row of hedges.

"We like wine," Kim said, turning around from the passenger seat, "so *we* are taking *you* on a small tour in celebration of all of your hard work."

"Oh, come on, guys, no. Renée, you've done far too much already for me to ever be able to repay you. And Kim, you just flew out here for a long weekend." My protests were cut off.

"Look! It looks just like a villa out of a storybook!" Kim exclaimed.

"Two to one, you lose," Renée said, opening the backseat door and dragging me out.

We sniffed, sipped, swirled, and spat our way back up north, finally stopping for a real meal in the restaurant at our last winery. Pizza ordered, they pounced.

"So, tell me, what's up?" Kim demanded.

"You've been awfully broody recently," Renée added.

"I know you were in contact with Patrick," Kim said.

"It wasn't me, I swear," I insisted, holding up my hands in surrender. "And it's not that." At Kim's look, I hedged, "All right, it's not only that. It's everything. Moving was harder than I imagined. Maybe because when I was here for my third year, I knew I was going back; this time it's permanent. No job offers from the few interviews I do get. Patrick being, you know, Patrick."

"What gives?"

"You know how he is, Kim. Hot and cold. Standoffish and clingy. His last email said how much he was thinking about me. And I just, you know, can't," I waved my hands as if trying to shake something off them.

"He's such a selfish asshole!" Renée's fist landed on the table. "He's the one who dumped you, he needs to man up and move on."

"Look," Kim tipped her hand, palm up as if in concession, "it's easy to get sucked into his vortex, especially when other things in your life aren't going great. He's a genuinely nice person, who has a lot of issues, and you don't like to see him hurting. He knows you really well now, and he knows exactly which buttons to push."

I nodded, some of my anger at myself melting away.

"Have you slept with Alex yet? Are you getting laid?"

"Mmeeeeeh ..." I rocked one hand back and forth.

"What does that mean?"

"Not since New Year's Eve."

"Oh, we know about that!" Renée teased. "What?" she asked at the expression on my face. "You were not quiet as a mouse. Besides, it's not like we expected that you guys were going to be able to keep your hands off each other once you were sharing a room."

I clapped my hands over my face as I felt all the blood rush to my cheeks. "Oh my God," came muffled from behind my hands.

"Right, so you haven't slept with him in what, five months?" Kim clarified.

I shook my head, still hiding my face behind my hands. "No, not since. We've just been taking it slow. Not that we aren't doing alllll the other things," I laughed. "It's kind of nice."

"There's your problem," Renée pronounced, sitting back like she'd just solved my whole life. "Okay, there's not the problem, but it would help."

"The bottom line is that nothing has changed, right? From Patrick?"

"Right."

"One of three things is going to happen here." Kim ticked the possibilities off on her fingers. "Patrick's either going to marry Bayless the Bitch, he's going to break up with her and want to get back together with you, or you're going to figure out how to not care so much, and what happens with him won't matter. You don't have control over what happens with him." She set her hand on mine as she finished. "But you do have control over what happens with you."

I sighed, and Renée poured me more wine.

"Ems, you have to recognize what you are worth. And it is so much more than this! I know you're afraid that Alex is going to get to know you and discover you're not perfect. Well, you're not, none of us are." Renée threw her hands up in exasperation. "But you are exactly the same with him as you are with me and Aaron. He already knows who you are. And you're not really interested in Patrick, you're just afraid that letting go of him will mean losing out on something. Don't think about never thinking about him, or talking to him. Focus on today. And when he wanders in, push him back out of your head. 'Back off, jerkface, this is my life!'"

"Guys come in different models, just like cars do," Kim added. "You have your high-end performance or luxury cars—like Porsche. They look great, they're good in town, they go fast, but they're a little pretentious. Which is fine if you always want to be dressed to the nines. Then there are the pickups. Great for hauling your shit around, fabulous on a sunny day, and can be dressed up if you work hard enough. But the problem with having room for all that shit in the back is that they often come with a lot of their own."

I nodded, listening intently. "But ..."

"Pay attention, little sister. Patrick drives a truck. He lit-er-ally drives a truck. He's got a lot of shit. You need to find someone who looks good with a decent wash job, but who isn't always dressed up. Like a nice SUV. You can go four-wheeling, or you can drive around the city with the windows down and the great sound system turned up. There's room for some stuff, but because it's in the same compartment with you, you actually have to deal with it."

Renée laughed. "That is an amazing metaphor!"

They each looked at me pointedly. "Fine!" I tossed my hands up but laughed. Her comparison was spot on—Alex did in fact drive a nice SUV.

That night, I sat on the back deck at Renée's house. It was late when we got home, but I couldn't quite sleep. Instead, I pulled a blanket around my shoulders, looked up at the stars, and listened to the faint sound of the ocean.

How could I have made it this far into my life and still know so little about myself? About life? Why couldn't I just be happy? Maybe most frustrating, was why couldn't I just move on from one relationship to the next like a normal person—why was letting go so hard? A million little moments tugged on my hands, my pants, untied my shoes. Just waiting to trip me up, even as I let myself take steps closer to Alex. Those memories would like nothing more than to see me fall just before I got close enough for him to catch me.

I concentrated on the tone of the waves beating the shore just a mile or so away. The sound was rhythmic and soothing. Every so often a skipped beat. There it was, in that tiny space, my opportunity to make something new and all mine from a plan foisted on me by someone who had never understood me. A moment to step into me. And more importantly, to recognize her when I see her.

Next to me, a little bell chimed, a text message from Alex. "I miss you, and I can't wait to watch you get sworn in. I'm so proud of you."

Getting sworn in to the Massachusetts Supreme Court register of licensed attorneys was in some ways like graduating again. There were no caps or gowns, but the participants and their supporters were all dressed up.

Unlike graduation, we did not parade across the stage, and names were not read individually. We listened to speeches, we stood, we swore to uphold the Constitution, we sat, we heard another speech, and then we all filed out into the humid air.

It felt strange not having my mother there, but she'd been unable—or unwilling—to rearrange her schedule to come out. She would have appreciated seeing the fulfillment of her desires, even if I had abandoned her and all the plans she'd had for my life in Denver. Still, it didn't matter so much as I'd anticipated it would. What did matter was that my friends, those people who had supported me as I had studied—both times—and failed, then made new choices and embarked on a life of my own, were there.

Alex had been there, as promised, leaving a deposition that was running long in the hands of a junior associate to make his flight back.

When Patrick's call rang through the next morning, I told myself I shouldn't be surprised, and answered with a weary, "Hey, Patrick."

"Congrats, Emmalyn! You're officially an attorney now! How does it feel? Feels good doesn't it, for it to be over?" If he'd been in front of me, he would have practically been bouncing, his tongue caught between his teeth in a smile.

"It does, actually," I agreed.

"And?"

"And it's a good feeling, you're absolutely right," I agreed with more brightness than I felt. "Thanks for remembering today was the day and calling. Kim is here though, and it's her last day, so I need to get going."

"Oh, sure." And then on a slow, sad exhalation, "Congratulations, Emmalyn."

I also hadn't expected the call from my mother. It sounded obligatory when she said she was proud of me. All at once I felt pulled in three different directions. I knew I disappointed her, and I wished that I knew how to be out East living my life, and please her at the same time. I wished that Patrick wasn't hurt as well.

And somewhere that nagging voice reminded me that just because I was sworn in now didn't mean I was any good—I still didn't have a job.

At the final dinner before Kim left the next morning, we piled around a bar table—just pizza and beer and the Red Sox on the TV so Aaron and Alex could keep an eye on the game.

"I have to admit, I was a little nervous about Emma moving out here all by herself," Kim said. "Clearly I didn't need to, and I wish I had come out sooner."

Five pint glasses chinked together. "Hear hear!"

We finished celebrating at the restaurant together, just a block from Faneuil Hall, where I was sworn in. In the evening, Kim and I sat on the deck together, the sky a light navy blue, a line of red along the edge of the horizon. Renée and the guys were sitting inside, having another round and chatting. Kim and I were having some last sister time together.

She called me brave and independent, but I couldn't see it. She explained herself: "I never would have driven so far away from home by myself, and certainly not for so long, when I was your age."

I couldn't imagine not having done it. Or rather I could, a little too well. "I was dying."

"I know."

In the darkness, we sat quietly together, for maybe the first time ever.

"You have to let him go, Emma. You have every reason to, sitting right there, thirty feet away."

"We're still figuring it out," I hedged, lifting a shoulder.

"You might be, but he's just waiting for you to get there," Kim said.

"I'm ready for a little downtime, where I'm not running everywhere at a hundred miles per hour. I need to really figure out who I am, who I can be. Those rocky months, years, with Patrick still linger in the deepest recesses of my heart. The rain and the beach and the green and the waves have all helped, but I want that sorrow to go away."

"They won't. Not ever. You will come back to visit and you will see him, or he will call and leave a voicemail and you will hear his voice and it will feel like the bottom is dropping out. But you are safe here. These people, not just Alex, love you. Almost as much as I do, little sister."

Chapter 53

September 3

I inhaled deeply as I stepped into the jetway, smelling the dust and dryness that defined Denver, and the early fall heat. Without me around, Mom hadn't gone to see her parents as we'd done every summer for as long as I could remember. Instead, they had decided to come to Denver. So here I was, too.

Over the days leading up to Labor Day, Mom wined and dined my grandparents at every high-end restaurant she could get a reservation for. On Labor Day she hosted a barbeque—catered of course—with the partners and senior associates from her new firm.

I skulked at the edge of the people assembled, trying to avoid being pulled into conversation about my career and why I'd moved to Boston, and was Denver not good enough for me. I watched my grandfather work the crowd, shaking hands, and trading small talk as well as I'd seen choreographed in any movie scene full of high rollers. Now I knew where my mom got it, although my grandfather was twice as charming as I'd ever seen her be.

As the sun set, I escaped to my room to call Alex.

"I don't know what was worse. Mom's forced laughter, Grandfather upstaging her, or my grandmother's pursed lips of disapproval. I'm sure she considered it a spectacle for Mom to be the host."

"Sounds like no one knew how to behave."

"I think Mom was too wrapped up in meeting and greeting to notice my lack of participation." I flipped over on my bed to lie on my stomach, kicking my feet in the air.

"At a party like that, if they were my co-workers, I can see the partners asking why you hadn't followed in your mom's footsteps."

I exhaled softly, letting go of the momentary fear that Alex would add something like, "Well, you never know who might know whom."

"Thank you."

"You're welcome. I wish I was there. I would tell everyone how great you are, and how they all missed an opportunity not hiring you. And then I would take you away and remind you just how special you are ..."

"I think I'd quite like that."

I repeated Grandfather's exhortation to myself as I drove to a law school alumni event at the end of the week. When my grandparents had left on Tuesday, my grandmother had seemed relieved to be going, all but patting me on the head for being such a good girl. Grandfather had been musing about when he might come back and have dinner with some of the partners.

"It's been good to see you, Emmalyn," he'd said, hugging me on the front porch before getting into the rental car. "You've been doing your best; keep doing that."

I held on to that thought, squaring my shoulders as I walked into the overflowing, glass, two-story atrium of the law building. Maybe someone knew someone in Boston that needed a lawyer.

It was good to get out, have a beer, catch up with people I hadn't seen since graduation day, and meet alums who had graduated years before me. But as I circulated, I realized that every single person I talked to was both married, and had a job that they loved. All my insecurities and self-doubt barged through the door I had closed behind me when I'd left for Boston. Why couldn't I get a job? What did they have that I didn't?

I dragged into the house after eleven, feeling sorry for myself. "How was it?" Mom called from the sitting room near the front door. She sometimes sat in there by herself, and I'd always suspected she reveled in the formality of the Chesterfield sofa.

"Enh." I wrinkled my nose. "It was good to see so many friends and meet some older alums. But, I don't know, they're all just in a different place in their life than me," I sighed, shoulders slumping.

"You need to keep looking for appropriate jobs," she insisted, still looking at the papers in her hands. As if job hunting would make me feel better. "This is what you always do." She looked up at me as if she was looking over the rims of glasses. "You retreat and hide instead of going and seeking."

"It's about more than just a job. It was like they graduated and magically," I swept an arm overhead, "their lives became what we were promised at orientation."

"You know, they had clerkships and other jobs which made them more marketable to employers and potential spouses."

"*I* had an internship."

"Only one. Then you flitted off to Europe, ran away to Boston." She continued to give me a penetrating look.

"Where I met a great guy." Of its own accord, my hand flung to the east. "Who happens to be a successful attorney in his own right!"

Mom peered at me, then changed the subject. "I noticed you had a nice conversation with Bob at the party."

The one conversation I hadn't been able to escape, with the partner that had invited Mom to join her new firm. "A brief one, yes." Where he'd, ironically, asked about my year at Harvard. And nothing else.

"If you moved back, he would hire you into his practice." She was back to looking at her papers instead of me. "If he doesn't, there are other firms we can connect you with."

Never mind that all the so-and-so's she'd mentioned in the past hadn't made me an offer, usually didn't even have a job to offer, and even if they had, I would have to pass the Colorado bar exam. If she'd been serious, she could have used her reputation, maybe called in a favor.

Into my silence she added, glancing at me again, "Focus on getting a job, you'll feel better."

"Thanks, Mom, that's really helpful," I said sarcastically.

"What else do you want me to say? That you're doing a great job?"

"It would be nice to hear you be supportive."

"But you're not," she said as if she was explaining a simple concept for the hundredth time. "You continue to slack off, and you're taking advantage of your friends."

"I think I'll go to bed." As I turned out of the room, I felt Mom watching me leave.

Behind the closed door, I imagined the derision my peers had for me. I lacked everything they had, that I was supposed to have, too. I had never had them—confidence, self-esteem, opportunities.

But aside from no real job, my life worked for me, I reminded myself.

Still I wondered if even now, my fellow attorneys were going home and saying, "Poor Emma." My mom was certainly saying other people didn't see me as good enough.

And neither did she.

Chapter 54

September 15

At about ten on my last Saturday in Denver, I rolled out of the guest bed at Kim's. Gone was the sun from the last couple of days, replaced by clouds and temperatures some twenty degrees cooler. Kim and John were just pouring coffee when I shuffled into the kitchen.

"We have eggs, bacon, biscuits, and gravy for breakfast if you'd like," John offered, as he started to warm a pan on the stove.

"Sounds great, I'm starving."

It was a pleasant morning, the little wood stove in the corner heating the house up from the overnight chill, bacon grease, and butter scents mixing with the coffee.

After a leisurely breakfast, John wandered off, leaving Kim and I with the dishes and no more coffee. She rinsed and loaded the dishwasher while I ground more beans.

"How was the alumni event?" she asked, pouring hot water into the machine.

"Good. Depressing. Fun, but ..." In lieu of describing the event, I told Kim what I had said to Mom, and the conversation that followed. "I guess I shouldn't be surprised it's challenging, not with seven law schools in the greater Boston area, several of them Ivy League."

Kim raised an eyebrow, like I should have already realized this.

"You're already doing what you need to. Your mom is wrong. You *are* working, you have a job; you are essentially a solo practitioner."

"Wait what?" I jerked, spilling coffee over the side of the mug.

"You're a solo practitioner." Kim handed me a towel, and I mopped the table as she continued. "You're hired as an independent contractor by small firms and other solo practitioners, right?"

"Yeah ..."

"Brand yourself. Emmalyn Edits—I write and cite your briefs for you."

I stared at Kim, mouth slack and in a half smile. She was either crazy, or brilliant.

"Whether you end up quitting law, or you decide you want to try out the partner track, the choice is back in your hands."

I wrapped my hands around my mug, pulling it close. "I don't know if I know how to do that," I whispered around the lump in my throat. Kim slid her hand toward mine and I grabbed on.

"I think that you're so intent on proving her wrong," she said quietly, "that you're doing things you don't want to do, and you can't see where you really want to go. And I'm sure that's affecting your re-lationships, too. Pushing through them to get where you want to be."

"My relationship with Alex isn't like that," I insisted, slightly offended.

"It isn't." Kim squeezed my hand. "But. Patrick really only want-ed to be friends after he broke up with you. He relapsed sometimes, I think, because, as he admitted, it was so easy to be with you. But you pushed for more, too. It's not like that with Alex probably because he's comfortable with himself and doesn't need for you to be any certain way. Also, you're different—out there, with him."

"I am?" I asked, surprised.

Kim nodded as she drank. "Completely. I think you like yourself better out there, perhaps in part because going to Harvard for your third year was a big ole *eff you* to your mother. And moving back out there was an even bigger one."

I fell back into my chair, our clasped hands jerking apart.

"And," she nodded, indicating this was important too, "I wonder how much of your angst with your mother is because you want to make her see things from your perspective, when she clearly isn't capable of that."

The wind beat against the side of the house, throwing leaves and spitting rain against the window. How much of my failings had been more my fault than I had been willing to admit?

Chapter 55

December 1

I'd been happy to get home, Mom's parting words a reminder that if I moved back, she could help me find a job. I knew what that meant. I might not have the kind of job she expected, but Kim's take, that I was a solo practitioner, was probably right. Even if I still wasn't sure what that meant.

What I did know was that I was happy where I was, even if I wasn't exactly living the life I had planned. There was no certainty I'd have that life in Colorado, even if I did move back and pass the bar.

Most importantly, there would be no Alex.

Whose couch I was now sitting on, waiting for him to return from a run to the office. We were expecting a nor'easter to come blowing in over the weekend, bringing with it a couple of feet of snow. There had been a few snowstorms already this year that would have been great for staying ensconced in his condo, had we been able to make it happen. And even though we spent most weekends together, for previous storms he'd been out of town, or I couldn't make it down to the city before the weather and roads were too bad, or one of us had too much work.

But this time we had planned ahead.

I heard the key in the lock and got up to pour him a glass of wine.

"Brrrrr," he said, shaking himself like a dog, sending snowflakes flying to the floor. "It's getting *cold* out there! The guy in the elevator at the office said meteorologists are predicting more snow now than originally thought."

"Oh, goody!" I still hadn't gotten over the novelty that predictions of lots of snow meant snow would actually be flying, and that it would hang around for more than a day or so.

"That's easy for you to say."

"Oh, grumble, grumble," I teased. "You sound like someone who'd rather be elsewhere."

"Nope." Alex leaned down to kiss me, his lips cold against my mouth, the tip of his nose pressing little cold spots onto my skin. "There is nowhere else I want to be right now, the rest of the evening, or for the weekend, than right here."

"Good, come over here to the couch and have some wine with me," I led him to sit in front of me, laying back against my chest so I could run my fingers through his hair as we talked. He clicked on the gas fireplace.

"You got it fixed!"

"I did. I know how much you like a good fire."

It was true. I'd had to pony up to Aaron for half a cord of wood, when he got tired of splitting enough to satisfy my habit of lighting one nearly every night. Renée had found the negotiations between me and Aaron funny, but he was right, fair was fair.

Now I was enjoying the firelight, the glow of the table lamp behind the couch, and our quiet conversation. For a long time I sat there, playing with Alex's hair, lost in thought.

Something broke me out of the spell, and I realized I'd been quiet for a long time. The silent spaces between Alex and me didn't bother us, so I didn't feel bad. I cued into his long deep breaths and realized he hadn't said anything because he was sound asleep. Smiling to myself, I tugged on his hair just enough to get his attention.

"Whazat?" he mumbled.

"It's late," I whispered, "and you're asleep on top of me. How about we go to bed?" I asked, kissing the top of his head.

"Hafta? Comfy." He shifted to the side to wrap an arm around my waist and cuddle.

"Yeah," I chuckled, "we do." Even if I didn't want to move, either.

When I finished my evening routine, Alex was already burrowed into the pillows, watching me. I smiled, stepping over to the window, where I pressed my palm against the cool glass, mesmerized by the scene outside. The streetlights reflected against the six or so inches of snow already on the ground. It looked like a snow globe, a sight that always made me peaceful.

Letting the curtain fall back into place, I climbed into bed. Curling up behind Alex, I wrapped my arm around his waist, trailing my hand across his abs until he rolled to face me. "Seems like a good night to warm up together."

"Oh, is that what you're doing?" he grinned, leaning forward to kiss me.

"I've been thinking," Alex began over breakfast on Monday.

The meteorologist had been right: we had gotten more snow and for now, the entire city was at a virtual standstill. The T was still running, but most of the businesses, and the government, were closed for at least today and probably tomorrow.

"Always a bad sign," I teased, pouring him more coffee.

"That you're such a good cook, I should keep you chained to the condo so you can make all my meals for me," he said, as he picked up the last cinnamon roll. "And at least clean the kitchen," he added, eyeing the spotless counter behind me.

"That seems very limited. Will I never be allowed outside again?"

"You have a good point. All right, I shall chain you to the building. That way you can go outside, or to the courtyard, and the fitness center. After all, I wouldn't want you to get fat while in service to me."

"That's very thoughtful of you," I agreed.

"I like to think of this as a win-win situation."

"I'm sure you do," I said dryly.

"Truly though," he set his hand on mine, grabbing my attention, "you need to be closer to Boston to make the most of employment opportunities, interviews, clients, and networking opportunities. I know you like living with Renée and Aaron, but I also know that you don't want to stay with them because A, you feel a bit like a burden, and B, you'd like to start moving in the direction you really want to be."

"All of that is true. But I'm not making quite enough to be able to afford to live down here." I swiped at the last of the frosting stuck to my plate.

"If only you had a boyfriend who had a place, and who was crazy enough about you to want to spend all of his time with you." Alex tapped his index finger against pursed lips, as if contemplating where I might find one of those.

Finger full of icing halfway to my mouth, I stopped. "You can't be serious."

"Why not?" he shrugged.

"Because we ... Because I ... There's not enough ... it's your space, and ..."

"See. No good reason," he said with a grin.

I continued to stare at him. This was not rational. Sure, the condo had two bedrooms, but it was a condo, in the middle of Boston; it wasn't huge. Yes, realistically, being closer to Boston would be better. And Renée had been right back at the winery, there wasn't anything we didn't know about each other already that would have made me think it was a bad idea. But ...

"Emma, there is no argument you can make that I haven't already thought of. And it doesn't matter anyway. I want you here with me. Will you move in with me?"

"I ... I will!" I clapped a hand over my mouth, my eyes widening with excitement.

Alex let out a whoop, jumped out of his chair to sweep me out of mine, and carried me back to the bedroom.

In bed, Alex hovered over me, dropping a variety of little pecks and nips across my face and shoulders. I stilled his movements by taking hold of his wrist. He stopped instantly, a worried look on his face.

"I'm scared," I whispered, tears leaking from the outer corners of both eyes.

"Of what?"

"That once I'm here, you won't want me anymore."

"Of course, I will," he reassured, wiping a fresh tear away. "How could I not, you're beautiful."

"I don't mean like that—like this. I mean ..." my free hand waved wildly out to the side.

"Emma, there is nothing you could say or do at this point that would make me think any less of you. Oh, shit—" he dropped his forehead to mine. "That is not what I meant, and you know it!"

I started to laugh. "That alone makes me feel better."

"Oh, good, I'm glad it makes *you* feel better." He shook his head, his forehead rolling back and forth across mine. "I'll say it again if it will help."

"Better not. It might lose its impact."

"I love you, Emma. I want to be together, not just when we plan for it, but always."

"Me too," I whispered. "I missed you so much when I moved back to Denver."

"I missed you, too," he whispered back, gazing into my eyes.

We stayed watching each other for a few minutes, and I moved my hand from his wrist to his cheek, tilting my head to kiss him lightly until we were back forehead to forehead.

"You were going to say I couldn't do anything to make you not like me. And maybe, that we will fight, but that's going to be fine too, because people do that."

"Yes, that's *exactly*," Alex gave a gentle push with his forehead against mine, "what I was going to say."

"We haven't really done that—fought, I mean. What happens when we do?"

"We talk," he said simply.

"That's it?"

"I guess we haven't talked about this much, either. Something's obviously bothering you." He rolled to the side to lie next to me, reaching to hold my hand.

"It's been one extreme or the other is all. My mother is a screamer. And my last relationship was ... too unattached to care. No, that's not fair. Too afraid to be able to care. And I was afraid, too: too afraid of him leaving for me to push to talk. That's my own fault, but it doesn't matter. So! I don't like extremes, how's that for how to fight with me?"

"I'd say that's fair. I doubt anyone likes them."

With the grey morning light filtering through the curtains, we were quiet. "Still want the girl who's sometimes afraid of her own shadow?"

"You are not that girl. You might be contemplative and sit back to observe from time to time, like that day I found you thinking about throwing yourself into the Liffey."

"You did not!" I rolled over to punch him in the shoulder.

"No, I didn't," he grinned. "And that's my point. You're not afraid, you're cautious. This might be better coming from Renée or Kim, but I think your being cautious gets you in trouble. You're afraid of making the wrong decision, so you don't make any decision."

I gaped at him. He was completely, one hundred percent right. Why had neither of my girlfriends ever pointed that out?

Taking in my expression, Alex added casually, "Think it over for a few more days if you want. We can talk about you moving in again later."

"No. I want to be here with you. I really, really do."

"Good," he kissed my nose. "Now, how do you feel about letting your soon-to-be 'roommate' talk you into consummating said new arrangement?"

"Favorable." I reached for him.

Chapter 56

December 25

Surveying the detritus left from opening presents, Mom and I each sipped our coffee. As I stared at the pile of wrapping paper, my gaze unfocused, and I fell back to my seven-year-old self sitting on the floor, the new show saddle I'd gotten propped in the corner, while Dad and I played with the Breyer horse model of Touch of Class, a famous show jumper, I'd unwrapped that morning.

"Emma?" I heard Mom ask, pulling me out of the warm glow of twenty years earlier. In my mind, I saw Touch of Class as she was now: standing on the bookshelf upstairs in my room. I smiled to myself before turning to Mom.

"Yeah?"

"You've been in Boston now for a year." She still sat straight up, only her head turned toward me.

"Mm-hmm," I nodded cautiously. "In two days, it will be exactly a year."

"And you're determined to stay, even though you're taking advantage of your friends, and haven't found a job."

"Mom," I sighed. "It is not taking advantage. We *like* the arrangement. Their house is plenty big enough for all of us."

"I still think—" she started, still watching me.

"No. Stop. I'm a roommate. I pay rent and part of the bills. I don't care what you think, and I'm tired of hearing about such a small issue!"

Mom pulled away from my vehemence. "There's no need to be angry."

"You never listen when I'm rational and nice." I finished the liquid in my cup. "More coffee?" I asked sweetly.

She held her cup out for me. As I poured, she attacked the only other thing she still had over me. "How are you paying them rent with no job?"

"You think the only way to make money is to have an eighty-hour week firm-bound job," I said.

"Or in-house, yes; it's the only stable way to have an income."

"Actually, it's not. There's a whole cohort of people who make their living as independent contractors."

Mom stared at me as if I had three heads.

"You know Sandy, at your office? She's not an employee, she doesn't get benefits, she's a 1099 employee."

"No, she's not," Mom scoffed. "She's a law student."

"No. She *was* a law student. She graduated at the same time I did. Now she's a full-fledged attorney, working just like I do. Only difference is she has one place of work." I paused. "And I know this because she wasn't invited to the Labor Day party. You only invited partners and associates."

"That's—"

"Elitist? Yep. But that's how it works when you're a contractor. I, and Sandy, aren't part of any employee group, so I'm not part of the fold. I don't get invited to holiday parties, or happy hours, which makes it harder to network." Whether she was too stunned by my revelations or was waiting for me to continue, Mom didn't say anything. "So no, I don't have a full-time job somewhere, as you want, and frankly, I would like. But I have my own business; I'm self-employed, just like any number of solo practitioners out there. The only difference is my clients are those other solo practitioners, and small firms, not people and corporations."

"You'd be able to network more if you lived in Boston, and not up in rural New Hampshire."

"Sure, Mom," I rolled my eyes. "That's definitely the only thing keeping me from getting a full-time job."

"Don't get sarcastic with me!" She set her mug down with a snap.

I mirrored her and set mine down with more force. "Then stop pretending you know everything about job hunting and networking, the number of jobs available versus the number of graduates. Stop acting like you know everything about everything! It's exhausting, and frankly boring! You are not the arbiter of how to be successful." I stood abruptly and walked toward the kitchen.

"Don't walk away from me," she called behind me. I imagined the frustration on her face that I didn't obey. "We are having a conversation."

"No, I'm done talking about my career with you. I'll come back if you want to talk about something more Christmas appropriate."

I could see her warring with herself before she finally said, "I guess the infinity scarf Bobby sent you will be handy in the New England winter."

"Absolutely!" I agreed, picking up the coffee pot as I headed back into the living room, secretly smiling to myself.

Being away from Denver, from my mother, from Patrick for an entire year had been good for me, I mused as I sat by myself at the kitchen table with my morning coffee on the second day of the new year.

Even as I had the thought, my phone buzzed, face down on the table next to me. I knew without looking that it was Patrick. Less than a week in town and he had already tracked me down. If ever there were a sign that I needed to not be in Denver, this was a big one.

"Hey, Emmalyn."

"Hi, Patrick. Merry Christmas! Happy New Year!"

"I heard that you were going to be in town for the holidays."

"I am." I was sure Kim hadn't told him.

"Yeah, you know how The Resort grapevine works."

"Right."

Silence. "What's new with you?" I asked, bailing him out.

"I finally got paid by The Resort. And now I'm working construction. I mean, I know it's not where I want to be long term. But I had to do something."

"Kim mentioned it."

"I feel like I need to justify my choices to people like you, who have been in my life for a long time."

I poured more coffee, preparing for a longer conversation. "You don't have to, shouldn't have to, justify to anybody! Shit happens. And when it does, sometimes you just need to do whatever you can to get yourself back on your feet."

Just as I'd lectured Mom about being an independent contractor. That had felt good, even if I did want the stability she was so fixated on.

"Right. I should have known that you would understand." I thought about the quotes I had seen on his door the first night we had gone out. Years later, was he still struggling to find himself capable of contributing to the larger world? "Could we meet up, get a beer?"

I stifled a sigh of resignation.

"I don't know when exactly, but sometime this week?"

I rolled my eyes at his typical inability to commit.

Part of me did want to see him—a test of my resolve and the life I was creating. Part of me never wanted to see him again, but clearly, that was like spitting in the wind. But maybe I could use this to my advantage, cleaning up things I didn't need or want anymore.

"Let me know when you figure out when works."

Chapter 57

January 3

The next morning, I woke up filled with motivation. I suddenly wanted the Emmalyn that Patrick saw in a couple of days to be different. I'd been brave enough to talk back to Mom over Christmas—although, mostly that had made me tired of defending myself.

Standing in front of the door to Mom's storage room, I pondered—what was in there that the Denver me had felt necessary, but the Boston me wouldn't? I had left a lot of threads hanging when I moved to Boston, and as much as I hated to admit it, that had been in part because I'd harbored some thought, deep in my mind, that maybe I wouldn't make it. That maybe I would have to admit defeat and come back.

I hauled my things onto the landing, unpacking each in turn. What did I need, and not? I flipped through old journals, carefully setting them to the side, and pitched old magazines. I set aside boxes of papers and dug into other ones packed with kitchenware. To my chagrin I found myself imagining what would look best in Alex's condo, and then what we would need or want if we moved into a house.

I grimaced at myself, smearing dust across my forehead. Not the baking dish held together with glue. Maybe the kitschy mismatched plates. Definitely my expensive pots and pans, and mixer. Not the sheets that were virtually the same color as his. His wine glasses were nicer than mine.

By the end of the day, my mother not yet home from the office, I had managed to sort through virtually all of my boxes of things and had a satisfyingly large pile to donate.

The following day I was still restless, and as I stirred sugar into my coffee, I argued with myself about Patrick.

Why did you even agree to meet him at all?

He's my friend.

No, he's not, and you know it.

Well, maybe we could be again.

He's unstable even as a friend, he's already proven that.

He's a good guy.

He is a good guy, he's just not a good guy for you. You know you were never truly friends.

Oh, shut up!

With Mom off to the firm, I sorted through the drawers in my old desk. They were filled with crap: piles of unfiled papers, receipts, and other office detritus from more than two years ago, when I had quickly dumped my things at Mom's before heading to Boston for my third year. I was tempted to stuff it all in the trash but knew better.

All the while my conversation with Kim from September percolated. I'd heard her, even used her words against Mom. Now, I turned her words around again. I didn't like that Kim might have been right, that I might have been acting like my mom, then compounding the consequences with self-sabotage.

Anything I didn't need any longer was getting dumped. Papers. People. The way I thought about my career. Maybe, I thought as I considered a wrinkled paper award from kindergarten I'd found at the bottom of a drawer, I could even let go of the need for approval on all fronts. As I unboxed and trashed, the pile of things to keep growing ever smaller, I thought about how my last five years had unfolded. Like I'd been holding on to the rearview mirror of my car as tightly as I could with both hands, staring into it to navigate my life, reluctant to let go, to take the steering wheel in my hands and focus on the future in front of me. I thought of Alex, of how tightly I'd held on to all these *things* in all these boxes. What would be so bad about looking forward, instead of looking backward?

With each piece of paper I put in the shred pile, I thought about what Kim had said about how I wanted to make Patrick whole. I had had real feelings for him, and I did genuinely care about him. But what if, I frowned at the thought, I had wanted the relationship more than Patrick himself? Had I romanticized everything? So that when the next thing I'd imagined didn't come true, I felt let down. By a situation that wasn't quite real. I cringed at the thought. And yet, these were things I needed to say to Patrick. I continued to roll them around in my mind, trying to coalesce my thoughts into something I could say without talking for hours.

Circles, I thought as I rubbed my thumb over the Celtic design on the door handle of the bar. Patrick and I had come here a few times when we'd been doing, well, whatever we'd been doing. Had I finally come full circle with him? I found a small booth and sat twisting my rings while I waited, smiling as I remembered doing this same thing on our first date. I started to wonder if maybe he wasn't going to show up, and then I thought maybe I didn't really want him to come, but what if he did, how was I going to feel about that ...

Oh, stop it, Emma! Whatever is right is what will happen. Just breathe. I took a deep breath. When I opened my eyes, Patrick was standing in front of me, holding pints of beer.

Oh thank God, now I don't have to decide.

We spoke at the same time, as I jumped up to give him a hug.

"Emmalyn—"

"Patrick—"

I didn't know where to begin, so we started with small talk. How's the job, how's life, how's ... anything? I couldn't hold up my end, though, so I just dived right in. "Did Bayless have a problem with you coming to meet me for a drink?"

"No." There was a long pause.

"I didn't know if she might, you know, given that you and I used to…" Perverse curiosity warred with embarrassment, and I swallowed some beer to cover it up.

"I don't really know what we are."

My insides cheered. Old habits. But then I remembered that this was the guy who couldn't assign labels to anything because they scared him.

Right. *So, here we go,* I thought to myself. "You remember that time when I said to you that all I wanted to do was go back to grooming horses and cleaning stalls and you said that I had made choices that made it so I couldn't do that anymore?" He nodded. "You were right. I did make those choices. Now I'm obliged to act on them. Part of doing so is taking responsibility for my actions and decisions, and where they got me, and how they helped shape where I am."

He interrupted me with a story about his house now being full of roommates, which threw me off track. I tried to get the conversation going in the direction I wanted. "You've interrupted my train of thought," I told him.

"Did you have anything to drink before you met me?"

"No," I said, confused.

"Well trains can't get derailed until you get to the bottom of your glass," he said, running his finger down the side of my pint.

I nodded and then took another drink before plowing on. "Anyway. One of the things that I realized was that I was a sham with you."

"People can't be a sham, only things—events."

"Sure they can."

He shook his head.

"Fine. I was a liar," I blurted out.

"I don't like you using that word about yourself."

"It's my story! Now, where was I?" He moved his finger down the side of my glass again and I took another drink. "So anyway, I realized I was a liar with you. I was a manipulative bitch."

He made a face at me and picked up my phone to play with it. "My boss is always texting people." He began telling another story to relieve tension. "Even from inside his own house, which we are currently doing work on."

The story was amusing, but derailed me again. "Patrick, you can't keep interrupting me. I keep losing my place and I need to get this out," I said with some urgency.

"It's nervous humor," he explained.

Yeah, tell me about it. "I know, that's your thing. Diffuse nerves with humor. I know."

He looked startled, so I let him go on, because maybe if he felt better, I would relax a little too. I took another drink while he finished his story.

"As I was saying: willful. Bitchy."

He made another face. "Those are big words," he scolded.

"Maybe not bitch. But the point is: I didn't listen." My voice was stern, but sincere. "You once said that you thought I would come throw hay only because I had an ulterior motive. That wasn't all of it. I did want to see you, but I also liked it, the connection back to being a crazy-psycho-horse-chick," I used his joking description for me and Kim, "that I lost when we took the horses to The Resort. And," I said pointedly. "I was reliable—for hay and for crises. After, we always seemed to end up in bed. So maybe I was manipulative, in some ways. I can only imagine the back and forth in your head between 'she's psycho' and 'she's great.'"

"You don't have any idea what was in my head," he spat, looking me straight in the eyes.

"Um, yeah, that's why I said *between* ..."

"Nope. You can't say anything about it. Even on a spectrum." His look hardened, even though I swore I wasn't trying to put words into his mouth.

"Right. Well, the point is that I'm sorry if you felt that way."

"Were you doing the best you could?" he asked, his voice softer and kinder.

"What do you mean?" I tilted my head as if doing so would bring his question into focus.

"Were you doing the best you could?" he repeated.

"Well, no. Isn't that the whole point? I may not have realized I was doing it, but that doesn't make it okay."

There was the face again. "I think you were doing the best you knew how."

Great, what did that say about me? "Why can't you just accept what I think about my own actions?" I spat back at him.

"But you really don't like chocolate, right?" he clarified.

"Right."

"And you really did jump four-foot fences?"

I rolled my eyes. I knew he was trying to prove I wasn't a liar, but that wasn't the point *I* was trying to make.

"Do you want another beer?"

"Sure," I sighed.

When he returned, I plunged on.

"My feelings toward you have been ... harsh. We'll leave it at that. I've been mad at you for all kinds of things—how you acted toward me at The Resort, the change in our friendship, how we were when we were in the same location at the same time."

"Emmalyn, you read all kinds of things funny. You see words that aren't there, read between the lines, read things in italics and quotation marks."

"Sure do. I'm a lawyer. It's my job to see the subtext." I frowned at him.

"Sometimes there isn't anything there but the words."

"Please stop. I need to finish this. I'm trying to say I'm sorry." I put up my hand. "Even if you don't think I need to. But here's the thing, you were a huge part of my life, for an important part of my life. You were my friend. I missed having you as my friend; I missed having you in my life. I really wanted to still be friends, and do this," I made a sweeping gesture to encompass the entire bar, "with some regularity."

Patrick narrowed his eyes at me. "Are you going to cry?"

"Do I look like I'm headed that way, or do I just have that reputation?" I asked dryly.

He shrugged.

"No," I answered, and he nodded once.

I'd relaxed in defending myself. I still had feelings, of some kind, for him. But they seemed fogged over. Misty and unfocused.

He'd been playing with his hat, hair, and sweatshirt since we'd sat down. I noticed it was a new Red Sox hoodie. From previous outfits I knew he would have looked better in blue, but the grey wasn't bad either. Which made me realize that I was staring at his eyes. A reminder as to why they were so dangerous, and I looked away, only to look back again immediately. To stave off traitorous thoughts, I brought up Bayless again.

"Don't assign labels for something you don't know about," he said sharply.

"Humph." I got up to get more beer. In response, he mumbled something I didn't understand, so I leaned closer to him, forgetting the drape to my sweater. Belatedly, watching his eyes drift, I remembered I only had a bra on underneath.

When I returned, Patrick was still watching me. "This reminds me of driving back from Cheyenne. The longest drive ever."

I gave a half laugh of agreement. "Yeah. I spent the whole time trying not to drive off the road I was so turned on. Every time I hear *Save a Horse, Ride a Cowboy* I think of that drive."

"And we had to stop at the store," he added, reminiscing.
For condoms. "Yep."

"And then you wouldn't let me touch you." Silence landed abruptly between us. "Good thing we're here," he said, moving his finger down my glass again, "or this would be really awkward."

There was something intimate about the way he kept running his finger down my glass. I tried starting the next thing I want to say in several different ways.

"Just say it," he instructed.

"I ... you, I always feel skittish around you," I blurted. I couldn't look at him for this, so I concentrated on the ruts in the table with my fingertip. "You make me edgy. I can never figure out exactly what kind of a reaction I'm going to get out of you. It's part of the reason I don't call. Because I don't know what you are going to say, or do. I don't even know if you want to talk to me. I always assume you're going to hang up on me, or reject me. And I can't handle that." I felt tears starting to prickle behind my eyes. But I wouldn't cry. I *refused*. I risked a glance at him and saw I had made him speechless.

The lines I had practiced were gone. Nothing he'd said had been what I was expecting. At which point it dawned on me that I didn't even know what I wanted from this meeting. That was better than what I was going to say, so I confessed that.

"I guess I just want you to know that I'm sorry for pushing you. It was obvious that you didn't want the relationship to go where I did. And in hindsight, I can see that you never felt about me the way that I felt about you, or the way that I wanted you to feel about me." I nodded to myself, a half smile on my face. "So, I'm sorry."

"I believe you." It was his turn to trace the grooves in the tabletop. "The truth is that you got weird, clingy while pushing me away. I couldn't be around that. It was too hard. I could see all of your fears, and I didn't know how to fix them."

"Oh, Patrick." I was even more sorry now. "And there I was, trying to hold you up, fix you, and heal you from your losses. God, what fools we were!"

"You know that heavy hole I described to you, laying on your floor?"

You mean the night you said I wanted people to pity me? Yeah. I remember that. "Mm-hmm."

"That's not there anymore." He paused, collecting his thoughts, taking another drink. "That heavy hole is gone, but there is still something there between us. I feel you inside me sometimes, or as if I am inside of you. Like we are tied together somehow."

"I know. It's the thing that has you call me when you see a bunch of cars just like the Little Car, the one that lets me know something is wrong in your life even though we haven't spoken a single word in more than months and I'm two thousand miles away. That won't let us drift completely apart. I know."

"Okay," he said again, still nodding.

We sat in silence as the waiter came by with our tab, and we stayed quiet as we walked out the front door.

I waited for him to say something, anything, but he just stood there in the middle of the street staring at me. I didn't want us to part tonight still hurting. But I couldn't be responsible for his emotional state anymore. I had come to say I was sorry, to answer for my part. I had never wanted him to simply be a page in my history, but we were different people now. I would now have to know him only as someone I used to love.

I took a single step forward for one last hug, but pulled up short, finally grasping the offshoots of my earlier thought: that I had missed seeing Patrick, the warmth of his presence in my life.

That feeling had been missing from my life for quite some time. He wasn't there anymore. Alex was. Alex, who was both closer and further away. He didn't hover, as Patrick had, and he didn't move around. He was consistently in the same proximity to me—never moving away, even when I got spooked, nor moving closer when he was feeling empty. The air around us was silent, save the quiet of the snowflakes that had begun to fall while we were inside, and the cars swishing by half a block away.

"Good-bye, Patrick."

Even here I could feel the tension of that rope of emotion that kept us tied. It was coming to its end, and I hoped it would break clean this time.

I drove back to my mother's house, and stood on the deck in the frosty air, waiting for the assault of emotions to hit me.

Days later I was still waiting.

Chapter 58

February 14

It was Valentine's Day by the time my boxes made it from Denver to
New Hampshire, and then down to Alex's. It would have made more
sense to ship them directly to Alex's, but they sat in Mom's foyer for
days, awaiting pick up, and I'd elected to circumvent any questions
about the address.

After hauling, loading, and unloading, the four of us grabbed a
drink at a neighborhood bar. I couldn't place why it seemed familiar
to me, and all that really mattered was that I had my friends, my boyfriend, and a properly poured Guinness.

Coming back from the bathroom, I slid on to the stool next to
Alex. Wine glasses marched down the bar, full of Valentine's candy
conversation hearts. I fished one out. *Cute boy*, it read.

I slid it in front of Alex.

He looked at me, down at the candy, then back at me. "Well hello
there, cutie. Is this for me?"

"Indeed, it is."

"That's really swell. But I should probably eat it before my girlfriend gets back. Wait—" he paused with the candy almost to his lips.
"Is this a roofie?"

"Darlin'," I drawled, "If I were aiming to sleep with you, I wouldn't need a roofie." I winked at him.

"You can't possibly think I'm that easy?"

"You're right," I fluffed my hair extravagantly. "But I do think I'm that hot."

He considered this. "You are pretty hot. But my girlfriend won't be much longer. How about if we slip out the back door for a few minutes?"

I punched him playfully on the shoulder, and he wrapped his arm around mine to pull me in close to him. "We can't leave Renée and Aaron here," I whispered back.

"No, I suppose not. Here, let's do this to kill the time." The music changed, and he pulled me off the stool and into a swaying hug.

"I think, Emma," Alex spoke my name deliberately, "that even though you are not a fan of this holiday, you should know something very important, on today of all days."

"What's that?" I asked in a teasing voice. I knew Alex was being serious, but it made me skittish.

"You are amazing. No, no, don't squirm away from a compliment. I just want you to know how awesome I think you are. I know you're going to disagree and say that you're the lucky one, but I feel lucky too. So, we'll have to agree that we're both lucky, and happy together."

"Okay, I'll agree to that," I acquiesced, resting my head on the front of his shoulder.

He wrapped his arms around my waist and just held me.

"Thank you for the dance. Thanks for being you," I added quietly.

Even with a long Christmas holiday, I had continued sending out job applications. By March I'd had one fantastic interview with a small firm near the condo, and I felt confident I would get a second.

Later that evening, I found I'd missed a call and voicemail during the interview. "Hey Emmalyn, it's Patrick. I've had a really confusing couple of weeks …"

Without realizing it, I hoped that meant he and Bayless the Bitch were breaking up. I frowned at the thought.

"I've been meaning to call you and talk to you after, you know ... And I've been meaning to pretty much daily since, and I haven't. So, I'm sorry it took me so long to get back to you. And I'm sorry to leave the apology as a message. But, I hope that you are well. Aaand ... I will talk to you later. All right, bye."

I dialed Kim immediately the next morning. "Can I just bitch for a minute?" I asked.

"Will I need coffee for this?"

"I can already hear it I your mug," I laughed.

She slurped noisily. "Fire away."

"Patrick called yesterday. Left a voicemail saying he'd been wanting to talk for days. And I just—why won't he stop!? We had what I thought was good resolution. And now ... ARG!"

"He's always found you a good place to unburden himself. Just because you're done doesn't mean he is."

"I don't know. It's odd to me that he'd keep coming for me after I admitted I didn't respect what he wanted, or didn't. I understood that he didn't want what I did, even before I really knew. And I told him that! The me he saw was one who mostly thought if I could just be what he wanted, then he would want me, and in return would be what I wanted. Like I did with Mom," I added dryly.

"Maybe he thinks the real you is better?" I could tell she was serious in her suggestion.

I gave this some consideration as I paced to the sliding glass door to the balcony. The snow was still around, but less in the warmer days.

"You just said it yourself: you learned from your mom to be what she wanted so that she would love you. But Emma," she said gently, "the real you, the you you are with me, is more interesting. Patrick probably sees that now. I'm sure Alex does."

I stared at the cars on the street below, unseeing for a moment. "Alex is ... something else entirely. He is exactly who and what he wants to be. I don't think he ever wondered if he was a product of his family's expectations. Not like me. He went to law school because he wanted to be a lawyer. Did I tell you he chose UVA for law school to stay close to his grandma? When he took his job with the immigration review office he did so because of Virginia's long history with slavery. He's a bit of a Southern gentleman, but he told me he wanted to do something to offset the wrongs that had been done. He didn't come to have the life he does because he's bouncing ideas off of someone else, like I was, or because he hasn't grown past an event that stunted him, like Patrick."

"You do know who you are," Kim insisted. "You're just used to hiding all of your quirks. But that's what those of us who know you love about you. I'm sure that's why Patrick could never walk away entirely. And still can't!"

I continued staring out the window, lost in thought. When I didn't respond, Kim continued, "You've already figured out how to do it. With me. With Alex. And apparently with Patrick. What would happen if you were all you in your career?"

After we hung up, I sat back down at the kitchen table and kept looking out the glass pane, at the trees, the little black birds stark against the grey sky. I replayed our conversation. Kim was right of course: life wasn't black and white, and neither was I.

I didn't sit around all day, but neither did I work on job applications like I might have told myself I should. I started cooking, the habit I'd discovered in law school that made all the random thoughts floating around seem to coalesce into a picture. By the time Alex got home I'd made not only spaghetti sauce, but also the pasta from scratch, as well as custard.

"What's this?" he asked, surprise and pleasure in his voice, as he came into the kitchen to kiss me.

"Dinner?"

"Sign me up!"

I smiled, but the smile didn't reach all the way to my eyes, I knew.

"What's wrong, Emma?" he asked, reaching up to tuck stray hair behind my ear.

"Nothing, *per se*. Come on, let's eat. You pour the wine, and we can talk about it."

"Nothing bad, I hope."

"No, nothing bad," I promised with a reassuring kiss.

Once we were settled down at the kitchen table and had talked about his day, he circled back to ask what was going on.

I swirled the wine in my glass, quiet while deciding how to begin. "What is it that you like best about me? As a person."

Alex frowned. "What do you mean?"

"Well, if you were to ask what my favorite thing about Kim is, I would say it's that she lets me do stupid things without judging me for it, and then turns around and makes me laugh at something else. If I were to tell you about Renée, I would say that she takes no shit, and champions the people in her circle."

"So, I can't just say that you're beautiful?"

"I'm not opposed to hearing that," I smiled, "but no, that's not really what I was going for. And maybe you don't have an answer," I added quickly.

"There are a lot of things I like about you. Not the least of which is how beautiful you are, but," he stopped me by putting up his hand, "I think it might be your way with people. Anywhere we go you come out with a new friend. In Ireland? Everyone liked you, wanted to hang out with you. You went to Harvard for a single year and how many new connections did you leave with? The fundraiser for The Resort where the matron gave so much money—I know you knew her going in, but she wouldn't have given without you. I think that's because you're so *real*. You give a part of yourself to everyone that you encounter. You're unfailingly loyal to your friends. If there's something you can do to help another person, you'll do it. Plus, you're a pretty good problem-solver."

I scoffed at that.

"No, you are! You just don't think you are because you haven't found solutions to your own challenges. But that's something that everyone struggles with. In a concrete and logical way, in the real world, you're great at thinking about something different and new. You do that with people, too."

With my chin propped on my fisted hand, I listened, rapt.

"Does that answer your question?"

"Uh-huh." I was enthralled with this new way of looking at something I'd never seen as more than just a personality quirk.

"You know, when I first came home and you were quiet and didn't want to talk right away, I was really worried. I thought you had decided that living together wasn't working, that you were going to tell me that you wanted to move back to Renée's."

"Oh God, no! That's the last thing I want!"

"Good. I'm going to put the dishes away, and then we're going to sit on the couch together, and you're going to tell me what brought this about."

As Alex stood up, I sank back into my chair, a small self-satisfied smile on my face. Yep, some pretty good stuff right here, right in front of me.

Chapter 59

March 25

With encouragement from Alex, I'd taken the next couple of weeks to go for leisurely runs along the Charles River, watching crocus push their heads above the ground, thinking about my conversations with Kim and Alex, about creating who I was and what Alex's take on my personality meant outside of our relationship.

Then I started completely from scratch on my resume and cover letter. This was who I was. Details, people person, puzzle pieces, and "what's next." I spent full days composing, printing, reading, scratching out, rewriting, consulting the thesaurus, and deciding who I wanted to be. Even if I didn't have much professional legal experience, I had other assets.

When I wasn't rewriting writing samples and reframing my experience, I was in the kitchen. When the creativity ran out in one area, I switched back to the other.

The phone rang. "Hello?" I asked distractedly.

"Emmalyn, have you booked your plane ticket yet?"

I was still halfway immersed in re-analyzing a case I'd refenced in a writing same. "Hmm ...? Uh, no."

"Have you even looked at fares?"

"No, actually, I've been a little wrapped up in research projects and writing memos these days. I don't even know if I've received a check recently." The instant the words were out I regretted not paying more attention to the conversation.

"Why not? That's irresponsible," my mother shrieked at me across the miles.

"It's still three months away." The annual summer visit to my grandparents', which I had forgotten in the excitement of my court appearance.

"I can't believe this. Why do I always have to tell you what to do? You are so damn careless."

"You know, I don't appreciate being yelled at like this. I know things are a little rough for you right now, but that doesn't give you any right to take it out on me."

"What?! How dare you accuse me of anything like that! I'm not yelling at you; you're just not listening. How did I manage to raise such an immature daughter? I'm done. You're on your own! I can't help someone who insists on being so incredibly irresponsible."

"I'm not going to sit here and be called names. If you'd like to finish this conversation later when you can be more reasonable, feel free to call me back." As always, her anger made me shake, though my voice remained calm. I counted to five, and the phone rang again.

"Are you going to stop telling me that I'm irresponsible?" I asked.

She didn't give me an answer, merely launched into more reasons why I was the "worst daughter ever."

"I don't trust you. I will find a ticket for your trip. Do you have the money to pay me back?"

"Maybe if you stopped treating me like a child and double-checking my work, you wouldn't be so disappointed when I don't do things the exact way you want," I said with more confidence than I felt.

"Answer the damn question! Do you have the money to pay me back for the ticket?"

"You will not buy my ticket. I will get my own. As you've just said, I'm on my own." I was impressed by my self-control, that I hadn't started screaming back at her, despite the anger vibrating in my fingertips.

"You're doing it to me again! You are ruining my life!"

"Okay, Mother, whatever you say," I sighed. "I'm going back to work now."

"Fine. We'll see how this turns out." Her tone was still harsh, but she'd backed off a little, which was more than she'd ever done before.

Alex stuck his head into the second bedroom we both used as an office. "Are you okay?"

I shook my head as I pressed my fingertips to my eyes in a vain attempt to keep the tears in. I felt Alex's hands on my shoulders.

"Come on, let's go for a walk. You've been sitting there reading the fine print of case citations for the last three hours."

The feeling of being hand in hand, strolling through the park, the grass just greening, the tulips waving in the cool breeze that ruffled the pond's surface, like a normal couple, made me feel like Mom was wrong. I wasn't a failure; I was already whole and loveable. Being with Alex proved that.

I squeezed Alex's hand and smiled up at him. "Thanks, you're right, I did need to get out of the house."

In some other lifetime, perhaps, I would have a mother who loved me.

Chapter 60

April 3

"Are you still in Boston?" Claire asked, breathless, when I answered her call.

"Yeah. Is everything all right? You sound a little stressed."

She laughed. "No, I'm just running through the airport."

"Your jetting-setting life!"

"Seriously! This trip is to Boston. Dinner tonight?"

"Yes!"

By the time we met for sushi, I'd calculated that aside from my brief stopover, we hadn't seen each other since we graduated law school. It didn't matter, though. For a few hours, it was just the two of us, the girlfriends who'd met next to a condom dispenser.

When we dipped into our mochi, she said, "I want to run something past you."

"Is this a good thing, or a bad thing?" I teased. Claire's plots were notorious for getting us into unpredictable situations.

"Definitely good. My firm is looking for someone to travel and sell us to various potential new clients. I immediately thought of you, and gave them your name. But I guess I didn't consider you might be doing something else equally interesting."

"You thought right. Tell me more."

"I don't know much more. Just that they're looking for client relations, but want someone who is licensed. I think the position is based here, but it might be out of Chicago, I'm not sure. Can I give my boss your name?"

"I thought you already did," I reminded her.

"Well, I just said I knew you and that I thought you'd be good at it."

"Mm-hmm," I teased.

"All right, maybe I said more than that." Her brown eyes were mischievous.

"Yes. Tell them all about me. Do you need me to send my resume to you for them?"

"They pretty much let me do whatever, and so would likely hire you on my word alone—but yeah. I'll have Greg, that's my boss, Greg Trafalgar, call you."

"Claire, thanks so much for thinking of me. I mean it. It's been really challenging, and I'm tired."

"I know," she sympathized, laying her hand over mine. "It's about to get loads better."

I decided to surprise Alex with a picnic in the park across the street from his office. It was a gorgeous April day. In the Financial District, modern buildings towered above the trees, and still, the city seemed to retain its stately character.

"This is a really nice break in my day. You know how I loathe Tuesdays," Alex said when he responded to the call to come up to the front receptionist.

"Yes, I know. First day of midweek, four more days until the weekend."

"You got it," he agreed. "Let me grab my wallet."

As I waited for him in the elevator lobby, my phone rang. "This is Emma."

"Emma, Greg Trafalgar here. I believe we have a mutual friend, Claire Campton."

"Yes, we do. How are you?"

Alex returned as the elevator opened.

"Fine, great. Listen, I don't have a lot of time before my next meeting, but based on your resume and what Claire has told me about you, I think we might have a great fit here. Are you available to come out to meet with us soon?" The elevator slid down the forty-three floors as I dug through my bag to find my calendar.

"Sure, sure, let's see," I grinned at the question written on Alex's face. "This week is booked, but I could do the first part of next week if that works for you."

"Great. It sounds as if you are en route somewhere, so I will have my assistant call you back later to make travel arrangements."

"Thank you, Mr. Trafalgar—"

"Please, it's Greg," he interrupted.

"Thank you, Greg," I corrected, "I look forward to meeting with you soon." I clicked off my phone and struggled to keep my face neutral until we were outside the office building.

"What was that?" Alex asked, feeling the excitement vibrating off me.

"That was Claire's boss. He wants me to fly to Chicago next week to talk with him!"

There was a slight hesitation before Alex's delayed, "Emma, that's great news!"

An hour later, I dropped Alex back at the front of his building and kissed him soundly. Watching him walk through the revolving door, I noticed a slump to his shoulders that hadn't been there before.

It was such a lovely day I decided to walk home, and the click and scrunch of my heeled sandals on the sidewalk kept time to my thoughts. I wondered what he was upset about. Alex was in nearly all circumstances optimistic, which was one of the things I liked best about him. Had he been so sad to leave me, our picnic, the sunshine, and go back to work? That seemed unlikely—as much as he might joke about waiting for the weekend, he did it more for form, and genuinely enjoyed his job.

I walked into the liquor store near the condo and perused the selection of sparkling wines. Then it hit me: he was happy for me. But he was also anxious about what this job would ultimately mean.

"Hi," I said softly, when Alex walked through the door that evening.

"Did something happen?"

"No, I was just thinking about lunch."

"Oh?" He dropped his bag by the door.

"Let's sit on the balcony. With wine," I said, handing him a glass.

Alex nodded, and I walked out with the bottle and my own glass. The clouds were a coral pink tonight, the lower sky a luminous gold. We couldn't see the harbor from here, but the light still reflected off the water. A few minutes later Alex joined me, now in jeans and a worn T-shirt.

"Well, cheers to the interview!" he saluted, but there was a false note in his voice.

"Alex," I stopped him, my hand on his arm, "don't fake it."

He exhaled strongly through his nose. "I'm sorry. I really am happy for you. I just ..."

"I know, me too. I was so excited that I didn't even think about any of the rest of it. Here's what I do know: this is only an interview—"

"Please. They're totally going to hire you. If Claire has as much pull as she says she does, plus this is the kind of stuff that you're amazing at doing. Why wouldn't they want you?"

"That's fair. But still, this is only an interview, it's not an offer. Secondly, I don't know where the job will be based. It might be Chicago. But their main offices are here."

"They are?"

"Yeah, pretty close to your building, I think."

"So you might not have to move?"

"Maybe not."

"I didn't know they had any offices here," he said, resting his forehead on his hands, elbows propped on his knees.

"I'm sorry." I reached over to rub his back. "I thought I mentioned that, but I guess I missed that part in all my excitement that there's a job someone knows I would fit."

He sat back up quickly and leaned over to kiss me. "I am *so* relieved. Stand up, I need to hug you!"

I jumped to my feet, propped myself up on my tiptoes, and wrapped my arms around his neck.

"It wouldn't have been fair for me to ask you to turn down a job simply because of me," he said, almost like a confession. "But I might have anyway, just because I love you so much."

"I'm not taking this job if I'd have to leave!"

We hugged each other closer.

Chapter 61

April 12

My travel arrangements were made, and I was leaving first thing Monday morning.

I'd spent most of the day after Greg's call looking at flights and emailing back and forth with Greg's assistant, coordinating arrangements, and getting a schedule.

Now, even though it was eleven at night, I was propped up on the couch, reading everything I could find on the internet about Greg. I'd talked to Claire, and she'd said she would call me in the morning and fill me in on everything she knew from working with him.

Then, I was planning on spending the rest of the days between now and when my flight left reading about all the firm's practice areas, their clients, and their clients' businesses.

If Trafalgar & Bridge, LLC didn't love me, I'd eat my hand.

I sat in the quiet, early morning terminal, holding a hot cup of coffee, eyes closed, thinking about all the good things that were happening.

I'd been so busy, not just preparing for the interview, but trying to make a life, that I hadn't taken the time to appreciate the life I already had. The pieces that had fallen into place even as I had wrested others where I wanted them. And then, when Alex had asked me to move in, all the changes had cascaded even faster. As if the universe had been waiting for me to step into the right place.

What if I hadn't been brave enough to accept any of it? But I had been confident that Alex had meant everything he said, sure that he was sure, understanding somehow that his stability made me feel safe.

I felt different. Confident that Trafalgar & Bridge would hire me, but knowing that regardless, I would survive. I might even be getting close to being someone my mother could be proud of. If I stretched my hand out in front of me, it was as if I could almost touch any one of a hundred different possibilities strung out before me. All I had to do was pick one.

I opened my eyes and watched the sun climbing higher into the sky across the harbor. It was going to be a beautiful day.

The flight was uneventful. I could not say the same for my interview. Or I should say interviews. Three days of round-robin left my head spinning. But I was glad to do them all at once, and not wait to see if there would be more.

"All we have left then are the terms of employment," Greg said. He'd been wearing a suit when I'd first met him, but today he'd lost the jacket and tie. The light blue shirt set off his hazel eyes and complimented his nearly black hair. He was exactly the kind of attorney my mom wanted me to work for, and in years past, one I would have given a wide berth.

I swallowed, nodding. I hoped I could restrain myself from accepting any offer they might give.

"The starting salary for this position, which as you know is a new one, is low six figures, with a bonus as well, providing for additional compensation depending on quarterly billables," Greg explained.

I nodded. This offer was more than I had dared to hope for.

"Naturally you'll have full health benefits, and the firm will contribute to your 401(k) at twice the rate that you do, up to four percent. There's also a tiered vacation allowance—two weeks your first two years with us, and increasing from there. What questions can I answer for you?"

Right now my most pressing question seemed petty. "Where is the position based? Here in Chicago, or elsewhere?"

"The position is based both out of Boston, and Chicago. As you know, many of our clients are in the Chicagoland area, and this was the founding office. But the majority of our corporate clients work with the Boston office. And, as this position would require meeting with current and prospective clients all over the country, and indeed all over the world, you would be required to travel."

"Sure, of course." I nodded.

"Is there a particular place you had in mind to work from?" Greg asked.

"Not specifically. I mean, I do enjoy Chicago, and I have friends and some extended family that live here. But, as you know, I currently live in Boston, and ..." I trailed off, not sure what else to say.

"And you have a relationship there." I opened my mouth to speak, to deny that was an issue, but Greg beat me to it. "Claire mentioned it, mostly as a detail of your personality than anything else."

"Mr. Trafalgar—Greg," I corrected myself, "I don't want you to think that that would keep me from accepting the position if it were offered, or that I must remain in Boston. But I did move there from Denver as a choice."

"That's perfectly reasonable. If I had chosen to move somewhere specific, I would want to think about what sacrifices I would or would not be willing to make."

"I—"

"It's a perfectly reasonable question is all I am saying," Greg cut me off before I could embarrass myself further. "Now, I'm sure after all our conversations the last few days, you are overloaded with information. Claire also mentioned that she was going to meet you this afternoon. I will excuse myself at this time and let you go back to your hotel."

"Yes, thank you," I said, standing. Greg walked me to the elevator.

"Please let me know if you have any questions or concerns. Let's plan on meeting for brunch tomorrow."

"Yes, I would like that. Thank you for your time. I will see you here in the morning."

The elevator doors slid shut in front of me and I stared blankly at my warbled reflection as I rode down seventy-six flights. I strolled back up Michigan Avenue, the rest of the way to my hotel, still not seeing anything in focus.

The next evening I walked into the condo, dropped my bags, and flopped on to the couch.

"That bad?" Alex asked, handing me a glass of whisky.

"That overwhelming. It was exciting, and I really like Greg, but man I'm worn out! How many people did you have interviews with? I had no idea it would be like that. I had dinner with Claire, and she gave me more information about the people I had interviewed with. Some were conferenced in from Boston, you remember?"

I had talked to Alex briefly each day I was in Chicago, but I'd been buzzing and exhausted at the same time, unable to form impressions. I'd slept the whole flight home.

"Did Greg tell you when they would let you know?"

I shook my head, taking a sip of the whisky. "No, and I don't have any idea how quickly they need this person. All I know is that it's a new position that they're creating to help manage their clients. It's sort of a customer service role, actually."

"How do you mean?" Alex asked, crossing his long legs in front of himself.

"Well, basically it's a legal concierge. This is what we can do for you, this is how we can do it, what do you need that's different, and how can we meet those needs? But then you have to keep serving those clients after they're in the door. What problems are you having that aren't legal, and then this person, this new role, figures out how to solve them. So basically, I would, this person would, fly around, meet people, find out about their lives and their company's lives, to maintain a satisfactory, a valuable, experience while working with the firm."

"Will people pay for that?"

I shrugged. "They seem to think so. And, they want this person to be an attorney so they can understand how the clients' non-legal concerns intersect with their legal needs."

"Huh." Alex gave a small frown, considering. "Well, if anyone can do it, you can!"

"I don't even know if they were interviewing anyone else. Surely, they must have been. Now it's wait and see."

I kept putting out feelers and resumes, but stayed positive I would be given good news.

A month later, I was still waiting to hear. Greg wouldn't return my phone calls, and the responses to my emails were short. No, they hadn't made any decisions, no they didn't need any more information, and no they didn't have any further questions. Claire didn't have any insight either.

I could feel myself sliding backward. I really wanted this job. And if they weren't going to give it to me, I wanted to know that too.

Chapter 62

May 25

The phone rang as I slathered peanut butter on toast. "Hello?" I asked distractedly.

"Emma?"

"Yes, this is she."

"Emma, it's Greg Trafalgar."

"Oh!" I nearly dropped my toast. "How are you?"

"I'm fine, thank you. I know it's been some time since you were here to visit with us about the possibility of coming to work for Trafalgar and Bridge. I wanted to follow up with you."

I had long since accepted that I wouldn't be going to work for them, but it was nice to hear from him in any case. "Thanks, Greg, I appreciate that."

"I know that it's very short notice, but I would like you to join the firm. I have a meeting in Brussels next week that I hope you can join me on."

"Ne-next week? I'm sorry, Greg, I'm just surprised is all. To be honest, I thought this was going to be a courtesy call."

"That's my fault. I should have checked back in with you weeks ago, and I let it slip through the cracks. I know you had some concerns about the position, specifically, where the job would be based. Selfishly I'd like you to be in Chicago, but as we talked about, most of our corporate clients are associated with the Boston office. It makes more sense for you to be based there. Will that work for you?" he asked, sounding concerned, as if I might actually turn him down.

"Is there anything I need to know, anything that's changed about the role and expectations for the job, or the compensation?"

"No, not at all."

"You'll have to forgive me for not being prepared for this conversation. Could I have a day to think through things?"

"Of course, of course. I just need to know that your passport is current, in hopes that you do decide to join us."

"Yes," I smiled, "my passport is always current."

"That's great. Let's touch base tomorrow afternoon then."

I agreed, hung up, and immediately picked up the phone again to call Kim.

"Pick up, pick up, pick up," I chanted quietly into my phone. "Kim! It's me. If I were in town, I'd be inviting myself over for dinner!"

"What's up? Everything okay with your mom?"

At that, I burst into tears.

"What! What's wrong?"

"Nothing's wrong," I shook my head, laughing at myself and swiping at the tears. "They finally called back and offered me the job. Greg wants me to go to Brussels with him next week!"

"Ems, that's great!" Kim exclaimed.

"I haven't accepted yet. I told him I needed a day to think about it."

"Why?!"

"Just because I wasn't prepared for him to call. I had moved on, you know? It'll be a big job, and probably a lot of travel. I can do this, right? You think I can do this? I mean what if I can't do this? What if they got the wrong person? What if I totally suck?"

"You? Suck at talking to people? That'll be a cold day in hell. Have you told Alex?"

"No, he's in a hearing all day today, and he probably won't be home until late. I had to tell someone!"

"Well, of course."

"And my mother. I don't know if I'm excited or terrified to tell her."

"You should probably be both. Look, call Greg back, accept the job, get the details, call your mother, and then go buy a really nice bottle of wine to celebrate with Alex tonight."

"Right!"

"Ems," Kim said sincerely, "I'm really proud of you."

"Thanks," I said quietly.

Chapter 63

May 26

I decided to wait a day. I needed to talk to Alex before I did anything. I did buy a bottle of wine to celebrate, and spent the afternoon singing in the kitchen, preparing a light summer dinner and key lime pie, making the kitchen smell like brown sugar and limes by the time Alex got home. The light from the sunset was fading, but there was still enough left for us to sit on the balcony and talk.

"You've been baking again," Alex noted. "What's up?"

"I got a call today," I answered cryptically.

"You did, huh? Either it was really good, or it was really bad."

"I finally got a call back from Greg."

Alex winced. "And?"

"And he said they want me to come work for them. Based in Boston, starting with a trip to Brussels next week." I paused to wait for a reaction.

"Emma, that's great!" He swooped over to grab me off my feet in a hug. "Are you going to do it?"

"Yeah, I think so. I mean, I wanted to talk to you about it first, but yeah, I want to," I said, excitedly.

"Why wouldn't you?" He set me down.

"It's going to be a load of traveling, I think. I mean I start with a trip to Europe. I wanted to make sure that you were all right with that." I looked into his brown eyes, hopeful.

"Why wouldn't I be? I want you to be happy. The travel is a bonus, but mostly I think it's a great fit for you. I know you've been depressed not having a job, not making 'real money,' as you put it. It's pulling you down; the longer you wait, the more unhappy you'll be."

I stared. I thought I had hidden it so well.

"I know you," he said, coming to smooth my hair back and press a kiss to my forehead. "I know all the little things you tell yourself to beat yourself up. That's why I haven't said anything about the job search. You put enough pressure on yourself as it is. You don't need to feel like I'm judging you, too." He wrapped his arms all the way around me as I laid my head on his shoulder.

"I don't know what to say to you."

"Just say you're going to take the job because it will make you happy."

"I do think it will make me happy. I won't be here as much, though."

"I managed to not starve before you moved in, I think I can manage when you're traveling," he said dryly.

I laughed against his shirt.

I was prepared when Greg called again. It was a short conversation, with him promising to send emails with a new employee packet, his travel information, his assistant's contacts again in case I needed help arranging my own travel, and the portfolio on the client we were going to visit.

A week! I was going to have a week in Brussels!

Crap, where were my power adapters?

But before that, I would have to call my mother. I was hoping for the best, but I was prepared for the worst. She picked up on the second ring. "Hello, Emma," she answered, her even tone making me wary.

"Hey, Mom. I have good news!" I decided to go with cheerful and ignore any possibility of her disapproval. "I got a job!"

"Finally. With one of the litigation firms in Boston?"

"With the firm that Claire works for."

"Aren't they in Chicago? You've finally gotten yourself slightly settled in Boston, and now you're moving again. Emma, when will you learn you need to be in one place in order to make connections?"

"I'm surprised you, of all people, don't know they're multinational. Yes, they are in Chicago. And Boston, which is where I'll be."

"Well, that's something," she conceded.

"Mom. I'm tired of having this fight with you. I'm tired of defending every single choice I make. I feel like I could get the highest paying job on the planet and if it wasn't in an area you saw fit, you'd still disapprove. Are you ever going to acknowledge my success?" I sighed.

She was silent.

"I guess that answers that question." In the space I left for her to refute it I heard a quiet sigh.

"Look, I get it." I paced to the window. "You don't understand why I don't want to be just like you, and you've never liked that I have so much of dad's people-person-ness in me."

"That's not true!" And then, more calmly, "I just don't think that will serve you well as an attorney."

"Don't you get it, Mom? That's just who I am. I don't want to be you, and I don't want to be Dad. I want to be me!" I threw a hand out in front of me in exclamation. "And 'me' has created a pretty great life out here. You don't have to approve, but I am taking this job, Alex and I will work through the travel, and I'll be in a city I love as much as you do Denver."

"You're still seeing him, then?" I heard her heels click on the hardwood floor.

"I am. We're good together. And you'd really like him. He's everything you ever wanted in a boyfriend for me: smart, successful, well-respected, handsome, polite. He's good to me. Good for me."

In the background, I heard her footfalls continue. "Mom, could you just stop and listen to me for a minute?"

"All right. Go ahead." I pictured her standing in the kitchen, looking out the back window to where the horses had once been.

I sank to the couch. "I'm never going to have the life you think is the one I should. I need you to get over that."

"Oh, Emmalyn," she sighed.

"Yes. Just like that," I said, releasing a long breath at her small acquiescence.

Chapter 64

June 17

"Hey babe!" I waved to Alex from the bar at Gavin's.

"Hi!" he greeted, kissing me soundly. "Man, what a day! Good thinking for a midweek pick-me-up."

The bartender slid Alex's usual Sam Adams across the bar.

I stood up to give Alex a better hug. As I pulled back, over his shoulder I watched Patrick walk into the bar with Bayless the Bitch right behind him. *Oh shit.* Patrick stopped abruptly, staring at me.

I looked squarely at him, and with a wry expression, nodded. "Patrick."

All at once, Bayless rushed forward to hug me, saying how great it was to see me, and she couldn't believe she was running into me in Boston. Patrick hung back.

Alex was his usual polite self, but I felt him surreptitiously reach down to grab my hand, and I relaxed fractionally.

"Hi, I'm Alex," he said, reaching his other hand out.

"Sorry! Alex, this is Bayless, and Patrick," I gestured to each. "Patrick and I, uh, used to date. In Denver."

"Nice to meet you two." Alex shook each of their hands.

"Alex is my boyfriend."

I noticed Patrick examining Alex. "Yeah. You too," he said with a curt nod and narrowed eyes.

I saw impending one-upmanship and shut it down quickly. "We're going to grab something. Have a good dinner."

"It was so good to see you!" Bayless gushed, leaning forward to hug me again.

"I know we were just going to sit here and have a chill beer and some burgers, but Bayless makes me uncomfortable. We were never real friends. Do you mind if we get something to go, and head home?"

"Of course," Alex agreed with a kiss to my forehead.

As we walked back into the condo, my phone buzzed in my hand. A few lines from Patrick lit up the screen and my blood pressure shot up. "Seeing you tonight was wild! Can we meet up for a drink tomorrow?"

I set the bottle of wine on the counter and opened the message. Sure, I *could*. But did I even want to? Curiosity and an ingrained ability for self-torture won out.

"I could meet you later in the evening," I typed slowly.

"Great! Can't wait to see you!"

I was frowning as I clicked my phone screen off. "Everything okay?" Alex asked, picking up the wine from in front of me.

"Yeah, I guess." I flicked my gaze up to Alex's face. "Patrick, you know the guy that you just met, wants to get a drink tomorrow."

"Sounds like fun. It's nice you can stay in touch with your friends from Denver. Wine?" he asked as he opened the cabinet door.

"Wine would be great!"

Why had I agreed to see Patrick? I could have pulled the card he'd pulled on me. I can't do this, we can't be friends, it's too hard. I don't want to see you. Classic Patrick. Hell, classic Emmalyn. Just waiting for him to call me up so he could tell me how much he wanted to see me. But I knew why. I wanted to see if Kim had been right.

When I walked into Gavin's Public House, the bartender waved. A coaster drifted in front of me as I slid on to a barstool. What could Patrick possibly have to say to me after all this time, after last night's awkwardness? Was there anything I wanted to hear from him?

"Hey," said a voice from behind me. I took a quick, deep breath before turning around.

"Hey, Patrick." I greeted him with a hug. "Have a seat." I gestured to the stool next to me as my Guinness appeared.

"Um, do you mind if we grab a booth instead?"

I glanced at the bartender, who gave me a funny look. I shrugged at him before turning back to Patrick. "Yeah, sure. Whatever."

The glass doors that lined the front of the pub were open to the light breeze, and the sunset filtering through the humidity in the air filled the sky with a golden haze.

"So!" he was suddenly bright and chipper.

"So," I mimicked back. When he only continued looking at me, I prompted, "What's this all about, Patrick? You were desperate to get together, but when I saw you here last night, you could barely say hi."

"So that guy is your boyfriend?" He was nearly sneering.

We were just going to lay it all out there. "Yes. Is that a problem?"

"Actually, it is." I sat back, surprised. "I needed to see you, to talk to you." I crossed my arms over my chest, waiting for him to elaborate. "I'm moving back to Massachusetts to help Dad out." Patrick sat forward, leaning on his arms. "In the past few months, as I've been dealing with his medical issues, and doctors and preparing for his hip surgery, I've been doing a lot of thinking about my life and what I've been doing with it."

I really hoped we weren't going to have to go through him apologizing for his behavior. I had long ago given up on that. "Okay ..."

"I know I was not always very good to you." *Crap.* "And I want to start by apologizing for not communicating better with you when it would have made a difference. But, as you said, we were significant parts of each other's lives for a long time." I nodded, acknowledging his acknowledgment, but he was staring out the open doors behind me.

"Anyway," he looked back to me, "I've spent a lot of time on my own these past months, and that's given me a chance to think. I, um, well, I missed having you in my life. When we broke up, I thought we'd still be friends. You've said you wanted that too," he almost accused. "To hang out and stuff. I'd like to do that." He took a deep breath.

Surprise silenced me.

"Actually, I'd like to do more than that. I'd like to get back together."

For a moment I just stared at him, unable to decide what to say. Silence hung until finally, I started to speak. "Um. Wow. Hm. What about Bayless?"

"What about her?"

"You were here with her last night. In from Denver," I said, prodding in my voice. *I mean, hello?* "Are you still dating her? What are you thinking you're going to do about that?"

"Oh," he shook his head, dismissing my concern. "We're not together. Dad really likes her, and she wanted to come along just to be nice to him, and to help me. I think she met someone, but we're still friends."

"Uh-huh." I couldn't believe he actually believed they were just friends. "Supposing that is true—"

"But it is!"

"All right, even with that being true, Patrick, last night you could hardly look at me, hardly speak to me. How do you think that looks?"

"I wasn't expecting to see you. Beantown's a big city, no?" He shrugged. "How was I to know you'd be here? And with someone?"

"You assumed that I hadn't been, wasn't dating anyone, since you and I stopped speaking nearly two years ago?" My eyebrows raised involuntarily.

"We haven't stopped speaking!"

"Patrick. I haven't talked to you in months, since just after New Year's. Before that we were only in contact sporadically by email. If you thought we were friends, you should have been talking to me regularly."

"You know I'm not good at staying in touch." He looked dejected as he said it.

I raised my eyebrows at the understatement.

"I realize I made a huge mistake by letting you drift out of my life. And if you need to be friends for a while before taking our relationship to the next level, I understand."

Had he thought I was going to leap back into his arms?

I sat back and closed my eyes, allowing myself a moment to relive all the wonderful things that we'd had between us. I opened my eyes and studied him. At the pure blue eyes that had gotten me into so much trouble with my heart time and time again. At the messy, curly hair I'd imagined our kids having. At the unabridged picture of the guy I had once thought was my whole world, and my only world. He was who he was, and as much as he wanted to change, or thought he had, it would never be enough. I would never be happy.

"Alex and I have been together a while. And even if we weren't, Patrick, I can't. Not only can't, I don't want to. I'm not the same person I was even at the beginning of the year. I need more. I cursed you up and down, but you don't hold my dreams anymore." I paused and considered. "When you said you wanted to see me, it seemed a little like you were just passing through to claim your lost and found. You can't think that you could just come waltzing back in and pick up where we left off five years ago. You hurt me, time and again. And I let you. I don't want to go back to being the girl that I was. Which is exactly what I'd have to do to be with you again."

"But—" Patrick began, expression imploring.

I cut him off before he could say anything else. "No, I've been up and down this road with you. I've worked hard to get here, and I wouldn't trade it back. The truth is, love doesn't live here anymore," I said, hand to my chest.

"Didn't you listen to a word I just said?! I was wrong, you were right. I miss you and I want to be with you!" I just shook my head. "Emma," I flinched at the shortened version of my name, "what you said was hurtful and unkind."

I considered him, tilting my head. It wasn't that I didn't care. I cared very much. But I knew that in the end, we would be miserable together. I had changed too much, and Patrick still had a long way to go. We might never be in the same place again.

"I'm sorry, Patrick."

I threw some cash on the table and stood up. Patrick stared at the table, sad and beaten. I laid my hand on top of his. "I didn't—don't—want to hurt you. Someday I hope you'll understand why this is my decision. Part of me will always love you." I kissed the top of his head. "Good-bye, Patrick."

When I got to the door, I stopped to look back. He was only twenty feet away, but we were so much further apart than that. I turned around again, and walked out the door.

Chapter 65

Fourth of July, one year later

The Fourth of July was an appropriate day for a celebration. Not only because it was my birthday, but because so much had changed in the last year and a half. I had been in so much pain at the beginning, so deep down in the emotions. But I had amazing friends who had dragged me kicking and screaming along.

It hadn't been all fun and games with my mother. After I'd told her I was living my life my way, she'd gone radio silent, and I imagined her insisting to herself she was still right. But in the spring she'd reached out and while she continued to question whether this job was good enough, we'd mostly come to a détente. In her birthday wishes she'd said she was happy for me, which was all I wanted now.

Ours was never going to be the kind of relationship I had envisioned, but I was doing the best that I could.

By the end of my first six months with Trafalgar & Bridge, Greg had been heaping me with praise. A year into the job, I spent most of my time with our multinational clients. Who was I to complain that the Europeans liked me best? Greg had been almost unable to believe the difference in the firm's relationship with nearly all its clients, and he was consistently saying I was the best thing they'd ever done for the firm. I suspected he was as surprised as my mother that anyone could care about the relationship so much, but I would take the flattery. I often joked with him that he needed to give Claire a finder's fee.

I split my time between traveling and working in the office in Boston, so I still didn't see Claire much, but Alex and I had settled into a routine. I missed seeing him when I was traveling, but on the other hand, we never got tired of each other. When I was home on the weekends, Greg respected it as time away from work, a fact I never took for granted.

As a result of a larger bonus from Greg, and our combined salaries, Alex and I had been able to buy an old saltbox house in Marblehead. The commute to work was longer, but now I could see the water from our balcony off the master bedroom. It had needed some renovation work, and there hadn't been much to the backyard.

Tonight would be our first opportunity to enjoy it with the repairs finished, the walls painted, and all the boxes unpacked. A night for celebrating. The Fourth of July and independence, my birthday, and the life I had created, another kind of independence.

Kim came out to the back brick patio Alex and I had put in shortly after we'd moved in. We'd used only old bricks, repurposed from buildings that had been torn down or repaired in the area. A brand-new engineered wood deck wouldn't have meshed with our house, but the herringbone brickwork was beautiful.

I smiled at Kim, glad that she and John had been able to come out. I had very little desire to go back to Denver—my life was here, in the Boston area and in New England. And I loved every hot, muggy, frigid, snow-filled day of it.

"Hey, lady, looks like you didn't pick up your mail yesterday. This was sticking out of the letter box." She handed me an envelope with no return address on it, post-marked Boston. "What it is?"

"I'm not sure," I said, frowning as I opened it. A CD fell out with a note that bore all-too-familiar handwriting.

Emmalyn,

I hope this finds you well, and that you have a happy birthday. You once said you hoped one day I would understand. I finally do. I visited Steven's grave when I was back in Denver earlier this year, and I realized just how much I had left to let go of. I'll never be able to love as fully as you, but you were right when you said I need to let my mom finish her transformation. You probably already know this, but I think that not letting her go was what caused that hole in me. I blamed you, but it was never you.

Bayless and I got back together just after I came back to Massachusetts, and now we're engaged.

I heard this song on the radio the other day and it really struck me as the truth. It's Kenny Chesney reminding me of you, once again. I think it says it all.

Always, Your Friend,

Patrick

I tipped back my head to prevent the tears that were threatening to spill over.

"Patrick?" Kim asked. I nodded. "Are you okay?"

"Let's see what he sent." I walked over to the stereo on the far side of the patio. That he had chosen a Kenny Chesney song was only appropriate. It reminded me of driving through downtown, him saying to me, "You know how Jimmy Buffett reminds you of me? That's how I feel about you and Kenny Chesney."

The first few notes fell out of the speaker, plucked loosely on guitar strings. I didn't need to hear more to know the song. The words were reminders of individual memories we'd had together, gathered from all our years together, and not.

When he'd broken up with me, he'd declared himself not fit to be with me, a giant hole in his chest where he should care, that place a sinner's prayer comes from. The time he dropped me off from the airport and joked he was only going to see the girl who lived across the street, insisting he was free and easy, that he didn't care, and bury-ing his acknowledgment of the mistake the next time I saw him.

He had warned me of the ending at the beginning of our time together, if not in words, then in intentions. He had never meant to hurt me, we hadn't meant to hurt each other, but staying friends had been a mistake neither of us had wanted to make, and I was sure that he had seen me leaning in the wind, wanting to fall toward him, into him, again and again. He'd say he was going, and instead, he'd stay. To comfort both of us, so many lonely nights we'd shared beer or sat on the couch, him telling rambling stories, me laughing as they carried on, sharing little pockets of himself. Still in all that time, I'd never seen him cry.

I sank down into the chair, my legs turned to jelly by what I heard in the lyrics and in Patrick's letter. This was the closure I'd wanted after he'd come barging in, asking me to rekindle our relationship. I sat and listened with tears rolling silently down my cheeks.

Good-byes with him had been like playing at a roulette wheel, never knowing where they might land. Were we still spinning, still clutching at each other, and the comfort we thought we had? Or were we finally standing still this time, left holding a losing hand?

In the end, our relationship, even our friendship, had closed with a fade out. A melody growing quieter and slower, fading to the end-ing, until you aren't sure if it's still quietly playing, or if it's just your imagination.

I was happy for him that he'd finally gotten closure, too. I hoped his seeking was done; he deserved to be as happy as I was.

At the end of the song the disc automatically ejected, and I reached to put it back in the sleeve. Scrawled across the face in Pat-rick's predictably illegible handwriting was the title. *Better as a Memory Than as Your Man.*

"Are you all right?" Kim asked again, quietly.

I nodded, still a little unsure. I patted at the tears on my cheeks and smiled at her.

"Yeah," I said quietly, "yeah, I'm really good. I guess he's always going to be embedded in here," I laid a hand on my chest, "no matter how much I want him gone."

"Probably. I'm sorry."

"Don't be. I learned a lot from him, and I wouldn't be me without that experience. Can you imagine where I might be now had I not needed to get away from him? I might not have gone to Ireland, not met Alex." I smiled again as I reached for her hand and squeezed.

Together we got up and headed up the back stairs of the house. Kim put her arm around my shoulder. "I love you, Emma, and I'm so proud of you. Happy birthday, little sis."

I leaned my head on her shoulder. "Thanks. I'm really glad you're my big sister."

"Anybody here?" Alex called awhile later. He and the guys had been out buying supplies for the evening. I didn't want to go into Boston this year. I had a beautiful house with a gorgeous widow's walk that had an incredible view. Marblehead would have its own show, and we'd be nearly underneath it. We'd watch the whole thing unfold from our own private balcony, and no crowds.

"Up here!" Renée called. Aaron waved up at where we stood on the widow's walk. John didn't respond, laden as he was with beer and who knew what else for the rest of the weekend.

"The sun's starting to slide, anyone want to come up and enjoy the show?" Kim called down to him.

I heard shuffling and then stomping, and the guys appeared with chairs and a cooler.

"Someone forgot we need to eat, too!" she complained.

"Not to worry, I will man the grill!" John exclaimed, holding tongs up as if they were a sword.

"Good, because the birthday girl is starving!" Renée laughed, pulling me sideways by the shoulders to herself.

"And that is why we have these," Alex said, presenting a container of cocktail shrimp with a bow.

"However did you know?" I teased him.

"Because I know you," he winked, kissing me on the forehead.

Hours later, after the last of the fireworks had ended, and all that was left was a neighbor's Roman candles in the street, I stood on the front porch, looking out over the front lawn, taking in the tiny pretty lights dancing in front of my new home.

I felt Alex's hand slide into mine.

I turned and smiled up at him as we walked to the other side of the street to look at our house together. "I was just thinking about the day, watching the last of the fireworks. Everybody celebrates the country's independence today, but I wonder how many people stop to think about their own while they're waving sparklers around."

"You mean like worship and arms and speech?"

"Well that, but I really meant more like the things that we over-come personally. Not just real trials and tribulations, but how we end up defining ourselves, and becoming our own person. Marblehead isn't cheap—how many people here created their own lives by forg-ing a start-up, or used family money to do something they might not otherwise have done, but that was right for them?" I mused.

"Heavy thoughts for such a lighthearted night," Alex observed.

"Perhaps. I'm just thinking about how I got here." I paused. I didn't really know how to describe what I felt. After a moment I be-gan again. "Do you remember our first Fourth together?"

"You mean watching the show in Boston, in person?"

"No," I shook my head, "I mean in Ireland." I smiled at the memory.

"I think I was a little more focused on you."

"Ha. Nice try."

"No really. You were so lonely. More than anyone else. I wanted to go over, pick you up, and give you a big hug."

"Really?" I asked, surprised.

"Yeah," he said with a serious nod. "But I didn't because of our history." Alex put his arms around my waist from behind, rested his chin on my shoulder, and spoke into my ear as we watched the teen-agers who were unwilling to leave a single firecracker unlit.

"I just didn't know what to do. I'd made such a mess of things by asking you up to my room that way. And then falling asleep! I moved on, but I always wondered what would have happened if I had done things differently. Now I know, of course, that I could have said anything to you. But I didn't know you then. I only knew that you weren't like any of the other girls on the trip. None of them would have gone halfway around the world by themselves, none of them had the kind of independence you did. I watched you take off on day trips by yourself, and I wondered what made you able to do that."

I turned around in his arms. I'd had no idea. "So that whole time you just—" I waved my hand around, "'What if?'"

"Yep."

"Wow. I just ... wow."

"I know. But now I can tell you as often as I like how beautiful I think you are. And how much I love you."

"Alex." I rested the crown of my head in the crook of his shoulder. "I couldn't have loved this much for anyone less than you."

The streetlight gave him a halo as he smiled at me.

"I love you, Alex, every day."

"I love you, too," he answered, kissing me on that midnight street.

This life, it was oh so sweet.

Author's Note

My parents read to me literally every night before bed, starting when I was about two. I took breaks while studying for the bar exam – also twice - by reading a chapter of a book. I have been telling stories for as long as I can remember. But whispering to yourself as you narrate your day can make you seem a bit . . . odd. At least the horses didn't mind.

Emma's story is a version of my own. I struggled with giving up hours training with my horses and summers spent crisscrossing the country to compete. I absolutely loathed every single minute of law school. The only classes I had any semblance of fun in were those in which my grade hung on writing. Preferably long-winded papers. And yet, somehow, I managed to get through. Probably owing to having a mother not unlike Virginia, although mine was not an attorney herself. Most of Emma's experiences are similar to ones I had, minus meeting a sweet, supportive, hot, successful soon-to-be lawyer boyfriend during my summer in Ireland. (Boo . . .)

Unlike Emma, I did not land a dream job at two-ish years out of law school. Mine took twelve. For most of my post-graduation years, I have felt like Emma does until she finds her niche: an incompetent blundering failure who knows she could have done better. If she really wanted to. Grad school *is* like that, as Virginia, and my own mother pointed out. But it can, and should be, at least as rewarding. Writing *Magnificent Mess* meant seeing my missteps as stepping-stones and not as something I tripped up on. That view of the Emma-version of me, the guys I dated and the experiences I had, was truly cathartic. The opportunity to have my alter-self do the things I didn't, to take the third year as a visiting student for example, let me see the challenges I had stumbled on as opportunities I could capitalize on, even years out. It's meant seeing my real life through a new lens.

If you're looking for unsolicited advice on the subject (mine), to anyone considering law school: only go if you're doing it for the education and are not set on making a career out of it or if being a lawyer is the only thing that will make you happy. Although I'm proud of my doctorate, I'm at least as proud (dare I say more?) of this book.

Acknowledgements

This book was never supposed to see the light of day. In fact, it was never supposed to actually *be* a book. It was a rambling garbage story I wrote for a personal growth class about a year after I graduated from law school. Every so often, I would feel it staring at me from its three-ring binder on the top shelf of my bookcase, where I'd stashed it after the class was over. And I'd feel judged for treating it so poorly. So here we are, seventeen years later.

Top of my list of people to thank is Kelly Walsh for reading drafts six through thirteen. I have no idea how she managed to read what was arguably crap, repeatedly, and not break up our friendship. I'm so glad I hated you! For additional readings and suggestions and encouragement, Lora Freeman Williams, who, owing to having been my babysitter and being someone who read to me, is also at least partially responsible for my love of books.

As much as law school was not fun for me, I had some extraordinary professors who inspired me to love different parts of the process. Kris Miccio, who was my professor for criminal procedure and criminal defense, is in Emma's criminal law professor. While I never worked for Kris, she said things to me during classes and in hallways that helped temper the moments when I felt like I would never make it through, and she helped me feel like all I needed was to find the area of law that fit. When I wrote about Emma's torts class, I thought of my own. Stephen Pepper terrified me. All my professors did, but none more than he. When I ended up in a small seminar with Professor Pepper as a 2L, I saw just how passionate he was about his students learning. Like Emma, I had a meltdown midway through my second year. I was in Marty Katz's constitutional law class at the time. He didn't so much as blink at me when I said I needed two weeks off to work through it. Not long after I graduated, Marty became the interim dean of the law school, and was eventually hired permanently. There is no one who deserved that honor more, and the students were lucky to have him.

When I finally got serious about doing something with this monstrous manuscript, something on the order of 150,000 words, Donna Mazzitelli at The Word Heartiste got me through my first professional edit. Then life intervened, and back on the shelf this poor manuscript went, until 2020, when Catherine Spader coached me through the first six months of the pandemic.

Many thanks to Polly Letofsky of My Word Publishing for introducing me to all these people who helped get the manuscript where it is today. To Victoria Wolf for walking through the first couple of rounds of cover design that helped me refine my vision for what I did and didn't want. And so much to Polly herself for believing in me when I was first introduced to her back in 2011, and who kept on believing I would eventually get something out into the world. Her support, encouragement, and help in the final stages prior to publication have been invaluable.

I eventually turned up on the doorstep of Alexandra O'Connell, Your Resident Wordsmith, who is ultimately the reason you hold this book in your hands. We combed through the entire manuscript at least three times before we got to line and copy editing, and I could not be more grateful for the hand-holding, cheerleading, and laughter as she parsed through the story I was trying to write, while simultaneously getting a master class on the inside of my psyche. Thank you for *getting* me.

Thanks to Jennifer Bisbing for her meticulous proof read, which went far beyond just a proof. And another thanks to Alexandra for introducing me to Katherine Patterson. I hired KP to do my branding, hoping it would help me know better what I was looking for in my cover. And then suddenly, there on my branding board, was Emma. And me. Thank you for seeing who Emma is and translating her from words to images. She absolutely deserved you.

I also want to recognize and thank the women who inspired Emma's friends in this story. Samantha for echoing my cry of "Discrimination!" upon seeing a condom dispenser only in the ladies' room. Christy for having been my big sister since college and for always having advice, even if I don't want to hear it. And Nicole for not hating me as much as she rightfully could have when I became the new roommate and for ultimately being the only friend from college I would ever want to keep.

Finally, I want to thank people whose storytelling has made me smile, laugh, cry, and hope that I too might do something I could be as proud of, write something so wonderful: Kathleen McGowan, Deborah Harkness, Katherine Center, Ali Hazelwood, Diana Gabaldon, Reese Witherspoon (as Elle Woods), Rebecca Serle, Colleen Hoover, Brené Brown, and Jane Austen. Something, or maybe everything, they have written has touched me, pushed me, changed me, and made me feel all the ways I hope my own readers may someday feel.

About the Author

Elizabeth Standish is an attorney based in Denver, Colorado. After giving up her appellate practice and getting tired of telling stories only to herself, she wrote her first novel. She shares her home with an ever-changing menagerie of animals.